## ALSO BY G. BRADLEY DAVIS

*Bellamy*
*Makin' Waves*

# SENSELESS

G. Bradley Davis

TELEMACHUS PRESS

Cover art and design by Bayley Ramos

Publishing services by Telemachus Press, LLC
7652 Sawmill Road
Suite 304
Dublin, Ohio 43016
http://www.telemachuspress.com

Visit the author website: www.GBradleyDavis.com

ISBN: 978-1-965121-27-6 (eBook)
ISBN: 978-1-965121-28-3 (Paperback)

Version 2025.09.09

For Emily Lauren, Myles, Bayley, and Emilie Clare.

*Thank you for listening to my endless list of stories. Each tale carries a fragment of life, a glimpse into the myriad experiences that shape us. Your patience, understanding, and love mean the world to me.*

# ACKNOWLEDGEMENTS

No manuscript goes from a writer's mind to laptop to print without many unsung heroes. The word patience is redefined when I think of my editor and friend, Rick Marsico. What seemed like an infinite number of conversations, suggestions, and re-readings never caused Rick to balk. Thank you, Rick—you are the best!

Steve Himes and everyone at Telemachus Press have once again gone above and beyond for me. I never heard a single complaint in response to my countless questions, changes, and requests. You are a joy to work with!

Bayley Ramos also demonstrated tremendous patience (do you sense a pattern here?) in creating both the front and back covers. You are a brilliant publicist, designer, illustrator, encourager—and, of course, a wonderful daughter. Thank you from the bottom of my heart!

As incredible as Rick and Bayley are, they did not have to live with me. That would be the job of the love of my life and best friend, Carolyn. Your advice, suggestions, and unwavering encouragement have always been the fuel that keeps my engine running. I can never thank you enough!

# SENSELESS

# CHAPTER ONE

*My heart throbs; my strength fails me, and the light of my*
*eyes—it also has gone from me.*
— Psalm 38:10

Martin's cell phone vibrated against the bedside table. He always placed it on vibrate when he went to bed in an attempt to be considerate of his wife. His thinking was that if the phone was on ringing mode, it would wake her up. The problem was, he never woke up when the phone was on vibrate. His wife did.

"Honey? Honey?"

"Huh?" Martin mumbled.

"Your phone," Mary Jo said.

Martin squinted towards the clock. Thirteen minutes after five. He didn't have to look to see who was calling. Only work would be calling him at this hour. Nothing good ever happened after midnight. The cloak of darkness seemed to inspire the evil in the world. It was as if evil waited patiently through the daylight hours till it could exercise its restrained passions after the sun set.

"Yeah," Martin said as he sat up in bed answering the call. "Alright. I'll be there as soon as I can."

Martin leaned over to Mary Jo and rubbed her in the hollow of her back.

"Murder?" she asked.

"Yes. Inside St. Frances Church, no less. I love you. I'll call you later."

Martin grabbed his clothes that were laid out on the footboard bench and went into the bathroom to get dressed. Years of getting calls in the middle of the night, his habit was to have his clothes at the ready so he would not disturb his wife. If he could only wake before she did when his phone vibrated, it would have been a perfect plan.

A sliver of light escaped from the bottom of the bathroom door, dividing the darkened bedroom in two. Mary Jo rolled away from the light and fell back to sleep.

Martin pulled his car out of the garage and realized only then it had rained during the night. The wet streets scattered the headlights randomly like cracks from a broken window, extending slivers of light randomly into the darkness. The autumn leaves, not wet and sticking to something, flew haphazardly with the wind.

Martin Wallace was a captain with the Philadelphia Police Department's Major Crimes Squad—a position to which he was promoted six years earlier. Being a captain in this police department was no small feat, considering the force included 6,000 sworn officers, making it the nation's fourth-largest police department.

Martin never attended college, which hindered his advancement in the police department. Although his skills and accomplishments were exemplary, he experienced difficulty in scaling the mountain of the chain of command which seemed insurmountable. Not only was it impossible for Martin to achieve a position within the hierarchy of the police department beyond his current status, he actually trained the current Chief of Police.

Bruce Conwell graduated from West Chester University and got a job at the police academy shortly thereafter. He spent a half dozen years there before being offered a cushy job in the Commissioner's office, where he made plenty of connections. He was then assigned to work under Martin as a detective. A few years later, Martin worked for Conwell when he became the Inspector of Detective Bureau Headquarters, and now, Bruce Conwell was the Chief of Police, a case study of fast tracking a career. Chief Conwell lacked the skills and experience of a good detective, but he excelled at playing the political game, something for which Martin had no stomach.

Martin could have retired when he reached 52. He had 25 years of service, but that was 4 years ago and here he was, off to a crime scene in the middle of the night. He had toyed with the idea of retiring, but then what would he do? He was good at what he did. Other than getting back into fishing, something he hadn't done since he was a teenager, Martin had no hobbies to occupy his retirement years. He would retire at 60, was the plan. One thing for sure, he wanted to exit on his own terms, and not be told to do so.

If it weren't his superiors pressuring Martin to retire, it was how rapidly the world was moving. Interconnectedness and speed of information exchange facilitated by technology, had led to faster innovation and cultural shifts, which was leaving Martin behind. Things were changing in the police department, too. Some bad, some good. Martin feared he was viewed as "old school" by some of the younger detectives; too stuck in his ways to embrace new technology which could aid in investigating crime. That wasn't necessarily the case, however. Martin used technology when needed, but he also had the "if it ain't broke, don't fix it" mentality. His techniques to solve crimes worked well in the past. Very well.

When Martin arrived at the crime scene, he positioned his car next to his new detective's vehicle parked awkwardly in front of the church. Maple trees displayed a kaleidoscope of red, yellow, green and orange, yet amid the riot of color, a black cape covered the city.

Martin was a little surprised that the newbie beat him to the crime scene. It was a good first impression. Martin had no say in the selection of the detective or his placement on Martin's team. It was a decision his boss, Inspector Jenson, made without Martin's input. His new detective transferred from the Criminal Law Division, a department responsible for investigating drug trafficking, child predators, organized crime, public corruption, and insurance fraud.

The Captain decided Martin would work closely with his new detective until he had some idea as to the type of asset this man could be. Martin would carefully watch the detective's strengths and weaknesses in order to evaluate his abilities. Although he was the supervisor of his team, Martin often paired up with his newest detective when working on assignments. He had a habit of working closely with any new member of the team. Otis, his new detective, would be his partner until Martin felt confident in the detective's abilities.

Martin was still reeling from the loss of his partner of four years. Before he had been promoted to captain, Martin worked with a detective he thought had the best instincts of any investigator he knew.

They had grown close. They had each other's backs, or so they both thought. Martin and Bobby had received a call to investigate a multiple shooting. A domestic. When they arrived at the house, the wife and two children were dead, and the husband was nowhere to be found. The two detectives separated as they searched the house. When Bobby went down to the basement he was ambushed by the husband who was standing behind the stairs.

The first shotgun blast took out both knees. The second blast tore a hole in Bobby's chest leaving him at the bottom of the stairs wallowing in pain. Martin heard the shots from upstairs and ran to the basement. There he saw the husband sitting next to Bobby. His hands raised and the shotgun in his lap.

Martin wanted desperately to put a bullet between the perp's eyes, but he was a detective of honor. He had integrity. He cuffed the man and took him in. A decision he regretted ever since.

No one blamed Martin for Bobby's death. At least not to his face.

All of that occurred years ago, but now Martin was at yet another murder scene in the wee hours of the morning. The harvest moon shone bright. It was near the time of the autumnal equinox. The angle of the moon's orbit relative to earth's horizon was at its minimum, causing the full moon to rise above the horizon much faster than usual. It provided a spotlight for the tragic scene.

Martin parked his car between a patrol car and Otis's unmarked car, both with their red and blue emergency lights still flashing and reflecting off the large church. The cathedral featured a grand Palladian façade, an aqua oxidized-copper dome, and was constructed of brownstone. The cathedral was modeled after the Lombard Church of San Carlo al Corso in Rome and exhibited elements of Italian Renaissance architecture.

Crouching beneath the yellow police crime tape, he entered the church. A gathering of police and detectives stood near the front of the sanctuary. A young man in his 30s wearing a vestment, who was much too handsome to be a priest, stood nearby.

"Good morning," Martin's new team member, Otis Gainwell, said as he handed Martin a coffee in the traditional Greek diner, blue and white paper cup.

"Nothing good about it," snapped Martin. "If this is a generic homicide, why did they call Major Crimes?"

"This is far from generic. Prepare yourself. I doubt you have ever seen anything like this, Captain. Especially gruesome."

"I've seen everything," Martin grumbled.

Walking over to the victim, Martin, who had been hardened by decades of murder scenes, stood in stunned disbelief. A deceased young woman had been posed in a kneeling position on the tuffet, her hands were clasped together with her fingers interlocked as if in prayer. Her eyes had been removed and were replaced with two cat's eyes marbles.

"What the..." Martin could not find the words to match his thoughts. "Maybe I haven't seen everything. Is that a Bible next to her?"

"Yes," answered Otis. "It's open to an interesting passage, Matthew 5:29 Listen to these verses. 'If your right eye causes you to stumble, gouge it out and throw it away. It is better for you to lose one part of your body than for your whole body to be thrown into hell.'"

"What in the world does this mean?"

"Jesus frequently used hyperbole in his teachings to emphasize a point. The phrase emphasizes the importance of taking drastic steps to remove oneself from situations or things that lead to sin, even if it means sacrificing something valuable."

"I don't need a sermon first thing in the morning, Detective."

"Understood, but you may find the next chapter in the Gospel of Matthew interesting, Sir. It is the origin of the phrase 'Eyes are Windows to the Soul.' Your eyes represent the focus of your life and what you are seeking. If you are simply seeking money and pleasure, rather than pursuing the love and truth of God, you will ultimately find despair."

"Gainwell, are you a priest who moonlights as a detective?"

The detective laughed. "No, Captain, but I do read my Bible every day and I teach Adult Sunday School at my church."

"What message is the perp sending us?" Martin said, not wanting the religious conversation to go any further.

"I have no clue," Otis said. "But she sure is a beautiful girl," Otis said.

"She certainly was."

Elaine Wu, the forensic pathologist, had walked up to the detectives when Otis was reading the Scripture. "Thinking of becoming a priest, Detective Gainwell?"

"Nope. That would be much more dangerous than this job," he said with a chuckle.

Looking at Martin, Dr. Wu said, "I thought I had seen everything."

"Not sure what those glass balls are," Otis said.

Martin turned to Otis with a confused look on his face. "You never played with marbles as a kid?"

"Marbles? Heck, no. We were too busy playing hoops or stick ball."

"This murderer has some issues," Martin said. "Have we identified the body?"

"No. There was no identification on her."

The remainder of the Major Crimes unit had arrived. Lane Wilton, both the IT specialist and photographer for the unit, walked in front of the tabernacle, genuflected and walked up to Martin with his camera. Looking at the dead woman he said, "What are those things in her eyes?"

"Marbles," Otis said. "And do not tell Martin you have no idea what marbles are."

"Make sure you take close up photos of the eyes, including the incisions," Martin said.

Turning to Dr. Wu, Martin asked, "What is the cause and time of death?"

"Her body is cool to the touch and rigor mortis has begun to set in. Her body is not completely stiffened. Hard to tell, but I would guess she's been dead for about 5 hours. There are no obvious wounds and no strangulation marks. I won't know the cause of death until I do an autopsy.

"She's been dead for about five hours. That would make the time of death between 11:30 and midnight last night. One thing we do know, she was obviously killed elsewhere and brought here. There is no blood from the removal of the eyes. Face wounds bleed like a faucet," Dr. Wu said.

"Why remove the eyes?" Otis asked.

"I have no clue, but I can tell you one thing," the pathologist said. "Whoever removed them had medical training. Look at this," she said, pointing to the incision around the victim's eyes. "Surgical precision."

"Dr. Wu, I'm going to need the results of the autopsy asap."

"I have six bodies ahead of her. Are you going to tell Inspector Jenson why the other autopsies are delayed?"

"I'll take care of Jenson. Please, Elaine. I really need to know how she died. I can't investigate the murder without knowing the cause of death."

Martin only used Dr. Wu's given name when he wanted something, or in social settings.

"Okay, but don't forget about the Inspector."

A uniformed officer walked up to the two detectives and asked, "What kind of sick son-of-a-bitch would do this? What the hell does he want with her eyes?"

Ignoring the rhetorical question, Martin said, "Watch your language. You are in a house of worship. Who found her?"

"Father Heller," Lane said. "Kind of a funny name for a priest, don't you think?'

The Captain was not amused.

Martin looked around the nave, his eyes immediately focused on the ornate stained glass windows that faced east, illuminated by the early morning sun that had just peeked above the horizon. The selection of reds, blues, yellows and greens drew one's eyes into the scene; Jesus being baptized by John, doves ascending to heaven. Even an atheist would appreciate the artistic beauty. The young lady sitting in the pew, however, would never have that privilege again.

Martin walked up to the priest who was sitting on the steps leading to the sanctuary.

"Father Heller, I'm Captain Wallace. Tell me what happened this morning."

"I always get up early to do my morning prayers. When I came into the nave, I saw this woman, kneeling in the third pew. I thought it odd that she had sunglasses on, but I left her alone, as she looked deep in meditation. I left her and prayed in the privacy of the sacristy. When I returned, about an hour later, I saw she had not moved. I mean, she had not moved an inch. I became concerned. I walked over to her and placed my hand on her shoulder. She slumped over on her side and her sunglasses fell off. I tried to find a pulse, but as soon as I touched her neck, I could tell she was deceased by how cold she felt. I then called 911."

"Have you seen this woman before? Perhaps at your services or at confession?"

"She does not look familiar but, those eyes…or, I mean…"

"I know what you mean, Father. This is a repulsive act. Tell me, do you keep the church unlocked all night?"

"No. We have evening mass only on Wednesdays and Sundays. Last night was Tuesday, so I have no idea how anyone got in here."

"Who all has a key to the nave?"

"Myself, Father Mark, the church secretary, the janitor, and Jeff Stapleton, the Grand Knight for our Knights of Columbus council."

"We are going to need contact information for each of these individuals."

"I understand. My secretary will be in at 8. I'll have her gather that together and get it to you right away."

"Thank you, Father. Here is my card. If you can think of anything else that may help us, please give me a call."

Martin walked over to the body where several of his team were gathering evidence.

"Detective, make sure they dust for fingerprints on the back of the pew where she was found as well as the pew in front of her. Swab the kneeler where she was positioned in prayer. I'll see you back at the station," Martin said to his new team member."

"Will do, Captain."

Martin opened the large door of the church and stood in front of the church. A cool autumn breeze blew between the buildings taking street litter with it. A pair of mourning doves fluttered away from scourging the last few crumbs of a soft pretzel someone tossed, sounding like their wings needed to be oiled. Martin looked up at the morning sky, pondering whether to ask for divine intervention.

Martin promised himself he would never become callous to the multitude of murder victims he had witnessed, unlike many of the detectives he had known. Yet, he feared perhaps it was inevitable. Just when he thought he had become numb to them, this idiosyncratic murder surfaced. Before he became a detective, he saw scores of deaths the result of drugs, car accidents, suicides, and gun violence. Most of the gun violence was perpetrated by gangs. It was hard to feel sympathy for those victims. Live by the sword… But murder victims, those whose lives had been snuffed out prematurely, those were different.

Martin walked around the outside of the church, then around the block, searching for anything that would indicate the scene of the murder: a pool of blood, evidence of a struggle; however, nothing seemed out of the ordinary. He got in his car and drove to the police station.

# CHAPTER TWO

*Believe half of what you see and nothing of what you hear.*
— "The System of Dr. Tarr and Prof. Fether" by Edgar Allan Poe

When Martin arrived at the precinct, Martin took the stairs instead of the elevator up to the offices of Major Crimes. He did so for the same reason he would park as far as possible from the grocery store. He was keenly aware how seemingly insignificant choices like that benefit one's health. He was in remarkably good physical condition for a man in his mid-fifties. When he walked into the open investigation room, Otis was already there.

Otis Gainwell was everything Martin was not. Tall, dark, handsome, and college educated. Otis was also a pious man, a devout Baptist. Martin had become a CEO Christian, attending church at "Christmas and Easter Only." His wife, however, attended mass several days a week. Otis was a black Republican. Martin, a white Democrat. Martin lived in the predominately white Northern Liberties section of the city, while Otis lived in Mount Airy, a black neighborhood. The differences did not bother Martin. His biggest concern was whether Otis had the moxie and intuitiveness to be a good detective.

The investigation room was a large, open area with room dividers and partitions to create cubicles. The detectives often called it the "Common Room." The freestanding panels were meant to act as visual and sound barriers between workstations, but they accomplished neither. Other than computers and lamps with LED light bulbs, the room looked pretty much the same as it did in the 70s.

Martin walked into his office. Several stacks of paper, a book on forensic science, scattered documents, and a photograph of his family adorned the desk. Organized chaos, Martin would say. Behind the desk was a white board with dozens of yellow sticky notes reminding him of minute details of a cold case he recently resurrected from the Central Records Unit.

Martin took a swallow of his, now cold, coffee. His thoughts were scrambled, uncharacteristic of him. He tried to focus on what he had just seen. There were more questions than answers. The motive, cause of death, location of the murder, and a viable suspect all needed answers. For some reason, he had difficulty focusing on the crime. Adjusting to his new partner, the estranged relationship with his son, and the death of his previous partner all jockeyed for his attention.

Looking out the large glass panels into the open office, Martin saw that his entire team had arrived. He made a quick note to speak to an optometrist and ask why anyone might want a set of eyeballs and left his office to address his team.

Martin was well respected among his investigative team. It is no wonder most revered their mentor. He was fair, relentless in his pursuit of discovery and had a reputation for closing cases. Some, however, did view him as an angry ex-drunk. Although he was proud he had quit drinking, like many sober alcoholics, he experienced a sense of loss. He had been in mourning. He lost his love. Her name was Vodka.

"Listen up," Martin said as he gathered the team. "I want to wait until the autopsy is complete before discussing how to proceed in this case, but there are some preliminary actions we can address. Santos, see if there have been any other homicides that reported the removal of eyes. We would have heard about such a bizarre murder in Philly, so I doubt any here, but check the surrounding counties. In fact, contact both New York and Baltimore, too."

"Got it," responded the detective sergeant.

Sergeant Diego Santos was built like a fire hydrant, short, thick, and hard. He sported a military style crew cut and a dark unibrow that formed a menacing "V-shape" when he got angry. Diego had transferred from Narcotics where he had been undercover for thirteen months infiltrating a drug ring operated by the notorious Esqueleto gang. Each member proudly wore a tattoo of a skeleton and crossbones with a knife in its teeth and blood dripping from it.

"Ewing," Martin said, as he turned to a blonde woman sporting a "bob" haircut. "Find out if there's a place in town that sells marbles and if anyone has recently purchased any cat-eyes. I realize the perp could have easily bought them online, but we need to check anyway,"

"I'm on it, Captain," she said.

Lieutenant Lillia Ewing had a natural type of beauty, in that girl-next-door kind of way. She didn't need any makeup to enhance her appearance, and as a result, she didn't wear any. Martin found her to be the brightest member of his team.

"Wilton, we are going to need a photograph of the girl without the marbles replacing her eyes. Can you...what do you call it... photoshop a pair of eyes on her to make her look normal? She's a natural strawberry blonde. I'm guessing she had blue eyes.

"Not a problem, Captain."

Corporal Lane Wilton was the youngest of the team. Standing a few inches taller than Martin, handsome with a chiseled jaw and dirty blonde hair, and a close-cropped beard, made him look more Hollywood heart throb than Philly detective. His technical know-how and stellar work ethic resulted in several promotions in a relatively short amount of time.

Turning toward the last two members of the Major Crimes Unit, Martin said, "Becton and Sinclair, scour a three-block radius of where we found the girl. See if there are any security cameras that picked up anything.

Detectives Jake Sinclair and Jordan Becton were both forensic scientists. Their work in the laboratory had proven to be essential in past murder investigations. Jake had dark brown hair and eyes to match. He had broad shoulders that tapered to an impossibly thin waist, clearly a fitness freak. He thought outside the box, something Martin liked about him. Jake had a sarcastic sense of humor which Martin tolerated.

Jordan looked more like a scientist. He wore black framed glasses that sat reluctantly on a rather large, aquiline nose, causing him to habitually push his glasses up to an appropriate sitting position. Some may think he has a tendency to over analyze, but when it came to the science of investigative work, Jordan stood alone.

"Let's meet back here by 3," Martin said. "We should have the autopsy report back by then. We have plenty of unanswered questions. We don't know the cause of death, which we should know by the end of the day. We need to know the weapon used, where the victim was killed, and how the body was transported to where the body was found. We also need to determine a motive. We have a lot of work to do."

~~~

A little past two in the afternoon, Otis walked into Martin's office holding a half-eaten tuna fish sandwich in his hand, Martin was pecking away at his computer keyboard like a chicken commandeering some scattered kernels of corn.

Never looking up at Otis, Martin said, "What do you have?"

"We have the perp on tape carrying a body bag up the church steps with a hand truck. He paused at the front door and pulled out a small pouch. It appears as though it was a lock picking kit. Within 30 seconds he had the door open. This was at 4:05 this morning"

"Could you see his face?"

"No. He was wearing sweatpants, a hoodie, and gloves. And get this, he had on a Barack Obama mask."

"An Obama mask? Hmmmm. Halloween isn't that far off. Let me see the video," Martin said. "And Otis…"

"Yeah?"

"Never come into my office with a tuna fish sandwich."

The two detectives watched the security camera footage a half dozen times.

"We need to find out where he parked," Martin said. "It could not have been far from where he placed the body. Has anyone checked the footage from the other cameras in the area? We need to know what car he drives. Maybe we can get a license plate."

"Jake and Jordan checked every camera in that area. Two cameras picked up the perp. One from a cell phone store across the street from the church, and the other at an Italian deli on the corner. They both show Obama carrying a collapsible step ladder. He places the ladder
~~~

under the camera, climbs it, and spray paints the camera lens until the video goes black. We assume he parked his vehicle on 10th Street."

"So you're telling me that our perp carried a telescoping ladder to both cameras, spray painted the lenses, carried the ladder back to his vehicle, pulled a hand truck out of his vehicle, placed the body on it, took it up the steps to the entrance of the church, picked the lock on the door, positioned the body in the pew, took the hand truck back to his vehicle and left, and no one saw a thing? And we have no footage of his vehicle?"

"It was around 4 a.m., Captain. Not exactly a lot of foot traffic at that time of the morning. I'm just telling you what we have."

"No! You're telling me what you don't have."

"Well, he had to have been driving a pickup or a large SUV."

"Yeah. How high up are those security cameras?"

"Twenty feet. I checked with Metro."

"Okay. Play the video again and stop when he climbs the ladder."

Otis identified the scene and started the video.

"There!" Martin yelled. "If the camera is positioned 20 feet up the pole, the collapsible extension ladder has to be 15 feet. Have someone go to all the hardware stores in the area. Print this part of the footage and have Ewing and Wilton show it to the store managers to see if they can determine the brand of ladder and if anyone has purchased this type of ladder in the past month."

"Detective Gainwell, find out the distance between the ladder rungs and calculate the height of the perp. We should be able…

Martin's phone interrupted the conversation. He picked up the phone and said, "Wallace…okay, we'll be right down."

Turning to Otis, Martin said, "Dr. Wu, the pathologist, has something for us. Why don't you join me?"

Martin and Otis took the stairs down to the morgue, located in the basement of the police station. Immediately upon entering the medical examiner's office, all of the detective's senses were hyper-awakened. The temperature controlled room was at least ten degrees cooler than anywhere else in the building. The sight of the corpse who had been cut from the collarbone to the lower abdomen, like cupboard doors, revealed the internal organs. The sound of an electric autopsy saw and a bone dust vacuum awakened their ears. And there was the smell.

There is nothing quite like the smell of a decomposing body. The putrid stench is similar to rotting meat and fruit. Martin would have preferred to be locked in an overflowing porta potty.

Otis immediately began to dry heave.

"Here," Martin said as he handed Otis a small jar of Vick's VapoRub, after putting some under his own nose.

Martin approached the pathologist and asked, "What do you have, doctor?"

"Take a look at her abdomen."

The detectives stared at a large number 5 which was painted on her stomach with orange nail polish.

"What the…" Otis could not find the word to finish his sentence.

"Five? What the hell does that mean? Is this his fifth victim?" Martin asked himself out loud.

Ignoring the rhetorical question, Dr. Wu walked over to a counter and retrieved a metal pan with half-digested food in it.

"About 4 hours before her death she had a pizza with pepperoni and mushrooms, a salad,
and some dark chocolate."

"There were no signs of trauma anywhere on her body. I did find these two needle marks on her arm. Someone gave her an IV. I took samples of blood, urine, tissue, and bile for toxicology testing. I just got the tox screen back. It showed she had succinylcholine in her system, a common drug used by anesthesiologists to block the neurotransmitter binding sites."

"English, please?"

"Succinylcholine is a paralytic that temporarily interferes with the messages that nerves send to the skeletal muscles of the body. The muscles completely relax and can't move until the drug wears off. The killer immobilized the young lady by giving her the succinylcholine, then he proceeded to dissect her while she was still alive. Martin, she was awake and aware when he removed her eyes."

"You've got to be kidding me!"

"But that isn't what killed her. At some point, after removing her eyes, he injected her with fentanyl."

"Did she have any recreational drugs in her system? What was her blood alcohol level?" Otis asked.

"There was no sign of recreational drugs. She did have a glass of wine or two. Her blood alcohol level was 0.02. She was not impaired.

"Gentlemen, you are looking for someone who has extensive medical training. The removal of the eyes was done with surgical precision. Not everyone has access to succinylcholine. These days, anyone can get their hands on fentanyl."

Otis looked up at Dr. Wu and asked, "Was there any sign of sexual assault?"

"No. I was a little surprised. She is a beautiful girl. There is some good news, however."

"We need some good news, Doc," Martin said.

"She had breast implants. All implants have a serial number and lot number associated with them. I wrote those numbers down for you. That will tell you what plastic surgeon performed the augmentation mammoplasty so you can identify this young lady."

"Excellent! That is good news, and much needed. Doctor, may I borrow your scalpel?"

Dr. Wu reached over to a metal tray displaying a variety of medical instruments and handed Martin the scalpel, handle first. Bending over the corpse, Martin delicately began scraping some of the nail polish from the girl's stomach and placed the shavings into a folded piece of paper.

Meanwhile, Otis presented a toothpick from his jacket pocket and with the rounded end, began to scrape the girl's fingernail to collect debris. He placed the scrapings in a zippered plastic pouch barely large enough to hold a penny.

Turning to Martin, Otis said, "I'll head back to my desk and check the NBIR." By the confused look on Martin's face, Otis could tell that the acronym meant nothing to Martin. To avoid embarrassing Martin, Otis quickly added, "the National Breast Implant Registry is a database that collects information on breast implant procedures and devices performed by plastic surgeons. We should know who performed the procedure in a few minutes and we can pay him a visit. By the end of the day, at least we will know who this young lady is."

"We're finished here. I'll go with you. Thank you, doctor."

As they were walking towards the door, Dr. Wu said, "Detectives," causing both of them to turn around. "Catch this sick son-of-a-bitch!"

~~~

"Do you always take the stairs instead of the elevator," Otis asked Martin in an attempt to get to know him better.

"I do, unless I need to go to the sixty-first floor of One Liberty Place."

Both Martin and Otis were trying to get to know each other; they simply had different ways to achieve that goal. Martin would ask Otis questions, sometimes personal ones, but he would wait till an opportunity presented itself. Unbeknownst to Martin, an opportunity was about to present itself. Otis, however, was more careful as he looked for casual moments when Martin seemed more relaxed. It was during shared lunches or dinners that Otis discovered more about who his boss was.

Martin followed Otis to his desk, anxious to find the plastic surgeon who performed the breast implant. On top of Otis's desk was a copy of Ebony magazine.

"You read women's fashion magazines?" Martin asked with a slight smile and a look of confusion on his face.

Picking up a framed photograph of the same lady, Otis said, "Don't you see a resemblance?"

Martin took the frame from Otis and studied the photo of an extremely attractive woman with skin the color of a penny, then looked at the magazine's front cover, and back at the photograph. "I do."

"She's my fiancée, Captain."

Handing the photograph back to Otis, Martin then picked up the magazine and turned the pages till he found the cover analysis of the model. After what seemed like hours, Martin finally lifted his head and stared at Otis for several seconds before asking, "Are you blowing sunshine up my skirt, Otis?"
~~~

Otis broke out in laughter. "No, Sir. Believe it or not, this goddess has fallen in love with me. The fact that I fell in love with her is not the surprise. Her name is Kalani Dantas."

"She's absolutely gorgeous! Not that you are some gargoyle-looking geek, but, come on…she is out of any man's league."

"Yeah, go figure."

Having overheard the conversation, Diego chimed in. "Last week Kalani graced the cover of Elle magazine."

Turning to Otis with a smirk on his face, Martin said, "I always respect a man who marries up."

Diego and Otis responded with a chorus of laughter.

"Okay, I'm on the NBIR website," Otis said as he turned his focus to his computer screen. The National Breast Implant Registry's database is extensive. According to the serial number Dr. Wu gave us, the vic's breast implant procedure occurred on January sixth of last year. The surgeon was none other than the esteemed Dr. Barnabas Albrecht."

"Is that name supposed to mean something to me?" Martin asked.

Lillia had been watching the interaction between the men and added, "He's only one of the most notable plastic surgeons in the country, if not the world. He's done work on scores of actors and actresses and even performed a nose job a few months ago on the Crown Princess of Jordan."

"Planning on having some work done, Lillia?" Otis said with a chortle.

"No need," Lillia said as she slapped Otis's back. "I'm perfect just the way I am."

"That you are," Otis said with a smile.

"Alright. Let's go pay the good doctor a visit," Martin said.

"That is going to have to wait till tomorrow, Martin. It's already 3:30 and his office closed at 3."

"Who in the world stops working at 3? Banker's hours. Okay, we'll go over there in the morning. Let's see what the rest of the team has come up with."

The two detectives walked over to the large white board where a photo of the deceased young lady was displayed, with bright blue eyes instead of marbles.

"Detective Wilton, excellent work!" Martin said. "Tomorrow morning we will have a name to go with this face. Lieutenant Ewing, what did you find out about the marbles? Is there any place in the city that sells them anymore?"

"Actually, there are. Walmart sells marbles and there is a little toy store on Passyunk Avenue that also sells them. I checked with the eight Walmarts in the area and the toy store. No one has asked about or purchased any cat eye marbles in the past two months."

"Of course not. That would make things too easy. Santos, have you found any similar murders where the eyes were removed?"

"No. Recently, New York had two cases where a person's liver was removed, and Baltimore had a kidney harvested. Most likely the motive behind these crimes was the illegal harvesting of organs for sale on the black market."

"Alright. Dead ends. Handing the folded piece of paper that contained the nail polish shavings to Jake, Martin said, "Sinclair, see if you can find out what manufacturer produced this nail polish, and what color it is."

"Not a problem."

"What is the significance of the number five? Is this his fifth murder? I want all of you to think about anything relevant to the number five. Once we have the name of our victim, we should have plenty of people to interview. Ewing, you can release the details of the murder to the press, but do not tell them anything about the removal of the eyes."

"Okay, Captain."

"Everyone go home and get some rest. We are going to have a busy day tomorrow."

On the drive home Martin's thoughts wandered but focused on beauty.

# CHAPTER THREE

*Where the lips are silent the heart knows a thousand ways to speak.*
— Rumi

Martin pondered the beauty of Otis's belle. On the aesthetics rating scale of 1-10, there would be no argument she was a ten. Good for Otis. Otis was a fine looking man, but he was a detective, not exactly someone who lived in the limelight. Kalani's life was completely different from Otis's. Everyone would want to be in Kalani's circle. Perhaps opposites do attract.

Men tend to be much more superficial than women. While men tend to be drawn first to a woman's physical attributes, women can fall in love with a man lacking in good looks, if he has other endearing qualities: a sense of humor, intelligence, fame, and…money. Some women can easily fall for a guy whose looks resemble a werewolf, as long as he is wealthy and/or famous. Case in point, there have been plenty of beautiful women who have married professional athletes that, if in a competition for looks, would lose to the likes of a toad, a bat or babirusa!

Mary Jo was still everything Martin wanted in a wife. She was beautiful, with that rare combination of dark hair and blue eyes. She was smart, a girl who should have gone to college, but was content being a mother, raising their three children, and getting a clerical job at a software company once all the children were in middle school. But Mary Jo was no longer that teenage girl Martin had swept off her feet. Although she still had those large, cornflower blue eyes, a smile that could melt the Cascades, and curves in all the right places, gravity had its inevitable effect on her breasts, fine lines appeared around her eyes and mouth, and cellulite clusters would magically appear on her thighs overnight. The inevitability of aging was obvious. Perhaps. It was obvious to everyone but Martin.

Martin appreciated Mary Jo's sensitivity. She would still become upset when a bird would break its wing when accidentally falling from its nest. She would serve the less fortunate, not just by donating canned goods or by writing a check, but by volunteering her time at the food pantry. She still giggled at Martin's silly stories and she still danced through the daffodils when springtime would make its long awaited return. He still viewed Mary Jo as his "ten" and knew he was a blessed man to call her his wife.

But what about those masses who could never hope to secure the love of a number 10 girl, Martin wondered. Ah, this is where "beauty is in the eye of the beholder" is enacted. Though some type of physical attraction may have sparked the suitor's interest, it is the authentic type of beauty that lies beyond what the eye initially sees.

These thoughts of beauty vanished as the ugliness of the girl's murder demanded Martin's attention. He could not make sense of the perp's obsession with the girl's eyes. The illegal harvesting organs reported in NY and Baltimore kept nagging at him like a dog wanting a ball thrown. *Are eye transplants possible? Why the eyes? Did he take them as a souvenir?* Martin knew he had to bury these thoughts as he pulled into his driveway. He had become very good at not bringing his work home with him, but sometimes…

As he opened the front door he immediately smelled the stuffed peppers simmering on the stove. Mary Jo was in the kitchen finishing her dinner preparation.

"Hello, Honey. You've had a long day. How bad was it?" Mary Jo said as she wiped her hands on her apron, put her arms around Martin's neck, and gave him a kiss.

"It was bad. Very bad, but you have a way of turning the worst day into a good one. I love you."

"I love you, too. Wash up for dinner and relax for a bit. Dinner will be ready in a half an hour."

Mary Jo learned many years ago not to ask Martin about the details of a murder. When they were newlyweds she had pushed him for details about one murder scene that had unnerved Martin. He was reluctant, but after she would not give up, he relented. That was a mistake. It took her weeks to try and erase the picture he had painted for her.

Martin went upstairs, took a quick shower, put on some old jeans, a flannel shirt and his slippers, and went back downstairs. He had twenty minutes before dinner would be ready. He looked at the television and thought whether he wanted to turn it on. Martin preferred to read rather than watch TV. His favorite authors were Agatha Christie, Arthur Conan Doyle, and especially Edgar Allan Poe. Sitting on a small table made of red cherry, was a book of the complete works of Edgar Allan Poe. Although he had read the short story a dozen times, Martin turned to "The Murders in the Rue Morgue," one of his favorites. Martin believed Poe invented the modern detective story. Poe's fictional detective C. Auguste Dupin was a reclusive character who is contacted by the police when they are unable to solve the crime.

Martin decided he was too tired to do any reading, so turned on the television. The 6 o'clock news appeared on the screen. He quickly turned the channel. He was in no mood to hear the press speculating, judging, suggesting about his case. Martin had disdain for the press, especially the pseudo experts with whom they were enamored. These so-called experts were self-proclaimed profilers and others who profess to have an expertise in high profile murders, when, in fact, their experience was limited or non-existent. The media often recruited talking heads, sometimes true experts, often pseudo experts, to offer their opinions on current cases, even when they have had no access to any of the intimate facts of the case.

When these people appear in the media and discuss ongoing cases, they have an enormous potential to negatively influence investigations and may even cause irreversible damage. Without factual knowledge, they speculate on everything from the motive for the murders to the personality traits of the offender. Such statements can misinform the public and may heighten fears in a community. Martin's experience is nothing good comes out of these media stunts. Often it results in mistrust and a lack of confidence in law enforcement and can possibly taint potential jury pools.

As much as the news tended to frustrate Martin, his channel-surfing was an expected disappointment. He thought good television had gone the way of the rotary dial phone. There was the extinction of gracious and considerate political discourse. Reality TV, an insult to anyone with even a minuscule brain, appeared upon the screen. The next channel displayed some surgically enhanced housewives discussing their indulgent lifestyles. Martin kept pushing the channel button. He paused for a few minutes to watch introverts living the hermit life in northern Alaska, but Martin wondered how isolated their lives really are if a film crew was there for months recording. Yet another channel showed the riveting relationships of ex-cons and their new online girlfriends who finally meet in person after they are released from incarceration. Another channel broadcasted a game show in the great outdoors where people are forced to perform degrading tasks in order to win a pile of money. *How could the entertainment industry sink to such a degenerate level so quickly?* Martin would have been happy with *Hogan's Heroes* and *Wild, Wild West* reruns. He was thankful when Mary Jo rescued him by announcing dinner was ready.

During dinner, Martin had difficulty paying attention to what Mary Jo was saying. Something about her friend Delores. Then something about bumping into someone, somewhere.

"What is the name of that excellent ophthalmologist your sister bragged about?" Martin asked.

"Nothing like changing the subject," Mary Jo said with a chuckle.

"I'm sorry, Honey."

Placing her hand on Martin's arm, she said, "That's okay. I can tell you are a million miles away. His name is Dr. Faulkner. He is the top surgeon at Wills Eye Hospital."

~~~

The next morning Martin arrived at the station early. Otis was already there.

"Good morning," Otis said. "Dr. Albrecht's office is located on the Main Line. Bryn Mawr to be exact. With the rush hour traffic being as it is, we should try and leave soon."

"Okay. You and I actually have two doctor appointments today. First, Dr. Albrecht, then Dr. Faulkner, an ophthalmologist. He is the
~~~

head of surgery at Wills Eye Hospital and one of the nation's best ophthalmologists. Last night I was giving thought to our killer's motive. I kept rewinding the video in my mind of the victim's eyes being removed. I thought we could ask an ophthalmologist whether or not eye transplants are possible. Mary Jo's sister had her eyesight restored by one Dr. Faulkner. She contacted the doctor's office and got us an appointment this morning.

"Man, I have no idea if an eye transplant is possible, but I guess we'll find out. I am ready when you are."

"Alright, let's go."

Otis got up from his desk, grabbed his jacket, walked past the elevators and toward *the stairs.* He was a quick study, Martin thought. They left the station and entered their unmarked Dodge Charger Pursuit. Otis got behind the wheel.

Martin continued his concerted effort to get to know his new partner, something that did not come naturally to him.

"Have you and Kalani set a date?"

"Yeah, February 29th. It's leap year. You and Mary Jo will be coming, right?"

"Of course. I want to be there when she has second thoughts and leaves you standing at the altar," Martin said with a deadpan look upon his face.

"You're a funny man, Martin. That is something I don't have to worry about. If it were up to Kalani, we'd get married this afternoon."

"I'm just kidding. I'm genuinely happy for you, Otis. There is nothing better than knowing you have found the right girl to spend the rest of your life with. I did. Not sure why I was so lucky, but I found the perfect lady."

"Saint Mary Jo."

Martin had to laugh at that. "Yeah, a saint, she is."

"Have you and Kalani selected the pattern for your china?"

"What?"

"You know, chinaware, for those holiday dinners."

"Why would we do that?"

Why indeed, thought Martin. Why request plate settings of fine china that one would only use twice a year. When Martin and Mary Jo were downsizing a few years back, none of their three children wanted their chinoiserie pattern china.

"I don't know why. I guess I was just wondering what to get you for your wedding gift."

Kalani has us registered at Williams-Sonoma, Macy's and Bloomingdales, but you can simply get us a bar of gold. 18 karat will do."

"Not a problem. You do know that because I am a Captain, I actually make a whole fifteen dollars a week more than you."

"Yeah, we're certainly not going to make it rich as gumshoes."

A silence permeated the car as Otis continued to navigate the morning rush hour traffic as he and Martin headed to see the plastic surgeon. Both men had a lot on their minds. Otis was thinking about everything Kalani was throwing at him, more specifically, the invitations to be addressed and mailed, and that he needed to give her a list of his family and friends he would be inviting. He also needed to find a day to go with Kalani to taste-test at the caterers. Oh, and the cake. She asked him a dozen times whether he wanted the golden butter layer cake with buttercream icing, or the Corkscrew Wedding Cake, whatever that is. The latter was recommended by Kalani's aunt who lived in New Orleans.

Martin was pondering the impromptu conversation he had earlier. Once upon a time, the Wallace family would have Sunday dinner together. They would go to church as a family, come home, and enjoy a big dinner, served on fine china. But things were different now. Two of his three children didn't attend church, and the variety of excuses they had for not coming over for Sunday dinner prompted Mary Jo to stop inviting them.

Even though Martin was not overly religious, it bothered him that his son and daughter-in-law, and his daughter and son-in-law had walked away from the church. He wondered where they would receive their moral compass if not from the values based on Biblical teachings that include love, compassion, and service. He was even more concerned about his grandchildren. Martin believed a strong spiritual foundation is essential for a child, but he realized many young people have largely isolated themselves from biblical thought, and they have become the most aggressive age group at rejecting biblical principles. *Maybe it is my generation's fault for not doing a very good job of practicing what we preach.*

Sometimes Martin felt as though their home was surrounded by a moat filled with alligators and no drawbridge to connect them to their children. It seemed as though Martin and Mary Jo would see their children the most when they needed a babysitter. That was always well received by Mary Jo; any excuse to be with the grandchildren. Martin also enjoyed spending time with them, but thought he and his wife were being taken advantage of. He tried to accept the fact his children had their own lives, consumed with work, little league, dance lessons and other obligations.

As Otis pulled the car into the parking lot of Bryn Mawr Aesthetic Plastic Surgery Center a canary yellow and white motorcycle roared past them and parked in a designated spot. A tall gentleman dressed in leather, took off his helmet, put the kickstand down with his foot, and dismounted the bike.

Martin and Otis walked up to the blue-glass building and entered the offices of the plastic surgery center. The waiting room was smartly decorated with cushioned chairs and couches, bright, original artwork on the walls, and a magazine rack which included a wide variety of newspapers and other reading material. In the far side of the room stood a refrigerator with a glass door displaying mineral water, soda and juices. Next to the refrigerator was a coffee and espresso machine. Clearly, this was a plastic surgeon catering to the upper echelon of Philadelphia society. The receptionist, an attractive lady in her early thirties, wearing a low-cut blouse that proclaimed she had been the recipient of a perfectly symmetrical set of breasts, compliments of Dr. Albreht, looked up from behind a large granite desk. Those who have received breast augmentation have something in common with those who have tattoos. If you have them, you need to show them.

"May I help you, gentlemen?" She asked with a pleasant smile.

"We are here to see Dr. Albrecht," Martin said.

"Do you have an appointment?"

"No, but we are with the PPD. This is Detective Gainwell and I am Detective Wallace," Martin said as he and Otis displayed their badges.

"Oh. Well, Dr. Albrecht has an appointment beginning in a few minutes. Please have a seat and I will see if he is available.

"His appointment can wait," Otis said with a smile. "This is a murder investigation, and the victim was one of your clients."

"Murder? Uh, okay. Please have a seat."

Neither of the detectives took a seat. Within a few minutes, the same man who they had seen arriving on the motorcycle appeared with the receptionist who was following him. In place of the leather pants and jacket, the doctor wore surgical green scrubs.

"Gentlemen, I am Barnabas Albrecht. How can I help you?"

Martin was adept at analyzing a person within the first few minutes of a conversation. Although not fond of the social sciences, Martin actually employed a variety of psychologies and thinking skills to solve cases. Of course, every detective uses analytical thinking in his investigations, but Martin also was a master of analects by Confucius, without even knowing it. He had a keen awareness of cultural diversity, that different cultures have different core values. Martin had also practiced the ABC principle even before he was a detective. *Assume* nothing, *believe* nothing, and *challenge* and *check* everything.

"Thank you for seeing us, Doctor. I am Detective Wallace and this is Detective Gainwell. We are trying to identify a young lady. Apparently, you had performed breast augmentation on her last year. We need her name and address. We have the serial and lot number from the implants," Martin said.

"I'd like to help, detectives, but you have to understand. My patients assume their privacy will be protected. We have some very high profile patients."

Martin looked at the doctor and felt like saying, "*You pompous ass. You make a life out of falsifying the inevitable aging of the rich and famous. You are not a surgeon who saves people's lives. You are going to give me the "privacy" line and not help us in our investigation?*"

"I'm guessing this lady will not be concerned about her privacy. She's dead."

"Oh. That is terrible. Okay. What is that serial number?"

Pulling out his cell phone, Otis looked at his notes and said, "344-7796."

The doctor leaned over the reception desk and began typing into the computer as the receptionist slid her chair to the side to give him more room. Martin wondered how much "work" the doctor had done on himself. There was no argument the doctor was a good looking man. Standing at 6' 2", he had broad shoulders which tapered down to a slim waist. It was obvious the man worked out regularly. He had wavy strawberry blond hair, a chiseled jaw and straight white teeth. Martin guessed that Dr. Albrecht was in his late 40s, early 50s. He was not wearing a wedding ring, Martin noticed.

"Oh…yes, I remember her. Her name is Farah Darvish. What a shame. She was such a nice girl. She was a student at Penn," he said as he wrote something down on a pad of paper. Tearing the top page off the pad, he handed it to Otis. This is the address we have for her."

"Doctor, did Farah ever indicate she had any personal problems, maybe with a boyfriend?"

"Not that I know of. Our conversations were mostly professional. She did tell me she was from California."

"Okay. Thank you Dr. Albrecht. If you think of anything else that might be helpful to our investigation, please give us a call," Otis said as both detectives handed the doctor their business cards. "Nice bike. What year is your Harley?"

The doctor's demeanor went from business-serious to elation as if he won the lottery. "It's a 2018 Harley Blue Edition. The rarest motorcycle in the world."

"Blue Edition? Wow! That is the bike that has a 100PS motor that is illuminated by heat-resistant LEDs, making it the first motorcycle to have an internally lit motor."

"You know your motorcycles, Detective. Correct, you are. It also has a rotating camshaft visible through a window in the camshaft housing, and gold throttle valves."

"I had a XLCH Sportster."

"Nice," the doctor said in a dismissive tone. "If there isn't anything further, I must prep for surgery now."

"That is all for now. If we have additional questions we know how to reach you. Thank you, Doctor," Otis said.

As the detectives were walking towards their car, Martin asked Otis, "What did you think of the good doctor?"

"He was accommodating enough, but a bit pompous. I felt he was speaking down to me."

"No, I saw the same thing. Some doctors are that way. I'm guessing, plastic surgeons more so."

"Clearly, you have never been to a plastic surgeon," Otis said, trying to hold back his laughter.

"Well, aren't you the comedian, Detective Gainwell."

"Hey, there's enough to cry about in our jobs. If we don't laugh…"

"Relax, Otis. We're good. Let's see what we can learn about eyes."

Martin said, "This visit to Dr. Faulkner is just to edify ourselves on why someone would want to harvest a pair of eyes. Mary Jo called the doctor's office this morning and asked if he would be so kind to see us. His secretary said he would make time for us between 10:00 and 10:30, so we need to get rolling.

On the way to Wills Eye Hospital, Martin picked up his cell phone and called the office.

"Corporal Wilton, our vic's name is Farah Darvish. She was a student at Penn. I want you to find out everything you can about her. Get her cell phone number, search her Facebook page, get her email address. Everything. Otis and I just left the plastic surgeon's office. We are heading to Wills Eye Hospital and then over to Penn's campus."

Soon after the call ended, they pulled up in front of the hospital.

Dr. Faulkner's office was on the sixth floor. Otis looked at Martin and said, "Stairs or elevator?"

"Stairs," Martin said.

Dr. Faulkner's reception room was quite different from Dr. Albrecht's. Although bright with light colored walls and contemporary prints of flowers, it had faux-leather seats, no refrigerator or coffee machine, and a television airing some inane talk show. This waiting room would not have appealed to the upper echelon, Martin thought.

After announcing their arrival, the detectives took a seat. An elderly white man with a younger, black woman, presumably, his caregiver, were seated on the love seat. Across from the detectives was a mother and young boy with a patch over his left eye. Martin wondered if the child thought it might be cool to play pirate for a while. Stupid thought, he realized.

"Detectives, Dr. Faulkner will see you now," the receptionist said.

A door behind the receptionist desk opened and a short balding man, with a nicely cropped beard appeared.

"Gentlemen, I'm Dr. Faulkner. Please come in and have a seat. Your wife said you have some questions I may be able to answer, Captain Wallace."

"Yes, doctor. Thank you for seeing us. This is my partner, Detective Gainwell. Mary Jo's sister thinks the world of you. You did some amazing things for her. She thought she had lost her vision for good."

"That is very kind of her."

"Doctor, we are investigating a homicide where the victim had her eyes removed."

"What? That is awful."

"Yes, and according to the forensic pathologist, it was done with surgical precision."

"A medical professional did this ghastly thing?"

"Apparently, or at least someone who has had medical training. Doctor, we are trying to determine a motive. Are eye transplants possible?"

"Yes, there are eye transplants, but they are limited to specific parts of the eye, such as the cornea. The most common type of eye transplant is a corneal transplant, where a damaged cornea is replaced with a healthy donor cornea.

"Last year, a team of over 100 surgeons at NYU Langone Health in New York City performed the first successful transplant of an entire eye and part of the face. The patient had suffered severe electrical burns to his face and left eye. Although the actual transplant was successful, the patient still cannot see. The main obstacle to restoring vision is that we have not yet figured out how to regenerate the optic nerve, which is necessary to transmit visual signals from the eye to the brain."

"Are there any other reasons why someone would want a pair of healthy eyes from a lady in her twenties?" Otis asked.

"Not that I can think of, but God forbid, if you begin finding more victims, you may have some twisted doctor who is trying to discover a way to transplant the entire eye. The blood supply and the critical optic nerve that must connect it to the brain, in order to cure blindness, is only a dream at this point in time."

"Thank you for your time, Doctor. You have been very helpful."

"My pleasure, Detective. Please do not hesitate to contact me if I can be of further help."

As the men walked out of the hospital, Otis's phone rang.

"Gainwell. Right. Okay, Great! Hold on. Let me write this down. What is his name again? Got it. Thanks." Turning to Martin, he said, "Lane and Lillia searched Farah's Facebook page. She did have a boyfriend. His name is Tanner Thrush and get this, he's a pre-med student at Penn,"

"Pre-med? Now things are getting interesting. Tell Ewing and Santos to go pay him a visit and have Becton and Sinclair interview her friends."

# CHAPTER FOUR

*Boys think girls are like books. If the cover doesn't catch their eye they won't bother to read what's inside.*
— Marilyn Monroe

Diego and Lillia drove over to Farah's boyfriend's apartment to interview him, hoping to gather information about the girl's murder. Martin thought Lillia's calm demeanor would counter Diego's intensity. Arriving in the Spruce Hill neighborhood that butts up against the University of Pennsylvania's campus, they parked their car and walked up to the building, a boutique complex with one- and two-bedroom apartments.

"This is it. 1395 Pine Street," Diego said. "He lives in apartment 9."

They knocked on the door, once, twice, when a handsome young man in a yellow and black flannel shirt and jeans walked up the steps behind them. His hair was the color of a crow's feathers, primarily black, but it appeared iridescent as it reflected the light from the stairwell window, giving off shades of blue and violet.

"Can I help you?" the young man asked.

"Tanner Thrush?" Lillia asked.

"Who wants to know?"

Both Lillia and Diego displayed their badges at the same time.

"I am Lieutenant Ewing and this is Sergeant Santos. We are with the Major Crimes Unit of the PPD. May we come in?"

"What's this all about?" the man said as he walked into the apartment. The detectives followed.

The living room was modestly fashioned. On the coffee table were several empty beer cans and several Chinese takeout containers.

"Are you dating Farah Darvish?" asked Lillia.

"Why are you asking? Is she alright?"

"We are in the middle of an investigation. Where were you last night between the hours of 10 and 2?"

"I was performing at Klein Recital Hall till about 10. I am a concert pianist. Farah came to hear me play. Afterwards, she said she was tired so I walked her to her dorm. I guess that was about 10:30 or so. Then I went to a bar down the street, picked up a six-pack and came back here to study for an exam I just took. What is this all about?"

"What is the name of the bar?" asked Diego.

"The Raven's Roost."

"Would you mind if we took a look around your apartment?' Lillia said.

"Would it matter if I said no?" Tanner asked.

"Not really."

Tanner motioned with his hand for them to go ahead and look around. Nothing seemed out of the ordinary. The two detectives searched aimlessly, like a writer looking for the appropriate metaphor but coming up empty.

Would you be willing to come down to the station to answer a few questions?" Diego asked.

"Questions about what? No, I'm not going anywhere until you tell me what is going on."

Looking at Lillia, it was obvious they would have to tell Tanner his girlfriend was dead. His reaction would tell them a lot.

"Mr. Thrush, I am sorry to inform you that Farah Darvish's body was found on Penn's campus last night."

"What? No! You've got this wrong! I walked her to her dorm room last night and she said she wasn't going out again," he said as he retrieved his cell phone from his pants pocket and put it up to his ear. "Answer your phone, Farah, please!"

Lillia handed Tanner a photograph that Lane had altered by adding a pair of eyes. "Is this Farah?"

Tanner said nothing. He lowered his head slowly and sat down on an ottoman. After what seemed to be several minutes, he said, "It looks like her, but she has green eyes, not blue. Maybe it's not her. How did this woman die?"

"We are not at liberty to discuss that at this time. Do you have a recent photograph of Farah?"

Tanner stood up, briefly thumbed through some photos on his phone, then handed Lillia his phone. Diego looked over her shoulder at the photo of Farah and Tanner standing arm-in-arm on the beach. The first thing Lillia and Diego saw were Farah's impossibly beautiful eyes.

"Would you mind air-dropping that photo to my phone? We don't have any photographs of Farah," Lillia asked.

"Okay," Tanner said as he transferred the photo.

"Mr. Thrush, why don't you come with us? We'll bring you back here after our discussion."

Getting up off the ottoman, Tanner said, "I have crew practice in a few hours. I need to be at Boathouse Row."

"Not a problem. Come down to the station, answer a few more questions and we'll drive you over there."

Tanner picked up a gym bag and his jacket and led the detectives out of the apartment.

~~~

Jake and Jordan left the precinct to interview Farah Darvish's roommate. As their car turned onto 34th Street and headed west toward the Penn campus, Franklin Field, the oldest college stadium in the country, stood off to the right. The stadium's high, open arcades, brick battlement parapet, and cast stone quoin-like bands, gives it a Colosseum-type vibe. Built in 1895, the grounds had previously served as a potter's field. *How appropriate,* Jordan thought to himself.

Once parked, the two detectives walked through the stunningly beautiful Kaskey Park enroute to Farah Darvish's dorm. The park was originally a botanical garden as part of a major transformation of the campus in the late 1800s. Over the years it had become a naturalistic garden home to hundreds of species of plants and even a refuge for wildlife.

"Should we speak to her roommate first?" Jordan asked.

"It's as good a place as any to start," responded Jake.
~~~

Entering the dorm, they took the elevator to the fourth floor. Finding room 421, they knocked on Farah's door.

"Emma just left for the library," a voice said from behind them.

The detectives turned around to find a young lady dressed in jeans and a sweatshirt, hauling a backpack. Taking one of her ear buds out, she said. "And Farah, well…"

"Yes, we are here about Ms. Darvish," Jake said.

"We saw it on the news this morning."

"Did you know her?"

"Not very well, but she seemed very nice. It's pretty scary, you know? My friends on campus are all freaked out."

"Yes, well, we are working day and night to find who did this terrible thing. You said her roommate went to the library. Where exactly is the library located?"

"Penn has nineteen libraries. She didn't say which one she was heading to, but I'm guessing it was Van-Pelt Dietrich Library Center. It's the Center for Global Collections. It is located in the 3400 block of Walnut Street. Fifth floor. Gotta go. I'm late for class."

"Thank you," Jordan said. Turning to Jake he said, "Nineteen libraries? The state school I went to had one."

"Go figure."

The detectives left the dorm and walked across campus towards Walnut Street.

"It didn't take long for the girls in her dorm to hear about the murder," Jordan said.

"Bad news travels fast," Jake said.

As they walked among the students, Jordan turned to Jake and said, "Man, to be twenty-one again."

"Were there many pretty girls where you went to college?" Jake asked.

"Not that I recall, but I went to Glassboro State and I commuted. I missed out on a lot of campus life. What about you?"

"I used the GI Bill to get my college education, but I also worked full time. If I wasn't in classes or studying, I was working. There were definitely some hot babes, but it seems to be that the ratio of women to men is better here at Penn."

The detectives entered the Van-Pelt Dietrich Library Center. Looking around, they both had the same impression, that they stood out like a nun at a NA meeting. The two men looked at each other, said nothing, and then looked at the photo of Emma McKinley that Lane had printed from a Facebook posting. They did not have to search very long before a young, redhead dressed in sweatpants and a turtleneck, walked up to them.

"Are you here about Farah's murder?"

"We are. Might you be Emma McKinley?" asked Jordan.

"I am. I am…was…Farah's roommate. The entire campus is devastated."

"I'm sure. Rest assured, we have every available detective working on this," Jake said.

"May we ask you a few questions, Ms. McKinley?"

"Call me Emma. Of course. Anything to catch this freak. I had reserved a study module to do some research. Let's go in there. We'll have more privacy."

Emma led the detectives into a small room with large glass windows and shut the door.

"Emma, did Farah have any enemies? Was anyone harassing her or did she receive any threatening phone calls?"

"No. Everyone loved Farah."

"What about her boyfriend?"

"Tanner? In my opinion, he was a little possessive, a little jealous, but he treated her pretty well. I mean, he could not have done this, if that is what you are asking."

"He told us that he walked her to her dorm around 10:00 last night. Is that correct?"

"I wouldn't know. I was at a concert at the Kimmel Center. Farah wasn't in our dorm room when I got back."

"What time was that?" Jordan asked.

"A little after midnight. Maybe 12:30."

"So, you cannot remember anyone having a problem with Farah? No jealousy, arguments, heated conversations?"

Emma tilted her head a tad, as she knitted her brow.

"Well, there was this argument she had with an older guy a few days ago."

"What was that about?" Jake asked.

"I heard the yelling as I approached our dorm room. When I realized it was coming from our room, I waited outside the door. I couldn't understand what the argument was about because they were speaking in Farci, but Farah was visibly shaken afterward. I asked her if she was alright, and who the older guy was. She said it was her uncle who lives in New York City, and that he was old school, a devout Muslim. I think she said he was a Principalist, whatever that is. I didn't pry, but from the little she told me, I think he was pissed off that she was becoming too American, too contemporary, in the way she dressed and acted. I think he's the type that believes she should be wearing a headscarf and anything that would cover her legs."

"Interesting. Well, thank you for your time, Emma. Here is my card. Please call if anything else comes to mind."

"I will. Please catch this bastard."

The detectives got on the elevator before they began speaking.

"What is a Principalist?" asked Jake.

"They are a conservative group who share traditionalist views. In Iran they control the media, they vet candidates for president, those kinds of things. Basically, they ensure that everything is in line according to Islam," answered Jordan.

"So, our victim was Muslim, but the killer dumped her body in a catholic church? What's with that?"

"I have no clue, but if the uncle was so pissed off that Farah was drifting from her Muslim upbringing, maybe he killed her and wanted to make a statement that she deserved to be placed in a house of worship that includes najas. I know, you are going to ask me what najas is."

"You took the words right out of my mouth," Jordan said.

"Items that are always defiling are called najas and include swine, blood, dog saliva, and wine. In the Catholic church you not only have wine, but the wine is believed to be the blood of Christ. If this uncle holds anti-Christian hostility, then maybe placing his niece's body there makes sense, in a warped way," Jake said.

"How do you know so much about the Muslim faith?"

"My roommate in college was a devout Muslim. We shared a room for three of my four years at university."

"I don't know much about Muslims. After 9/11, I am suspicious of anyone who embraces Islam."

"Most Muslims regard Christians as Mushrik, one who associates partners with God. So that's not a bad thing, but they believe Christians are committing shirk, or polytheism, because of the Trinity, and so they contend that they must be dhimmis, religious taxpayers, under Sharia law."

"Would the uncle object to Farah's lifestyle enough to kill her?"

"Nothing would surprise me anymore, but I think we need to have a little chat with him."

"Let's check in with the Captain and see if he wants us to take a road trip to New York," Jake said.

"Good, I could use a nice hot pastrami sandwich."

~~~

Back at the office, Lillia and Diego had just returned with Tanner Thrush in tow.

"Place Thrush in interrogation room one," Martin said to Lillia. "I want you and Detective Gainwell to interview him.

"Okay. By the way, Jake has some answers on the orange nail polish, Captain."

"Good. Let Thrush wait for us. I want to be in the observation room when you do the interrogation."

Martin walked into the forensics lab and saw Jake with his eyes pressed against a microscope.

"Detective Sinclair, what did you find?"

"I used the Energy Dispersive X-ray Fluorescence Spectrometry for elemental analysis of nail polish. After extensive research on this specific nail polish...well, let me ask you this. Do you have any idea how many different colors and manufacturers of nail polish there are out there?"

"No. Let's get back to what you found."

"Oh, right. Well, the nail polish the perp used is called Pumpkin Spice, it is a seasonal offering, only available in the fall, and it is only sold at two high-end stores in the Delaware Valley: Stowman's Department Store, and Chic Exposed, a little cosmetic boutique on
~~~

Spruce Street. All of the credit card purchases were by women, but get this. I visited both stores and a girl at the cosmetic desk at Stowman's, I think they call her a beauty advisor, was the only person remembering a man purchasing that specific nail polish a few weeks ago. All she could recall was that he was a tall, friendly, middle-aged white man. He paid with cash. No credit card receipt."

"Alright. Thanks, Detective."

Detective Becton walked up to Martin and said. "Captain, we were able to determine what type of ladder the perp used to get close to the security cameras and spray paint over them. It was an aluminum one-button, retraction collapsible extension ladder. The problem is that all the hardware stores in the city and surrounding counties carry them. We have a list of everyone who purchased one in the last 3 months, and we are interviewing them, but so far we have no leads. The perp may have had this ladder for years."

"Oh, and speaking of ladders," interrupted Otis, "by calculating the distance between the ladder rungs, we determined the perp is 6' 2."

"That should narrow down our search a little. Only a fraction of men are that height. Good work, all of you!"

Martin walked down the hallway to the observation room where most of the team had gathered. Otis and Lillia were waiting for Martin to return from the lab before interviewing Tanner. Through the two-way mirror Lane would be recording the entire conversation. The detectives could see Miss Darvish's boyfriend hanging his head low between his knees.

"See what he has to say," Martin said.

Otis and Lillia left the room and reappeared through the two-way mirror in the interrogation room.

"We are so sorry to keep you waiting, Mr. Thrush," Lillia said. "And I am so sorry for your loss. Can we get you something to drink?"

"Yeah, well I need to be at crew practice soon. I will take some water."

Turning to Otis, Lillia said, "Detective, would you get Mr. Thrush a bottle of water?"

"You can call me Tanner. Is this going to take long?"

"Okay, Tanner. No. We just have a few questions. I would think you would be happy to help us find out who killed your girlfriend."

"I am, but I don't know anything."

"I understand you are a pre-med major?"

"Yes. I'm a senior."

"Are you minoring in music? I heard you play classical piano."

"No. I love to play, but I didn't want to make that my career. Medicine is my passion.

How was Farah killed? Was she killed in her apartment?"

"We're not at liberty to say quite yet. Exactly how long have you and Ms Darvish been dating?"

"Since the beginning of the year."

Otis entered the room and handed the suspect a bottle of water. He took a swallow and placed the bottle down. Otis made a mental note to swab the bottle for Thrush's DNA.

"What was Ms. Darvish's major?" Lillia asked.

"Civil Engineering with a minor in International Relations."

"She must have been pretty smart."

"She was very smart. I don't see how that is going to help you catch her killer. I told you I do not know anything about her death," Thrush said, with obvious agitation.

"Well now, Tanner, that's where you may be wrong. My experience has shown that the person closest to the victim often knows little things that can often break the case. Everything matters, Mr. Thrush," answered Otis. "What was your relationship like?"

"It was fine. We had a great relationship."

"Did you ever argue?"

"Occasionally."

"Did you argue the evening she was killed?"

"No. Look, I would never have hurt Farah. Are you trying to pin this murder on me? Am I a suspect? Do I need a lawyer?"

"Sir," Lillia said as she leaned forward in her chair and looked directly at him, "Everyone is a suspect. You were the last person to see Farah alive. That makes you a suspect. I'm sure you can appreciate the need to interview everyone who had contact with your girlfriend. Of course, you are free to call a lawyer, but there is no need, if you have nothing to hide."

"I understand, but I have to get to crew practice. We have the Navy Day Regatta in a week and if I miss practice I will be replaced."

"We are almost finished here."

"Hey, someone needs to contact her parents. They are Iranian immigrants living in L.A. I never met them and I don't have their number," Thrush said.

"Do you know anyone who would want to harm her? asked Otis. "Did she have any enemies? Did she mention anyone who was following her or harassing her?"

"No. She had a very small circle of friends. She was careful with whom she hung out."

"Was Farah a Muslim?" asked Lillia.

"Well, by birth, but not by choice. In fact, in many ways, she was more American than a lot of the students who were born here"

"How so?"

"She was a contemporary dresser, always wearing the latest fashion. She loved going to concerts and football games. She even got breast implants. She said her father would kill her if he ever found out."

"Why did she get breast implants, and where did she get the money for that?

"Funny. The only real argument we ever had was about her implants. She thought her boobs were too small. I told her she was perfect just the way she was. And the money? Money was never a problem. Her father is loaded and he wires money to her bank account monthly," he said as he stood, picked up his gym bag, and grabbed the bottle of water. "I'm not answering any more questions without a lawyer."

Martin walked out of the Observation Room and met Tanner who had entered the common area.

"Thank you for coming in, Mr. Thrush. Detective Becton, will you please drive Mr. Thrush to Boathouse Row?"

Extending his arm to indicate the direction of the exit, Jordan said, "This way, Mr. Thrush."

After they left the room, Martin turned to Otis and said, "What do you think?"

"Well, I was hoping he would leave the water bottle behind so we could check it for DNA. Anyway, my thoughts about him? Since he is a pre-med student, he certainly understands the intricacies of the human body, and I'm sure he knows how to handle a scalpel, but I find it a bit odd he is more interested in rowing his shell than he is in helping us find the person who murdered his girlfriend."

"I was thinking the same thing. He was not overly cooperative and he did not seem very distraught, either. Otis, there has to be some significance with the eyes. We have seen perps cut off the hands of their victims so they cannot be identified by their fingerprints, but why the eyes?"

"I have no clue. I laid awake last night till after two trying to figure that out. Farah was found in a church, with an open Bible. The good book says to remove your eyes if they cause you to sin. Maybe the boyfriend thought she had gazed upon something or someone with sinful desire. You know what I mean. What if he became jealous because she had eyes for another man?"

"And to punish her, he killed her and removed her eyes?" asked Martin.

"Exactly."

Martin was curious about Otis' faith. Most devout Christians Martin knew were very good at turning on and turning off their spiritual faucet depending upon the situation and their environment. Martin had lost any faith he had for God and the church. He believed religion was mostly a good thing. It kept some men from any tendency to break the law. He had seen the evil humans can do to one another. He understood some killing. Death is an inevitable, if not, necessary ingredient of war. It is the killing that occurs within a "civilized" society that lacks answers. And why does God turn His back on the victims of horrific crimes? Where did Otis find his faith?

Otis walked his talk. Martin didn't know any cops or detectives in this ugly business who were not hypocritical Christians. It wasn't that he expected Christians to be perfect, but he didn't expect them to cheat on their wives, lie whenever it benefited them or, at the very least, practice that Jesus thing about loving your neighbor as yourself.

Otis interrupted Martin's thoughts.

"Maybe the perp is a religious zealot, and that is why he uses scripture to quote or as a prop."

"The fact that Thrush is a pre-med student is what has me thinking. Dr. Wu said the dissecting of the eyes was done with surgical precision. I wouldn't rule Thrush out quite yet."

"Right."

"Well, let's see if their friends think the relationship was really so wonderful.

~~~

Martin gathered the team together to review the case.

"Well, we have not made much progress on this case. I know it's early, but we basically have nothing: no murder weapon, no idea where the actual murder took place, and few suspects." Martin looked up at the white board where a photograph of Tanner Thrush was placed. "Okay, let's have a little brainstorming session on the number five. Anything that pops into your mind. Anything. Go!"

"The Olympic rings representing the five inhabited continents of the world: Africa, America, Asia, Europe, and Oceania," Jake said.

"Good," Martin said as he drew the five rings on the board. "Keep them coming.

"The English alphabet: There are five vowels in the English alphabet: A, E, I, O, and U," added Lane.

"Basketball. There are five players on each basketball team," Diego said.

"Okay. We are on a roll," Martin said.

"The quincunx. The pattern of five dots on a dice is called the quincunx," suggested Lillia.

"Ooooh! What a show-off," chuckled Jordan.

"Okay, smart ass, what do you have to add," Martin said.

"The high five," Jordan said as he clapped hands with Diego.

"The number five is the sum of the first even and odd numbers, two and three," shared Lillia.

"She's on a roll," Otis said. What about the five-finger discount, theft?"

"Excellent. Anything else?" Martin asked.

"Five-speed transmission," Jake offered.
~~~

"These are great!" Martin said. "I have one. Five stones: the game of jacks is played with five stones."

"Now, who is the smart guy?" Jordan asked.

"Alright. I want you all to keep thinking about what significance the number five is to this case. Corporal Wilton, we now have Farah Darvish's parent's phone number. Please notify them."

Martin walked back to his office where he saw a 5 x 7 manilla envelope sitting on his desk. He was about to toss it aside, when he felt something other than paper inside. Opening it he found a cassette tape, nothing else. Martin flipped the envelope over. No return address. Yelling toward the open office door he said, "Detective Gainwell, do you have a minute?"

"What's up, Captain?"

"Take a look at this."

"Ha! I haven't seen one of those since my dad would pop one into his cassette recorder and listen to Harold Melvin and the Blue Notes. Do we even have a cassette recorder in the building?"

"I doubt it." Martin walked out of his office to the common area. Otis followed.

"Sinclair, I would like you to head down to that vintage record shop on South Street. I forget what it's called."

"The Vinyl Jukebox," Lane said. Martin gave him an odd look. "Hey, I'm a music connoisseur. I'd rather listen to vinyl than I would digital or a CD. More authentic. Better sound."

Turning back to Jake, Martin said, "Give them a call and see if they have any used cassette players we can pick up."

# CHAPTER FIVE

*The world is never quiet, even its silence eternally resounds with the same notes, in vibrations which escape our ears. As for those that we perceive, they carry sounds to us, occasionally a chord, never a melody.*
— Albert Camus

artin inserted the tape into the portable cassette player. After listening to the first seven words recorded on the tape, he stopped the tape, rewound it and called Otis into his office.

"Close the door. This tape is from our killer. I only listened to the very beginning of it where he introduces himself. He is using some kind of voice altering software. I want you to hear this.

*Hello, Martin. You can call me "Five." By now I am sure you are hard at work to solve the riddle I have imposed upon you. This is a game of wits. Mine against yours. Now, why the eyes? The eyes are the window to the soul. It is the eyes that draw us in, is it not? This young lady had, in fact, a quintessential set of eyes. Perfection. Flawless.*

*Are you a fan of things that cannot be improved upon, Martin? Ahhh, what makes a perfect set of eyes, you may ask yourself. Well, to begin, there is the palpebral fissure length. Oh, I'm sorry. Am I talking over your head, Captain? Let me simplify it for you. The palpebral fissure length is the distance between the inner and outer canthi of the eye, or the opening between the eyelids. Eyes that are wider than they are tall, are much more attractive.*

*Then there is the issue of eye color. Green eyes are both rare and beautiful. Did you know that only about 2% of people worldwide have green eyes?*

*Now we come to the eye shape: Almond-shaped eyes, which are symmetrical and resemble an almond, are the most attractive and desirable shape. Iranians tend to have this type of eye.*

*This lady also had perfect iris exposure. To be flawless the iris should be around 90% exposed.*

*Lastly, the inner and outer half of the eye should have an optimal ratio of 4:5. I had to search for months, no, years, but my patience was rewarded when I found Farah's idyllic eyes.*

*Well, my fine antagonist, I am now off on my next scavenger hunt. Stay tuned!*

*Sincerely,*
*Five*

The click from the off button was the only sound in Martin's office. Martin and Otis were silent. Neither wanted to interrupt the other's thoughts. Finally, Otis broke the silence.

"What does he mean that he is off on his next scavenger hunt? Is he insinuating he will go after more victims?"

"It would seem that way. We need to get ahead of this before he kills another innocent lady."

Martin got up from his desk and opened the door to his office.

"Wilton, do you have a minute?"

"What's up, Captain?"

"What do you know about voice altering technology?

"Well, there are some pretty sophisticated software programs out there that will disguise a voice. There are also VPNs and encrypted voice apps."

"This isn't about a phone call. The Captain received a prerecorded tape from our killer," Otis said.

"Play the tape again for the corporal," Martin said.

Lane listened intently to the recording, working hard to analyze what he was hearing.

"Sick puppy," Lane said. "Voice changing software is a type of AI application that allows users to alter pre-recorded audio. The software used can provide different effects, such as changing the pitch or speed of the voice, or transforming the user's voice to sound like a famous celebrity, or a cartoon character. Basically anything."

"Thanks, Corporal. I knew you would have the answer," Martin said. "Let me ask you something. Can forensic voice comparison software be used to identify the person whose voice is on this tape?"

"Well, kind of. We can use specialized software to analyze the voice recording and attempt to identify a speaker through voice characteristics; however, completely removing the distortion from a voice altered by distortion software is not readily achievable with current technology. In other words, we won't be able to hear the person's voice exactly as it naturally sounds. With advanced forensic analysis, we may be able to reveal subtle clues about the speaker's identity even with the distortion present. That's accomplished by analyzing the unique features of a voice like pitch, intonation, and pronunciation patterns, potentially to identify a speaker, but a voice to compare it to is needed."

"Alright. I'm going to take this tape down to Dr. Zimmerman. As a forensic psychologist she may be able to give us a criminal profile on the type of person for whom we are searching. When she is finished with it, get it to the forensics lab and see what anyone there can do with it.

~~~

The next day provided more challenges.

"Captain, Mr. and Mrs. Darvish are here," Diego said.

Informing people their loved one was, not only dead, but was the victim of a homicide, is clearly the most difficult part of a homicide detective's job. Interviewing family members while they still grieve is second. No matter how many times one does it, it never gets easier.

"Mr. and Mrs. Darvish, I am Captain Wallace. I am so sorry for your loss," Martin said with sincerity. "I am heading the investigation into your daughter's death. Please, let's go into my office."

"Who would do such a horrible thing?" Mr. Darvish said.

"That is what we are trying to determine," answered Martin. "When was the last time you spoke with your daughter?"
~~~

Mr. Darvish turned to his wife, looking for an answer. She was dressed in more traditional Islamic attire, including a shawl to cover her hair.

"Last Tuesday evening she called," she said.

"Did she indicate that anything was upsetting her? Did she mention that anyone was giving her problems or following her?"

Mrs. Darvish looked at her husband as if she were seeking his permission to speak. He nodded.

"No. She said everything was fine and that she was looking forward to coming home during the long Thanksgiving weekend."

"What do you know of her boyfriend, Tanner Thrush?" asked Otis.

The question clearly stirred Mr. Darvish's anger. He turned to his wife and said something in Farsi in an indignant tone.

"Did you not know she was dating anyone?"

Reluctantly, Mr. Darvish answered the question. "No, we did not. She would not have wanted us to know she was dating an American. She knows we would not approve. No offense."

"No offense taken. We understand her uncle may have paid her a visit recently. Do you know what that was about?"

"We know nothing about that, but my wife's brother travels to Philadelphia occasionally. He owns a restaurant in Great Neck, New York. I would think he may have been wanting to take her to dinner if he were in town."

"A witness said their exchange became pretty heated, and he left Farah without taking her anywhere," Martin said.

The silence was as if someone had just dropped a test tube of nitroglycerin.

"You have to understand our culture. We are modest people. We are not, however, extremists. We allowed our daughter to attend university and we have not pursued an arranged marriage, but dating is a sensitive issue. We would prefer her to marry an Islamic man."

Turning to Mrs. Darvish, Otis asked, "Would your brother have been upset enough to harm your daughter?"

Crickets. Finally, Mr. Darvish spoke. "No. He would do no harm to Farah. Now if there is nothing more, we would like to take our daughter's body home for burial. According to Islamic teachings,

Muslims should bury the deceased as soon as possible, ideally within 24 hours of death. We do not practice embalming. We believe the body should decompose naturally in the ground. It has already been three days. This is troubling."

"I'll see if the pathologist is ready to release the body," Martin said.

~~~

After Martin escorted Mr. and Mrs. Darvish to the elevator, Lillia approached him.

"Captain, Dr. Zimmerman is asking for you. She said she is available till 4, then she will be in a meeting."

"Thanks, Lieutenant." Turning to Otis, Martin said, "Let's go, Watson. Hopefully, she can give us a profile to go on."

"Watson?" Otis said with a look of confusion.

"Forget it."

While on their way to the doctor's office, Otis's cell phone rang.

"Hey there, Kalani. I'm a little busy right now. May I call you later? …Yes, that date is fine. Okay, I will see you tonight. Love you."

Turning to Martin, Otis said, "That was my fiancée. We are going to change the date of our wedding. She now wants a spring wedding."

"A woman's prerogative. Spring is a good time to get married. Everything begins anew."

The department's psychologist's office was on the same floor as both Inspector Jenson and Chief of Police Conwell's offices. The nameplate on the doctor's door reads:

<div align="center">

DR. REBECCA ZIMMERMAN
FORENSIC PSYCHOLOGIST

</div>

The door was open.

"Doctor," Martin said.

"My two favorite sleuths. So, I understand you have a real gem."

"We want you to listen to this audio tape our killer sent us. If you can share your perspective on this guy, it should prove to be beneficial.
~~~

It just may give us an understanding of the kind of creep this perp is and give us a clearer direction in finding him."

Martin placed the tape recorder on the doctor's desk and pushed "PLAY." Dr. Zimmerman listened intently to the tape, rewinding several sections that caught her attention.

"I can tell you he is educated. He obviously has no remorse or guilt. White, middle-aged male. Employed. He is a perfectionist. I do not think he is impulsive, like most serial killers. I say serial killer assuming he acts on his promise. He has a need for power and control. Clearly he is egocentric. He may have experienced trauma in early childhood. I wouldn't be surprised if he has mommy issues."

"Married or single?" Otis asked.

"That's a tough one. If he is single, I do not expect him to be a loner. He could also be married with children and living a secret life. He likes being the center of attention. Elaine Wu showed me the girl. His obsession with eyes has me a bit baffled. Gentlemen, if the eyes are the windows to the soul, this perp is soulless. I wish I could be of more help to you."

"No, you have been very helpful. It's just such a strange case. We need to catch him before he acts again. His comment on the tape that he was off on his next scavenger hunt scares me."

"It unnerves me, as well. Good luck, detectives."

~~~

Heavy clouds hid the moon, the streetlights offering sporadic light. The cool autumn wind had yet to be warmed by the anticipated sun. It was Halloween, a perfect evening for someone wearing a mask to hide in full view of others. Yet, Martin thought an Obama mask would be easy to spot since Barack had not been president for over 8 years. Half of the trick-or-treaters never even heard of him.

Martin wondered if, perhaps, the perpetrator was bluffing about more victims to come; however, the letter did suggest the killer was not finished with his ghastly endeavor. What exactly did he write? *I am now off on my next scavenger hunt. Stay tuned!* Would Halloween inspire the murderer to act once again?
~~~

Three weeks passed with no new victims, and there had been very little progress in solving the case. Martin was beginning to feel the pressure. He had a feeling his time was being spent as much to keep his boss at bay as it was trying to solve the murder. A few days earlier Inspector Jenson wanted to lend Jake and Jordan to help homicide with a case of murder-suicide that forensics believed to be a double murder. Martin argued he was being pressured to solve this case and the last thing he needed was to do so with fewer resources. The inspector relented.

Martin walked into the common area where his detectives were busy on their laptops or on their phones.

"Sergeant Santos, when you see Detective Gainwell, send him to my office."

"Sure, Captain."

Martin headed toward his office when Santos said, "Here he is now."

Detective, grab your jacket. We are taking that road trip to New York to interview

Farah Darvish's uncle, with whom she had an argument a few days before her death."

As a courtesy, I will contact the Nassau County Police Department to inform them of our desire to interview Mr. Ahmad.

Jake overheard Martin's decision that he and Otis would be going to New York.

Turning to Jordan, Jake said, "So much for our hot New York pastrami."

Otis and Martin left the precinct, got in their car and drove up the New Jersey turnpike while they discussed the case. They crossed the Verrazano-Narrows Bridge and headed northeast toward the village of Kings Point in Great Neck. There, the highest concentration of Iranians in the United States reside. What is surprising is the population in Great Neck is almost exclusively Jewish.

It was still an hour and a half before the restaurant would open for their lunch patrons. They parked the car in front of the small Persian restaurant. An entrance canopy identifying the restaurant's name, The Sunset Colbeh, moved reluctantly with the late autumn wind. The door was locked. Otis knocked. When no one answered, he knocked again, a little harder and a little longer. A figure emerged from the darkened dining room.

"We do not open till eleven," a man yelled through the glass door.

Otis pressed his badge against the glass, prompting the man to unlock the door. He opened the door just a crack.

"Officer, what seems to be the problem?"

"Detective," Otis said, correcting the man. "This is Captain Wallace. I am Detective Gainwell. We are with the Philadelphia Police Department. May we have a few words with you?"

"Philadelphia? We have our own police department here."

"Are you Mr. Ahmad?"

"Yes, I am the owner. What is this all about?"

"I assume you heard about your niece's murder?"

"Yes, of course. Terrible."

"May we please come in?"

"Yes. I apologize."

Mr. Ahmad turned on the lights. A paper Thanksgiving turkey honeycomb and small tri colored pumpkins were joined by some gourds that contorted themselves around the display on the hostess counter. A dozen tables with white tablecloths created a clean, elegant look. On each table, a small vase of flowers accompanied napkins standing upright in a folded pyramid-style.

"Please have a seat."

"Thank you. Mr. Ahmad. When was the last time you saw your niece?" asked Martin.

The restaurant owner tilted his head and looked away as if he were trying to remember.

"I think it was a few months ago at a dinner my sister had to celebrate Milad un Nabi."

"Milad un Nabi is in September, is it not?" Otis asked.

"Yes, Detective. Are you akhi?"

"No, but there are plenty of Muslims in my neighborhood."

"Funny thing is we have a witness who puts you at Farah's dorm room a few days before her death."

Hesitating, as if trying to decide how to respond, Mr. Ahmad said, "Oh, yes, of course. How forgetful of me. I come to Philadelphia from time to time to purchase items for the restaurant. I just wanted to say hello to my niece while I was in town."

"Items? What items do you purchase in Philly that you cannot get in New York City?" asked Otis.

"The glassware and silverware are much less expensive in your fine city."

"And they cannot be shipped to you from Philly? Mr. Ahamd, I have to tell you that if you are not completely honest with us, not only will you become our number one suspect, but you will be taking a ride with us down I-95." Martin said, as he leaned toward the man. "Do you want to try answering that question again?"

An obvious discomfort came over Mr. Ahmad as small beads of perspiration appeared on his brow.

"Gentleman, my trips to Philadelphia are of a personal nature. I would rather keep it that way."

Tired of the dance the uncle was orchestrating, Martin stood up.

"Get up, Mr. Ahmad. Perhaps you will be more comfortable answering our questions at our precinct."

"Okay, okay, but please use discretion. There is a girl I go to see in Philadelphia. She dances at The Striped Pony. You can understand my embarrassment and reluctance to share that with you detectives."

"How was your visit with your niece?"

"Fine, she is…was a lovely girl. She had so much promise."

"We understand you had a pretty heated argument with her that evening."

A silence permeated the dining room, only interrupted by ice falling in the ice machine located in the kitchen.

"Detectives, it is important for my sister and brother-in-law, as well as for me, that our children adhere to the traditions of our faith. Farah had begun assimilating into a society whose values are sharply at odds with our religious heritage. We have a problem with Western cultural practices, such as the celebration of birthdays, Halloween, and prom night. My niece was drifting from what she has been taught. This has been a terrible burden for my sister."

"And so, when she resisted your lifestyle, you killed her. Maybe it was an accident. Something you did not mean to do; it just got out of hand?" Otis asked.

"No! No! I would never hurt Farah. We disagreed, I reminded her that nothing is more important than the welfare of her soul. That her soul is eternal and her actions have consequences."

"You must understand, if Farah was to marry outside our faith she would have become dead to her family."

"Well, now she *is* dead to you, and not figuratively. Where did you go after you left her room?" Martin asked.

"It was late. I went back to my hotel."

"Mr. Ahamd, you may be seeing us again. Thank you for your time."

Martin and Otis got back in their car and headed back to Philadelphia. They had been driving on the New Jersey Turnpike for over an hour when they received a call from Jake. Martin put the call on speaker so Otis could hear the conversation.

"Captain, we have another murder and it looks like it may be the same perp as the guy who removed the eyes from Ms. Darvish. This time it wasn't the eyes. He removed the victim's ears. She looks like she is in her mid-twenties."

"Look at the victim's stomach and see if a number five is painted on it. I'll hold." Turning to Otis, Martin said, "Our worst nightmare just happened. May God help us. So, this time he went for the ears."

"First the eyes and now the ears?" Otis asked rhetorically.

Jake's voice came back over the speaker. "Captain, she has the same number five painted on her stomach in orange nail polish, and that's not all. The scene was staged. There is a scarecrow sitting next to her. The victim and the scarecrow are positioned arm-in-arm. She was found in Chinatown. I'll text you the address."

We are five minutes from the Betsy Ross bridge. We'll be there in ten."

# CHAPTER SIX

*Men trust their ears less than their eyes.*
— Herodotus

Rain began to fall as Martin and Otis drove underneath the Chinese "Friendship Arch" and turned onto Cherry Street. Philadelphia's Chinatown stretches from Arch Street to Vine Street, and from 11th Street to 8th Street. The 20-block neighborhood is densely packed with various businesses and an assortment of restaurants representing several East Asian cultures. Yellow police tape, and several unmarked police cars with flashing lights attached to their dashboards were parked in haphazard positions. Several members of the press were already there.

"What do we have?" Martin asked Jake.

"The girl had over-the-ear headphones on when she was found. When we removed them we saw her ears had been cut off. There were no visible signs of trauma, just like we found Farah Darvish. There are a lot of similarities to that murder. The perp concealed the area where he removed a body part, in this case, with headphones. You'll remember that Ms. Darvish was found wearing sunglasses which concealed her eyes."

"I remember, Detective."

"This young lady's name is Lan Nara. She is twenty years old and of Manchurian descent. She lives in a small apartment above the Golden Moon House restaurant on Race Street," Jordan said, handing the girl's driver's license to Martin. Pointing to a frail looking old lady, he continued. "That lady over there works in the fabric store across the street. She came out the side entrance to take out some garbage. She found our vic propped up between the two dumpsters, arm-in-arm with this scarecrow."

The corpse was an attractive young lady dressed in a pair of tight, black leggings and an oversized Temple University sweatshirt. She was shoeless. Both of her ears had been removed with meticulous accuracy. A scarecrow slouched next to her. No blood splatter was found anywhere near the body and not a drop of blood was anywhere on her face, indicating the girl was murdered elsewhere and later dropped in the alley between the dumpsters.

Jake bent over the girl's body and lifted her sweatshirt to reveal the number "5" painted on her stomach in orange nail polish. Turning to Diego who stood behind him, he asked, "Have you ever had the feeling of déjà vu?"

"What do you mean?" asked Diego

"That strange sensation of feeling like you've already experienced a situation before, even though you know you haven't."

"I know what déjà vu means, knucklehead! What I meant was— what specifically are you déjà vu-ing about?"

"There are a lot of similarities to the Farah Darvish murder. A facial feature was removed and covered with something. The body was murdered elsewhere and, not only dumped somewhere else, but the body was positioned carefully. And this creepy '5' painted on their tummies."

"Yeah, well, are there similarities with the Darvish murder? Yes, but there is no such thing as déjà vu. What you are experiencing is a false memory where your brain incorrectly signals familiarity with a current experience, despite it being new," Diego said.

"I didn't know you are an armchair psychologist," Jake said.

"There are a lot of things you don't know about me. What I do know is we need to catch this filthy snake who is killing these girls."

"We do. Speaking of snakes, did you know, according to the Chinese zodiac, this is the year of the snake?"

Diego performed gongshous, a praying hand gesture with a bow, and said, "Grasshopper, you mighty wise detective."

"This is not the time or place for that kind of humor, Diego," Jake said.

"I was just trying to lighten the mood.'

The rain continued to fall. Martin went back to his car for a hat. Late autumn in Philadelphia means sporadic rain showers, and when it rains, any evidence is washed down the sewer grate along with cigarette butts, empty crack vials, used condoms and bubble gum wrappers.

Jordan could be seen getting out of his car and walking toward Martin.

"Glad to see you could finally join us, Detective," Martin said.

"The early bird may get the worm, but the second mouse gets the cheese," responded Jordan.

"You better start looking for some cheese. I want everything swabbed for any trace DNA. The headphones, the scarecrow, everything. See if you can lift any prints off the headphones, Detective."

When Martin walked back to the body, Elaine Wu, the forensic pathologist, was kneeling over the young lady.

"Dr. Wu, have you been able to determine the time of death?" Martin asked.

"It's hard to say. At first I thought anywhere between 36 and 56 hours."

"Doctor, that's not much help."

"Her body is cold and hard. Martin, despite all of the advancements made in science, time of death is still one of the least reliable methodologies we have. Once I do an autopsy, I'll have a better idea. Her stomach contents can give us an approximate time of death based on the degree of digestion that has taken place. The absence of insects, flies and maggots specifically, tells me the flies did not have access to the body immediately after death, so I'm guessing she was not murdered anywhere outside. She was probably murdered inside a building and very recently placed here.

"I suspect she could have been murdered weeks ago. She may have been placed in a freezer after her death. I say that because there is skin slippage; the superficial layers of skin start to fall away. As I said, I'll know more when I do the autopsy."

Their conversation was suddenly interrupted by a screaming middle-aged Asian woman who was running towards them. Two uniformed police officers held the woman back, trying to convey it is a crime scene and she could not go any farther, but the woman did not seem to understand English. She did, however, seem to know the victim, because she repeatedly yelled out the name "Lan."

"Dr. Wu, do you speak Chinese?' asked Martin.

"I speak some Cantonese, but this woman is speaking Manchu. Hardly anyone speaks Manchu. Good luck finding an interpreter. I'll get back to you after I perform the autopsy. Meanwhile, I'm sure you will find out who saw her last, and when that was. That may be the best indicator of when she died," Dr. Wu said.

Martin turned to Diego and Jake, saying, "When we are done here, I want you to check out Miss Nara's apartment. When you are finished there, meet us back at the station."

The corpse was being placed in a body bag as Martin noticed Otis speaking to a young Asian woman who was trying to comfort the older woman in distress. Walking over to them, Martin listened in on the conversation.

"This lady is Lan's mother," the younger woman said.

"Do you speak her language? Otis asked.

"Yes, we are both Manchurian. I knew Lan. I cannot believe someone would hurt her."

"What is your name?"

"Abahai, but my American friends call me Abby."

"Abby, please ask her when she last saw her daughter."

The young lady spoke to Lan's mother, then turned back to Otis.

"She said she hasn't seen her for nearly a month. Her daughter attended an evening class at Temple University nearly four weeks ago and has not been seen since. She filed a missing person's report but, according to her, Lan is nothing more than a statistic to the police."

"It's comforting to know the police are held in such high regard in Chinatown," Martin mumbled.

Martin motioned for Lane to come over to him.

"Wilton, when you get back to the office I would like you to find out who, if anyone, investigated the disappearance of Miss Nara. Oh, and find out if Miss Nara and Farah Darvish knew each other, or if there is any connection other than the fact they both were college students."

"Okay, Captain."

"Did Lan have a boyfriend?" Otis asked Abby.

"Yes, his name is Guo Kong. He works at the fish market on 12th Street. I think they were planning a wedding."

"Abby, would you be willing to accompany Lan's mother to the precinct and act as an interpreter?" Martin asked.

"Yes, of course."

Turning to Lillia, Martin asked, "Would you please take these two ladies to the station? See if you can find anything more about our victim. Make sure you get both of their contact info."

"Ladies, my car is over there," Lillia said as she gently placed her arm on Lan's mother's shoulder.

"Detective Becton, I would like you to come with Detective Gainwell and me. Let's go pay this boyfriend a visit."

~~~

"This is Miss Nara's apartment," a gray-haired Chinese man said as he unlocked the door.

"You mentioned you have not seen Miss Nara's boyfriend around here lately. Is that correct?" Diego asked.

"I'm the building super, not Miss Nara's matchmaker," the man said.

As soon as the door was open, a little brown and white dog came running up to the three men. Its ribs were showing and it appeared extremely malnourished.

"When was the last time you saw Miss Nara, Mr. Chen?"

"I haven't seen her for a while. Maybe 2 weeks ago. No, it must be longer than that. Please lock the door when you leave."

"This dog is obviously starving," Diego said as he walked into the kitchen no larger than a small walk-in closet.

The dog had chewed the corner of the pantry door enough for him to retrieve a box of crackers. Wood shavings and the cracker box, which was in a thousand pieces, were scattered around the kitchen floor.

A wok and other pans hung from the ceiling. Everything in the room was positioned neatly to utilize every inch of the kitchen.

Opening a cabinet above the sink, Diego said, "Here is some dog food."
~~~

The dog cried as Diego operated the handheld can opener. He filled a small bowl with water, which the dog drank quickly, then placed the bowl of food before him."

"I think it is a chihuahua or maybe a shih tzu," Diego said.

"A chihuahua or a shih tzu? You don't know anything about dogs do you?"

"Not really."

"It is a Jack Russell Terrier. Call the Animal Care and Control Team and have them pick up the dog. I'm going to search the back bedroom."

A few minutes later, Diego came back into the small living room.

Thankfully, the toilet seat was up and by the water that was splashed around its base I am assuming the dog has been drinking water in there. And we know where the dog was relieving himself. It reeks back there,"

"I called Animal Care and Control. They can't pick the dog up. Ever since the budget cuts took place at the beginning of the fiscal year, they are down to two units. One is rescuing an eagle that nests underneath the Walt Whitman bridge. A semi struck it and it broke its wing. The other unit is dealing with a rat infestation at a private prep school in Chestnut Hill. We're going to have to take the pooch with us to the precinct."

"Great," Diego said.

"His name is Stewart," Jake said.

"How do you know that?"

"Because I just named him that."

~~~

Even though there was a steady drizzle of rain, the Gongsun Fish Market was busy with customers and workers scurrying around refilling the baskets of Chesapeake blue shell crabs and a variety of fish. Bins of scallops piled high, three different sizes of shrimp, and squid and octopus occupied the sidewalk. A young man dumped ice into the wooden troughs that displayed the smorgasbord of seafood. Martin and Otis walked up to an older gentleman wearing a blood-stained apron who appeared to be the person in charge.
~~~

"Excuse me," Otis said. "Can you tell me where to find Guo Kong?"

The man said nothing, but with his hands occupied with a bin of mackerel, he turned his head and nodded to indicate Kong was inside the store.

Inside the fishmonger was a young man filleting a weakfish. The detectives watched as he deboned the fish with surgical precision, a most challenging task, particularly with smaller, bony fish like small whole trout due to their delicate flesh, small bones, and intricate structure. This type of deboning required precise knife skills and a high level of dexterity to remove the bones cleanly without damaging the meat.

"Sir, would you please put down that knife?" Otis asked.

"Who the hell are you?"

Showing their badges simultaneously, Martin said, "We are detectives with the Major Crimes Unit. Now put down the knife."

The man put his knife down on the table and wiped his hands on his apron.

"Major Crimes? I have done nothing wrong."

"Are you Guo Kong?" Lane asked.

"Yeah."

"What is your relationship with Lan Nara?"

"Did you find her?" Kong asked anxiously. "Is she okay?"

"Answer our question," Otis said.

"We are engaged to be married. Now answer my question. Did you find her? Something bad has happened to her, hasn't it?"

"Why would you say that?" Otis asked.

"Why? Are you kidding me? She has been missing for over three weeks. Twenty-three days to be exact. I called the police station every day for the first two weeks, but the cop I kept talking to, a Sergeant O'Malley said, 'Do you know how many missing person complaints we get every year? Over four thousand!' I told him I am only concerned with one missing person, Lan. Now, for the last time, did you find her?"

The three detectives looked at each other. Martin gave Otis a slight nod of the head.

"Sir, I am sorry to inform you that your fiancée was found dead this afternoon," Otis said softly.

Kong took hold of the counter to steady himself, his knees buckling beneath him. Lane put his arm underneath Kong's arms and guided him to a chair in the back of the room. Kong put his head between his legs and wept.

"How?"

"We don't know that yet. When did you last see her?" Lane said.

"On the twenty-sixth of last month. She had an evening class at Temple till around 8:30. We met outside Alter Hall and then went down to The Birdhouse for a few beers and something to eat. I walked her back to her place, saw her enter her apartment, and I went back to my apartment and crashed."

"What time was that?"

"I don't know. Maybe 11:30…midnight? She only lives a few blocks from here. Who did this to her?"

"That is what we are trying to find out. Was there anyone you can think of who would want to hurt her?"

"No! No! Lan was a quiet spirit. Shy. Everyone loved her."

"Okay. Thank you, Mr. Kong." "Do her parents know?"

"Her mother arrived at the location where we found Lan, at the corner of 9th and Cherry Streets. She is currently at the police station answering a few questions."

"You have to catch this guy. Lan was the love of my life. She was going to be my wife," Guo said as he began to weep.

"We have every available detective on this case. I want you to know this is a high priority case. One more thing, Mr. Kong, please do not leave town. We may need to ask you more questions when we know more."

Martin and Otis walked back to their car and sat there for a few minutes, discussing what they had just seen and heard.

"What do you think?" asked Martin.

"I don't think he did it. He was obviously distraught, and they were not fake tears.

"I agree, but he sure is comfortable around knives. I know eyes and ears cannot be transplanted to another human, but something keeps bugging me.

"What's that?"

"The Chinese regime's practice of forced organ harvesting. In China, they use prisoners of conscience as a living organ bank. What if they are opening a branch in the States? What if our perp is practicing on the eyes and ears only to move on to kidneys, liver or lungs? Maybe even hearts."

With a look of discovery, Otis asked, "Hey, both of our vics were college students. One at Penn and now this girl at Temple. What if the perp's obsession with the number five has something to do with the Big Five association of local college athletic programs?"

"Good observation, but now the Big Five includes a sixth team, Drexel University. Let's give this more thought."

"Captain, you have been a detective a lot longer than I have. Is this the most bizarre case you have ever seen? I mean, this is absolutely absurd and we have so little to go on."

"It is, and yeah, the lack of evidence is not helping us. Hopefully, Dr. Wu will be able to give us something to go on."

As Martin and Otis were about to drive back to the precinct, Jake and Diego pulled up in their car. Diego jumped out of the car and walked up to Martin's side of the car. Martin pulled down his window.

"Nothing of interest at Miss Nara's apartment, other than a starving dog, but something dawned on me, Captain."

"What's that?"

"When Lillia and I were interviewing Tanner Thrush, Farah Darvish's boyfriend, I noticed there were several half-empty Chinese takeout containers. Guess from what restaurant? The Golden Moon House."

"The restaurant below Lan Nara's apartment," Martin said. "Bring Mr. Thrush back in. I have some more questions I would like him to answer." Turning to Otis, he said, "Let's get back to the precinct."

# CHAPTER SEVEN

*People are like stained-glass windows. They sparkle and shine when the sun is out, but when the darkness sets in, their true beauty is revealed only if there is a light from within.*
— Elisabeth Kübler-Ross

When Martin got back to the precinct, the boss was waiting for him in Martin's office. Martin glazed across the common room, then a double-take, thinking he had seen a dog. In fact, he had. Jake and Diego were introducing Stewart to the rest of the crew.

"Aren't you the most adorable thing in the whole wide world?" Lillia asked the dog whose tail was wagging at an impressive speed.

"What's with the dog?" Martin asked.

"Animal control could not pick him up and the poor thing was starving to death," Jake said. "I'll drop him off at the animal adoption center on my way home."

"If Jenson sees that dog, you know what will hit the fan," Martin said as he walked to his office. "He's already on the war path. He wants the case to be wrapped up in a neat little bow."

Martin walked into his office and looked with disdain as Inspector Jenson sat with his feet on Martin's desk.

"Martin. Come in and close the door," Jenson said.

Mark Jenson, Inspector of Detective Bureau Headquarters, was a clueless bureaucrat, concerned with both political and procedural correctness at the expense of the people who worked beneath him. Kissing up to his superiors was something at which Jenson excelled. He had a Napoleon complex, an adipose stomach that overlapped his belt, and he used the few remaining oleaginous hairs as a comb-over to hide the ever-increasing receding baldness.

"Glad to see you made yourself comfortable."

"Actually, I'm not comfortable. Have you gotten anywhere on this case? I understand we now have two victims who had body parts removed. Two! A serial killer is on the prowl and now the press is all over this. The city is going to be in a panic. Both the Chief and the Mayor are on my back, although Chief Conwell seems to think you can handle this case. I don't like unnecessary attention from my superiors. We need this case wrapped up."

Martin always felt law enforcement administrators should not run the investigation, but rather ensure the investigators have the resources to do their job. And when it came to the mayor, Martin believed supervisors should act as buffers between investigators and the other levels of command. But Jenson was the quintessential brownnoser; incompetent, with no humility and with little desire to run interference for Martin.

"The Mayor is demanding some answers and a progress report," the Inspector said.

"You mean the same mayor who has allowed The Kessington area to become the Philadelphia Badlands? A cesspool that has become an open-air recreational drug market that perpetuates drug-related violence and has hand-tied law enforcement so we can do absolutely nothing about it. That mayor?"

"That mayor is my boss, and my job is to make him happy, and guess what, Martin? Your job is to make me happy."

"If you keep the Mayor out of this my team will make progress. All he can do is make things worse. I don't trust him. There is still that issue with the disappearance of the Mayor's mistress a few years back," Martin said. "I still think he had something to do with that. It is more than coincidental that she was going to expose their relationship and then suddenly, she disappears. His long-suffering wife gives him a flimsy alibi and we are told not to pursue the case further,"

"I don't care if you don't like him, and besides, he was cleared of any participation in that case. The Mayor knew you were pushing to continue investigating his lady friend's murder. You are on his shit list."

"Good, because he's on mine! So much for nobody is above the law."

"I need to give him something. Where are you in this case?"

"We are not as far along as we would like to be. Mark, there was absolutely no forensic evidence, no DNA…nothing for us to go on. There is almost always something a perp leaves behind, but this guy is both cautious and methodical in his approach to these murders. He is intelligent and he plans his murders down to the last detail. Elain Wu is performing an autopsy on the girl we found today. We are hoping that reveals something."

Jenson got up and walked towards the door. "It better. Oh, and don't forget that Saturday night is the annual Mayor's Ball. Rent a tux," Jenson said as he opened the door to leave.

It was just then that Stewart freed himself from Lillia and headed straight for the Inspector. Without hesitating, he lifted his leg and peed on Jenson's pant leg.

"What the hell?" the Inspector yelled as he jerked his wet leg abruptly from the dog.

"Sorry, Inspector. The little fellow was victim number two's pet. The Animal Care and Control Team is shorthanded and could not pick him up. We're watching him until they can come and get him," Diego explained.

"Get rid of that mutt!" Jenson said as he stormed out of the office.

As soon as the inspector entered the elevator, the entire detective team broke out in laughter. In Martin's office, things were much more subdued.

Martin walked around his desk and sat down. He felt as though a fly had landed in his soup. He *had* forgotten about the Mayor's Ball, and he hated wearing a monkey suit. His wife, Mary Jo, was much better at small talk and smiling on demand. The ball would be one of the many situations requiring Martin's self-discipline, and self-disciplined he was. He had mastered it out of preservation and necessity.

As a child, he could conquer the Christmas Eve temptation of sneaking a peek at the presents hidden underneath his parent's bed, when his two siblings could not. He quit smoking cold turkey, and when he was beginning to see love handles appear in the mirror, he began habitually going to the gym.

Martin's self-discipline was never more evident than when he had conquered the demon of alcoholism without the aid of AA or a rehab facility. Although Mary Jo had mentioned he was drinking too much, no one made him quit. Mind over matter. Martin's strong will gave him the ability to scale many problematic mountains he had faced.

Martin's discipline, however, was not selective. Unlike the actor who displays discipline in learning his lines, only to act like a spoiled child who cannot control his emotions when the cameras have been put away, Martin was disciplined in all aspects of his life. Focused. He was not overly animated. He was more of a loner, forced into an arena where gladiators, kings and queens, jesters and entertainers, executioner and clergy would cohabitate. That was one reason he despised the artificial social gatherings where people pretended to like everyone else.

Martin was better suited to be a bachelor, discussing his thoughts with only himself. It was not that he was a bad husband, or he regretted marrying Mary Jo. He never cheated on her, though God knows he had ample opportunity. It was not that he regretted having children. He adored his children, even Martin Jr, who had not spoken to him in 14 years. It was more that he felt he was living his life for an audience of one, watching a theatrical performance in which he was the only actor. He often felt unattached to the scene being played. Perhaps it was the fact that his mind was always on a case—dissecting every nuance, every minute piece of evidence, every word of a suspect's alibi. He would need those traits to break this case.

Martin's thoughts were interrupted as Lillia walked into Martin's office with Otis.

"Jenson is going to have to change his pants. That pup went straight for him, as if he knew the inspector was unlikable," Lillia said.

"I'm not much in a laughing mood," Martin said.

Changing the subject, Otis asked, "I'm guessing he thought this case would be all wrapped up in a pretty little bow by now?"

"But, of course."

"Boss, I had a good conversation with Lan's mother and father," Lillia said. "Her father came down to the station after receiving the news from his wife. I don't know if they gave us anything that will help with the case, but I did find out a few things. Manchurian girls are given three ear piercings on each ear soon after they are born. Apparently, during the Qing dynasty, this became a law. All Manchurian ladies were required to have three ear piercings on each earlobe. A long time ago in China, ears were considered very intimate."

"Actually, this could be important, Ewing. Good job."

"I also learned a few things about Manchurian culture from Abby, Lan's friend. Manchurians are an ethnic group different from the Huan Chinese majority. Lan means "orchid." Lana's parents are traditionalists. They were not thrilled at the idea of their daughter dating or marrying a Huan Chinese. Lan Nara is Manchurian. Her fiancé, Guo Kong, is Huan Chinese," Lillia said.

"So we have a similar situation with Farah Darvish. Traditionalist family members who oppose their daughter or niece who were deviating from their family values," Martin said.

"And both of the suspects have expertise with knives, but don't we agree we are looking for one perp and not two?" asked Otis.

"It would appear that way, but we do not want to rule anything out," Martin said. "Speaking of not ruling anything or anyone out, have they brought Tanner Thrush in yet, Lieutenant Ewing?"

"No. I'm sorry about that, Captain. We got sidetracked when we got back to the office."

"Okay. Why don't you go now and take Becton with you. I don't like coincidences and I find it more than interesting that he got takeout from the Golden Moon House, the restaurant located below where our second vic lived. Will do, Captain. Oh, I almost forgot, Dr. Zimmerman called. The forensics lab tried improving the quality of that tape recording the killer sent you. They said there was little improvement in the audio quality."

~~~

Jordan and Lillia returned from Tanner Thrush's apartment. Jordan walked up to Martin who was in a conversation with Diego.

"Am I interrupting anything?" Jordan said.

"No, detective. What do you have?"
~~~

"Ewing and I went to pick up Tanner Thrush, as you had instructed us to do. He's gone, Captain."

"What do you mean, gone?" asked Martin.

"Gone, missing, skipped town. His landlord said Thrush loaded boxes into a SUV about a week ago and he hasn't seen him since. The rent was due last Monday and Thrush never gave the landlord a check, which he said was odd. Thrush has never before been late on the rent. Get this. When we contacted the university, we discovered he took a leave of absence. We contacted his parents in Ohio. They have not seen him and they are worried that he seems to have disappeared."

"Thrush said he was in his senior year at Penn. It is surprising he quit school when he is so close to graduating," Otis added.

"That's what we thought, but the university confirmed Thrush took a leave of absence for, what he called, personal reasons."

"Becton, I want you to notify the inspector of this and have an APB put out on Thrush. Have them use his driver's license photo. I want this alert to notify officers across jurisdictions to be on the lookout for him. He just jumped to the head of our suspect list."

"I'm on it, Boss."

~~~

The week ended with more roadblocks than progression in the murder cases. Instead of having the luxury of a day off to unwind and ease his mind, this Saturday was more like a workday. That evening would be the annual Mayor's Ball, an *optional* event Martin was *expected* to attend.

"The blue one or the green one?" Martin asked as he held up two neckties for Mary Jo to see.

"Neither. I rented a tux for you since I knew you would forget. This is a formal affair, my dear man," she said as she closed the bathroom door to reveal the tux hanging from the door in a clothing bag.

As much as Martin was dreading the Mayor's Ball, Mary Jo was looking forward to it. Opportunities to "dress up," mingle with the
~~~

upper echelon, and dance the night away were rare for her. The longer Martin worked in homicide, the less he wanted to socialize. He was, however, aware of this trend and so he tried hard to agree to the social events that interested Mary Jo.

As they entered the Union League, located just south of City Hall, Martin took a good look at his wife. She wore her hair up, a style Martin loved. Her full-length iris gown highlighted with sparkling sequin embellishments hugged Mary Jo's shapely figure. A lengthy side slit revealed her beautiful legs and her fabulous heels completed the outfit. Martin may not have relished the idea of having to rub elbows with those who never did any dirty work, but he was proud to be seen with his lovely wife.

The evening would revolve around "social" drinking, of course. Martin would be nursing a glass of club soda with a slice of lime. It wasn't that he resented other people drinking, it was the drinking to excess that annoyed him. There was a direct correlation between those people who drank excessively and their new-found ability to be talkative about inane topics. Martin had a distaste for undisciplined people. He would put on a happy face, say the appropriate things and, hopefully, make an early night of it.

The Union League of Philadelphia is a private club founded in 1862 by Philadelphians as a patriotic society to support the policies of Abraham Lincoln. The main building was built in 1865. The Mayor had given Chief Conwell an extra pair of passes for the event, who then passed them on to Inspector Jenson, who gave them to Martin, who, in turn, gave them to Otis.

As they entered the private club, it was obvious no expense was spared for the annual cocktail party. The coterie all wore sophisticated attire, while a selection of fine cocktails and hors d'oeuvres were being served by a half dozen butlers. The Union League venue was tastefully decorated with elegant, yet subtle touches, including soft lighting, candles, fine linens, and floral arrangements.

Martin found the butlers to be a bit over the top. They certainly had a formal, refined appearance, each wearing a black suit with tails, a waistcoat, and a crisp white shirt with a bow tie. They exhibited grace, decorum, and impeccable manners, all of which added to the refined atmosphere of the ball. Martin thought about the aesthetics, the appearance of the ball, or more correctly, the appearance for which the mayor was striving. *When you are the highest ranking politician in the nation's sixth largest city, I guess you can splurge when you have a party. All at the taxpayer's expense.*

Martin saw a small gathering at the coat check. Moving closer, he realized what had garnered people's attention. Several couples were enamored by Otis's model fiancée.

Martin and Mary Jo walked up to Otis and his fiancée. "You must be Kalani. I am Martin Wallace and this is my wife, Mary Jo," Martin said.

"Watch out for this guy," Otis said with a chuckle. "As you can see by Mary Jo, he has a fondness for beautiful women."

"Then we are birds of a feather," responded Martin.

"Hello Mary Jo. I am so happy to meet you," Kalani said. "And Martin, I have heard a lot about you."

"Martin took her hand and kissed it. You cannot believe everything this man says."

"Oh, so you aren't the smartest, most intuitive man in the Philadelphia Police Department?" she said with a smile.

"Like I said, believe everything this man tells you."

The two couples laughed.

"I love your dress. Is that a Miuccia Prada?" Mary Jo asked.

"It is. You have a good eye for fashion. It is one of the perks of being a model. Free clothes. The downside is the attention a model draws. I'm fine with walking down a runway, where no one speaks to me and I'm not required to engage in small talk. No matter how many of these types of functions I attend, I never feel completely comfortable. I much prefer getting together with a group of friends and having a barbecue in the backyard."

"Kalani and I have a lot in common, I see," Martin said. "Maybe we should swap dates for the evening."

Mary Jo gave Martin a soft punch on his arm.

"Oh no you don't!" Mary Jo said. "I'm not competing with this gorgeous lady."

The smile on Martin's face disappeared when he saw the mayor walking toward them.

"Here comes trouble," Martin whispered.

"Captain Wallace. And this must be the lovely Mrs. Wallace," the Mayor said.

"Good evening, Mayor Foerster. This is my wife, Mary Jo," Martin said.

The mayor took Mary Jo's hand and dipped his head as a courtesy. "It is a pleasure meeting you, Mary Jo. May I steal your husband for a minute?"

"Only for a minute, Mr. Mayor. Martin has some dancing in his immediate future."

"I promise I will not keep him."

The mayor led Martin by the arm to a corner of the room. Standing tall and thin, the chain-smoking, highest-ranking official of the city, reeked like a day old ash tray. His after shave and the breath mints he had eaten were impotent to the malodorous odor.

"Lovely lady. I understand you have been spinning your wheels on the two high profile murders that have surfaced. I'm sure you know most homicides must be solved within the first 48 hours or they may not be solved at all. The press has gotten wind of the horrendous nature of these murders and all hell is breaking loose. That is the last thing I need. I am running for reelection this coming year. I have made the decision to bring in the FBI so they can assist you before this butcher kills anyone else."

"That is a bad idea, Mr. Foerster. My experience has been that the FBI tends to ignore the suggestions of the local investigators and often make things more complicated."

"Captain, you would not be subordinate to the FBI, and they will not take over your investigations, I can promise you that. The investigative resources of the FBI can work with your people so you can pool together in a common effort to investigate and solve the case."

"Please give us another week before doing that, Sir. I think we are close to getting a break in the case," Martin said.

"I'll talk to Inspector Jenson and Chief Conwell about this. If they agree you are making progress, I'll hold off. Enjoy the evening." As the mayor turned to walk away he added, "You have to try those baked Malaysian-style curry puffs the waiters are serving. They are to die for. Pun intended."

Martin had the deflating sensation of impotency. With few leads, and the high profile nature of the case, he knew his team was making little progress. He had experienced just about everything in his 29 years working for the Philadelphia police. He had used his gun three different times, twice ending in deaths of criminals. He had solved numerous murders, safely brought home two kidnapping victims, infiltrated an Uzbekistan drug ring, and delivered one baby in the back of a minivan, but Martin was a realist. A detective is always judged by the "what-have-you-done-for-me-lately" mentality.

Mary Jo walked up to Martin and handed him a club soda with lime. She held a flute of champagne.

"What did he want?" she asked.

"He wants the most difficult case the city has ever encountered to be solved yesterday. He wants to call in the FBI."

"What do you think of that idea? Can they help?"

Before Martin had a chance to answer, Otis and Kalani appeared.

"Let me guess. Just like his puppet, Jenson, King Tut is upset we haven't solved the case yet," Otis said.

"But, of course. Now he wants to bring in the FBI."

"That's just perfect. Actually, I'm not surprised. Did you see this morning's *USA Today*? Our case is now getting national attention. Somehow they found out about the severing of the eyes and ears. They are calling the perp "The Broad Street Butcher."

"That would make sense if the victims were all found on Broad Street."

"You know the press. They need to give the murderer a name. Broad Street is probably the best known road in Philly."

"Someone is leaking confidential information to the press. That, in itself, presents problems for us. Much of the public's knowledge concerning serial murders is what they get from Hollywood productions. The way movies portray these monsters creates story lines to heighten the interest of audiences, rather than to accurately portray a serial murder. By focusing on the atrocities inflicted on victims by deranged offenders, the public becomes captivated by the criminals and their crimes. This only results in misconceptions and confusion."

Patting Martin on the arm, Otis said, "Try to enjoy yourself tonight, Martin. You've been under tremendous stress."

"That is what I told him," chimed in Mary Jo. "Where is Kalani?"

"Everyone and his uncle wants a photo with her. I wish they would let her be."

"She's a celebrity, Otis. You better get used to that."

"Oh, I am used to it. I just don't care for it. Kalani is always gracious towards these people who want a piece of her, but all she wants is to enjoy herself and be left alone when she is away from the modeling business. I guess I'm just surprised it is happening here."

Kalani walked up to the three of them.

"This place is teeming with every high profile lawyer, doctor, politician and celebrity. It is a who's who of Philadelphia."

"As far as I'm concerned, you are the most prestigious person here, Kalani," Martin said.

"Oh, you are a charmer, Martin."

# CHAPTER EIGHT

*Since love grows within you, so beauty grows. For love is the beauty of the soul.*
— Saint Augustine

Monday morning came as if the weekend never existed. Martin took one last swallow of office coffee, crumbled the paper cup in his hand, and tossed it in the trash can as he exited his office. He motioned for Otis to join him as he walked toward the door.

"Dr. Wu has the autopsy report. Let's see what she found."

Inspector Jenson, Martin's boss, was reaching for the door when Martin opened it.

"Captain, I was just coming to see you," Jenson said.

"Inspector."

"Do you have any leads?"

"Nothing worth mentioning. We haven't cleared the first victim's boyfriend, but we don't have enough to make an arrest. We are convinced the two murders were committed by the same guy. There hasn't been even a spec of DNA. The fact that our perp killed the ladies someplace else and then transported the bodies to where we found them is why we haven't found any DNA. This guy is smart and extremely careful, but we may have found a connection between the killer and the two victims. The first victim's boyfriend had empty Chinese takeout containers in his apartment that were from the restaurant below where our second victim lived. I have Ewing and Becton bringing him in for more questioning.

"Good. Let me know how that pans out. We need to start making some progress, Captain. Keep me in the loop."

"I will."

Otis waited till the DA left the offices before walking up to Martin. "He didn't say anything about the FBI being called in?" Otis said. "Maybe he wasn't privy to those discussions."

Martin took the flight of stairs down to the autopsy room as Otis followed. He was hoping for some significant forensic evidence, but his hope was fading. Martin was afraid it was more like wishing to win the lottery. Naturally, he was optimistic, but his senses provided a reality check that the chances appeared slim. Dr. Wu was not in the autopsy room, so Martin and Otis walked over to the mortuary adjacent to the room where the autopsies are performed. It is there where they found her.

"Dr. Wu, tell me you have some good news for us."

"I wish I did, Martin. As I suspected, Miss Nara's body had been frozen after death and then partially thawed when she was found. This was confirmed by testing the activity of the enzyme short-chain 3-hydroxyacyl-CoA dehydrogenase, SCHAD. This technique was initially designed to test meat quality in the food industry, but it has successfully been transferred to forensic pathology. Frozen tissue has distinct damage when viewed under the microscope. Ice crystals form within the cells and rupture the cell membranes causing catastrophic structural failure."

"So, after killing Miss Nara, the perp froze her body for nearly a month and then transported it to Chinatown. He must have a chest freezer, or have access to a walk-in freezer like the ones restaurants have," Martin said.

"Or, like fish markets have. Guo Kong, Miss Nara's boyfriend, works at a fish market in Chinatown," Otis added.

"Dr. Wu, did anything else stand out to you? Any DNA?"

"Unfortunately, no. I combed through the girl's hair, swabbed each of her orifices; nostrils, eyes, mouth, ear canals, anus, urethra, and vagina. I came up with nothing."

"What about her tox screen?"

"Same as your last vic. You will notice these two small needle marks on her arm. One was for the IV where the succinylcholine paralyzed her. The second was where she was injected with fentanyl which killed her. There is no evidence of any sexual assault.

"Martin, the man for whom you are looking, is highly intelligent, meticulous, and skilled. I have been doing this for nearly twenty years and never have I seen anything like this. It baffles me that he would immobilize these ladies and take the time to dismember them, but did not sexually assault them. Odd. What in the world could be his motive? I'm sorry I can't give you anything to go on."

"Me, too, Elaine. Me, too."

As Martin was walking back to his office, ADA Linda Bryson intercepted him.

"Captain, may I have a word?" she asked.

"Do I have a choice? If this is about the case, I just spoke to your boss this morning and have already been accosted by the Mayor, the Chief, and Inspector Jenson. Everyone is on my ass."

"I'm not here to pile on, Martin. I just want to know if you have any viable suspects. I'm also getting pressure from my boss. DA Malerba wants updates on the case and I have no answers. You need to give me something."

Martin stopped walking and turned toward the woman. Tall, slender and attractive, he knew not to underestimate the ADA. Her looks often would distract and disarm an adversary so he would let his guard down, to his own peril. She was quick, bright and witty.

"You know everything I know, other than the mayor wants to bring in the FBI. He also is having a press conference later today. Miss Bryson, I promise you we are exhausting every lead. If you need to tell Malerba something, tell him our last victim, Ian Nara, was frozen soon after she died. Her boyfriend works with knives and has access to a walk-in freezer, which would naturally make him a suspect, but we don't think he's our guy. He was genuinely devastated at the news of his girlfriend's death. And his alibi checked out. We are bringing in the boyfriend of our first victim. We think there may be a connection between him and our second victim, besides the fact they both attended local colleges.

"I hope something concrete surfaces, for your sake," she said as she turned and walked back the way she came.

~~~
~~~

Elsewhere, the killer was hard at work. The bright lights made it difficult to see the man standing over her, but her eyes revealed the terror she was experiencing. The metal table she laid upon was cold, not that she could feel it. The succinylcholine flowing through her veins caused the intentional loss of sensation. The paralyzed victim stared wildly at her offender. She knew this man!

Pulling his surgical mask down, the man whispered into the woman's ear, "My dear, instead of my proper name, you may call me Five, like the number. I must tell you, your lips are absolutely perfect, my dear. They are flawless. I noticed them immediately when I laid eyes on you."

Leaning over, he gently kissed her.

"Now, we are going to perform some surgery here, but do not be afraid. You are in a very prestigious position...or dare I say enviable position, my love, for I *chose* you.

The lady's eyes moved rapidly. Panic and dread were as evident as if she were screaming for her life. But no sound would emanate from her lips.

"No, this is not lip augmentation. This is not a vermillion advancement. No need. Your lips are the quintessential shape and size. No doubt, you are pondering my intentions. I must have your lips, my dear, but do not fret. I am highly skilled with the ability to make clean, precise incisions with minimal damage to the surrounding tissue."

A tray with scalpels, forceps, and both Mayo and Metzenbaum scissors, sat on a small table next to where the girl lay. A CD player accompanied the surgical tools.

"What, my love? You look confused. The music? Are you wondering about the selection? Quite moving and harrowing, would you not agree? It is a requiem. Requiem aeternam dona eis, Domine. Oh, pardon me. That is Latin for 'give them eternal rest, Lord.' It is a mass for the dead. This enchanting, if not intriguing, piece is Mozart's Requiem in D minor. I purposely chose this for you. Did you know that Wolfgang Amadeus died midway through its composition, leaving some movements complete? Franz Xaver Süssmayr finished the work."

"Yes, this is, in fact, a scalpel, my beautiful subject. But don't worry, you will not feel a thing," the man said with a theatrical sigh."

Five began meticulously cutting around the girl's lips, frequently dabbing gauze to absorb the blood. Abruptly, the man stopped and looked off, as if he were the one paralyzed.

"Ah, listen carefully. This is my favorite part, the emotional heart of this exceptional work. This is the most poignant movement of the requiem, the Lacrimosa. Mozart wrote only eight bars before breathing his last."

Five continued his incursion by cutting around the circumference of the lips and with forceps, removed them and placed them in a basin filled with a solution. He placed a large absorbent cloth over her mouth where it was bleeding profusely.

"I have placed your exquisite lips into this UW solution. Yet again, you look confused. Allow me to explain. UW stands for the University of Wisconsin. This organ preservation solution was developed there. The UW solution is effective because it uses a number of cell impermeant agents that prevent the cells from swelling during cold ischemic storage."

The girl's facial expression was unchangeable due to her paralysis by the succinylcholine; however, a tear appeared in the corner of her eye, slowly traveling down her cheek and resting in the corner of what once was her lips.

"Unfortunately, this is where we must say goodbye, my darling."

Five picked up a needle and injected it into a small vial of a liquid drug, flicked the needle to remove any air bubbles that may have been trapped in the syringe, then injected the girl with 5.1 mg of fentanyl. As the lethal dose of the synthetic opioid flowed through her veins, her eyes closed. Within a minute she was gone.

Five placed the woman's lips into a small container making sure they were immersed completely in the solution. He then placed the container in a small cooler packed with dry ice. Five rolled the girl's body off the surgical table, hitting the floor with a thud. He then positioned her body in a large black bag, zipped it up, and dragged it to the door where his black SUV was parked. Going back inside the building, he retrieved the container with the lips and took them to a walk-in refrigerator located in the next room. He then hosed down the table and watched the pink water flow down the floor drain. After wiping off his surgical instruments and placing them into a glass container with undiluted sodium hypochlorite, he turned out the lights and left the building.

~~~

The next morning Martin awoke earlier than usual and could not get back to sleep. He got dressed and went down to the kitchen. A large white bowl held a few oranges, apples and bananas. Martin selected a banana and peeled back its skin. Martin was a man of routine. His daily breakfast was a prime example: A piece of fruit, a cup of strong black coffee, a tall glass of water, a bowl of yogurt, sprinkled with granola, and a handful of blueberries. He topped the yogurt off with a sprinkle of cinnamon and a drizzle of honey. The only addition that fluctuated was the fruit that accompanied the yogurt. Today it would be blueberries, tomorrow, perhaps strawberries. The days of three eggs, scrapple or pork roll, home fries and toast were long gone. Martin's brutal dictator of a cardiologist laid down the law regarding his high fat diet and Mary Jo was the enforcer.

After breakfast, Martin left for work.

When he arrived at the station, the inspector's secretary walked up to him.

"You are a hard man to track down, Captain. The inspector wants you in his office right away," she said.

"Alright. I'll be there in a minute."

"He emphasized *right away*."

Martin tossed his portfolio brief onto a chair and headed for the Inspector's office. He knocked on the Inspector's door. Chief of Police, Bruce Conwell opened the door.

"Captain, come in," Conwell said.

Mayor Foerster was there with the Chief and Inspector.

"Martin, I believe you know the Mayor?

"Yes." Martin extended his hand to the mayor who responded with a limp handshake. Martin then gave a head nod to Chief Conwell. "Chief."

"We have been discussing your current case. The press, and more importantly, the public, want answers. We think you need some help finding this serial killer. I asked the FBI to assist in the investigation. I
~~~

don't want to hear your objections to this, so please save your breath. The decision has been made. At the very least, it will give you additional investigators and some fresh eyes to take a look at the case."

Knowing he was outnumbered, Martin said, "That's fine. Just to be clear, they will be taking all responsibility for the case. We are just there to do their leg work."

"That is not what I said. You are still in charge. They will be working alongside you.

And one more thing. We are having a press conference at 2 p.m. today. Put on a tie and jacket. I want you there. We need to warn the public of this serial killer. Specifically, the female students attending the local colleges."

"Sir, I think that is premature. We have no proof the perpetrator is targeting only college women. Announcing this to the press will only create panic."

"Captain, is it not true that the only connection you have between the two victims is they attended two of the Big Five schools?" the Mayor asked.

"We may have another connection, but it is too premature to mention. Yes, both of our victims attended Big Five schools, but assuming our killer is only targeting college girls is a large leap. This could backfire on us."

"Let me worry about that," Chief Conwell said. "Alerting the public about the killer's desire for college girls will decrease the impetus for the killer to continue committing these crimes. If another murder occurs at one of these schools and I did not warn the public, they are going to have my ass, not yours.

"Need I remind you that this is an election year? We need Mayor Foerster to win. The press is already saying a serial murderer is preying upon college age girls. We will show photos of the hooded man in the Obama mask, the ladder and the black SUV he drove. We'll ask the public for their help identifying him. Meet us in front of the station at 1:45. Dismissed."

Martin left the Inspector's office and walked to the common area. Entering the room, he stood for a few minutes to look at his team members scattered about the room, all busy at work. They each had different personalities, which Martin appreciated. Varying approaches of deduction, opinions on motives, and ways to accomplish a difficult task were what made his team successful. Unlike those who either were victims of the Peter Principle, or so incompetent they were promoted to positions of authority, his team members were sharp and astute, hardworking and determined.

They had not contracted the disease of government laziness, nor did they enjoy the play of politics. Martin hoped they had been immunized from the egotistical, grandiose mentality of self promotion. They worked well together. How they would work with the FBI was a concern for him. All were protective of their investigative team.

Otis was on the phone when Martin walked up to him.

"Alright, I will meet you there at six tonight. Love you," Otis said as he hung up the phone.

The look on Otis's face made Martin ask, "Is everything okay?"

"Yeah. Kalani has been bugging me for weeks for a day when we can go to the caterer for a taste-testing. She wants everything to be perfect, including the reception. I told her I didn't care what is served for dinner and she should decide, but she is adamant I am there for this."

"Otis, a wedding is the most important day in a girl's life. Go! Believe it or not, we can survive a few hours without you, and I have no intention of working past five tonight anyway."

"Yeah. You're right. Thanks, Captain. What did the Inspector want?"

"It wasn't just the Inspector. I got ambushed when I walked into his office. The Mayor and the Chief were there as well. Not only have they asked the FBI to join in the investigation, they are holding a press conference this afternoon."

"Great! Add more confusion to an already complicated case."

"Unfortunately, we have no choice."

~~~

Both the local and national press gathered in front of City Hall. Otis decided to attend, more as emotional support for Martin. He knew his boss does not relish the attention. Martin hoped he would not have to
~~~

speak, but being the lead investigator, he knew he would be expected to comment. The mayor walked up to the podium first.

"Thank you all for coming this afternoon. As you are all aware, there have been several horrific murders in our city. Due to the specific nature of these homicides, it has garnered much national attention. We believe both murders are connected and the perpetrator is not going to stop until he is caught. I'll let Bruce Conwell, Chief of Police, discuss the progress his detectives are making on the case, and then we will take questions."

*Questions?* Martin thought to himself. *Not a good idea.*

"Thank you, Mayor Foerster. Our Major Crimes unit has been diligent in pursuing every lead and have been interviewing dozens of individuals. Although we do not have one suspect, there are several persons of interest. We believe the killer is targeting college females from the Big Five schools. One of the victims attended Penn and the other, Temple. That is the only connection between the two. We would strongly urge all female students to walk in pairs. Never walk alone, especially at night."

Turning around, Conwell was handed several photographs from ADA Bryson.

"We are asking for the public's help in identifying this man."

The photograph was of a tall man with a hooded sweatshirt and a Barack Obama mask.

"Although this photograph does not show the perpetrator's face, we are hoping his clothing may look familiar to someone. Perhaps someone knows an individual who has a President Obama mask. The man in this photograph is 6 foot 2 inches tall. We have no idea of his ethnicity. He could be white, black, Hispanic, Asian. He may have been seen carrying a large ladder."

"This second photograph shows the vehicle he drives. We ask anyone who has seen this man or a suspicious 2024 black Cadillac Escalade, especially in or around Chinatown or St. Frances church, to contact the Philadelphia Police. We have a toll-free number we will share with you. The smallest detail may be extremely important to our investigation. We need the public's help identifying this perpetrator. Captain Wallace who is directing the investigation will take your questions."

*Great! Nothing like throwing me to the wolves.*

Dozens of hands went up, followed by numerous questions asked at the same time. It sounded like a kindergarten free-for-all. To Martin, it seemed more like a piece of meat was being tossed to a cackle of hyenas, and he was the meat!

Pointing to a local reporter he knew casually, Martin said, "Bret?"

"Captain, can you confirm that the FBI has been asked to help you with the case?"

"Yes. We expect them here tomorrow morning."

Following up on the response, the reporter asked, "Is that an indication your team's investigation has stalled?"

"No. It is an indication we welcome any and all help to put this killer behind bars."

"You," Martin said, pointing to an eager journalist.

"Can you tell us how these women died? What weapon was used?"

"The cause of death was fentanyl poisoning, but there is no indication either of these women were addicts. These are not women who lived on the fringe of society. They were not hookers wandering the streets at night."

Recognizing another face representing a national news organization, Martin pointed to her and said, "Elana."

"Captain, can you confirm that one of your suspects is your first victim, Farah Darvish's boyfriend, Tanner Thrush and that he has left town?

*Who in the world leaked that?*

"We have several suspects. Mr. Thrush is a person of interest. We just learned he put a hold on his studies and has disappeared. We have some questions we would like to ask him; unfortunately, he is nowhere to be found."

Martin pointed to an attractive blonde representing CNN, allowing her to launch the next arrow.

"Captain Wallace, is it true the killer removed the eyes of one of the victims and the ears from the other?"

*How in hell did that get leaked?* Martin wondered with exasperation.

"I am not going to confirm or deny that. This is an ongoing investigation. That's it folks. Thank you for coming. When we have something new to report, we will let you know."

Martin looked at his superiors posing for photographers and walked away.

"Well, that went well," Otis said with a hint of sarcasm.

Martin said nothing.

The two investigators walked from City Hall to the police station, a distance of less than a mile. Otis remained quiet, knowing Martin was more than perturbed. When they arrived at their offices Lane and Lillia were arguing over the correct pronunciation of the word *niche*.

"Really?" Martin said with anger and frustration. "You clowns have nothing better to do? The mayor and the chief have decided to bring in the FBI since, apparently, we do not have a *niche* for solving this case. They will not tolerate tomfoolery. And if I find out who leaked confidential information on the investigation to the press, I'll have his badge!" Martin went into his office and slammed the door.

"Tomfoolery?" Jordan said with a chuckle.

# CHAPTER NINE

*Beauty is power; a smile is its sword.*
— Charles Reade

Inspector Jenson and Chief Conwell entered the detective's workspace with two men in suits.

"Well, people, we can relax. The cavalry has arrived," Jordan said loud enough for everyone to hear.

"Look at them," Jake added. "They could be picked out of a massive crowd in a second. They scream "Feds!"

"Listen up!" Chief Conwell yelled to the team. "This is Special Agent Doug Huffman and this gentleman is Special Agent Kevin Buchanan. They are from the FBI and both men have worked cases involving serial killings. They are here to help."

Martin's team had an instinctive reaction to outsiders infiltrating their investigations. Bringing in the FBI was viewed as an insult, that they could not solve the murders on their own, and they took offense to that. The detectives scrutinized the agent's appearances. Huffman looked more like he should be playing the piccolo and marching with a drummer and a flag bearer, than he did a FBI special agent. He was short, bald, wore glasses and had a pale complexion. Special Agent Buchanan was tall, standing 6 foot 3, had a full head of chestnut-brown hair, an unusually large forehead, and deep dimples that appeared when he smiled (which is, perhaps, why he did not smile very often).

"Mutt and Jeff," added Detective Becton.

"Alright! Enough!" Martin said. "Show them the same respect you would expect."

"Thank you, Captain," one of the two men said. "I know you didn't ask for our help, but we're here nonetheless. Title 28, Code of Federal Regulations Section 540 B—a request by an appropriate state official is required before the FBI has authority to investigate this matter. In other words, we would not be here if we were not invited. The FBI's National Center for the Analysis of Violent Crime partners with local law enforcement in combating serial murders."

"Partners?" Jake asked.

Martin gave Jake a look that needed no explanation.

"Seriously, we are just here to help," Special Agent Huffman said.

"As the Chief just said, Special Agents Huffman and Buchanan have experience in working serial murder cases. You may recall the Cornfield Killer, Michael Thomas McDonald?" Inspector Jenson asked. "He had abducted and strangled seven teenage girls in Nebraska. These two men brought McDonald to justice."

"Inspector Jenson told me he shared with you everything we have thus far. Are you up to speed?" Martin asked.

"We are. It seems as though the perp has been careful not to leave any DNA or evidence behind," Buchanan said.

"That's right. The surveillance videos and the cassette tape recording are all we have."

"I'm sure you swept the crime scenes for any trace evidence, but it's odd that absolutely nothing was found. If you will indulge us, Special Agent Huffman is very experienced in serial killer profiles and he has some thoughts on this guy."

"Thank you all for this opportunity to share my thoughts."

"Like we have a choice," mumbled Diego.

"I'm not a fan of the media given too much information," Huffman said.

"Neither are we, but that came from our superiors," Martin said as he looked at the Inspector and Chief Conwell.

"I get it. In high profile serial murder cases, the media may attempt to interact with members of the victims' families, which we understand already occurred. The victims' families are obviously suffering emotionally from their loss and want the case closed quickly. A lengthy investigation, particularly one seemingly with no conclusion in sight, exacerbates the situation. I suggest we establish a liaison for each of the victims' families so we can head off the media. Whoever is assigned will need to keep open communication with the families to make sure they do not give into the media's tenacious demands for information, unauthorized information, that can hinder the case."

Huffman continued. "Just about all serial killers suffer from a variety of personality disorders, including psychopathy. The guy we are looking for is very good at manipulating others. He most likely displays superficial charm, a grandiose sense of self-worth, and is a pathological liar.

"Let me share some misconceptions about serial killers. Not all are dysfunctional loners, in fact, the majority of serial killers do not live alone and are not social rejects. This perp is hiding in plain sight. Most likely, he is gainfully employed and appears to be a fine upstanding member of the community. That is why most serial killers are so easily overlooked by law enforcement and the public.

"Another misconception is that all serial killers are white males. The truth is they span all racial groups. They also are not always motivated by sex. I believe you found none of the victims was sexually abused, is that correct?"

"That is correct," Martin answered.

Buchanan took his turn sharing his thoughts on the murderer. "We believe this killer is a local and not someone transient, traveling interstate. Normally, a serial killer has a defined geographic area in which he feels safe and where he operates.

"Since the victims have been found on opposite sides of the city, we believe the killer has great confidence he will not get caught. The logistics involved disposing of the body in multiple sites is complex. If he continues to do that there are greater chances someone will see him."

"The motivations for his killing have stumped us, as well. Financial gain certainly isn't a factor. I believe the key to solving this case lies in answering the question of why he removes facial features from his victims."

"That is all very helpful, but what are your thoughts on how to proceed with the investigation?" Martin asked.

"Sometimes it's good to go back to the beginning. Why don't we reinterview the friends, neighbors, lovers and work colleagues? Perhaps they remember something. If you can divvy up that list, Special Agent Buchanan and I are going to visit the crime scenes.

Captain, can you lend us one member of your team who knows the exact location of where you found the victims?"

"Sergeant Santos, go with them. Sinclair and Ewing, visit Miss Darvish's circle of friends and relatives. Becton and Wilton, you cover Miss Nara's associates. People, it's three days before Christmas. Be sensitive with your questions."

"We have created a team of six uniforms to monitor the toll free tip hotline," Chief Conwell said. "Calls are already flowing in."

~~~

Martin and Otis decided to reexamine both Farah Darvish's and Lan Nara's clothing while Lane and Lillia paid a visit to the store where the killer bought the nail polish. Both were dead ends.

"Hey, since Mary Jo is at Kalani's wedding shower, what do you say we grab a cheesesteak for dinner?" Otis suggested.

By the look on Martin's face, he was oblivious of the fact that his wife had plans for the evening, even though she told him twice.

"Eh, yeah. Sure. I'm partial to Jim's on South Street," Martin said.

"Fine by me. Ya know, I don't think I ever ate at Jim's."

"Best cheesesteaks in the city. I've been going there for 30 years."

"Damn! You are old!"

As soon as they entered Jim's Steaks, Maxine, a rather large black woman, saw Martin and waddled up to him.

"Well hello there, Baby. Aren't you a sight for sore eyes," Maxine said while giving Martin a big hug. "And who might this handsome man be?"

"This is Otis Gainwell, our new detective."

Visually inspecting Otis from head to toe, she shook her head and said, "Mmm, mmm, mmm! Mighty fine! You can investigate me anytime you like, Detective," Maxine said as she threw her head back and let out a belly laugh. "Now, what can I get you two gentlemen?"

"Well," Martin said. "There is a line out the door that ends almost to Washington Avenue."

"You know you don't belong in no line. Not when Maxine is here. Now, you having the usual, Martin?
~~~

"You know, I'm feeling adventurous today. I'll have a special Italian hoagie, with prosciutto"

"And you, Mr. Stud-muffin?"

Laughing, Otis said, "I'll have a mushroom cheesesteak with provolone."

"Anything to drink?" Maxine asked.

"I'll take a Pepsi," Otis answered.

"And I'll have a birch beer," responded Martin.

The two detectives tried to talk about anything besides the case, but no matter how much they tried, the conversation kept circling back to the murders. The sun had already set when they left the restaurant. They felt the early winter cold as simultaneously they pulled the collars of their jackets up to protect their necks from the biting cold.

~~~

An easterly wind rose off the river and flowed down Market Street like a rogue wave. As darkness fell over the city, Christmas lights appeared, giving the appearance that all was well. The holidays would decorate the city of death by placing a mask of joy and thanksgiving over what was a skeleton's face of fear and suspicion. Martin hoped for a silent night.

Christmas morning came unexpectedly for Martin. His preoccupation with the case made him nearly oblivious to the approaching holiday. In fact, he had to rush about on Christmas eve to purchase gifts for his wife. It was quite different for Mary Jo. She made sure Christmas would not be forgotten. Two of the three children, their spouses and the grandchildren would be dropping by after they had their own morning celebration. Martin's son, his wife, and their children would not be coming.

The tree was decorated, as was the remainder of the home. Garland draped the banister, cut greens and Christmas ornaments adorned the fireplace mantle, the ham was in the oven, and cookies in the shape of bells, snowmen, and Christmas trees were on a plate resting on the coffee table. Presents sat under the tree, waiting for the children and grandchildren to arrive. Martin's daughters would be there, but his son would refrain from joining the celebration. It was his
~~~

way of punishing his father for something Martin was still trying to understand. Martin had accepted that. His wish was a happy Christmas to all, and to all a *good* night. All he wanted for Christmas was a respite from a phone call announcing another death. Not today. Not ever.

No call came on Christmas. It came the morning after.

~~~

The black walnut trees, bare of leaves, like the skeletons of the psychopath's victims, stood in contrast against the background of the newly fallen snow. The snow arrived a day late for there was not to be a white Christmas this year. A day late and a dollar short, Martin liked to say.

Martin drove down Front Street swerving to avoid the cavernous potholes. As he approached the Old City's historic district, the emergency lights from police cars sprayed their red and blue warnings across the surrounding buildings. Charming cobblestone streets and an aura of 18th-century charm surrounded Washington Square, a small park located in close proximity to the Liberty Bell, Penn's Landing, and Benjamin Franklin Bridge. Fashionable boutiques, restaurants, eclectic galleries and theaters bordered the park. A statue at the Tomb of the Unknown Revolutionary War Soldier stood guard. Apparently, he had fallen asleep during his watch that evening, for nearby a woman's body lay cold and stiff. Martin walked past the monument memorializing Washington and the soldiers of the American revolution. An inscription reads, "Freedom is a light, for which many men have died in Darkness."

The full moon illuminated the yellow crime scene tape securing the area. Martin's breath smoked in the frosty air. His shoes crunched on the snow. Otis, Lillia, Jordan and Lane were already there. Lane was taking photographs of the victim and the surrounding crime scene. A uniformed police officer walked up to Martin. Small clouds of warm, moist air were visible as they spoke against the chilly, early morning air.

"What do we have?" asked Martin.
~~~

"A Hispanic female in her mid to late thirties," the officer said. "No obvious signs of how she died, but take a look at her mouth."

"Are those wax lips?" Martin asked as he leaned closer to the corpse.

"Yeah. Never seen anything like this."

"We used to buy them at the penny candy store in Pennypack when we were kids."

"Penny candy?" Martin had not seen Otis walk up from behind him. "You are old."

Ignoring the humor, Martin took a pen out of his coat pocket and nudged the wax lips to reveal that the woman's lips had been surgically removed.

"She has no winter coat on and it's got to be in the teens," Martin said. "No blood evidence. Once again, he did his dissection elsewhere, killed her, and transported the body here. Have you ID'd her?"

"Yes. The only thing she had on her was a driver's license in the pocket of her jeans. Her name is Katrina Alvarez. She lives in the Fairhill neighborhood," the officer said.

"El Centro de Oro," Diego said, having just walked up to the conversation. "For you Anglos, it's also known as 'The Golden Block.' It's the hub of Latinx culture centered along North 5th Street."

Diego walked over to the body. She was positioned on a park bench, legs crossed and her eyes closed. Martin bent over the body and pulled the victim's sweater up to expose her stomach. The number five was drawn in orange nail polish.

"Detective Becton, are there any surveillance cameras in the area?"

"Only on that building over there."

"I want you to look at the past 24 hours of film. See if the video caught anything. Go!"

"He who hesitates is lost," Jake said with a chuckle."

Who found her?" asked Martin.

"That man over there," the officer said, pointing to a man leaning on a white box truck. "His name is Ben Patterson. He was filling that newspaper vending machine next to the bench."

Martin looked at the vending box that was still open, a stack of that morning's *Philadelphia Inquirer* sat nearby. The top few pages flickered from the breeze. Martin walked over to the newspaper man who was obviously shaken.

"Mr. Patterson, I am Detective Wallace. Tell me what happened."

"Like I told the officer, nothing like this has ever happened to me before. I've been delivering newspapers for twenty-five years, filling these machines from Delaware Avenue to Broad Street."

"I was minding my own business. I brought a stack of newspapers over to the machine to fill it, like I do every morning. This lady was just sitting on the bench. It's freezing out here and she wasn't wearing a coat. Her eyes were closed, so I thought she was asleep. No one is ever out here this early. I said, 'You're going to catch a cold, Miss. You need a coat,' but she didn't respond. I don't think it's safe for a woman to be out here all alone at this hour. I told her that, too. When I got closer to her I saw she was wearing a pair of those wax lips we used to buy when we were kids. I thought that was really weird. I offered her a free paper, but when I held it out, she didn't take it. I touched her shoulder and asked her if she was alright. That's when I knew something was wrong. She was hard as stone! That's when I called 911."

"Okay. You did the right thing. Did you give your name and number to the officer?"

"Yes, Sir."

"Thank you, Mr. Patterson. We'll be in touch if we need to speak with you further."

A black unmarked car with a blue flashing light pulled up to the dead end street. The two FBI agents got out of the car and walked up to Martin.

"The same guy?" Special Agent Huffman asked

"Yeah. This time he removed her lips. The same number five is painted on her stomach. This makes three."

"If you strike out in making any obvious connections between the offender and the victim, we will need to discern the motivations behind the murders, as a way to narrow our investigative focus," Huffman said.

"That's fine, but that is also a problem. How in the world are you going to determine a motive for a guy wanting to collect various facial parts. I would say he's keeping them for trophies, so he can relive the crimes, but you would think he would stick to one feature. If only the eyes were removed from each victim we could surmise he has an eye fetish."

"Captain, I'm not going to pretend I have any answers. In my thirty plus years in the FBI, this is the most bizarre case I have ever worked."

"That makes two of us. I feel like I'm eating soup with a fork. We're not getting anywhere."

Turning to his team of detectives, Martin said, "Alright. I want a methodical search of the surrounding area. Anything, and I mean anything, you find needs to be collected and bagged. I don't care if it's a gum wrapper."

"Jake, see if you can get any fingerprints off the bench and the vending box. Lillia, let's see if we can get any DNA evidence. Swab the vic's hands, the wax lips, and her neck. Make sure you bag that cigarette butt that's on the ground next to her."

"Detective Gainwell, let's get to the station. All hell is about to break loose."

"Okay, when we get back to the office I'll check her marital status and anything else about her online."

As Otis and Martin were walking back to their car, a slender young lady, bundled up in a down parka, a scarf, and a stretch cap walked up to them.

"Well, if it isn't Captain Martin Wallace!"

"Breanna Drexler! Look at you!" Martin said as he gave the woman a bear hug of an embrace. "This here is my newest and brightest detective, Otis Gainwell."

"Happy to meet you, Detective. Don't let Captain Wallace fool you. Under that gruff appearance is a sweet, ol' puppy dog. A few years ago I was strung out on heroin and working as a prostitute to finance my habit. Instead of busting me, he worked a deal with the judge to get me in rehab and he even got me a job when I got clean. He and his wonderful wife, Mary Jo, would check on me weekly to make sure I was staying on track.

"Martin, you will be happy to hear that I am a sophomore at La Salle University."

"Outstanding! I am not surprised, Breanna. I could see your potential even at your lowest moments. What's your major?"

"I'm in the nursing program."

"I am so proud of you. What are you doing up at this hour?"

"We are on winter break from school. I'm working the breakfast and lunch shift at the All It's Cracked Up To Be restaurant on Arch Street. I'm running late," she said as she gave Martin a kiss on his cheek. "Call me. I'd love to have lunch with you and Mary Jo!"

As Otis and Martin watched Breanna hurry away, Otis said with a smile, "Who woulda thunk it. Captain Wallace is a softy."

Otis and Martin got in their car and proceeded down Christopher Columbus Boulevard when Martin told Otis to pull over.

"Look at that," Martin said as he pointed to several city workers removing a statue of Christopher Columbus. "There was an endorsement of a city proposal by the Philadelphia Historical Commission to remove the statue. They cited public safety and susceptibility of damage to the statue as a result of the George Floyd protests. Maybe I cannot see past my whiteness, so let me ask you what your perspective is on this, Otis."

"Wow! You really want a heavy conversation, Martin?"

"Seriously, I respect your opinion."

"Well, for some minorities, some statues are reminders of the city's complacency with systemic oppression and colonialism. On the flip side, members of the Italian American community want to celebrate their heritage. Personally, I think the answer is in diversity *and* inclusion. It doesn't have to be *if/or*. It can be *both*. Philly also has statues of Martin Luther King, Jr, the All Wars Memorial to Colored Soldiers and Sailors, and the Octavius V. Catto Memorial, which depicts the bravery of the 19th-century Civil Rights advocate."

"You're wiser than you look," Martin said.

Otis laughed.

Martin stared at the statue being hoisted upon a flatbed truck. "Maybe I'm just an old fart. I fear we are becoming the Russia of the 1930s and 40s. We topple statues of our old heroes, and erase their names in the streets.

"Things are changing, Otis. I get that, but not all changes are necessarily good."

"I don't disagree with you. Once politics gets involved in something, you can normally expect things to move slower and they will always upset half of the country."

Changing the subject, Martin said, "This case is convoluted, to say the least. We have more questions than answers, and we better start getting some answers."

"Hopefully, we will be able to garner some evidence that will point us in the right direction," Otis said.

"Yeah, hopefully."

# CHAPTER TEN

*A thing of beauty is a joy forever; its loveliness increases; it will never pass into nothingness.*
— John Keats

On the way to the office the next morning, Martin tried to shake his frustration. He wanted to tell the mayor, the chief and the FBI special agents, "I told you so," but he held back. He had shared his professional opinion that it was premature to assume the killer was targeting young college women. With the exception of asking the public for help identifying the suspect, all it did was create fear and panic across the city.

As soon as Martin walked into the common area, Jordan ran up to him, obviously excited.

"We caught a break! Forensics identified two separate DNA profiles from the wax lips.

One was from the deceased, Katrina Alvarez, and the other an unidentified male. There was also DNA on the cigarette butt that matches the same male. They are running the samples through CODIS to see if we can identify the male."

"Excellent! We needed this! Let me know the instant Forensics calls us with the results. Stay on top of them."

Looking at his team, Martin said, "Alright people, we finally have some concrete

evidence to go on. What else do we have?"

"Miss Alvarez is a Cuban-American and was employed at City Hall. She was an administrative assistant for Parks and Recreation. She is not a student at any university. She lives with her boyfriend, or I should say he lives with her. His name is Jorge Navarro. He is unemployed—living off his girlfriend. Then again, he may have a side job off the books, like dealing on the street. He's no stranger to law enforcement. His rap sheet includes aggravated assault, drug possession with an intent to sell, and car jacking. He spent 3 years in Graterford."

"Ah, yes, Graterford. Pennsylvania's finest correctional facility. Detective Gainwell and I will pay him a visit. What else?"

"We've received hundreds of calls on the tip line," Lane said. "Most of them were either dead ends or worthless, like the lady who stated she is positive the perp is her ex-husband. When I asked her how tall he is she said 5'8". Not quite the 6'2" we're looking for, but just before you walked into the office, we got a promising call. A Judith Applegate called in. She said very early yesterday morning she and her husband saw a man with an Obama mask walking toward a large black SUV. They wrote down the license number. When I asked her for it she said her husband has it and he had just gone to the market. I told her we would come to their home this morning to interview them."

"That's incredible. Maybe today we will finally turn the corner on this case. Okay, Corporal Wilton and Lieutenant Ewing, visit Mr. and Mrs. Applegate. See if they remember anything else about the black SUV or the perp and get that license number. Don't wait till you get back to the office to run the number. Call Detective Sinclair back here so he can do it."

"Captain, we now have three victims. One had her eyes removed, another had her ears removed and now this one had her lips removed. There is some kind of connection among the three, but I couldn't put my finger on it, but it finally came to me. See no evil, hear no evil, speak no evil."

"The monkeys symbolize the idea that if we don't hear, see, or speak evil, we can be spared from evil. The phrase is often used as a message of peace and tolerance," chimed in Lane.

"Well, well, well. I never knew you had a degree in Sino-Japanese relations," chuckled Lillia.

"Wasn't one of our vic's Manchurian?" asked Lane.

"Let's not discount anything," Martin said. "That's good thinking, Corporal. This is exactly the outside-of-the-box thinking we need. Our perp is unorthodox. We need to think in an unorthodox way."

"Let's make some progress before our FBI friends return to the office. They went to McGuire Air Force base in Jersey. Apparently, the military was testing some drones the evening the victim's body was transported to Penn's Landing. They are going to review the video tapes from those drones. Special Agent Huffman told me the tapes are classified and although they cannot share them with us, they would allow the FBI to view them."

"So, we are ugly stepsisters?" asked Diego.

"It is what it is," Otis said.

Turning to Otis, Martin said, "Why don't you and I pay Miss Alvarez's boyfriend a visit?"

~~~

Martin and Otis entered the apartment building where their latest victim lived with her boyfriend. It was an older building, fairly well maintained and provided an affordable option to the newer, high-rise apartment/ condo buildings in the city.

The knock at the apartment door was met with vicious barking.

"What do you want?" a man yelled from within the apartment.

"It's the police, Mr. Navarro. Please open the door. We'd like to ask you a few questions."

"Wait a minute."

Martin and Otis were not about to wait for Navarro to exit on a fire escape or to destroy evidence.

"Sir, if you don't open this door immediately, we will break it down," Otis yelled with a voice of authority.

The door opened a crack. A white and black pit bull was pushing between the man and the door, trying desperately to get to the detectives.

"May we come in?" asked Martin.

"No, you may not," the man said over the barking dog.

"We have a few questions about Katrina Alvarez."

"What about her?" the man asked, while trying to control the dog.

"We can have this conversation here or at the precinct, your choice."
~~~

Mr. Navarro opened the door with his foot, while trying to hold the dog back by its collar. "Back, Satan!"

"If you don't control your dog, I will. I really don't want to waste a bullet," Otis said.

Navarro dragged the dog into a back room and shut the door. The barking continued. Jorge Navarro was short, with long, thick anthropoid arms. He wore a white, slightly stained, wifebeater t-shirt and dungarees. Tattoos covered both arms and half of his neck. He walked over to a couch covered by a stained, grey blanket, and threw a pile of dirty laundry on the floor. A coffee table was cluttered with empty beer bottles, a marijuana bong and a five dollar bill that had been rolled to be used as a straw to snort speed.

"What's this about?"

"When was the last time you saw Miss Alvarez?"

"I dunno. I think it was Tuesday."

"You think?" asked Martin. "Four days and you didn't think of notifying the police that she was missing?"

"I don't trust the police. Besides, she was probably whoring some place with her good-for-nothing sister."

"Do you mind if we take a look around?" Otis asked.

"Do you have a search warrant?"

"No, but we can come back with one."

"Then I guess that is what you'll have to do. I'm not answering any more questions."

Getting up from the couch, Otis picked up the bong and rotated it in his hands.

"Do you have a medical marijuana license, Sir?"

"Really? You actually give a shit about a couple of grams of grass? Don't you have criminals to catch, brother?"

"I'm not your brother."

"Yeah, you're more like an uncle. Uncle Tom. You that white man's boy?"

Picking up the five-dollar bill on the coffee table, Otis unrolled it and rubbed his pinky along it and touched it to his tongue.

"Have you been snorting some meth, Mr. Navarro?"

"I don't do drugs. They're bad for your health."

"Put your hands behind your back. You are under arrest for possession of a controlled substance. You have the right to remain silent. Anything you say can and will…"

~~~

Lillia and Lane drove over to the house of the couple who had called the tip line to report they had seen the man wearing the Obama mask. They parked their car in front of the home of the Applegates. If they had, indeed, written down the license plate number of the black Escalade, the case would be sent into hyperspeed.

As they walked up the stairs to the front door they heard a woman screaming inside. Lillia tried opening the door, but it was locked. Lane knocked on the door, but there was no response. The woman's screams continued. Backing up a few steps, Lane kicked the door, just below the door knob. It budged, but did not open. He tried again. The third time the door splintered and opened enough for Lane to reach in and unlock the door. The detectives entered the house. Another scream!

"It's coming from upstairs," Lillia said.

The two detectives pulled out their handguns and quickly ran up the stairs, two steps at a time. The screams directed them to the last room down the hall. The bedroom door was open. They entered.

"Oh," Lillia said

"Oh, no," added Lane.

To their astonishment, an elderly couple in their late sixties were in the middle of some vigorous love making. The woman was perched upon her husband who was lying prone. Without any modesty, the woman turned from her position, looked at the two detectives and said, "Why do you think they call those of us in our sixties, sexagenarians?" Both she and her husband laughed. "You must be the detectives who called about that man in the mask," she said with no attempt to cover her nudity.

"Yes, Ma'am," Lane answered.

"Okay. Give us a moment and we'll meet you downstairs in the living room."
~~~

Lillia and Lane walked down the stairs, sat on the sofa and looked at each other as if they had just seen an implausible event. For the two of them, they had.

Lane broke the silence. "Have you ever…."

"Don't finish that sentence, and never bring this up again," interrupted Lillia.

The lady came downstairs first.

"Look what you did to our front door!" she said.

"I am so sorry, Ma'am. We heard you screaming and thought you were in danger. That maybe our suspect found out you had seen him."

"How old are you, detective?"

"Twenty-nine."

"And you are telling me you cannot distinguish the difference between cries of pain, and squeals of pleasure?"

Lane was speechless. Lillia rescued him.

"Ma'am, we will have someone replace the door. Are you Mrs. Applegate?"

"Yes, dear. How rude of me. Would you folks like a cup of coffee or tea?"

"Coffee would be nice," answered Lillia.

The lady disappeared into the kitchen.

"Can't we just ask for the license plate number and get out of here?" asked Lane.

"No. Relax. Let's find out if they saw anything they failed to mention on the phone.

Mrs. Applegate returned carrying a silver tray with a pot of coffee, cups and saucers, cream, sugar, and Christmas cookies. Her husband came down the stairs wearing a bathrobe and slippers.

"Now, then, what can we do for you, Detectives?"

"Mrs. Applegate, you called the 800 number to say you and your husband believe to have seen the suspect we're looking for?" Lane asked.

"Yes, we're snowbirds. We spend the winter in Florida. The cold weather is hell on my arthritis. We normally stop in South Carolina for the night, but Henry wanted to drive straight through. We come home for two weeks to celebrate the holidays with our family. We love to be around those grandkids during the holidays. You simply cannot celebrate Christmas where the temperature is in the 70s. We don't like driving through snow, but we always wish for a white Christmas. Do you like snow on Christmas, detective?"

"Yes, Ma'am, but you were telling us about spotting the suspect?"

"Please, call me Margaret. Well, it was about 4:30 yesterday morning when we exited I-95. We were driving north on Christopher Columbus Boulevard when we saw a man wearing a President Obama mask pulling a hand truck. Henry and I both thought it was odd, didn't we, Honey?"

"Yes, dear," the man replied.

"Anyway, I had Henry pull over and I wrote down the license plate number."

"Do you have that number, Margaret?" Lane asked. "When you called into the station you said your husband had it and that he was running errands."

"Honey, where is that license number you wrote down?"

"I was not very good at science," replied Mr. Applegate

"Not science, Honey, license. That *license* plate number you wrote down."

"Yes, I did write it down."

"Where is it, Darling?"

Looking up and to the side, Mr. Applegate was in deep contemplation. Lillia was also doing some thinking. *Don't tell me he has no idea where he put that piece of paper.*

Henry stood, walked over to a credenza near the front door, and opened the top drawer. After rummaging through the drawer, he picked up a small piece of paper and looked at the detectives.

"She is just as beautiful and sexy as the day I married her!" he said.

"And you are still a beast in bed, my love," Margaret said.

Henry walked up to Lillia and handed her the piece of paper.

"Henry has horrible handwriting," Mrs. Applegate said. "Chicken scratch. That's a 'D', not a zero."

"Thank you. This is very helpful. Can you remember anything else?"

"No, I don't think so. He had one of those very large SUVs. Black as coal."

"You have been very helpful. We will be in touch if we have any further questions."

~~~

The autopsy of Katrina Alvarez had yet to be completed when Martin was given the search warrant for her apartment. Otis, Martin, and a few uniformed officers were accompanied by two officers from the Philadelphia Police Department's Animal Care and Control Team (ACCT) to handle Navarro's vicious dog. When the door was opened the two Animal Care officers ensnared and removed the dog as it whipped its body in distorted positions trying to escape. The officers entering the apartment could hear the dog barking even after it was removed from the building.

The dog was the least of their problems. As soon as Otis opened the door to a spare bedroom, they were hit with an overpowering odor.

"What in hell is that smell?" an officer asked.

Immediately, each reached for his handkerchief and placed it over his nose to help filter the smell. In the spare bedroom they found the walls decorated with mounted pigeons, rats, and squirrels. The origin of the offensive odor was a large plastic trash can containing the skin of two raccoons lying in a solution—a pickle bath made with equal parts distilled white vinegar, water and salt. A card table and one chair were positioned in the middle of the room. On the table was a stuffed racoon waiting for some finishing touches. Otis pointed to the racoon's eyes.

"Marbles," he said.

Martin picked up a scalpel from the table. "And surgical tools," he added.

"Take a look at this," Otis said as he pointed to a small bowl sitting on the kitchen counter. "A variety of fake eyeballs."

"Let's bag the marbles, the eyes, and the scalpel, finish our search of the apartment, and get back to the station."

~~~

Temperatures hovered around freezing as rain began to fall upon the city of brotherless love, making the roads treacherous at best. It took Lillia and Lane twice as long to get back to the station as they decided to follow a city Public Works truck, their car being pelted by flying salt along the way. When they arrived at the office, the two FBI Special Agents had just walked into the common area.

"Damn, it's cold out there," Special Agent Huffman said as he rubbed his hands together rapidly.

"You are from Arizona, Mr. Huffman. Anything would be cold to you. How did you make out with the Air Force?" Martin asked.

"We reviewed hours of tape and we were able to find the perp. As you had suggested, he did use a hand truck to transport the victim from a black Escalade to a park bench in Washington Square. After he placed the body on the bench and returned to his car, we were able to follow his route up I-95 where he got off at the Woodhaven Road exit. That's where the drones lost him," Huffman said.

"So he was heading toward the Northeast Philly, Bensalem, Bristol area."

A chorus of sirens interrupted the conversation. Special Agent Buchanan walked over to the window and gazed down at the streets.

"Fire engines and ambulances. Must be a big fire somewhere."

Ignoring the obvious, Otis said, "We have Jorge Navarro, Katrina Alvarez's boyfriend, in interrogation room two. We're letting him simmer for a while before we interrogate him."

"We'd like to listen in on that," Huffman said.

"Of course," responded Martin. "We can arraign him on drug charges, but with such little evidence of any controlled substance, his lawyer will have him back on the street within a few hours. The search warrant revealed he is an amateur taxidermist. Small sharp knives were lying on a card table, but the most interesting find was a bowl full of marbles and a selection of artificial eyes. Navarro said he was trying to find the perfect eyes for a raccoon he was working on. You'll remember that our first victim whose eyes were removed were replaced with marbles."

"Do you like him for all three murders?"

"I think we are in agreement that all three murders were committed by the same perp. He is probably the best suspect we've had thus far, but I still have my doubts. I don't think he is smart enough to elude us thus far or to have sent that audio tape. I still think Tanner Thrush is at the top of our list. We have yet to find him. People don't run unless they have reason to run."

"There are too many unanswered questions. Neither he nor his girlfriend owned a car, so where did he get his hands on the Escalade and where does he keep it? I doubt he's going to shell out $300 a month for a parking garage. We searched his apartment and used luminol. The only room that lit up was his taxidermy room and although we detected 4 different types of blood, they were all animal blood. Detective Gainwell and I are going to interrogate him. You can listen in the observation room."

More sirens could be heard from the street below. Martin glanced at his watch, then to Otis. "Navarro's been in there for over an hour. Let's see what he has to say."

The two detectives walked into the room to find Jorge Navarro asleep with his head resting between his arms on the table. Martin lifted the end of the table and let it drop with a bang.

"What the hell, Man?" Navarro said. "That ain't no way to treat me."

"My apologies, Mr. Navarro. I wanted to make sure we have your undivided attention."

"You ain't got nothin' on me, and I ain't got nothing to say. You want to charge me with possession of a gram of pot and a hint of meth? Go ahead. My lawyer will have me out of here before dinner time."

"We aren't going to charge you with possession. We just want some answers. Your girlfriend has been missing for four days. Naturally, we have some questions," Otis said.

"Yeah, well maybe I should have my lawyer here."

"Sure, you may call your lawyer. In fact, I think you should call your lawyer if you are guilty. Then things will change. They go from a friendly chat to officially charging you, and you won't go back to the cage. We'll make sure that you are sent to the general population and who knows, maybe we will make the mistake in what crime you were charged; you know, instead of drug possession, it could state child molestation. Clerical mistakes happen all the time. It would be terrible if it leaked that you are a child molester," Martin said.

"Yo, I'm no chomo! You can't do that!"

"Shit happens, Mr. Navarro."

"What is this, good cop, bad cop? You the bad cop?"

Otis walked over to the table, and walked behind Navarro with an anger Martin had not seen. "No! He's the bad cop, and I am the bad cop! You don't get a good cop!" Leaning forward he whispered in Navarro's ear, "We are going to book you for child rape. It's going to take at least three or four days to correct that paperwork."

"Yo, what do you want from me?"

Now, are you up for a friendly conversation?"

"Yeah. Whatever."

"Tell me about your taxidermy hobby."

"What's there to tell? I'm teaching myself with YouTube videos. I'm more comfortable around animals than people."

"Dead animals?" Martin asked.

"I find some dead, some alive."

How do you trap and kill them?" asked Martin

"Nighttime is when the rats and raccoons come out. The rats are easy. You corner them in a alley. You can't get too close or they'll jump for your throat. You get close enough, then throw a blanket on them. I gotta use a baited trap for the coons."

Martin leaned over the table so his face was only a foot away from Navarro's.

"Ever practice your taxidermy skills on a person, Jorge?"

"Ew! You have that old man smell," Navarro said as he tilted his chair back on two legs.

Otis stood up and walked behind Navarro, kicking the chair. He then grabbed the suspect's shoulders and pinned him and his chair against the back wall.

"Look, you little piss ant, do you really want to play games with us? Go ahead and we'll charge you with murder and I guarantee you won't be given bail. You can play dominoes with your friends at Curran-Fromhold."

"Murder? Yo, Po-Po, I ain't done no murder!"

"No? That's not what our evidence shows."

"What evidence? You think I don't know when you're capping? Dude, I not only been around the block a few times, I *own* the block!"

"When was the last day you saw, Katrina?" Martin asked.

"I dunno. Day before Christmas Eve. We were supposed to go over to her mama's. When she never came home I guessed she went without me. That old bitch don't like me, no how."

"That last day you saw her, did she say where she was going?"

"No. She said something about meeting her doctor, but I know that was a lie. No doctors have hours at night."

"What doctor?"

"How the hell am I supposed to know?"

"What time was she supposed to meet this doctor?""

"It was halftime of the Sixers game. I dunno. Maybe 8:30. That's why I know she was lyin'. Nobody goes to the doctor at night. What's all this about Katrina?"

Martin slid photographs of Katrina Alvarez's murdered body in front of Navarro, one at a time."

"Oh, man! What the hell? Is she dead?"

"You sound surprised," Otis said.

"Yo, you aren't gonna pin this on me. I loved her."

"Yeah, you loved her so much that you didn't even report her missing for four days."

"What's wrong with her mouth?"

"Someone practiced taxidermy on her. Any idea who that would be, Jorge?"

Abruptly, the door to the interrogation room opened and Jordan walked in. I need to see you both. It's urgent."

"Make yourself comfortable, Mr. Navarro. We'll be right back," Martin said.

Otis noticed the look of horror and fear on Jordan's face. Jordan looked only at Otis.

"Otis, those sirens we've been hearing for the past hour? There was a horrific accident on the Schuylkill Expressway. It was icy and apparently a fuel tanker fishtailed and collided with numerous cars, causing a nine car collision and huge explosion. Five were pronounced dead at the scene and dozens more injured. Kalani was one of the injured."

"Kalani? Where did they take her?" Otis asked with sheer panic.

"Temple Burn Center."

"Go! Go!" shouted Martin to Otis who was already nearly out the door.

# CHAPTER ELEVEN

*The five senses are the ministers of the soul.*
— Leonardo da Vinci

Martin arrived at the hospital around seven that evening, after he finished interrogating Jorge Navarro and meeting with the two FBI Special Agents to discuss the direction they wanted to take the investigation. Also, before leaving for the hospital, he and ADA Linda Bryson discussed whether they had enough evidence to formally charge Navarro with the murders. Bryson decided they did not.

Martin took the stairs to the 4th floor of Temple University Hospital where the Burn ICU is located. Walking over to the nurses' station, he showed his badge to the lone nurse and asked her for Kalani Dantas's room number.

The nurse said, "Room 8, but her fiancé is in with her. We only allow one person in a patient's room at a time, and all visitors must be completely donned in PPE—a disposable hat, disposable protective clothing, long shoe cover, N95/FFP2 mask, and double-layer gloves."

"Thank you. I will not be entering her room. Detective Gainwell is my partner. I'm here for emotional support."

"I understand. There's a waiting room just outside the double doors, to the right."

Martin walked over to room 8 and looked through the large window. Kalani looked like a mummy, her face and hands completely wrapped in white gauze. Her arm that was not wrapped was bare and red, with obvious blistering and skin sloughing. She wore an oxygen mask, had an IV in her arm and various tubes and wires were going in and out of her body. Martin could not tell which tube did what. Monitoring equipment and two video screens were mounted on the wall.

Otis sat next to the bed with his head in his hands. Martin gently tapped on the window. Otis looked up and walked toward the door and came out to meet his boss.

Taking off his mask, Otis said, "Thanks for coming, Martin."

"How is she, Otis?"

"Not good. She received burns over 30% of her body, including the left side of her face. She's been placed in a medically induced coma to manage pain and facilitate the healing process while her body recovers from the extensive damage caused by the burns. The next 72 hours are the most critical. She's touch and go. The doctors say if she makes it to the weekend, she'll live."

"I am so sorry, Otis. Needless to say, take as much time as you need. We'll manage without you."

"Yeah. This is the worst possible time for me to be absent from work."

"I don't want you worrying about the case. Family comes first. Kalani is going to have a long road of recovery in front of her. She's going to need you, Otis."

"Well, I have learned a lot about burn victims over the past five hours. A general rule of thumb is that a burn patient will spend one day in the hospital for each percentage of her body that is burned. With 30 percent of Kalani's body burned, the doctor said there are many factors that can affect a patient's length of stay. She will need numerous operations and skin grafting and burn excisions, which will all contribute to a lengthy stay."

"She will need blood transfusions. Apparently, patients who have suffered smoke inhalation injuries can also expect a longer recovery."

"Do you know her blood type?"

"A+. I'm B+."

"I'm A+. I'll be by tomorrow to donate a pint. Otis, anything you need, anything, just say the word."

"Thanks, Martin."

~~~
~~~

The next morning FBI Special Agents Huffman and Buchanan were waiting for Martin when he walked into the common area.

"Good morning," Agent Huffman said.

"Not really. Detective Gainwell's fiancée was one of the victims in that fiery crash on the Schuylkill Expressway yesterday afternoon. She's severely burned and they don't know if she's going to make it."

"I'm so sorry, Captain," Huffman said.

"Yes. Let us know if we can be of any help," added Buchanan.

"Thank you. What can I do for you, gentlemen?" Martin asked.

"You were right, Captain," Huffman said. "It was premature to assume that the perp was targeting college girls. Miss Alvarez was 34 and never attended college. It was a mistake to announce to the press that was his motive."

"Tell that to the mayor and the Chief. They were adamant about it."

Lane walked into the room and gave Martin a familiar look.

"What is it, Corporal?"

"We ran the license plate the Applegates gave us. It's registered to a Darius Banks-Marsette. He lives on Harlan Street in West Philly. Jake and I are going to pay him a visit."

"Bring Mr. Banks-Marsette in. I also want that SUV to be processed for blood, saliva and other bodily fluids or DNA."

"If the killer murdered the girls in one location, placed them in a body bag, and then transported the bag into the SUV, maybe forensics will find something, but I doubt it," Lane said.

"And since we do not assume anything, we will still run a thorough inspection of the vehicle. Right, Corporal?"

"Right, Captain."

When Lane left the room, Mr. Huffman continued his thoughts.

"Captain Wallace, we have been here now for nearly two weeks. We are spinning our wheels as badly as your team has. This perpetrator is obviously shrewd. He's careful and very intelligent. Kevin and I spent most of yesterday looking at old serial killer files and through the Bureau of Justice Statistics, the BJS database of Federal statistics, and two statistical databases maintained by the FBI. We are looking for anything that will help break this case. We know that 75% of all murder victims knew their offender. I think we need to start there. We should check to see if these ladies attended the same church, belonged to the same fitness club, had dated the same man, had the same mailman. We need to review our notes from all interviews you have had with friends and family members of the three victims and thoroughly vet every friend, coworker, lover, and neighbor. Perhaps they frequented the same coffee shop or restaurant. There has to be some connection among the suspects, or at the very least, between each victim and the killer."

"That's fine. We can interview the associates of the victims again, and spread the net wider, but we are spread pretty thin. I'll try to convince Chief Conwell to lend us a few more uniforms to man the tip line."

"Special Agent Buchanan and I will be searching the city's database for vacant buildings and other possible places where the perpetrator could have dissected his victims, specifically looking for places with large refrigeration units. Clearly, this guy could not have performed his surgeries in a building frequented by people. We're going to search in Northeast Philly, Bensalem and Bristol. That is where our drone lost the black Escalade."

"Speaking of drones, the FBI is loaning us one of their larger drones so we can search for that car from the sky. You would think the killer would conceal the Escalade in a garage, but you never know," said Buchanan.

The conversation was interrupted by the forensic pathologist who walked into the common area.

"Dr. Wu, for what do we owe the pleasure of your presence? You seldom leave the comforts of the catacombs," Martin said playfully.

Dr. Wu's demeanor was serious and pensive.

"Martin, I need to speak with you. Privately."

"Excuse me, gentlemen," Martin said as he escorted the pathologist into his office.

"You look serious."

"We have a problem. There was DNA evidence from the Alvarez crime scene. She was raped. The wax lips, the discarded cigarette, and the rape kit all had trace DNA on them. We ran it through the Combined DNA Index System and got a hit."

"That's absolutely wonderful," Martin said with elation. "What's the problem?"

"Martin, the DNA is a match for the mayor."

~~~

Martin was trying to process what Dr. Wu just said.

"Elaine, are you absolutely sure? Run the DNA samples again."

"We have. Twice. Martin, the DNA was found at three different places on the victim. She was sexually assaulted. The rape kit revealed semen from the perpetrator. We also found trace DNA evidence on the wax lips and the discarded cigarette butt. All three identified the same assailant through a DNA profile match. The mayor. I don't know what to tell you."

"Who knows about this. Right now?"

"Just you, me, and Denise Kowalski. She is a Crime Laboratory Analyst who ran the DNA tests. She has been working here for three years. Denise is young, but an excellent analyst."

"Are you certain she has told no one else?"

"I was extremely clear about that. She assured me she would keep the results to herself; however, she is required to fill out a report on the results of every DNA test she performs."

"Tell her to fill it out and give the paperwork to me. If anyone questions her about where the report is, tell her to send him to me. This is an absolute cluster. Elaine, I need your lab, actually, I need this Denise Kowalski to determine the brand of cigarette that had the Mayor's DNA on it. Can she do that?"

"Yes, our forensic lab can determine the brand of a cigarette butt. They will analyze the cigarette ash through techniques like X-ray fluorescence (XRF), which can identify the unique elemental composition of different cigarette brands, as long as the condition of the butt is half-decent. Then they will compare the data they receive with the comprehensive brand reference library."
~~~

"Okay. Tell Miss Kowalski that I want her to hand deliver the results to me. No phone call. No paperwork. And tell her she needs to keep this confidential. Tell her to do her best."

"Alright. How is Otis holding up? How is his fiancée?"

"I plan on heading over to the hospital when I finish here. Kalani has third degree burns over a third of her body. She is touch and go. Say a prayer for her."

"I already have. Martin, do you really believe Mayor Foerster could be involved in this?"

"I have learned over my 29 years of crime investigation that anyone is capable of anything. Anyone."

~~~

The next morning, Otis was busy at his desk when Martin arrived at the office.

"I'm surprised to see you. How is Kalani?" Martin said.

"Yeah, well, idle time has been my enemy. I've been going crazy. Too much time to think. When my thoughts are consumed with Kalani, I become angry and I feel hopeless. I need to get back to work. She has a long road ahead of her, Martin, but the doctors say she is going to make it. They expect her to be in the hospital for at least another 45 days, then she will be moved to a rehabilitation facility. She is still in a coma."

Martin took a step closer to Otis so they were only a foot or two apart.

"Otis, I'm going to say this again. Anything you need… anything. If there is anything Mary Jo and I, or for that matter the department, can do for either of you, please let me know."

"I will. I promise. Now back to work. What have I missed?"

"Actually, a lot. Let's go into my office."

The two detectives walked into Martin's office and closed the door behind them. Otis could sense something was not right.

"This ought to be good," Otis said. "I can always tell when something has gotten under your skin."

"Yeah, well, prepare yourself. Forensics got a DNA match off of Katrina Alvarez. Three matches to be exact. They lifted DNA
~~~

from the wax lips, the discarded cigarette butt, and semen from the rape kit. They ran it through CODIS and got a hit."

"That's great, Captain! So, has an arrest been made?"

"Not yet. The DNA came back as a match for Mayor Foerster."

Otis said nothing, for what seemed like a month of Sundays. He tried to process what he heard.

"I know," Martin said, breaking the silence. "This is going to get ugly in a hurry."

"How are you going to handle this?"

"I have a meeting in an hour with Inspector Jenson, Chief Conwell and Special Agents Huffman and Buchanan. Conwell called the meeting before the DNA results came back. I figured I would wait for the meeting before dropping the bombshell. He called the meeting to see what progress we have made and, I think, to see if we are cooperating with the FBI."

"Have you informed the special agents?"

"No. The only people who know about this are you, me, Dr. Wu and the forensics analyst who discovered the match. Her name is Denise Kowalski. They have all been instructed to keep the information confidential."

Martin's attention was drawn to his window where he saw Special Agent Buchanan walking towards Martin's office.

"Here comes Buchanan. I'm going to have to let him know about the DNA. I don't want to blindside him and Huffman when we meet with the inspector and the chief."

Before Buchanan had a chance to knock, Martin waved him in.

"Good morning, gentlemen," Special Agent Buchanan said. "Detective Gainwell, how is your fiancée?"

"She is still in intensive care, but she's going to make it. She has a long road ahead of her."

"That's great news. I feel badly for her."

"Thank you."

"I thought you two would like to know that Huffman and I had dinner with the mayor last night. I think he wants to know if our assessment jives with what you have been telling him. I don't like the idea of him setting you up like this behind your back. I thought I would give you a heads up."

"I appreciate that, Special Agent," Martin said.

"I know we have a meeting with the DA scheduled for this morning, but I wanted to touch base with you before that. Any new developments?"

Martin second guessed his decision to tell the FBI agents about the results of the DNA tests. In a preemptive attempt to thwart criticism for not revealing the devastating news about the mayor to the FBI agents before the meeting, Martin said, "I am going to ask that the DA and ADA are at the meeting as well. We should have the results of the DNA analysis by then."

"Let's keep our fingers crossed they find some trace evidence. Oh, and he acknowledged telling the public the killer was targeting college women was probably premature."

"Ha! Monday morning quarterback," Otis said. "I assume you did not say that Martin told him so."

"No need."

"Well, I'm glad he came to his senses."

The look on Martin's face was one of a child who comes down the stairs on Christmas morning and sees an abundance of wrapped gifts under the lit tree.

"What? You're not glad the mayor came to his senses?" Otis asked.

"That's it! Otis, you nailed it! The number five represents *the five senses!* We've been focusing on the wrong features. Our perp's obsession with eyes, ears and mouth has to do with sight, hearing and speech. His next two victims will have their nose and hands removed."

"How do we alert the public about that?" Otis asked.

"We don't." Changing the subject, Martin turned to the FBI agent and asked, "Special Agent Buchanan, by chance, did you notice what brand of cigarette the mayor smokes?"

"He smokes Newports, just like my sister-in-law. Funny how the city has a smoking ban within any public building, but he smokes in his office. Perhaps he thinks he is above the law," Buchanan said. "Why do you ask?"

"I'm just curious. Maybe I'll buy him a carton as a peace offering."

~~~

Jake and Lane left the office and drove to the address associated with the black Escalade. They pulled up in front of a brick-faced rowhome and walked up to the door. Paint was peeling off the window frames like the skin from a tangerine. Across the street sat a black Cadillac Escalade.

"Let's check out the license plate number on that Escalade before we knock on the door," Lane said.

Looking at his cell phone, then to the license plate, Jake said, "Ladies and Gentlemen, we have a match."

"Let's hope Darius is home."

Jake knocked hard on the front door. No response. He knocked again.

"Who is it?" a female voice asked from inside the home.

"Police!"

"The door cracked open."

A terribly thin woman with a mouth full of decaying teeth peeked out.

"What'd you want?"

"Does Darius Banks-Marsette live here?"

"He ain't home."

"Who is that in the back room?" Jake asked.

"No one."

Jake pushed the door open and ran to the back bedroom where a cadaverous frame was halfway out an open window in an attempt to go down the fire escape. Jake grabbed him by the back of the shirt and dragged him into the room.

"Darius, today's your lucky day. You get a free ride to Curran-Fromhold Prison. Unfortunately, you will not pass go, and you will not collect $200."

"Yo, man, I done nothing!"

"Yeah, but you just so happen to own a black Cadillac Escalade associated with three murders."

"Oh no you don't! I know nothing' about no murders!"

"You can tell us all about it down at the station."
~~~

# CHAPTER TWELVE

*There are no better cosmetics than a severe temperance and purity, modesty and humility, a gracious temper and calmness of spirit; and there is no true beauty without the signatures of these graces in the very countenance.*
— Arthur Helps

It was an hour before sunrise over Philadelphia. The man sat at his desk focused intensely on a stack of photographs, portraits of beautiful women. With the aid of a magnifying glass, he carefully scrutinized each face, in search of the perfect nose.

He listened to Edvard Grieg's, *Peer Gynt Suite No. 1 Op. 46: Morning Mood in E major* as he worked. He paused his search tilting his head back as he listened to the melody which alternated between flute and oboe, with the unusual climax occurring early in the piece, at the first forte, signifying the sun breaking through. The man loved symbolism and ironicism. The four-minute piece ended and was followed by Beethoven's Symphony No. 5, widely recognized as the "fate knocking at the door" motif due to its distinctive four-note pattern of "short-short-short-long."

Yes, fate indeed was knocking. The man believed his destiny, his fate, was to create the perfect woman. He had no choice in the matter. It was beyond his control. It had been predetermined by a power much greater than himself. He was simply obeying his master's commands.

The man pondered the origins of the five senses. Was it first mentioned in the Bible, or other holy scrolls, polyglot codices, or palimpsests? He was not religious by any stretch of the imagination, but he respected the ancient writings. Picking up a book that included writings from Rabbeinu Bahya around 1300 C.E., the man turned to Devarim 4:28. He read out loud, "The reason that God provided man with five such senses is that they correspond to the five Books of the

Torah… The soul displays its activities by means of these five senses. This is why the Torah/Bible condemns idolatry by pointing out that these idols cannot use any of their senses. How can idolaters say to their deities in times of stress: 'arise and save us!' These idols are unable to rise, much less save."

The man sat there contemplating. Perhaps the five senses can be traced back to ancient Greek philosophy, especially to Aristotle. The Greek philosopher prescribed them into a hierarchy. Sight and hearing were designated as the most important of the senses as they are the most useful to the soul and mind of man. Taste and touch were located at the bottom. Smell was assigned the position at the middle of the hierarchy. Depending upon the context, it could move up or down on the list.

The man's eyes were tainted by his perspective that his victims, the women he chose, were but inanimate objects like the concrete and steel structures that towered over the city.

What governs the idyllic nose? The man was a student of sensory science. For him, the perfect nose must be 1/5 the width of the face, and no wider than the distance between the eyes at its widest point. The bridge of the nose should be about 80% the width of the nostrils.

Then there is the issue of the length of the nose. A nose that starts at the inner corners of the eyes and ends above the lip line was what the man longed to find in the photographs. Proportionate, is the word he used to describe the length of the nose as it complimented the face. The tip of the nose needed to be refined, and the nostrils, small and symmetrical. Who, but who, would be the lucky lady?

Photo after photo he rejected and added each discard to a second pile with the photograph facing down. Finally, a smile came over the man's face. The quintessential nose: flawless, utopian, inimitable. He looked at the bottom of the photograph for the name identifying the woman, *Susan Cranford*.

<center>~~~</center>

Although Martin was five minutes early for the meeting with the DA, everyone was already seated. It made Martin wonder if Chief Conwell had called a meeting before the meeting. DA Edward Malerba sat behind his desk. ADA Linda Bryson, Inspector Mark Jenson, FBI Special Agents Buchanan and Huffman were seated in a semi-circle facing the DA. They all turned and looked at Martin when he walked into the mayor's office. It was abundantly obvious they had been discussing him, or his performance.

"Captain. Have a seat," Chief Conwell said. "Special Agent Buchanan just shared with us your theory that the killer is preoccupied with the five senses and that you believe his next two victims will have their nose and hands removed, respectively."

"I would say that it is more than a theory, and the perp is more than preoccupied with the five senses. He is obsessed with them."

"Preoccupied, obsessed—semantics."

"Have you any viable suspects, Martin?"

"Actually, we do," answered Martin.

The expression on everyone's face was one of surprise. No new revelations had been shared to this point, and Special Agent Buchanan appeared the most surprised, having met with Martin a few hours earlier.

"We just received the forensic report on the latest victim, Katrina Alvarez. We have a DNA hit and a match through CODIS."

"Finally! That is wonderful news! So, who is this degenerate?"

"Mayor Foerster."

Like the perfect strike in bowling, Martin's revelation "ball" hit the pocket, between the 1 and 3 pins causing a chain reaction knocking them all down.

"There must be some mistake," DA Malerba said. "You need to run the tests again."

"We did. Twice. And there wasn't just one piece of trace evidence. We found the mayor's DNA on the wax lips, a discarded Newport cigarette butt, and semen from the rape kit. Miss Alvarez had been sexually assaulted before she was murdered."

"I hear Pandora's box creaking open," ADA Bryson said.

"Captain, isn't this a complete diversion from the other murders? What I mean is the other victims were not sexually assaulted and the perp was extremely careful not to leave the most miniscule trace of evidence," DA Malerba asked.

"You are correct, and I have not discounted that. It could be the killer is getting sloppy; he is feeling bold and more confident and so he is letting his guard down. It could also be he is trying to throw us off his trail. It doesn't make sense, but the evidence is the evidence. DNA does not lie. If the killer is the mayor, it would explain why he is a step ahead of us."

"Who knows about this, Captain?" DA Malerba asked.

"Just Dr. Wu, Detective Gainwell, the forensic analyst Denise Kowalski, and all of us in this room. Dr. Wu, Gainwell and Kowalski have been sworn to secrecy. How do you want to handle this? Should we make the arrest?"

"No. Not yet, the DA said. "Let me have a private conversation with the mayor to let him know what is coming. We are going to need more evidence, so keep digging."

"You mean, finding DNA on three separate places at the crime scene isn't enough evidence to make an arrest?" Special Agent Huffman asked.

"What I mean is, if we are wrong about this, everyone in this room, minus you two FBI agents, will be looking for a new job. When I do approach the mayor, I want this to be an open and shut case. We have no idea what his motives are. Did he have the opportunity to kill each of these girls? What about the weapon? Does the mayor have any experience with scalpels or surgical cutting?"

"What he has is a reputation for being a womanizer," Bryson said.

"If we arrested every man in Philadelphia who is a womanizer we wouldn't be able to fit them all into Lincoln Financial Field."

The DA's office and Major Crimes too frequently had disagreements on investigations. Though on the same team, so to speak, the two parties would often come to an impasse, like two rams head butting. Both had the same objective, but they did not necessarily agree on how to accomplish their shared goal. It's like that sometimes. In a manufacturing company, everyone wants to increase sales and profitability, but production wants to make products the sales department cannot sell, and the sales people want to sell products production cannot manufacture. The DA always wants more evidence, a case tighter than a camel's ass in a sandstorm.

"Put a tail on the Mayor and make sure your people are discreet!" Inspector Jenson said.

"Chief, can I assume you will approve the overtime this is going to take?" Martin asked.

"Of course," Chief Conwell said.

"Alright. That's all for now. I don't have to tell you to keep this information to yourselves. We'll know better how to proceed by the beginning of next week," Malerba said.

~~~

With everything the investigative team was handling, the last thing they needed was another intrusive and meddlesome individual. Enter Miss Fields.

"I know who has been committing these murders," the lady said. "He has the women's confidence and so, naturally, they lower their guard. He is handsome and clever, and works in the medical field."

Otis and Lillia looked inquisitively at the woman with wildly tossed hair wearing large hoop earrings, a silk, paisley-print blouse in bold colors, and fuchsia-colored harem pants. Their curiosity was followed by skepticism. Otis spoke first.

"And how do you know this, Miss…"

"Fields. Autumn Fields is my name. My parents were hippies. Call me Autumn."

"How do you know these things about the killer, Autumn?"

"I saw him."

"You saw him? Where?" asked Lillia, her eyes widening in disbelief.

"In my mind. I am clairvoyant."

"Clairvoyant?" Otis asked rhetorically.

"Yes, I have the ability to see clearly beyond the physical realm. You have five senses. I have six. I experience vivid visions and I have a strong sixth sense, a supernatural sense that gives me a unique perception about events and people."

"Sixth sense, eh?" Otis asked rhetorically.

"The sixth sense is called proprioception, which is the ability to sense where your body parts are in space. It is also known as the
~~~

'silent sixth sense' because it operates largely unconsciously," Lillia interjected.

Looking at Lillia, then Miss Fields, Otis said, "Yes, well, that may be true, but we live in the physical world. When the DA and ADA bring a suspect to court, they need physical evidence to get a conviction. We rely on the tangible, not the abstract."

"Of course you do, but I can offer intuitive insights about the case not readily accessible through the five senses."

The mention of the five senses caught both Otis and Lillia's attention.

"For example, I know you are experiencing trouble in your romantic relationship, Detective," Autumn said as she looked sympathetically at Otis.

Otis felt hot anger building up within him. Lillia sensed it and dove in to save him.

"Miss Fields, I mean Autumn, give us your contact info and we will be in touch."

"He's going to kill again."

"If you have this sixth sense that can see things we cannot, where and when will this murderer strike next?" Otis asked.

"It doesn't work that way, Detective. I don't tell this power what information to give me. These visions are given to me as a gift. I make no demands."

"Thank you, Autumn. We'll be in touch," Lillia said, clearly having had enough of the self-proclaimed psychic.

As Autumn Fields was leaving the offices, Martin walked in, and the look on his face was one that garnered the attention of his entire team.

Slamming that day's *Philadelphia Daily News* on Jake's desk, he said, "I want to know who is leaking our investigation to the press! Now!"

Otis picked up the paper and read the headline.

SENSELESS SERIAL KILLER TARGETING LOCAL WOMEN

The subheading read: "Serial killer collecting eyes, ears, mouth, from female victims and fixated on the 5 senses. Authorities fear he will harvest a nose and hand next."

Otis stared at the paper as Martin walked into his office and slammed the door. Looking up at the team of detectives, he said, "You may think you're doing the public a favor, but in reality, you're sabotaging our case," Otis said. "This makes us look incompetent, as though we cannot make a 2-foot putt!"

"Why do you assume it was one of us?" Diego asked.

"Let's see. The only people who were privy to the idea the perpetrator is obsessed with the five senses are the DA, ADA, the Chief, Inspector Jenson, the mayor, you two FBI agents, and you detectives. God help you if we find out which one of you is leaking this information. We need to work and trust each other, folks! Martin is under tremendous pressure. He doesn't need this crap!"

"I thought we agreed that Mayor Foerster is our killer," Jordan said.

Special Agent Huffman shook his head. "He is a *suspect!* There was no sexual assault with the first two victims. Why would he suddenly change his modus operandi? The evidence may point to the Mayor, but something doesn't add up. We keep digging, doing the leg work, in other words, we keep investigating until we have a conviction. Got it?"

Martin came out of his office and stood in front of the white board. He looked at the photographs of the three women who had been murdered, then turned to his team.

"I want a 24-hour surveillance on the mayor. I want to know everywhere he goes after he leaves City Hall. I want to know everyone he encounters and I want photographs. Damn it, I want to know what he has for lunch and how many times he blows his nose. Corporal Wilton, I want you to head this up, and make sure no one working with you blows his cover. Understand?"

"Captain, is the mayor our guy?" Lane asked

"His DNA was found on Miss Alvarez and on the cigarette butt we found at the crime scene. He also drives a black Cadillac Escalade, so yes, he is a suspect. Listen to me carefully, if anyone outside of this room finds out about this surveillance, each of us will be looking for a new job. Got it?"

"Got it," the detectives responded in unison.

~~~

Darius Banks-Marsette had been sitting in the interrogation room for nearly an hour when Martin and Otis walked in. His head, cradled in his arms, was resting on the table.

"Mr. Banks-Marsette. You have quite the rap sheet," Martin said as he looked through a manilla file folder. "Let's see, breaking and entering, grand theft auto, possession with the intent to distribute. Hmmmm…mostly meth and pills."

Darius looked up nonchalantly, pushing his tangled strands of dreadlocks out of his face. Raising his eyes, but not his head, he said, "I did my time."

"And you are going to do more!" Otis said. "Killing three young women. You are going to be strapped to a gurney. Then a member of the execution team will insert two needles into your veins. You will experience pain and suffocation caused by pulmonary edema as well as the tortuous burning of potassium chloride."

"Man, I already told those other two detectives, I ain't done no murders!"

"Tell me, Darius, I can call you Darius, can't I? Tell me how you can afford a nice, new Cadillac Escalade when you are washing dishes at a diner? I see here you own it outright. No car payments. Impressive. Are you selling drugs again, Darius?" asked Martin.

"Look, man, I'm looking to go clean."

"Yeah, then why were you climbing out of your bedroom window when we came for a house visit?" Otis asked.

"Because you guys are cops. You always looking to pin something on a brother like me."

"Where did you get the car?"

"Can't say."

"Can't or won't?"

"I'm not saying nuthin."
~~~

"Captain, I wonder what we would find if we were to do a blood and urine test on Darius. I mean, it would be a shame to book Darius on a parole violation just for having smoked a joint or drinking one beer."

"Come on, man. That ain't right. What do you want from me?" Darius said.

"Let's begin with where you got the car," Martin said.

"Some old white guy. Younger than you," Darius said, nodding his head at Martin. "I'm sitting on my stoop having a cigarette when he pulls up in this shiny, black Escalade. He says he will give me the car for free, but I need to do somethin' for him."

"What did he want in return?"

"All he wanted was my cell phone number and for me to go pick him up whenever he calls me. I'd always pick him up on the corner of 15th and Market. He would drive me back home. A few days later he would call me and tell me where he parked the car. It was always somewhere near the zoo. He had a set of keys for the ride and I had a set."

"You want me to believe that some stranger gave you an $84,000 car and all he wanted was for you to loan him the car on occasion?" Otis asked.

"You can believe whatever you want. It's the truth."

"Since you said you were trying to keep your nose clean, why would you agree to this deal?" Martin asked.

"I mean, it's street math, dude. Trying to make a livin'."

Martin pushed photographs of the three victims in front of Darius.

"Damn, man!" Darius said, pushing the photographs away from him. "What, are you sick? Don't show me that stuff."

"Darius, these three women were murdered and the only evidence we have are witnesses and video showing your car at each scene. That makes you our number one suspect."

"Why would I make them dead?"

"What did he look like?" Otis asked.

"Who?"

"The guy who gave you the car, numbnuts!"

"I don't know. Like I said, old like you," Darius said while nodding toward Martin. "White. A doctor, I think."

"Why would you say that?"

"His hands were clean and his shoes dirty. His hands look like they've been washed a million times. Nobody has hands like that, man."

"Alright. Today really is your lucky day," Martin said. "We are not going to book you, but what you're going to do is call us the next time this man wants the car. Got it?"

"Yeah, that's cool. Oh, and one more thing. He didn't want the car to be tracked and because I told him I once worked for a chop shop, before I changed my ways and went straight, he told me to do my magic. I disabled the location services within the MyCadillac app, and physically disconnected the OnStar telematics unit. It wasn't rocket science."

"I'm sure it wasn't," Martin said.

"Here is my card. Anytime, night or day, you call me immediately after this guy calls you."

"Got it."

"And, Darius?"

"Yeah?"

"Don't leave town."

# CHAPTER THIRTEEN

*If I, deaf, blind, find life rich and interesting, how much more*
*can you gain by the use of your five senses!*
— Helen Keller

Martin left the office and drove over to the hospital to see Kalani. She was scheduled that afternoon for the first of what would be several surgeries. Martin donned the surgical mask, gloves and gown and knocked on her door and waited for permission to enter. Otis opened the door.

Martin was delighted Kalani was conscious.

"Martin! You didn't tell me you were going to drop by today," Kalani said in a raspy, garbled voice, evident it was painful for her to speak.

"I hadn't decided until I left the office. How are you?"

"I am doing well," Kalani interjected. "And look at you, bringing me flowers! Mary Jo is a lucky lady!"

Kalani breathed heavily as if she had just come back from a ten-mile run.

Martin looked beyond Otis to Kalani lying in bed. Martin had seen scores of horrendous murder scenes over the past 29 years, but the sight of Kalani unnerved him. The third-degree burns affected the deep layers of skin making them appear stiff, waxy white, and leathery. Keloids, scars, and ridged areas created by an overgrowth of scar tissue, covered her neck and the left side of her face. Her aesthetics altered from beauty to beast. Martin tried not to act horrified. *Act natural!*

"Well, I am so glad you are on the mend. I know you have a long road ahead of you."

"Thank you, Martin. Now go home! You had a long day. Mary Jo is waiting for you."

Walking closely to Kalani's bedside, he touched the sleeve of her nightgown, conscious not to touch her hand.

"Kalani, what can Mary Jo and I do for you?"

"Keep this wonderful man from falling apart," she said as she looked at Otis. "Help him to understand this is not the end of the world and that the future is bright. Oh, and I almost forgot. Thank you for donating that pint of blood."

"It was my pleasure. You do realize this means we are related now, don't you? Now that you have my blood pumping through your veins."

"Okay, Cuz," Kalani said with a painful chuckle.

"You have an incredibly positive attitude, Kalani. I'm not sure I would have such a frame of mind."

"Having a positive outlook promotes healing. At least that is what I have heard."

"Get better. We all love you," Martin said.

"Thank you for coming, Martin."

Otis walked Martin to the door. In a soft voice he said, "Martin, you cannot believe the pain she's in. I am amazed by her optimistic spirit. She is thankful she is alive and believes this is all part of a bigger plan God has for her."

"That kind of perspective is going to help her get through this, Otis. That, and having you by her side. I'll see you tomorrow."

When Martin left, Kalani asked Otis to sit on the side of her bed.

"Otis, baby, I want you to listen carefully to what I am about to say. I do not want an argument. In fact, I do not have the energy to argue with you. I have given this much thought, and I have made up my mind. I am not going to marry you."

Kalani's words were the last thing Otis expected. Breaking off their engagement *never entered his mind*. Hearing Kalani's words took his hope-fueled expectations, and replaced them with crushing disappointment. Kalani could see the sadness on his face.

"Look me in my eyes and tell me you do not love me," Otis said.

In an attempt to change the subject, Kalani said, "Jean-Jacques dropped by this morning.

He is the only person from the modeling industry to visit me, and that was to let me know he would pay me for the complete cosmetic shoot I had just begun, but he could not honor my contract since I will not be able to fulfill my part of the agreement. Do you want to know what hurts more than the pain from the burns? The realization that people saw in me were my looks. It is degrading knowing I was nothing more than an inanimate object."

"Of course, I love you, Otis. That is why I cannot marry you. I do not want you to carry this burden. You deserve better," Kalani said with softness in her voice.

"Do you actually think that little of me? Do you really believe I fell in love with you because of your physical appearance? Do you really believe I am that shallow? Of course, I was attracted to your beauty. Your outward beauty drew me to introduce myself to you and ask you out on a date. That is it! Kalani, I never would have asked you to marry me if your inward beauty did not match, or exceed, your external beauty. I don't love you one iota less than before your accident. When I look at you I still see the beautiful woman you are. I always will. Your beauty is intertwined with my love for you. You cannot be ugly to me, and there is no force in this world strong enough to take my love for you away. It matters not what the world thinks or sees."

"You are so sweet, Otis. You need to understand that no amount of time, healing, or plastic surgery will ever be able to take away this scarring. My surgeon told me I am lucky to be alive and that I will always have visible scars because the third-degree burns damaged all layers of the skin, so the body can only heal by forming scar tissue."

"I don't want you to be embarrassed when we are out in public, and, by the way, once I am out of rehab I am not going to be a hermit locked up in a closet for the rest of my life. I would never want our children to experience the horror on people's faces when they look at me, or when little children point at me and say, 'Look at the monster.' You don't deserve that. Sure, you will be kind to me and will try to ignore the insensitive remarks people will make, but it will slowly eat at you. I know you, Otis."

"The wedding is still on," Otis insisted.

"Well, then, you better hurry to find a bride because I will not be attending. Go now. I am very tired and need to sleep…and, Otis, please do not come to visit me anymore."

~~~

District Attorney Malerba had the inevitable task of confronting the mayor about the overwhelming evidence found at the crime scene. He decided to visit the mayor unannounced. Since he knew the restaurant the mayor frequented when dining alone, Malerba surprised the mayor when he approached him seated at the white, linen-covered table in the corner of the room.

"Edward," the Mayor said with a startled look on his face. "Have a seat. This Veal Oscar is the best in the city. Let me order one for you."

Mayor Foerster raised his hand to get the waiter's attention.

"No, thank you. I can't stay long."

"Your loss. The food is consistently amazing here. Have you made an arrest in the Senseless murders?"

DA Malerba sat down.

"Not yet, but possibly soon. That is why I am here, Ron. Forensics found your DNA at the crime scene."

"That is preposterous! Clearly, they made a mistake."

"No mistake. They found *your* DNA on the wax lips Miss Alvarez had on her mouth to cover the fact that the murderer had removed her lips. The rape kit revealed *your* semen in the murdered woman. And they found *your* DNA on a Newport cigarette butt found at the scene. If that were not enough, you just happen to drive a black Cadillac Escalade, the same make and model we know the perp drives. Three strikes. What would you do?"

"This has to be some kind of joke. Someone is setting me up!"

"No, there's no humor to be found in this. Ron, look me in the eye. Did you commit these murders?"

"Who the hell are you to come in here and make these accusations? I've known for years that you want to be mayor, but this is not the way to go about it. Play by my rules and I will guarantee you will be sitting behind my desk."
~~~

"Trust me, I have absolutely no stomach, or aspirations, for your position."

The mayor put down his fork, wiped his mouth, and continued to act like a petulant child.

"You're serious?"

"I am. The police are simply following their leads. If you turn yourself in I am willing to work a plea deal for you, Mayor."

"I am being framed. Make this go away, Ed."

"It's not that simple. You brought the FBI in on this. You can't just sweep this under the rug when they're involved."

"Exactly! *I was the one that brought in the FBI.* Do you really think I would bring in the nation's top investigators if I were guilty? Come on, Ed. You are smarter than this."

Getting up from the table, Malerba put both hands on the back of his chair and leaned forward.

"Ron, I came here as a courtesy. I didn't have to. Try the crème brûlée. I hear it's to die for."

~~~

Martin returned to the office after having met the DA to discuss the mayor's suspected involvement in the murders. When he saw Otis, he immediately knew something was off. Otis's demeanor and body language spoke volumes. He was leaning back in his chair with his feet on the desk. Otis threw a crumbled up paper towards the trash can. It hit the rim once, twice and dropped outside the can. Martin saw his detective stare at nothing in particular.

"Hey, are you alright?" Martin asked. "You never miss your trash can 3-pointer."

"Yeah. No. I'm fine."

"Yes and no. I think I'll believe the no. Come into my office for a minute," Martin said as he placed his hand on Otis's shoulder.

Reluctantly, Otis followed his boss into his office. Martin closed the door and took the seat next to Otis rather than behind his desk.

"Want to tell me what's going on?" Martin asked.

"Not really."

"Is it Kalani?"
~~~

"Yeah. She broke off our engagement."

Martin debated how to respond. Was it because she had a change of heart? Martin knew the trauma of a near-death experience can drastically shift a person's perspective on life. It can lead them to re-evaluate their priorities and relationships, often questioning whether their current romantic relationship aligns with their newfound values and desire to live life to the fullest. Maybe it was simply that she felt "unloveable" and ugly. Martin decided to say nothing and see if Otis would elaborate on the break-up.

"Martin, I love her so much. She thinks that now I only want to marry her out of loyalty, or obligation, or even worse, out of pity. She thinks I will not want to be seen with her because her face is permanently scarred. Do I project that kind of shallowness? Be honest with me?"

"Otis, I'm not one to be very warm and gushy, but I need to tell you I have known few men with as much integrity as you have. I have been watching you. The way you handle difficult situations. Your commitment and desire to be ethical in all you do. The fact that you still want to marry Kalani demonstrates clearly your love is genuine. It is authentic. It is so much more than skin-deep infatuation."

"Yeah, well, I don't think Kalani sees it that way."

"Maybe she does, but she is afraid. So, what are you going to do?"

"I don't know. When I left her hospital room last night she told me not to come back."

Martin chuckled.

"You find that funny?"

"No, my friend. She is trying to protect you. She wanted to give you an 'out.' That shows *her* integrity and how much she truly loves you. Do you remember how you pursued her when you were falling in love with her?"

"Yeah?"

"Well, do it again. Romance her. If this is the girl of your dreams, then the Otis I know will not give up. Pursue her. Wow her. Convince her by your actions."

A smile and a tear came over Otis's face.

"You're right. I will."

A knock on the door interrupted the conversation. Martin looked through his office window to see Special Agents Huffman and Buchanan at the door. He waved them in.

"Captain, do you have a minute? We'd like to discuss the mayor and also the senseless motive."

"Sure."

Otis stood and walked toward the door.

"Detective, why don't you stay," Martin said.

"I spoke with Corporal Wilton to see if the mayor's movements have revealed anything. He had nothing interesting to report. Do you think it would be worth interviewing an ENT doctor? Maybe he could give us something more to go on. Something we may be missing," Agent Huffman asked.

"Ear, nose, and throat? We have victims whose eyes, ears, and mouth were removed. So far, the nose hasn't come into play," Martin said.

Before Martin could finish his thought, there was another knock on the door. Dr. Wu cracked the door open and stuck her head in.

"Is this a bad time?" she asked.

"No, doctor, please, come in."

Looking at Huffman, Buchanan, and Otis, she said, "Gentlemen."

"We were just discussing if it would be worth our time to meet with an ENT doctor to see if he or she could, perhaps, shed some light on the perp's motives. Specifically, why he is focusing on the five senses."

"If you ask me, you need to spend more time with Dr. Detrich, our forensic psychologist. This killer has a particularly twisted mind. If you want to pursue the ENT route, I know a very good otolaryngologist. An otolaryngologist is an ear, nose, and throat doctor, but the work encompasses more than the care and keeping of the senses. These doctors are also concerned with maintaining the ability to swallow, with ease of breathing, a sense of balance, and much more. I'll email you Dr. Dosik's contact info when I get back to my office. She should be able to help you."

"Thanks, Doctor. Why did you come to see me?" Martin asked.

"Oh, I almost forgot. Miss Alavrez was six weeks pregnant."

~~~

After everyone left his office, Martin looked at the stack of mail he had ignored for the past couple of days. A monthly police magazine, administrative nonsense, an envelope that had a return address from Homeland Security, and a 5 x 7 envelope, made up the majority of the mail. Martin intuitively put on a pair of disposable plastic gloves and picked up the manilla envelope. It had something rigid inside. He could tell it was too thick to be a ballpoint pen accompanied by a request for a donation. There was no return address. He had a sickening feeling in his stomach.

Martin tore the envelope open and pulled out a letter and a vial of something that appeared to be blood. In block letters the letter read:

MY DEAR CAPTAIN WALLACE,

'BLOOD WAS ITS AVATAR AND ITS SEAL'. I SPEAK NOT OF THE FICTITIOUS RED DEATH PESTILENCE, BUT OF AN AUTHENTIC PLAGUE OF MY OWN DOING.

PURPOSEFUL DISMEMBERMENT MAY SEEM CRAZED BY YOU. THERE ARE TIMES WHEN I MIGHT AGREE WITH YOU. 'I BECAME INSANE, WITH LONG INTERVALS OF HORRIBLE SANITY'. YET, THERE IS AN ERUDITION THAT HAS TO BE ADMIRED.

I MAY BORROW SPECIFIC FEATURES OF A WOMAN, BUT I DO SO TO GIVE ANOTHER A PERFECTION THAT IS UNKNOWN IN THIS WORLD.

I AM SENDING YOU THIS GIFT, AS I AM AWARE OF YOUR INTEREST IN MY QUEST. YES, HAVE IT TESTED. YOU WILL FIND THAT IT ONCE PUMPED THROUGH THE VEINS OF KATRINA ALVAREZ.

YOU NOW KNOW MY MOTIVE IS TO ACCUMULATE THE WORLD'S MOST PERFECT EYES, EARS, LIPS, NOSE AND HANDS. THEY WILL BE TRANSPLANTED ONTO A, THUS
~~~

UNDETERMINED, LADY. SHE WILL BE THE EVE OF MY CREATION.

WARM REGARDS, FIVE

"Otis, put on gloves and check this out," Martin said as he handed him the letter."

"Who sent this?"

"Our killer. There is no return address. It came with this vial."

"Is that blood?"

"I think so. I'm guessing it is one of his victim's?"

"He says it is Miss Alvarez's blood."

Martin got up from behind his desk and walked out to the common room followed by Otis.

"Becton!" Jordan lifted his head which was buried in some papers. "See if this is blood and if it is, get down to forensics. Have them check to see if it matches Miss Alvarez's DNA and see if there are any fingerprints on this envelope."

"Blood? Where did you get that?" Jordan asked.

"We believe our killer sent it to me. He is taunting us."

"There is no return address on this envelope. I guess the Mayor waited till everyone went home and dropped this off on your desk, Captain," Jordan said with a smile.

"Becton?"

"Yes, Captain?"

"Just do it, please."

"I'm on my way."

# CHAPTER FOURTEEN

*Memories, imagination, old sentiments, and associations are more readily reached through the sense of smell than through any other channel.*
— Oliver Wendell Holmes

Martin abruptly sat up in bed. Sweat dripped slowly down his forehead. His eyes were large and wild.

"Honey, it's okay. It was a nightmare," Mary Jo said in a comforting tone.

"Yeah," Martin said as he got out of bed and walked into the bathroom. Seconds later he came back to the bed, sitting on its edge while wiping his face with a hand towel.

Over the years he had been a homicide detective, Martin was subjected to many horrific sights. Witnessing the dreadful came with the job and unfortunately, Martin could not be desensitized. Images often plagued him, especially at night. No matter how hard Martin tried to bury certain pictures, those troubling scenes still haunted him.

"This case is slowly killing you," said Mary Jo. You have never heard me say what I am about to say, Martin. Never. But I cannot keep these thoughts to myself. I want you to retire when this case is over," she said, knowing he would never consider laying down his badge until the perpetrator was caught and brought to justice.

"I may just do that."

Mary Jo was a bit surprised by Martin's response. He had never seriously considered retirement. Fully awake now, she decided to change the subject.

"Have you seen Kalani recently?"

"Not since Sunday. Will you join me when I go to the hospital tomorrow?"

"I will. I know you will have to pick me up and then double back, but I really want to show her some love," Mary Jo said.

"It's okay. I don't mind."

Mary Jo had not seen Kalani since the accident, but from what Martin told her, she had an idea of the damage the burns had done to her body. Martin had also shared Otis's reaction to his fiancée's physical appearance. The fact that nothing could sever his heart from Kalani's heart impressed her. Pausing for a minute, Mary Jo then asked Martin, "Honey, would you still have married me if my face was scarred in a fire?"

Martin pondered the question. He loved Mary Jo. She was his confidant, friend, lover, wife and the mother of his children. She was everything he ever wanted in a wife, and more. Martin really did not know how to answer the question, because he really did not know what he would do in that situation.

Leaning over to her, he took Mary Jo's face in his hands.

"Mary Jo, you are asking the wrong question. If I truly loved you enough to marry you, then I would be with you as you faced your health challenges, no matter what that entailed. I believe if I would have wanted to avoid that experience, then quite arguably, I was never really in love with you."

Mary Jo kissed Martin and whispered, "I adore you."

Martin's phone began to vibrate on the end table.

"Victim number four," he said before answering the phone.

"Wallace," Martin said into his phone. "Was it the nose or hands removed?

Right. I'm on my way."

Mary Jo reached over to touch Martin's back.

"The maniac strikes again. This time he removed the nose. I'll call you later, honey."

Martin dressed, got in his car and headed toward Rittenhouse Square, the center of the eponymous Rittenhouse neighborhood. The square is one of the five original open-space parks planned by William Penn and his surveyor Thomas Holme during the late 17th century. Martin looked at his watch. It was a quarter to six.

On his way to the crime scene, Martin wrestled with the hypothetical question Mary Jo posed. If it had been Mary Jo disfigured in a fire, would he have married her? As much as he loved his wife, he could not honestly answer the question. The possibility he may not have followed through with the wedding made Martin sad and disappointed in himself. *Relationships are by far the most difficult thing in life.*

His mind then raced to thoughts of his mother, of all people. Little seemed to phase his mom. She was a strong, no-nonsense Polish woman who, at times, seemed more rigid than the statue of Billy Penn who stood watch above Philadelphia's City Hall. It was a frantic phone call from his mother, one autumn afternoon, when she turned to her law enforcement son for help.

During an impromptu session of dalliance, his father had a massive heart attack and perished while perched on top of his mother. Although a premature death, Martin viewed his father's demise as the best possible way to depart this earth. His mother did not share Martin's favorable view. She blamed her husband for dying in such a position as to demean her, as if he chose to conclude his pleasurable orgasm by dropping dead.

Like a hummingbird stopping at a flower just long enough to get a drink of nectar before moving on to the next bloom, Martin's thoughts refused to rest on any one subject for very long. His thoughts went back to Mary Jo. She always had a perspective Martin found refreshing. As perceptive as Martin was on cases he worked, often he was oblivious to the cause and effect they had on him. He was incognizant of their impact. But this case was like no other. Martin was profoundly aware as he navigated the strange and convoluted Senseless murders.

The investigation consisted of an unabated maze of dead ends along the winding path towards justice, or was it righteousness? Martin wasn't sure. Regardless of what laws are decreed in a civilized land, they are devised by imperfect man, or are they? Martin thought that what one person may find offensive, or even illegal, another may perceive as not only acceptable, but pleasurable. He knew that truth within a Judeo-Christian society, it is God who decides right from wrong, and it is passed down to the people. The problem therefore is, in a godless society, evil thrives. And yet, Martin was fighting a war of push and pull, one not of right versus wrong, or good versus evil, but rather of beauty versus the grotesque.

Beauty. Something so obvious and lucid had become more complicated and mystifying.

Martin pondered what beauty actually is. *Is it that goodness which ignores obvious aesthetics? What if we all looked the same, like mannequins? Then beauty would have no choice but to be beyond skin deep. Are we really that blind that we can see only with blinders on, preventing us from gaining a complete understanding of a person?*

Otis once told Martin that the global cosmetic surgery market was valued at over $80 billion dollars. *The never-ending quest for aesthetic perfection. Why is our society so obsessed with one's physical appearance? It had to be more than just that beautiful people have a clear advantage. True beauty becomes more apparent in old age when wrinkles, receding hairlines, gravity, and elongated ears have kidnapped youthful beauty. Shame on us!*

Martin parked at the corner of Walnut Street and South 19th Street, between two police cars whose emergency vehicle lights were bouncing off the high-rise residences, luxury apartments, and office towers that surrounded the park. Martin was glad he finally beat Otis to a crime scene.

"What do we have?" Martin asked the two uniformed police officers.

"It looks like the work of our serial psycho. Her nose has been surgically removed with precise execution and replaced with these Groucho Marx novelty glasses. You know, the ones with an attached nose, moustache, and eyebrows? Besides the removal of her nose, she has signature marks on her neck. They appear to be small puncture wounds from a taser. Here you can see the marks at the site of the probe contact. There are no other signs of trauma. She had no identification on her, but she did have a set of keys in her coat pocket," the officer said, handing the keys to Martin.

"Who found her?"

"That man over there, talking to your detective."

Martin looked to where the officer was pointing and saw Otis talking with a well-dressed man with a Bichon Frisé on a leash. Martin walked over to them.

"Thank you, Mr. Shackleton. We'll be in touch if we have any additional questions," Otis said.

"What did he have to say?" asked Martin.

"He walks his dog early every morning, since he likes to be in his office by seven. Rittenhouse Square is a popular dog walking destination for area residents. Mr. Shackleton is the Chief Information Officer at the Philadelphia Stock Exchange, and lives with his partner who is an art dealer. He said he knows the victim. Her name is Susan Cranford. She lives two doors down from his place. Here is her address," Otis said, as he handed Martin a piece of paper. "He only sees her on the weekends when she walks her dog. He sleeps in on the weekends and walks his dog later on those days. He said the woman's dog is a boxer."

"Is she married?"

"He thinks she is divorced. He's not sure, but he has never seen her with a man."

"The use of a taser is a new twist for our killer. Did you check the victim's stomach?"

"I did. It has the orange number five."

This park is very well-lit. Our perp is becoming more confident and reckless. That is a good thing. Overconfidence will be his downfall."

Almost, as if on cue, the park lamp posts extinguished their light as the sun peaked its head over the horizon. Martin looked around the perimeter of the park surrounded by restaurants and residences. Dozens of benches were scattered throughout the park, a popular lunch-time destination for residents and workers in Philadelphia's Center City neighborhood. Lion and goat statues were favorite gathering spots for small children and their parents, but murder turns the most idyllic place into a cesspool.

Turning to Lillia, who had just arrived on the scene, Martin said, "Lieutenant Ewing, I need a search warrant for 1936 Chancellor Street. It is the address of Susan Cranford, our fourth victim. Get a warrant for her cell phone, too."

"Will do, Captain."

Martin started walking towards the victim when, for no apparent reason, he abruptly stopped and looked up at the full moon which was still visible.

"What is it, Captain?" Lillia asked.

"Did each of the other three murders happen under a full moon?"

"I'm not sure, but it would be easy enough to check."

"Please do that.

"Sergeant Santos, I want the park bench dusted for prints, as well as the fake nose and glasses. Every security camera that faces the park needs to be checked out."

Otis and Martin saw Dr. Wu walking towards them with only a sweater to keep her warm.

"Aren't you cold, doctor?" Otis asked, himself wearing a heavy peacoat.

"No. This is the warmest morning we've had since early November. It is a friendly reminder that spring is not far off. You know what they say—March comes in like a lion and goes out like a lamb." Looking at Otis she said, "Detective, you look like you're ready for a blizzard in Siberia."

"Black people are from Africa. We cannot stand the cold."

"Africa? You are from Mount Airy," the doctor said with a laugh. Quickly she changed her tune. "I assume Mr. Five has his fourth victim?"

"Yeah," responded Otis. "This time he removed her nose."

As Dr. Wu turned and walked toward the victim, Martin said, "Dr. Wu, please let me know if they get any hits on trace DNA. I'm especially anxious to see if it reveals DNA from you-know-who.

"I will, Martin."

"Elaine?"

"What is it, Martin," the doctor said in a voice suggesting she was getting impatient to inspect the body.

"What about DNA transfer? That's a possibility, isn't it?"

"Are you referring to the mayor's DNA we found at the last crime scene?"

"I am."

"Well, absolutely; DNA transfer is a real thing, but the mayor's DNA was found on the wax lips, the cigarette, and from the rape kit. It's pretty unlikely all three locations would be the result of transfer."

"Humor me," Martin said.

"Secondary transfer occurs through an intermediary. For example, if two people shake hands, then one person handles a gun, DNA from the first person may be transferred to the second person and then deposited on the gun. There's also tertiary transfer; DNA is transferred indirectly through two intermediaries. For example, one person touches a chair, then a second person touches the chair, and then handles a gun."

"So. it is possible."

"Anything is possible, Martin. I should add that it can be difficult to determine if a DNA profile is from primary, secondary, or tertiary transfer. There are factors that impact DNA transfer, which include the freshness of the biological material, the amount of DNA deposited by hands, and the type of substrate. Now, if you will excuse me?"

"Of course. The young lady is waiting for you."

~~~

The team arrived back at the precinct in time to see Inspector Jenson walking out of the common room with Chief Conwell.

"What were they doing in here while all of us were at the crime scene?" Lillia said.

"I haven't a clue," responded Jake as he stared at the white board. "I'm sure they heard about the latest murder."

The white board in the common room now had three suspects posted, Tanner Thrush, who abruptly quit school in his senior year and since disappeared, Jorge Navarro, who had a violent streak and a fondness for operating on dead animals, and Mayor Forester, a trifecta of his DNA retrieved from the third victim. Photos of Thrush and Navarro were posted next to a solid black image of a man's head and the initials M.F., representing Mayor Foerster.

Martin was discussing the latest crime scene with the two FBI Special Agents when Lane caught Martin's eye.

"What is it, Corporal?"
~~~

"We have been following the mayor for five days now. Nothing overly suspicious surfaced, but we did see him meeting a much younger young lady at the Gladstone Hotel on Thursday evening. What we found interesting is that he did not enter the hotel at the front entrance, like everyone else. He entered the hotel through the delivery door in the back of the hotel, and he drove himself; no chauffeur or bodyguard accompanied him."

"Mayor Foerster is married. If he is having an affair, he would want to do so discreetly," Martin said.

"Yeah, well, Jake followed him up the stairs to the ninth floor and the mayor had a key to the room. We questioned the hotel manager who was more than reluctant to give us any information. When we threatened him with us questioning every one of his guests, he was more forthcoming. Apparently, the mayor has been meeting a hooker named Crystal Cummings, no pun intended, for the past fourteen months. The mayor was given his own room key. They meet at the same hotel, same room, every Thursday, at the same time. Jake got some photos of the two of them in a kissing embrace behind the hotel. They exited the hotel from the garage at the loading dock."

"Good. Jake and Lillia, I want you to bring in Darius Banks-Marsette. He was supposed to call me if our perp contacted him for the black Escalade. He reneged on his promise. If our killer stayed consistent with his ritual, he killed the girl elsewhere and used the black Escalade to transport her here."

Turning to Diego, Martin said, "Sergeant, I want to talk with Miss Cummings, but we don't want her to reveal our investigation to the mayor. I want you and Lillia to bring her in."

"Okay. Do you have an address for her, Lane?" Diego asked.

"I do."

Lane handed Diego his business card with Crystal Cumming's address written on the back, then turned to Martin.

"Captain, may I speak with you in private?" Lane asked.

"Of course." Turning to the FBI agents, Martin said, "Excuse us, gentlemen."

Martin closed the door to his office and said, "What's up?"

"I was going to meet my wife, Karen, for lunch today. I suggested we meet at that Greek restaurant on South Street, but she really wanted to go to a small bistro in Society Hill. When we walked into the restaurant I saw Jordan at a table in the corner. He was having lunch with a reporter from the *Philadelphia Inquirer* at a cafe. The reporter is Robert Newell."

"The investigative reporter?"

"One and the same. I'm sorry, Captain."

"Did he see you?"

"No. I explained the situation to Karen and we left before he saw us."

"Where is Detective Becton now?"

"He's on the mayor's surveillance detail."

"Call him and tell him I want to see him immediately. Detective Gainwell and I have an appointment with the otolaryngologist. Tell Becton not to leave the office and to wait for me."

"Will do."

After Lane left Martin's office, Otis walked in.

"Everything alright?" asked Otis.

"No. Not close. Becton is our leak. He's been meeting with Newell from the *Inquirer*."

"Becton? The same Newell who broke the story on the Public Works bribery case for the paving of Roosevelt Boulevard?" Otis asked.

"Yes. I'll deal with him later. Let's go visit Dr. Dosik and see if she can give us any insight on the motive concerning the five senses."

<div align="center">~~~</div>

Dr. Dosik's offices were located eight blocks from the police station, so Martin and Otis decided to walk rather than drive; a walk that afternoon with the temperature in the high 50s, the warmest day of the new year, was an opportunity for the men to enjoy some much needed fresh air.

"Do you really believe this doctor can provide us with anything useful?" Otis asked.

"Are you asking if this is a waste of time?"

"Yeah, I guess that is what I was trying to say, just in a more tactful way," Otis said with a chuckle.

"The short answer is, no. I'm not sure this is worth our time, but at this point, we need all the help we can get. I'm still not convinced Mayor Foerster is our guy. He has no motive and it just doesn't add up."

The two detectives entered a blue window skyscraper and took the elevator to the forty-ninth floor. Otis was thankful Martin did not opt for the stairs. They entered the doctor's office, introduced themselves and were told to have a seat, and that Dr. Dosik would be with them momentarily. The only other person in the waiting room was a young man with white surgical tape X'd across his nose.

Dr. Dosik entered and greeted Martin and Otis.

"Philadelphia's finest! I'm Miriam Dosik," the doctor said as she led the detectives into her office. "Dr. Wu said you would like my perspective on this serial killer who has been terrorizing our city."

"I am Captain Wallace and this is Detective Gainwell. Yes, Dr. Wu thought if anyone can shed some light on a person's obsession with the five senses, it would be you. Thank you for taking time out of your busy schedule."

"My pleasure. Elaine and I did our pre-med studies together, but we attended different medical schools and lost touch. I do see her from time to time at medical conferences. So much for past history. How exactly may I help you gentlemen?"

"Well, I'm sure you have heard this serial killer is intent on dissecting women's features related to the five senses. So far he has removed eyes, ears, lips, and a nose from four different victims, respectively. What is your take on the obsession with the five senses, doctor?"

"The Five Senses, sight, hearing, smell, taste, and touch, can be traced back to ancient Greek philosophy. Aristotle ordered them into a hierarchy. Sight and hearing, designated as of most use to the soul and mind of man, were at the top of his list.

"The nervous system is designed to receive and process information about the world outside in order to react, communicate, and keep the body healthy and safe. The sensory organs: the eyes, ears, nose, tongue, and skin help to accomplish that. Nerves relay the signals to the brain, which interprets them as sight (vision), sound (hearing), smell (olfaction), taste (gustation), and touch (tactile perception). That is your medical lecture for the day."

"I would look for someone who is obsessed with human aesthetics…beauty…the physical appearance of women."

"Isn't that the entire male race?" Martin said with a chuckle.

Dr. Dosik joined in the laughter. "You said that, not I, but yes, actually. Let me be a little more specific. There are occupations that, by their very definition, center attention on the physical appearances of women. Fashion photographers, hair stylists, pimps, and talent agents, for example. Your killer may be either in the porn industry or, or addicted to pornography."

"What about a taxidermist?" Otis asked.

"Now that is an interesting possibility. They are interested in the aesthetics of their project. They need to manipulate the eyes, mouth, hands…I don't know. Maybe. Your killer has yet to remove the hands from a victim, is that correct?"

"Not yet," Otis said.

"If your murderer only removed the hands, I would suggest you look for a Hindu from India. They symbolize super-humanity by the multiplication of the most important parts of the body. Since arms and hands are extremely useful, a twelve-armed god demonstrates the power and the strength denied a two-armed god. This may not make sense to us, but in the Near East it recognizes that power and wisdom and strength may be expressed quantitatively. Sometimes you will see a Muslim wearing a small image of the hand around his neck to ward off the evil eye."

"Our first victim was Muslim," Otis reminded Martin.

"I don't know what else I can tell you," the doctor said.

Getting up from his chair, Martin said, "You have actually been very helpful, Dr. Dosik. Thank you for your time."

"You're very welcome. Good luck catching this man, detectives."

As the two detectives were leaving the doctor's office, Otis received a call on his cell phone.

"What's up Lillia? Okay. Great! Thanks!"

Turning to Martin, Otis said, "We have the search warrant for Susan Cranford's home. Lillia and Diego are going to meet us there.

Oh, and she said you were right. All four murders occurred when there was a full moon."

"So, our killer is obsessed not only with the five senses, but with full moons. Let's head over to Miss Cranford's place."

# CHAPTER FIFTEEN

*The only time you really live fully is from thirty to sixty. The young are
slaves to dreams; the old servants of regrets. Only the middle-aged
have all their five senses in the keeping of their wits.*
— Theodore Roosevelt

Lillia and Diego were waiting for Martin and Otis when they arrived at Miss Cranford's home.

"The people who live around here have some serious money," Otis said. "See that restaurant over there? Believe it or not, they have a $100 cheesesteak on the menu."

"Yeah, well I will stick with Jim's steaks," Martin said.

Susan Cranford's condo was a luxurious 4500 square foot gem. Surrounded by some of the city's swankiest mansions and a slew of restaurants, it was clear Miss Cranford had, or came from, money.

When the detectives entered the condo they were met with a putrid odor.

"Ugh! What is that smell?" Lillia asked.

No one needed to respond. A brindle-colored boxer was dead on the parlor room floor; a half-eaten ribeye steak next to him.

"Santos, bag that steak and have it tested for poison. I want the dog placed in a body bag and taken for an autopsy. This time the killer had to improvise. The other three victims went with the killer willingly. There were no signs of struggle either on their bodies or at their homes. Here, we have the opposite. The killer came to Miss Cranford's home, had to eliminate the dog who was probably protecting its master, and then used a stun gun or taser to subdue her."

"Captain, here is her cell phone," Lillia said.

"Let's take a look at her texts, emails, and calls from the past month. Perhaps her killer first tried to invite her to join him somewhere and when she refused, he came to her. It appears the other three victims willingly met with him. She obviously did not."

Martin scrolled down the dozens of texts on Susan Cranford's phone. A short text conversation caught Martin's attention. "Listen as I read these exchanges of texts," Martin said.

**Person A:** As I stated over the phone, there was an overcharge and you have some money coming your way. I could send it to you via USPS, but I might as well drop it off at your home.

**Susan Cranford:** That's great, but I hate to put you out. You can just drop it in the mail.

**Person A:** I have a lunch date just around the corner from your place. Besides, I hate the U.S. mail. It took them nearly three weeks to deliver a birthday card to my friend, and he only lives in Maryland!!!

**Susan Cranford:** LOL. Yeah, I get that. Well, if it's not too much trouble…

**Person A:** No trouble at all! See you in about an hour.

Martin reached into his jacket pocket for his cell phone and called Lane.

"Hey, Boss. Find anything interesting at Miss Cranford's home?" Lane asked.

"Our perp killed her dog. I'm thinking he gave the poor thing a poison injected steak. The dog only finished half of it before its demise."

"Hey, I want you to run a phone number. Ready? 358-855-0011. I'll hold."

After a few minutes Lane came back on the line.

"That number is from a burner phone."

"Of course it is. Okay, thanks for checking, Corporal."

"Let's head back to the office."

~~~

As FBI Agent Buchanan walked out of the police station he bumped into Otis and Martin who were returning from Miss Cranford's home.

"I was just going to grab a bite to eat, but that can wait. You are not going to believe the news I just received," Buchanan said.

"At this point Mr. Buchanan, I would believe anything," Martin said.

"Let me walk back to the office with you," the agent said as he followed the two detectives to the stairs. "Why are you taking the stairs?"

"Exercise. What is this unbelievable news?"

"One of our suspects, Jorge Navarro, is on surveillance camera footage at the Devon Race Track and Polo Grounds. He went into one of the stalls where a horse was kept and, apparently, electrocuted it in a certain manner. We spoke to a veterinary pathologist and he told us that if you know what you are doing you can electrocute a horse and it would be very difficult to find signs of foul play and the death would be chalked up to colic. By the various surgical tools Navarro had with him, his intent most likely was to render the horse unconscious for exsanguination."

"I know what you are thinking, because it was my question to the veterinary pathologist. What is exsanguination? Believe it or not, it is the bleeding out, which typically occurs while the body is still alive. It's the loss of a significant amount of blood, usually from trauma or other serious injuries, that results in death. Whatever Navarro's motive was, he never got to finish what he started. Navarro got spooked when one of the equine veterinarians entered the stables to check on a horse who had been operated on the previous day."

"This horror story never ends," Otis said.

"So, I assume they do not have Navarro in custody?" Martin asked.

"No. When Navarro saw the vet, he took off running, leaving his tools behind. The veterinarian yelled for Navarro to stop. An old stable hand was walking between stables and heard the vet call out. He tried to stop Navarro, but instead got hit hard over the head and Navarro
~~~

got away. The man is okay. He received a concussion and several stitches."

"Stupid question, but did anyone go over to Navarro's apartment to see if he's there?"

"Yeah, two uniforms went. No one was home."

"So now we are looking for both Thrush and Navarro, both who are on the lam," Otis said.

"This case has more twists than Chubby Checker," Martin said.

"Who is Chubby Checker?" asked Otis.

~~~

As soon as Martin, Otis, and Agent Buchanan walked into the office, Lane approached them.

"Everyone wants to see you, Captain. Jordan has been waiting at his desk for you, Dr. Wu called and said she has the results from the autopsy of Susan Cranford, and we have Crystal Cummings, the mayor's prostitute in interrogation room two."

"A trifecta. Alright. Offer Miss Cummings a cup of coffee or a bottle of water. Make her comfortable and let her know I will be with her shortly."

"My pleasure!" Lane said with a smile.

"Hey Lane, don't get too worked up over her," Otis said with a chuckle.

Martin turned and caught Jordan's attention from across the room, motioning for him to come into his office. Martin held the door open for Jordan and closed it behind them.

"Have a seat."

"Did I do something wrong, Captain?"

"You tell me."

A look of confusion, or perhaps fear, swept over Jordan's face.

"Why did you leak information on our case to the press?"

Jordan hesitated to speak, perhaps contemplating whether or not to deny the accusation.

"Let me first say if I did speak to the press, it was motivated only by having the best interest of the department in mind."

"You ignored a direct order from me, your superior."
~~~

"Perhaps I was overly influenced by our nearly six month-long investment in the case. I have been frustrated about the inaction of the investigation."

"And how would you have done things differently?"

"Well, first of all, I would have arrested the mayor."

"Those orders came from DA Malerba, and besides, I don't think he's our perpetrator. Tell me you did not leak to Robert Newell that the mayor is a suspect."

Jordan hesitated before answering Martin's question. "The public has a right to know their top government official is a suspect in four murders."

"Jordan, I believe the evidence was planted. It was transfer DNA, which I am about to prove, but now you have jeopardized the investigation."

"I was just trying to sway public opinion before charges against the mayor are filed."

"You just don't get it, do you, Detective? Every piece of evidence must be verified. Every suspect must be investigated thoroughly. Do you think I am the least bit afraid to arrest and charge the mayor if the evidence proves he is our killer? Why do you think we have not brought charges against him? I'll tell you why. It is because we don't have enough for the DA to prosecute. Remember that 'innocent until proven guilty' thing? Well, we cannot prove the mayor did anything other than commit adultery."

"Thanks to you, we now need to handle anecdotal information with the press. The FBI was brought in because those of us involved in this case, investigators, prosecutors, and pathologists, have limited exposure to serial murder. Most of our experiences are based upon a single murder. That includes you. You have taken your limited experience with a single murder case, as well as the factors in that case, and extrapolated to our existing serial murder. As a result, certain stereotypes and misconceptions take root regarding the nature of serial murder and the characteristics of serial killers."

"Captain, I had no place to vent my concerns internally, despite the alternatives you will say existed."

"Are you trying to say I am not approachable?"

"You are not exactly the most personable guy, Captain."

"Jordan, you are fired," Martin said. Extending his palm, he added, "Let's have your gun and badge. You have ten minutes to leave the building."

Jordan sat in front of Martin's desk as if he were told his family left on vacation without him.

"That's it, Mr. Becton. You are dismissed."

Jordan walked over to his desk, grabbed a framed photograph of his girlfriend and his coffee mug, and walked toward the elevator. The entire team stopped what they were doing to watch Jordan leave. They did not need an explanation as to what was happening.

Martin came out of his office and asked Otis to join him in the interrogation of the prostitute. As they were approaching the interrogation room, Special Agent Huffman caught their attention.

"Captain, may I speak with your witness when you are finished questioning her? I would like to see if she will be willing to wear a wire. If we think she can pull it off, I want her to ask the mayor some specific questions about the murders."

"Sure. That may be a good idea. Let's see what she has to say."

"I'll be listening in the observation room," Huffman said.

"I am so sorry to keep you waiting, Miss Cummings," Martin said.

Crystal Cummings was a buxom blonde, with equally large eyes and pouty lips. She was tall, thin, and had legs that seemed to go for a Philadelphia mile.

"Am I in some kind of trouble? As I told the other detective, I am not a call girl and I have never met the mayor."

"Well, you *were* a call girl, because you have been arrested twice for solicitation of prostitution," Martin said, matter-of-factly.

Otis reached into an 8 x 10 manilla envelope and pulled out photographs of the mayor and her kissing on the loading dock at the rear of the Gladstone Hotel."

"Never met him, huh?" Otis said.

With hesitation, Crystal looked like a child who had been caught cutting school.

"Okay, I may have told you a little white lie, but I was not having sex with the mayor for money. I am his girlfriend."

"A girlfriend who he sees only for an hour a week to have sex? Has he ever taken you to a restaurant, a movie, or a concert?"

"Well, no. He's married, so we had to keep things quiet."

"Tell me, Miss Cummings, did you use a condom when you had sex with the mayor?"

"Yes, I always practice safe sex, and Ronnie does not want me to get pregnant."

"I am going to ask you this next question once. If you lie to me, you will be charged as an accessory to murder, so I want you to consider your response carefully before offering it to me. Do you understand me?" Martin asked.

"Murder?"

"You heard me correctly. Did someone pay you for the mayor's semen?"

Otis turned and looked at Martin as if he were the one surprised by the question.

"I don't know how to answer that question."

"Just tell me the truth."

"I plead the fifth."

"You cannot plead the fifth. This is a friendly conversation, an interview. But the friendly part is starting to disappear. Miss Cummings, I had a difficult day, I am tired, and my patience is thin. If you do not cooperate, I will have you arrested and charged with accessory to murder. Do I make myself clear?"

"I think I should call my lawyer."

"Well, you are certainly free to do that. Who would that be?" Martin asked.

Crystal rummaged through her pocketbook and came out with a business card.

"Mr. Robert Roth."

"What a coincidence," Martin said. "Mr. Roth just so happens to be the mayor's attorney."

Martin stood up and turned to Otis, saying, "Detective, book Miss Cummings for accessory to murder and have her arraigned."

"Wait. Okay. Look, a man approached me and said he would give me $3000 for a condom with the mayor's semen. He threatened me about keeping my mouth shut. The man told me the mayor had killed some people and he was going to get away with it. I was scared out of my wits! Just so you know, I decided to end my relationship with Ronnie."

"What did this man look like?"

"I don't know. Black, medium height, maybe mid-thirties."

"He was a black man?" Otis asked.

"Yes."

Would you recognize him if you saw him again?" asked Martin.

"Yes, I would."

"Okay."

Leaning close to Otis, Martin whispered, "Now that she says the man was black, there is no sense in having her look at a photo lineup. Thrush, Albrecht, and Navarro are not African American, and we have no black suspects."

"Miss Cummings, do not speak of this meeting with anyone, not the mayor, no one. Do you understand?"

"Yes."

"Here is my card. Call me if that man contacts you again."

"Alright. Sit tight. FBI Agent Huffman has a few questions for you."

"FBI?"

Otis and Martin walked out of the interrogation room to find Jake walking towards them.

"Dr. Wu called again while you were interviewing Miss Cummings, Captain. Dr. Wu has the results of Susan Cranford's autopsy."

"Thanks, detective." Turning to Otis, Martin said, "Let's see if Dr. Wu has found something we can use."

# CHAPTER SIXTEEN

*Beauty must appeal to the senses, must provide us with immediate
enjoyment, must impress us or insinuate itself into us without
any effort on our part.*
— Claude Debussy

EVEN BEFORE MARTIN and Otis entered the medical examiner's laboratory they could hear loud noises that included the buzzing sound of an electric saw. When they entered the autopsy room, Dr. Wu was bent over a corpse with a power saw, making precise cuts on the cranial cap. The sound of the saw was joined with a bone dust vacuum. Otis had to turn and take a deep breath to prevent from retching.

"Dr. Wu!" Martin yelled.

The doctor could not hear him, and Martin was afraid he might be decapitated if he surprised the pathologist, so he waved his arms frantically. That did not work either, so he walked over to the light switch and turned the lights on and off rapidly which finally caught her eye. She turned off the saw and removed her goggles.

"Well, hello, Gentlemen."

"What's with cutting into this guy's head?" asked Otis.

"I need to create a cover that can be pulled off to expose the brain. I will then remove the brain. This man died by blunt force trauma. The damage to the skull and brain may provide clues to the nature of the murder weapon, since no weapon was found at the crime scene. I take it you are new to autopsy procedures, detective?"

"I worked with the Criminal Law Division for the past five years. Most of the cases I worked involved either drug trafficking or insurance fraud. I was getting bored with that and requested a transfer to homicide."

"Lucky you. Well, I have an autopsy to finish by the end of the day, so let me tell you what I found on the victim."

"Her name was Susan Cranford, Doctor," Otis said.

"Miss Cranford," Dr. Wu said, correcting herself. "These marks on her neck are from a taser. Your killer used it to immobilize his victim. The taser delivered an electrical waveform that caused neuromuscular incapacitation by stimulating both the sensory nerves and the motor nerves, causing involuntary muscle contractions. The nose was amputated with meticulous accuracy. She had been dead for at least 36 hours when I inspected her at the crime scene. Her body was cold, but not stiff. If the body had felt cold and stiff, death would have occurred 8-36 hours earlier."

"I would have thought just the opposite. That if the body is cold and hard, her death would have occurred more than 36 hours ago," Otis said.

"That is why I am the forensic pathologist and you're not," Dr. Wu said with a smile. "By the way, the ribeye you brought me had been laced with rat poison, more specifically, arsenic. We found it in the dog's tox screen, as one would expect. Shame. What a beautiful dog."

Turning to Martin, Otis said, "Lane looked at Miss Cranford's phone records. Someone called her an hour before the time we believe she was killed. It came from a burner phone and the call lasted 73 seconds. I am guessing the killer tried to convince her to come to him. When she refused, he paid her a visit and was well prepared to eliminate her dog. He must have known her well enough to know she had a dog, and boxers are very protective of their owners."

"Gentlemen, as you would expect, the number '5' was painted in orange nail polish on her stomach," Dr. Wu said. "Speaking of stomach, she had an abdominoplasty."

"Abdominoplasty?" interrupted Martin.

"A tummy tuck. Tissue samples and blood samples were sent to the forensic laboratory. The toxicology report looked specifically for drugs and poisons. Just like the other three ladies, fentanyl and succinylcholine were found in her system; however, unlike the others there is a lot of postmortem bruising. It looks as though she was dropped on her back and hit a very hard surface, like concrete.

Bending over the corpse, a frown came over Otis's face.

"Did he cut out her tongue, too?"

"No, I did that. The tongue is removed during autopsy to thoroughly examine the oral cavity, document any abnormalities, and so I could take tissue samples for further examination."

"Doctor, I wanted to let you know that the mayor's DNA was planted at the crime scene of Katrina Alvarez," Martin said. "We discovered he has been meeting with a prostitute for the past year and a half. Someone got wind of that and paid her to give him a condom filled with the mayor's semen."

"What about the wax lips and the cigarette?"

"Anyone could have picked up the cigarette butt after the mayor put it out. The DNA on the wax lips was probably transferred."

"Someone must really hate the mayor," Dr. Wu said.

"If we arrest everyone who hates the mayor we will have to build a new prison. A large one," Otis said with a chuckle.

~~~

Otis and Martin went back up to their offices where Jake informed Martin that Darius Banks-Marsette would be at the precinct soon and that Diego and Lillia were bringing him in.

"What a day! I would like you to have vehicle forensics place a GPS tracking device on

Banks-Marsette's black Escalade," Martin said.

"Not a problem."

Seconds later, Darius Banks-Marsette could be heard before he was seen in the detective's common room. ADA Bryson had arrived a few minutes earlier when she was informed of Darius's arrival.

"Yo, I don't want nothin' to do with your murder investigation. I know somehow you all are going to lay this on me and that old white guy you are looking for will walk. It's racial injustice."

"Take him to Interrogation Room 2," Martin said.

"Do you think he'll cooperate?" asked Miss Bryson.

"I don't know. I'm not sure he'll help us willingly, but if he thinks we will charge him with the murders, he'll sing. We have a new photo
~~~

line-up that includes all three of our suspects. Let's see what he has to say."

When Martin and ADA Bryson entered the interrogation room, Darius's face was pressed against the mirror with his hands cupped around his eyes as he tried to see if he could look through the two-way mirror.

"Darius, I am very disappointed in you," Martin said. "I thought we had an agreement."

"Look, man. This guy is scary. He told me he would kill me and my girlfriend if I talked to you guys. You are putting my life in danger. I want witness protection."

Otis entered the interrogation room and stood behind Darius.

"Sure, witness protection. We can do that," Martin said sarcastically. "But first, I want you to look at some photographs to see if you can identify your used car salesman. Detective Gainwell, would you please do the honors?"

"I already looked at those mug shots and I ain't gonna help you no more. Lawyer!"

Ignoring Darius's request for a lawyer, Martin said, "Now that is a shame, Darius. Since you will not cooperate, you have now become our number one suspect. Congratulations for moving to the front of the class."

"Darius stood up and said, "I think I will leave now."

"Shut up and sit down. Would you like a cup of coffee?" Martin asked.

"No, but I'll take a glass of Crown Royal."

Martin ignored Darius's request and turned to Otis. "Detective Gainwell, would you please bring in that newest photo line-up?"

Otis left the interrogation room and returned with a sheet of paper with eight photos of middle-aged white men including one of the Mayor.

"I told you. I already looked at those pics. I dunno any of them guys."

Otis placed the lineup sheet in front of Darius. "These are different mug shots. Do you recognize the man who gave you the car?"

Darius turned the sheet of paper over without looking at the photos, crossed his arms and said, "I ain't looking at those mug shots and I ain't gonna help you no more. Lawyer!"

Darius got up from his chair and said, "You ain't got nothing on me. Are you chargin' me? If you ain't, I'm out of here."

ADA Bryson motioned for Martin to step outside the interrogation room with her.

"Let him go. If he's going to lawyer-up, there's no sense in keeping him here. We can't make any charges stick. Once we solidify the evidence, we can bring Mr. Banks-Marsette back in."

Martin and Linda walked back into the interrogation room. Before they could say anything, Darius spoke.

"Look, I didn't commit no crime! If you ain't gonna let me walk, you better call my lawyer."

Martin was discontented. "Let's go, Darius," Martin said as he escorted the suspect out of the interrogation room.

As they were walking out of the room, Crystal Cummings and FBI Agent Buchanan were walking past the interrogation room on their way to the elevator. Abruptly, Miss Cummings snapped her head back to look at Darius.

"That's him!" screamed Crystal Cummings as she pointed to Darius. "That is the man who paid me for the Mayor's semen!"

The look on Miss Bryson's and the detective's faces was one of astonishment.

"Mr. Banks-Marsette, let's go back into interrogation room 2. You have a lot more explaining to do," Martin said. "Miss Cummings, you have been very helpful. Thank you for your time."

"Okay," Crystal said sheepishly.

"Lieutenant Ewing, would you please walk Miss Cummings out?

"Sure, Captain," Lillia said as she motioned for Crystal to follow her.

Otis, Martin, ADA Bryson, and Darius Banks-Marsette entered interrogation room 2.

"Well, well, well. The evidence is starting to pile up against you, Darius. Planting evidence, kidnapping, murder."

Darius began speaking before he was asked the obvious question. "Look, the same guy who gave me the Escalade called me the other day and said if I could convince that hooker to keep the Mayor's love custard he would give me five grand cash. He said whatever it took to convince her to do it, the rest of the cash was mine. I started with one G, but she wouldn't budge. Finally, when she got me up to $3000, she said she'd do it and keep her trap shut."

"Detective Gainwell, please bring in that photo lineup you showed Miss Cummings."

Otis got up and left the room.

"Mr. Banks-Marsette, planting evidence is a serious offense. You are going to do time. The question is, how much time. If you cooperate, I will put a good word in for you with the DA."

"Man, I have done everything you asked me to do."

"Now, that is not exactly true, is it? You did not call me when your car buddy contacted you for the car, and you didn't call me when he contacted you to frame the Mayor."

Otis walked back into the interrogation room.

"Three strikes and you're out, Darius. Take a look at these photos and tell us if you see your car buddy."

"He's no buddy of mine. I wish I never met the freak. Ever since I did, I've had nothin' but trouble."

Darius looked through the photos one at a time. It didn't take long for him to strike gold.

"Him! This is the dude who is behind all of this."

Martin and Otis looked down at the photograph of Dr. Barnabas Albrecht.

~~~

Otis left the office earlier than usual so he could get back to the hospital to see Kalani. Otis commandeered Kalani's surgeon who was walking down the hallway of the hospital.

"Dr. Weisman, may I have a minute of your time?"

"Certainly. You are Miss Dantas's fiancé, aren't you?"

"Yes, Sir. Otis Gainwell. Doctor, how is Kalani doing?"

"She is responding well to the skin grafts and burn excisions. Burn excisions are surgical procedures that remove damaged tissue from a burn wound. They do that to reduce the risk of infection and promote
~~~

healing. She has already been through four surgeries and there are more to come. She is a fighter. I am convinced she is going to be fine. There will be permanent scarring. There's not much we can do about that, but she should live a long healthy life."

"Thank you, doctor…for everything."

"You are welcome."

Otis walked over to Kalani's hospital room and knocked softly on her door. Although her eyes were closed, she was awake. Not wanting to rehash the conversation about their engagement she canceled, Kalani pretended to be asleep. Otis walked in and sat by her bed hoping she would awaken from her slumber.

Nearly an hour passed when Otis got up from the chair and knelt by Kalani's bed and began to pray.

"Dear Heavenly Father, I come before you with one request. Only one. I know You are the Great Physician. I know nothing is too difficult for You. I know You love Kalani. And You know how much I love her. As much as I want to spend the rest of my life with her, if I may, I ask for one thing, I ask You to heal her—completely—not only physically, but also emotionally. Please! And let her truly know how much I love her. In Jesus's name I pray, Amen."

Otis stood, kissed his finger and then placed it gently upon Kalani's forehead, turned and left. Once he was gone, Kalani placed her hand on her bed sheet where Otis had rested his head as he prayed. It was wet from his tears.

~~~

Back at Police Headquarters, the District Attorney entered Chief Conwell's office with purpose.

"Did you see the front cover of this morning's *Philadelphia Inquirer*, Chief Conwell?" DA, Malerba said with a raised voice, slamming the newspaper on the desk.

The Chief of Police picked up the paper and saw the headline, "Mayor Ronald Foerster Prime Suspect in Senseless Murders."

"The mayor wants to see Wallace immediately, and I am not covering for him."
~~~

"Mr. Malerba, Captain Wallace discovered one of his detectives had been leaking information to a reporter from the *Inquirer* and he fired him," the Chief said.

"Well, the damage has been done!"

"The mayor is no longer a suspect. Wallace believes the mayor's DNA found at the scene was planted."

"I'm sure that will be a comfort to the mayor. Remember, he wanted to see Wallace in his office five minutes ago," the DA said as he walked out of Conwell's office."

Chief Conwell picked up the phone and called Martin.

"Captain, the Mayor wants to see you immediately. He is more than pissed. I assume you have seen the front page of today's paper?"

Martin hung up the phone and walked the five blocks to city hall.

The mayor's office was immense. The intentional layout drew one's eyes to the large, dark brown, Brazilian Rosewood desk, and its grain that featured a distinctive spider webbing enhancing its beauty. Behind the desk was a large painting of Philadelphia's first mayor, Humphrey Morrey, who was appointed by the city's founder, William Penn, in 1697.

"Captain Wallace. I'm glad you could make it," the mayor said.

*I bet he is! Buckle your seatbelt, Martin, cause here comes the bumpy ride,* Martin thought to himself.

"Of course, Mayor Foerster."

"So, you think I am a serial killer."

"Actually, no, I do not."

"But you were investigating me?"

"Yes. Sir, your DNA was found at the crime scene of Katrina Alvarez. Not just once, but in three separate places: the wax lips, the Newport cigarette butt, and semen from the rape kit. What would you have thought?"

"Yes, Mr. Malerba paid me a visit. I told him I had nothing to do with this, and now, you have leaked your suspicions to the press!"

*This guy just can't be wrong. He never apologized for announcing to the press and thus, the public, that the killer was targeting college women. He blames us for the planted evidence supplied by his girlfriend. This guy is the definition of arrogant!*

"I will hold a press conference today informing the press you are innocent and that the police made a mistake."

"You don't get it, do you? The damage is already done. The public cannot unhear what they have been told! Your department is incompetent and worthless! I would fire you right here and now if it did not look like I were retaliating."

"You are welcome to do that, of course, Mr. Mayor. For what it's worth, I fired the detective who leaked this information to the press. And if you want to blame someone, look at your girlfriend hooker, Crystal Cummings. She took the condom filled with your semen and sold it to our killer for $3000."

"Get out of my office!" The mayor screamed.

Martin stood up, gave the mayor one last look, and left the office.

# CHAPTER SEVENTEEN

*The senses deceive from time to time, and it is prudent never to trust
wholly those who have deceived us even once.*
— Rene Descartes

"We need corroborating evidence," Martin said. "Corporal Wilton, there was a photographer at the Mayor's Ball Otis and I attended just before Christmas. I want to see every photo he took."

"I'm on it, Boss."

"Otis, do you recall seeing Dr. Albrecht there that evening? I wonder if that is where he gathered the mayor's DNA, that is, other than his semen, which we know Miss Cummings collected. It would not have been that difficult to follow the mayor outside and pick up a cigarette butt after he discarded it."

"I do not recall seeing him at the Ball, but that doesn't mean he wasn't there. I bet there were at least 150 people at the event."

Thinking out loud, Martin said, "Our first victim, Farah Darvish, was identified by her breast implants. Our last victim, Susan Cranford, had a tummy tuck. Santos and Ewing, I want you to interview the families and friends of Lan Nara and Katrina Alvarez and find out if either had any plastic surgery done and, if so, by whom. Let's find out who performed the procedure. Oh, and you are going to need a translator when you visit Lan Nara's parents."

~~~

Lane entered the Hocus Focus Studios located on Chestnut Street. A young woman and a man in his late forties were busy tearing down light modifiers that included reflectors and diffusers from what had
~~~

been a recent photo shoot. An attractive, but overly thin, woman came out of a dressing room, fussing with her hair.

A man, clearly the photographer and owner of the shop, was bent over a table looking at photographs through a flat video screen.

"Owen, darling, please email me the proofs as quickly as possible. The deadline is the day after tomorrow," the model said.

"Do not stress, Callista. It causes premature creases in your face. Every photograph I take of you is flawless. You are the quintessential model, my love, my favorite subject. You will have them by the morning."

The woman blinked exaggeratedly slowly, threw her chin towards her shoulder, and left the studio without a response.

"Are you Owen Dahlquist?" Lane asked.

"I am. What can I do for you?"

Lane showed the photographer his badge and said, "I am Corporal Wilton with the Major Crimes Division. Were you taking pictures at the Mayor's Ball a few months ago?"

"I was. What is this all about?"

"I would like to see every photo you took that night."

"Do you have a warrant? I'm sure you can appreciate that my clients expect complete privacy from me. There were quite a few high profile people there that evening."

Lane walked over to the review table and purposely got very close to the photographer.

"Please, detective, you are invading my space!" the photographer said.

"I'll be invading more than your space if you refuse to cooperate! There were over 150 people at that party, Mr. Dahlquist. If they wanted privacy, they should not have attended such a gala where they knew photographs would be taken. In fact, you were not the only photographer taking pictures that evening. Photographers from several local papers were there taking shots for their society pages. The reason high society people come to these galas is *for the publicity!*"

"Nonetheless, I do not feel comfortable sharing my photos with you."

"Fine, I'll be back with a warrant, and we will go through every single photo you have in this place. That should keep your business shut down for at least a week."

Tilting his head to his left, and offering a sheepish smile, Owen said, "You don't have to work yourself up into a tizzy. Maybe I can have you look at the photographs I took that night right here, instead of taking them with you."

"Now, see, that is the cooperation I had hoped for, Owen. Isn't it much nicer working together?"

The photographer was not amused, and displayed a look of vexation. He retrieved a thumb drive from a drawer and plugged it into the computer. A photo of the Union League, the location of the Mayor's Ball, came on the screen.

"Use this button to scroll through the photos. There are 332 in all."

Lane pulled over a bar stool and sat down. Several hours of slowly reviewing the photographs required frequent breaks for Lane to rest his eyes. His tedious labor paid off. What appeared to be a waste of time, finally paid dividends. Lane found four photographs that proved the plastic surgeon, Barnabas Albrecht, was at the ball. Two of the four photos were of the mayor and Dr. Albrecht together.

Owen Dahlquist was preoccupied with photographing a new client for his modeling portfolio when Lane called out to him.

"Mr. Dahlquist, I found several photos I would like you to print for me."

"Can it wait? I'm in the middle of a shoot."

"I have been here for over two hours. No, it cannot wait," Lane said with obvious irritability. "Get me those prints and I will get out of your hair."

Letting out a sound that was a cross between a sigh and a grunt, Owen turned to one of his assistants and said, "Tommy, darling, would you please print the photos the detective wants so we can get rid of him?"

Without a word, Tommy walked over to the review table, printed the photos, handed them to Lane, and with a motion of his hand, dismissed Lane.

~~~

Meanwhile, Diego and Lillia arrived at Lan Nara's mother's home. The drapes were drawn, giving the appearance the house was vacant. They stood on the stoop of the rowhome and rang the doorbell.

"Lillia, are you surprised at all that Otis still wants to marry Kalani? I'm not trying to be the average American guy who is only obsessed with a woman's looks, but from what the Captain said, the entire side of Kalani's face is permanently scarred."

"So, he should just dump her when she needs him the most?"

"No, well, not exactly. I mean, he can be there for her…be her friend…but that doesn't mean he has to marry her."

Diego rang the doorbell again.

"Otis has really impressed me with how he is reacting to all of this, Diego. Otis is treating her like a beautiful goddess. He understands something most men do not. If a man *believes* you are beautiful and *treats* you like you are beautiful, then no matter what a woman looks like, she will begin to *believe* she is beautiful. It warms my heart when I see a couple, well into their 80s, long after the woman's beauty has passed, and the man looks at her, kisses her, sees her as that beautiful woman he fell in love with 50 plus years ago. Otis sees the *real* Kalani. He sees beyond the scarring. She is just as beautiful to him as she was before the accident."

A short, overweight, middle-aged woman pulled back curtains and peered through a bay window. Diego showed her his badge. Several locks could be heard before the door opened a crack. Not being able to find a translator who speaks Manchu, the detectives accessed a cell phone app that translated Manchu into English, and vice versa.

"Yes?" the woman said, using one of the few words of English she knew.

"Mrs. Nara?" Lillia asked.

"Yes?"

Lillia spoke into her phone and a digital voice responded in Manchu with, "I am Lieutenant Ewing, and this is Sergeant Santos. May we come in?"
~~~

The door closed for a second to allow the woman to slide the chain so she could open the door completely.

"Have you found our daughter's killer?" Mrs. Nara asked.

"Not yet, Mrs. Nara, but we believe we are very close to doing that," answered Lillia. "Please accept our condolences."

"Do you have a suspect?"

"That is why we are here. We need a little more information that will help us narrow our list of possible suspects, ma'am," Diego said.

"Please, have a seat. May I offer you some tea?"

"No, thank you. We won't be here very long. Mrs. Nara, do you know if your daughter was seeing any doctors?"

"No. Not that I know of. Lan was a healthy girl."

"She did see a doctor about five months ago," an English-speaking voice from the stairs said. "I am Lan's cousin, Alioth Nara. My American friends call me Alice. I am here to comfort my aunt."

"Where is your uncle?" Diego asked.

"He is working. He works seven days a week at the restaurant."

"So, you were saying Lan had seen a doctor recently?"

"Yes, but she did not want her parents to know. She saw a plastic surgeon to have

liposuction. She tried everything to lose weight. Nothing seemed to work."

Alice's answer caused Lillia and Diego to look at each other in one of those "Ah ha" moments.

"Do you know the name of the doctor who performed the liposuction?"

"No. I just know his office is somewhere on the Main Line. I think he is some kind of famous doctor. Lan said movie stars go to him to get some work done."

"Thank you, Alice. You have been very helpful. Here is my card. If you can think of anything else, please give me a call."

As the two detectives were walking to their car, Diego said, "Do you think the plastic surgeon Miss Nara went to is the same guy who did the work on Farah Darvish?"

"I wouldn't be surprised. By the end of the day, after we interview the friends and families of Katrina Alvarez and Susan Cranford, we should know for sure," Lillia said.

"Why would a plastic surgeon be twisted enough to commit these murders?"

"Who in the world knows? Diego, tell me, why does anyone take the life of another person?"

"I guess there are a lot of answers to that question. I understand why some murders are committed, but these murders seem senseless."

The two detectives got in their car and drove from Chinatown to the Fairhill neighborhood.

"Katrina Alvarez's boyfriend, Jorge Navarro, is in county, waiting for his trial on killing that horse out at the Devon Race Track and Polo Grounds. We could interview him again, but he was less than cooperative the last time the Captain and Otis interrogated him," Diego said.

"I'm afraid you are right. That would be a waste of time. Katrina worked for Parks and Recreation. Let's head over to City Hall and see if she confided in one of her workmates," Lillia said.

~~~

Back at the precinct, Martin had noticed Otis's spirits needed a lift. He walked out of his office and over to Otis's desk.

"Let's grab some lunch," Martin said as he laid his hand on Otis's shoulder.

"I was just reviewing the pictures Corporal Wilton brought back from the photographer. Our friend, Dr. Albrecht, was at the event and some photos show him chumming up to the mayor."

"I heard. Wilton told me. Let's take a break. You need to clear your head. What are you hungry for?"

"I don't know. No, actually, what I am hungry for is breakfast for lunch. I had one of those bird seed granola bars and a cup of coffee this morning and it's just not doing it for me."

"Breakfast it is. Let's head over to the Penrose Avenue Diner."

~~~

The men parked their car and walked into the diner where they were met by a dessert cabinet showcasing cakes, eclairs, cannoli, and cream puffs.

"Maybe I'll skip breakfast and just have dessert," Otis said.

There were no tables available so the two detectives sat at the counter.

"Coffee, Gents?" asked a past-middle-aged woman with large breasts and cleavage that extended south for a block and a half.

"Please," responded Martin.

Turning to Otis, Martin said, "How are things between you and Kalani?"

"Well, every time I visit her she is asleep. I am not stupid. I *am* a detective after all. I can pick up on clues. I'm starting to think she pretends to be asleep when I visit, hoping eventually I will stop coming to see her. At least she hasn't told me not to visit her again. You may recall, that is what she said when she blindsided me with her desire to break off the engagement."

"I wouldn't give up if I were you."

"I'm not."

The waitress came back to the detectives, looked at Otis and asked, "Are you ready, hun?"

"I'll have cream chipped beef on toast, hash browns, English muffin, and a side of scrapple."

Martin took a sip of coffee which was hotter than he expected, causing him to dribble a little on his pants.

"Oh, let me wipe your lap for you, sweetheart," the waitress said with a broad grin. "Now don't get too excited before you eat, darlin'. It's not good for digestion. Whadda you having, handsome?"

Martin was delighted with the waitresses' ribald banter.

"I'll have two poached eggs on rye toast, pork roll, hash browns, and a peach Danish."

The waitress turned her head and yelled back at the cook, "Shit on a shingle, scrapple in the alley, home fries, burn the British, Adam and Eve on a raft, home fries, Taylor ham in the alley!"

"They do have their own lingo, don't they?" asked Martin.

"Indeed they do. Hungry, Captain?"

"Actually, I'm starving. Don't tell Mary Jo about the Danish, or the waitress for that matter."

Otis laughed. A moment of silence brought both of the detectives back to the more serious conversation.

"Martin, although Kalani was a model, she was never obsessed with her looks. I know that makes no sense at all. I mean, sure, she made her living with her physical appearance, but she was never going to go under the knife to enhance her appearance or to provide longevity to her career. Did you know that the average model's career is only 5 years? Kalani is very bright and she had plans on getting a degree in architecture."

"She can still do that," Martin said.

"She can. With her modeling career over, that would be a great avenue for her to pursue. I just want her to be happy and…" Otis paused, as if he were trying to find the right way of finishing his sentence.

"What?"

"Is it selfish to want to be a part of her happiness?"

"I don't think so. Your goal is to make her happy and, should you succeed, you will be happy."

"Martin, when I lie in bed at night, besides thinking of Kalani's long and painful recovery, my mind keeps dwelling on the topic of beauty, sometimes in philosophical terms, and I am no philosopher. What is beauty? Why do we put so much emphasis on beauty? Do I subconsciously value beauty above substance?"

Martin said nothing, allowing Otis to purge the thoughts that were haunting him.

"If beauty is in the eye of the beholder, then who is entitled to decree what is not beautiful? Beauty can be found in the most mundane things. Proper lighting and the right perspective removes veils from one's eyes and reveal a world of beauty unknown to those who will not take the time and effort to look beyond the mere surface. I remember in high school science class when we took a handful of sand and looked at it under the microscope. Those gritty particles transformed into colorful, geometrically diverse wonders. Truly beautiful! But people are not grains of sand."

"When it comes to the beauty of humans, it seems as though our objectivity is often tainted. If people would take off their blinders, perhaps they would see that many people who may not possess aesthetic beauty, are in fact, fantastically beautiful people. But that requires the investment of time to get to know the person and the willingness to have an open heart."

"I have often wondered, if there were only two people left on earth, or if two people were stranded on a deserted island, would a person's aesthetics matter? If the answer is no, if one's physical beauty, or lack of, would not matter in those circumstances, then one must ask himself a question that demands an honest answer—Is the need for an aesthetically pleasing partner more for the positive opinion of others and the approbation an individual might receive?"

"Otis, you *are* a philosopher," Martin said as he placed his hand on his partner's shoulder. "You have already invested time into your relationship with Kalani, and you have a heart that controls your mind, eyes, and speech, and that, my good man, is a beautiful thing."

They finished their meal, paid at the cash register and walked out of the diner.

"Thanks, Martin."

"For what?"

"For caring. It means a lot to me."

"Alright, don't get all mushy with me."

~ ~ ~

The office was empty except for Jake and Lane. Jake was on his computer trying to access the county's title and land records to determine who owns the Schuylkill Meat Packing Company.

"You have got to be kidding me!" Jake screamed.

"What now?" asked Lane.

"The County Recorder's Office website is down. I swear, no city in the world has more issues with its websites than Philly! I'm surprised we aren't still working with dialup internet."

"Don't you miss what they used to call the handshake—those screeching and hissing sounds followed by a series of chirps and whistles?"

"I'm too young to remember Alexander Graham Bell's internet," Jake said sarcastically.

"Well, I guess you'll have to call them," Lane suggested.

Jake picked up the phone and dialed the Official Recorder's Office. It didn't take long before Jake's agitation shifted to overdrive.

"Title and land records," Jake said over the phone. "No! Title and land records. No! That is not correct! Land records, not band records! I hate these recorded messages with so-called instructions! What, are you a music store or the County Recorder's Office? No! Title and land records."

Turning to Lane, Jake said, "Morons! I'm on the phone with the Philadelphia County Recorder's Office. I am trying to find out whose name is on the title for the Schuylkill Packing building. I'm riding a merry-go-round with their recording instead of speaking to a human being."

Speaking into the phone again, Jake yells, "No! Not human resources! Forget it! Give me an operator! Operator!

"Yes, hello. Is this Customer Service?... Yes, this is Detective Sinclair with Major Crimes. I need to find out the legal ownership, or whose name is on the property deed documents, for the Schuylkill Packing Company located on Mantua Avenue...What? No, this is for a police investigation. It is very important that we have this information...You're kidding me, right? Well, you have been wonderfully uncooperative!"

Jake slammed the phone down in frustration.

"I swear the government only hires idiots!"

"*We* work for the government," Lane said.

"Case in point."

"If you are heading over there, I better go with you. I'm afraid you will come back with someone's head on a platter," Lane said.

Otis and Martin walked into the office just as Jake and Lane were leaving.

"Where are you two heading?" Martin asked.

"We are heading over to the mental institution they call the Philadelphia County Recorder's Office to find out who actually owns that closed slaughterhouse on Mantua Avenue. I would have accessed the information online IF THEIR FREAKING WEBSITE WASN'T

DOWN AGAIN! If we don't return this decade, assume we are buried beneath miles of paper archives in the basement of the County Recorder's Office!

"You may want to take a deep breath before you enter their offices. They are known for being the black hole of information," Martin said.

"Great!" Jake said as he and Lane walked into the elevator.

~~~

While Jake and Lane were heading for City Hall to find out who owns the meat packing plant, Diego and Lillia were already there to interview Katrina Alvarez's coworkers. They entered the elevator where a short, dark-haired man asked them, "What floor?"

"Sixth, please," answered Lillia.

A small sign directed them down the hall to the Parks and Recreation department. Inside the office were six desks, three next to the wall, an aisle, and another three next to a bank of windows. A young woman in an orange blouse and hair to match, looked up and with a smile asked, "How may I help you?"

"I am Sergeant Santos and this is Lieutenant Ewing."

"Are you here about Katrina?"

"Yes, we are. Were you close to her?"

"I wouldn't say close. You should talk to Donna Hampton. The two of them were friendly."

"Where will we find Donna?" Lillia asked.

"The last desk on your right," answered the woman.

Donna was on the phone when the detectives walked up to her desk.

"That is correct." Donna said. "You can get that form on our website or at our office. We are located in City Hall on the sixth floor. You're welcome."

"Donna Hampton?" asked Lillia.

"Yes?"

"I am Lieutenant Ewing and this is Sergeant Santos. We are with the Major Crimes Division of the police department. Do you mind answering a few questions for us?"
~~~

"Is this about Katrina?"

"Yes, it is."

"I was devastated to hear of her death. Let's go into the break room. It will give us a little privacy."

Walking into the break room, Donna asked, "Would you two like a cup of coffee?"

"Not for me," Diego said.

"No, thank you," echoed Lillia. "Were the two of you close?"

"As close as anyone in this place, I guess. Occasionally, we would grab a drink after work together. Have you looked at her worthless boyfriend, Jorge?"

"We have and he has been arrested, but not for her death."

"I told her she should dump him. He is creepy and has an obsession with dead things."

"We found that out. Did Katrina ever share anything about cosmetic surgery she may have had?"

"Actually, yes, she did. Jorge pushed her to get a butt lift. She had no desire to surgically alter her looks, but she wanted to make him happy, so she did it. He paid for it."

"Do you happen to know the doctor who did the surgery?"

"Of course. That famous guy you see on TV sometimes. Doctor…"

"Albrecht?" suggested Diego.

"That's it. Dr. Albrecht. Jorge wanted her to go to some quack in West Philly who would do it for a third of the cost, but Katrina was adamant that if she were to go under the knife for him, she would only have it done by the best. It was one of the few times she stood up to Jorge. Anyways, rumor has it that guy in West Philly doesn't even have a license to practice medicine in the States."

"Thank you, Miss Hampton. You have been very helpful."

"Please catch this madman. The entire city is on edge."

"We will. Thanks again," Lillia said.

# CHAPTER EIGHTEEN

*The best part of beauty is that which no picture can express.*
— Francis Bacon

The doctor stared at the mannequin posing in the window of Wanamaker's department store. The window dresser was arranging merchandise and incorporating visual elements. Being undressed, the human figure was nothing more than a prop. But as the window dresser used her artistic skills to garnish the mannequin with stylish clothes, jewelry, handbag, heels, and a wig, the doctor's imagination morphed into an appreciation for the mannequin's beauty; although inanimate and devoid of emotion, still beautiful with manmade perfection. She had high cheek bones, perfectly positioned eyes, ears that were not obtrusive, full lips, and a nose with a nasolabial angle between the upper lip and the nose at 95 degrees. The doctor admired the proportions of the nose, a balanced ratio between the width and length of the nose, that obediently followed the "Golden Ratio" of 1:1.618. But it was the hands that captured the doctor's interest.

The power of touch, the doctor thought to himself. The impact of human touch on emotional well-being is undeniable. In a world where feelings of isolation and loneliness are on the rise, physical touch becomes a powerful antidote. Of all the five senses, touch is the most underappreciated. I need to find the perfect set of hands—femininity of shape, perceived fattiness and skin healthiness, and the appearance of nail vicinity. The heart line should curve at the end up between the index and middle finger.

~~~
~~~

Jake and Lane navigated their way to the lost cavern of the County Recorder's Office. There was a line of 7 or 8 people waiting for the clerk to assist them. One of the perks of being in law enforcement is not having to wait in line, or at least that is what Jake thought. He bypassed the line and went to the front where there was a plump, white-haired woman, barely tall enough to look over the counter. A Q-Tip.

"Excuse me, ma'am, I need to find out the owner of a warehouse property."

"Back of the line," she barked without looking up at Jake.

Jake opened his jacket to reveal his detective badge.

"This is official police business."

"And this is official city business. See all these people. They have been waiting for quite some time. Get to the back of the line."

"You don't understand…"

"No, you don't understand. I am in control here, not you. I have been doing this job for the past 42 years, and I have dealt with many law enforcement types much higher than your rank, Sergeant, so if you don't mind? You are wasting my time. I'll be with you just as soon as I help these other folks."

Forty minutes later the woman behind the counter pulled a cord that changed the illuminated number above it. "143!", she hollered.

"That's me!" Diego yelled back. Turning to the person behind him in line, he mumbled, "I feel like I'm in a deli."

"I heard that!" the woman said. "Look, I run an organized records department. If you don't like it…"

"No, no. It's fine. We appreciate how competent and professional you are," Jake said to the lady who was not quite sure how to respond to the verbal honey.

"What can I do for you, detective?"

"We would like to know who owns The Schuylkill Meat Packing Company. Here is the address," Diego said as he handed her a piece of paper.

The woman started typing away at her keyboard as her eyes were focused on the computer screen in front of her. She extended her head a bit and scrunched up her face that made the detectives think either she saw something on the screen she did not like, or she was having difficulty discerning the information in front of her.

"It says here that a Mr. Cecil Tobiason is the title holder. There is a mortgage on the property. He purchased the property from a bank, Gwynedd Savings and Loan, on August 25th of last year."

"You have been very helpful, Miss…?

"Coulter," she said before yelling out, "Number 144!"

~~~

As they were leaving the offices of the Parks and Recreation, Diego turned to Lillia and said, "Two down, one to go. Do you want to grab lunch before we head to Rittenhouse Square to interview Susan Cranford's neighbors and friends?"

"I'd rather get this done, unless you are starving," Lillia said.

"No, I probably can lose a few pounds anyway."

"You can, and don't make me feel guilty."

Diego chuckled.

When they arrived at Miss Cranford's house, Diego asked Lillia, "Do you want to divide and conquer? I'll take the house to the left of Susan Cranford's place and you take the one to the right, that way I will be enjoying my lunch sooner rather than later."

"You really do think of eating 24/7."

"Maybe 23/7. Hey, there's a gyro on South Street calling my name."

"Alright. We'll split up, but remember that women will only share personal things like getting a tummy tuck with other women. Interviewing men probably won't get us anywhere."

Twenty minutes later, Diego was waiting for Lillia in front of Susan Cranford's house.

"No one was home next door," Diego said. "How about you? Have any luck?"

"No. The lady in this building said Susan is very nice, but quiet. They only shared pleasantries."

"Would you happen to have Miss Cranford's keys to her place?" asked Diego.

"Yeah, why?"
~~~

"Well, if she recently had plastic surgery she would have a receipt for the surgery. Let's take a look at her financial records."

"You know, I think you get smarter when you are hungry."

"And you get funnier."

The two detectives entered Susan Cranford's home. The stench of death still seemed to drip from the walls. The home felt cool and damp from the wet Pennsylvania spring weather. They entered a room which had several bookcases, a desk, and a display cabinet. An antique grandfather clock in need of winding, stood silently on guard. Lillia sat at the desk and began opening drawers.

"Well, the good news is she was very organized. Here is an accordion file of receipts. Here, you take this pile and I'll look through these."

Rummaging through the stack of receipts, Diego said, "Wow, she keeps everything. Here is a receipt for an Argosy magazine renewal. Is Argosy still around?"

"Heck if I know, but here is an airline receipt for a flight she took last year to Arizona," Lillia said.

"Bingo!" Diego said. "How much do you think the abdominoplasty surgery cost?"

"I have no idea."

"$12,000, and Dr. Barnabas Albrecht performed the surgery."

"We are 4 for 4! Let's head back to the station."

~~~

ADA Bryson dropped by the Major Crimes offices to garner any new evidence the team had. The entire team congregated in the common room for an assessment of where they stood on the murders. Miss Bryson's timing was ideal. Martin was happy to see her. It saved him from having to go to the District Attorney's offices.

"Linda, I was just going to pay you a visit. I need a search warrant for the doctor's penthouse," Martin said to ADA Bryson. "I can't believe he was performing these amputations and no one in the building saw or heard anything."

"If a bear farts in the woods, and no one is there to smell it, does it still stink?" asked Jake.
~~~

"What is that supposed to mean?" responded Lane.

"The key point is that the sound and smell of a fart is the vibration of air molecules created by the rush of gas exited from the bear, regardless of whether someone is there to perceive it. If no one heard the evil doctor perform these warped surgeries, does it mean they were never performed in his penthouse?"

"Who is this guy?" asked Lane.

"He minored in physics in college," answered Diego.

"I did my thesis on Kinetic energy," Jake said. "I changed majors three times."

"Can we get back to the case, folks?" Looking at the ADA, Martin asked, "Miss Bryson, do we have enough for a search warrant of the doctor's penthouse?"

"Barely. You can try Judge Nabors. He is your best chance of getting the warrant. Do you have anything new for me?"

"We do. All four of our victims had cosmetic surgery performed by the same plastic surgeon, Dr. Albrecht and, as you know, each murder involved the surgical removal of a facial feature. Isn't that enough to show ample cause for a search warrant?"

"It should, but, you never can tell," Mrs. Bryson said as she walked towards the door. "Good luck, Captain."

"Alright. Jake, go see Judge Nabors. He knows who you are, right?"

"Yeah. He directed me to put Keith Searcy in the general population rather than segregation when we arrested him for kidnapping and sexually abusing those two young sisters last year. He got beaten to an inch of his life."

"Go! It's getting late, and make sure the warrant also includes Albrecht's financials. Once you have the warrant, call Lieutenant Ewing and Sergeant Santos. I want the two of you to look at the doctor's finances. Follow the money trail with a fine-toothed comb. Look for any large payments, any unusual payments, mortgages, everything."

"Captain, we just got a call from New York Police. They have Jorge Navarro in custody. He was arrested at a meth hall in the Bronx," Lillia said.

"Okay. He is obviously not our prime suspect, but we'll see if DA Malerba wants him extradited to Philly so he can face charges. Otis and I will pay Dr. Albrecht a visit at his office tomorrow morning. It's been a long day. Let's hit the ground running first thing in the morning."

~~~

Otis drove over to the hospital as he did every day after work and each day Kilani had either pretended to be asleep, or she told Otis he would have to leave because the doctors were about to perform another procedure on her. On this day, and to Otis's delight, Kalani was more engaging. She turned her head slowly and gave Otis a smile, something he was not sure he would receive.

"These are for you," he said, as he displayed a bouquet of yellow roses he was hiding behind his back. I know yellow is your favorite color."

"Thank you, Otis. That is very kind of you, but I thought I told you…"

"Stop. Please. You can no more make me stop loving you than you can make the wood thrush mute and refrain from its poignant song. It's like asking the sun to stop shining or the stars to grow dull. Some things are impossible, my love."

Tears appeared in Kalani's eyes.

"I know you are a romantic, but I didn't know you were a poet," Kalani said. "Did you know that Thoreau wrote a love letter praising the wood thrush's evocation of, quote, 'the liquid coolness of things drawn from the bottom of springs?' Unquote."

"I did not, but, then again, I am not the reader you are. You look more alert today. How is the pain?"

"Better. Not gone, but anything is better than what I experienced that first month. The doctor told me I will be moving to rehab within the next couple of weeks. I can't wait. Everyone has been wonderful here, but I need to get out of this room."

"I understand. You have had such an incredible attitude through all of this. I am proud of you. I don't think I would have been so gracious."
~~~

"Kalani, tell me our engagement is back on."

"We'll see. I am very tired and need to get some sleep. Thank you for coming, Otis."

Otis got the hint and left Kalani's room. He removed the gown, gloves and mask, placing them in the hamper outside her room and walked down the hall to the elevator. When the elevator door opened, Kalani's parents appeared.

"Mr. and Mrs. Dantas. How are you?"

"Otis," Mrs. Dantas said, as she leaned forward to give him a kiss on his cheek. "How is she?"

"She is progressing. Slowly. She is still experiencing pain, which I assume will continue for some time, but she says the pain level is much more tolerable. At least she is off the morphine drip."

"She has a long road ahead of her. Thank God she has you."

"She has me for as long as she wants me," Otis said solemnly.

"What exactly does that mean?"

"She has broken off our engagement. Mr. and Mrs. Dantas, I love your daughter. I do not care about the scarring on her face and body. She is still as beautiful as the day I met her and always will be."

"Otis," Mr. Dantas said as he placed his hand on Otis's shoulder. "Give her time. She thinks she looks like a monster and cannot fathom anyone would want to look at her for the next 50 years. In her mind, how would any man want to make love with her while looking at the horrific scarring. Just keep loving her. She will see your heart is what controls your eyes. You are a good man, Otis. She's lucky to have you."

"No, Mr. Dantas. I am lucky to have her."

~~~

Martin left work early enough to have dinner with Mary Jo, something that had not happened in over a week. He opened the door to his house and was greeted by a wonderful smell drifting from the kitchen. He threw his keys on the foyer table and walked towards the kitchen.

"Is that my favorite meal of pot roast and my wife's wonderful crusty bread I smell?" Martin yelled out.
~~~

Mary Jo came out from the kitchen wearing an apron and a wide smile. She walked up to Martin, locking her arms around his neck and giving him a warm kiss.

"You really are a good detective," she said with a laugh. "Yes, we are having pot roast and I made a loaf of that bread you enjoy so much. Happy Anniversary, Honey!"

The look on Martin's face went from jocose to regret.

"I, eh…it's April 3rd? I am such a jerk."

"Honey, it's okay. I knew you had forgotten before you got home. Every year you have flowers delivered on our anniversary. I was not surprised when they didn't arrive today. In fact, I would have been surprised if they had! This case has consumed you. I love you so much and I know you love me. That is all I need."

A sense of sweeping disappointment and remorse washed over Martin. A sense of personal failure overwhelmed him. He had let the city down by not catching the butcher responsible for the series of murders and now, worse, he let Mary Jo down.

"Honey, I feel terrible. I promise I'll make it up to you. As soon as this case is over, you and I are going on a vacation. Anywhere you want."

"Sit down, my love. Light the candles while I bring dinner out. Tonight, you are mine."

# CHAPTER NINETEEN

*What is beautiful? That which makes the soul of the observer dance.*
"Thus Spoke Zarathustra"
— Friedrich Nietzsche

The next morning Philadelphia received a corn snow, spring snow with a coarse, granular texture that resembles corn kernels. It is a wet type of snow that disappears once the midmorning sun has a chance to warm the pavement.

Martin and Otis arrived at the Plastic Surgeon's offices before it opened and waited in their car.

"Hey, are you alright? You look a little off this morning," Otis inquired.

"I'm fine."

"Fine? You haven't said five words to me this morning. Look, I'm not prying, but you have been consistently concerned about me and Kalani. And I appreciate that. I really do. I was just trying to reciprocate. I've spent a lot of time with you over the past five months, Martin. And I think I'm a pretty good detective, so tell me to mind my own business, but don't insult my intelligence by saying you are fine."

Martin laughed.

"Yeah, you are a damn good detective and no, I'm not alright. I'm a jerk. Yesterday was my anniversary. I have never…never, forgotten Mary Jo's birthday or our anniversary…"

"Until yesterday," Otis said, finishing Martin's sentence.

"Otis, I really do love Mary Jo. I never want to hurt her."

"I won't say the obvious. Was she hurt?"

"She didn't act like she was, but how couldn't she be? If she *were* hurt, she wouldn't tell me because she knows it would make me feel worse. That is so Mary Jo. And you didn't have to state the obvious.

Mary Jo did. She said the case has taken over my life. She said she understands, for me not to worry about it. She made my favorite dinner and gave me this new wallet," Martin said as he pulled his new billfold out of his pants pocket.

"She is a good woman, and I know a good woman when I see one," Otis said. "You are a blessed man, Martin, and I know you know that. You'll make it up to her. It may have to wait till this case is over, but you will make it up to her."

"You're right. I will."

In an attempt to change the subject, Otis asked, "Do you think this is our guy?"

"I guess I am protecting myself from any foolhardy optimism. My gut says yes, he is our killer, but my mind isn't so sure. Logically, it doesn't make any sense. He certainly had the means. He obtains the surgical skills needed to commit a crime, but even if he had the opportunity, what could possibly be his motive?"

"We are not arresting him, right? Just questioning him?"

"We don't have enough to make an arrest, according to Bryson. That may change once we search his penthouse. I am more interested in how he answers our questions and his demeanor during that questioning."

"Looks like the assistants and nurses are arriving," Otis said. "Oh, and here comes our doctor."

A Jaguar F-Type convertible, British racing green with camel-brown interior, pulled into a reserved parking spot in front of the building.

"Nice car," Otis said. "I guess it's still a bit cold for the top to be down or for him to ride that yellow and white motorcycle we saw him when we came here back in October."

"Obviously, he likes to impress people. Grandiosity is one of the signs of a serial killer.

Let's wait for 5 minutes, then we'll go in," Martin said.

Martin and Otis entered the Bryn Mawr Aesthetic Plastic Surgery Center. The receptionist's desk had a vase displaying the perfect spring arrangement of forsythia and pussy willow branches. The same receptionist was at the desk.

"Good morning. Detectives Wallace and Gainwell, right?" the woman asked.

"I'm impressed. With that kind of memory, you should be in our line of work," Martin said.

"No thanks. I think it's safer here. I have an eidetic memory. It can come in handy, but it can also be a curse. I find it difficult to relax and forget information sometimes, but so much about me. I assume you are here to see Dr. Albrecht?"

"Yes, we are," Otis answered. "But before you tell the doctor we are here, may I ask you a question?

"Sure."

"What can you tell us about Dr. Barnabas Albrecht?"

No patients had arrived yet, but the receptionist still looked around to make sure no one was listening. Lowering her voice she said, "Professionally, or socially?"

"Both."

"Well, he is very good at what he does. He is a perfectionist. I guess that is a good thing if you want him to work on your physical appearance. He does have a god complex. Maybe a bit over-confident. He has that swagger, if you know what I mean. He plays classical music when he is in surgery. He says flawless surgery requires flawless music. He is not married and I don't think he dates much. No woman is good enough for him," she said with a chuckle. "Oh, and whatever you do, do not call him Barney!"

"Thank you, Miss…"

"You can call me Kirsten."

"Thank you, Kirsten. One more question," Martin said. "You said the doctor is single. Does he have any family? Any close friends?"

"He is an only child. He's kind of a loner. He does have a cousin who came in here about a year or so ago for a facelift. Her name is Marilyn Rowan. She lives somewhere up in Bucks County, Pennsylvania. I think near New Hope. I can look for her address while you're with the doctor, if you would like."

"That would be great. Thank you, Kirsten."

"Just make sure you don't tell anyone I spoke with you. I could lose my job. Let me tell him you gentlemen are here."

Kirsten picked up the phone and explained the detective's objective. A young lady with shoulder-length blonde hair came out to the waiting room and walked over to the detectives.

"Detectives, follow me. I'll take you to Dr. Albrecht's office."

When the detectives entered the doctor's office, he immediately stood up from behind his desk and greeted them.

"Detectives! It's good to see you again. Please, have a seat. May I offer you some coffee? Water?"

"No, thank you. We're fine," Martin said.

On the doctor's desk was a bust of a human head. Both detectives made a mental note of it.

"What may I do for you, Detectives?"

"Since we came to visit you after Farah Darvish's murder, there have been three additional murders with a similar modus operandi. Instead of removing the eyes from the other victims, the killer removed the ears from Lan Nara, the lips from Katrina Alvarez, and the nose from Susan Cranford."

"Thus, the title 'The Senseless Killer.' But what does this have to do with me?"

"It just so happens all four of these ladies had work done by you. That is their only connection with each other."

"Really? I wouldn't know that. I have had thousands of patients over the years. What a coincidence."

"Coincidence? We like to call it a lucky break," Otis said.

"Certainly, you do not think I had anything to do with these murders. I spent my entire career enhancing beauty, not destroying it."

"We would like to know where you were the evening of each of the murders, Dr. Albrecht," Martin said.

"I will have to look at my schedule, but I have a busy schedule this morning, detective."

"Well, then, let's start with the most recent murder. Where were you on the evening of March 11th?"

"I was watching a performance of The Cleveland Orchestra at home. It was broadcast live from Severance Hall. The orchestra is one of the five American orchestras informally referred to as the 'Big Five'. They played an exquisite rendition of Samuel Barber's, *Adagio for Strings*."

The doctor began humming the piece of music.

"Dr. Albrecht. You just so happened to know what you were doing two and a half weeks ago without consulting your calendar?" Otis asked.

"March 11th was the second Tuesday of the month and that means the special concert series on PBS is televised. I never miss it. If there is nothing else, detectives, I must prepare for my appointments. I have a VIP who flew in from France to meet with me."

"One last question, Doctor. How tall are you?"

"Six foot, two. Why do you ask?"

"Of course you are," Otis said.

"What is that supposed to mean?"

Ignoring his question, Martin said, "Thank you, doctor. We'll be in touch."

As the detectives were leaving, Kirsten, the receptionist, walked up to them and handed Otis a piece of paper.

"Here is Dr. Albrecht's cousin's contact info. Remember, you didn't get it from me."

"Promise," Otis said.

As the detectives walked outside, the spring sun shone brightly in their faces. Along the sidewalk, a half dozen crocuses, like new born chicks breaking free from their shell, popped their heads through the quickly melting layer of snow.

"Man, it hasn't been this warm in five months," Otis said.

"They say it may reach 60 today."

"I'm trying not to be paranoid, but with the number five being so important to the case, did you pick up on when the doctor said the Cleveland Orchestra is one of the five American orchestras informally referred to as the 'Big Five'?"

"I did," Martin said. "It was almost as if he were taunting us."

~~~

As soon as Otis and Martin arrived back at the office, Jake met them at the door.

"I was just about to text you, Captain. Judge Nabors granted the search warrants, but he said we are treading on thin ice," Jake said.
~~~

"He would not issue the phone tap. He also warned us this better not be a fishing expedition."

"Does the warrant include the doctor's financials?" asked Martin.

"Yes, Captain."

"That's good news. We just came from Dr. Albrecht's offices, so we know he will not be home when we search his penthouse." Turning to the rest of his team, Martin continued.

"Alright, folks, we have three different objectives today and we will be dividing up to get these accomplished. Corporal Wilton, I want you to search the doctor's financials."

Turning to the two FBI Special Agents, Martin asked, "Would you two be willing to help the corporal on this? You may have access to information from the federal government that we don't."

"Absolutely," said Agent Buchanan. "We partner with law enforcement and regulatory agencies including the Securities and Exchange Commission, the IRS, the U.S. Postal Inspection Service, the Commodity Futures Trading Commission, and the Treasury Department's Financial Crimes Enforcement Network."

"I know from experience financials are haystacks difficult to navigate. Make sure you take a metal detector so you can find the needle," Martin said. "If Dr. Barnabas Albrecht is everything we think he is, then we are dealing with a very intelligent, cunning man."

Just then, Lillia walked into the office.

"Lieutenant Ewing, don't take off your jacket. I want you to pay a visit to the doctor's cousin, Marilyn Rowan. She lives in Lahaska, a few miles west of New Hope. It's about an hour's drive. See what you can find out about Dr. Albrecht's personal life."

"The rest of us will be searching the doctor's penthouse. Let's go!"

~~~

Lillia drove across the tranquility of Upper Bucks County. Bordering the Delaware River to the east, the surroundings offer up huge helpings of rolling hills, river towns, meandering streams, hardwood forests and preserved farmland. Although only an hour drive from center city Philadelphia, the peaceful countryside seems a world away from the congestion and violence of the city.
~~~

Lillia drove past Buckingham Friends School, a private Quaker school, and came upon Peddler's Village, a storybook village with charming colonial-style buildings, romantic lodging, award-winning gardens, distinctive shopping, and exceptional dining. Not far from Lahaska stands New Hope, a preferred destination for New York's rich and famous to escape the squalor and chaos they helped create. As confirmation the locals were suspect of their New York immigrants, Lillia noticed a bumper sticker on a passing car, "DON'T NEW YORK MY NEW HOPE!"

Following the directions on her cell phone, Lillia turned onto a dirt road that led to a 10-acre farmette. Out in the field, two miniature horses, five sheep, and a goat took turns feeding from a trough as deer and wild turkeys feasted themselves on the winter wheat, eating the seedheads in the milk stage. Lillia parked her car and walked up to the house. The sidewalk was protected on either side by lines of red tulips that stood at attention like the King's Guard at Buckingham Palace.

Lillia knocked on the door. An attractive woman in her early 50s came to the door wearing jeans and a t-shirt that read, "I prefer 4-legged sheep to the 2-legged kind."

"Mrs. Rowan? I am Lieutenant Ewing. I spoke to you on the phone?"

"Yes, Lieutenant. Please, come in. Make yourself comfortable," the lady said as she motioned for Lillia to sit on the couch.

"Thank you, Mrs. Rowan."

"Please, call me Marilyn. Would you like a glass of lemonade?"

"Thank you. That will be nice."

As Marilyn walked into the kitchen, she said, "You said on the phone you wanted to ask me a few questions about Barney."

"I was under the impression Dr. Albrecht did not like to be called Barney."

"Hmmmmm, well, maybe. That is what Auntie Bernice always called him. They had a tumultuous relationship at best," Marilyn said as she handed Lillia a glass of lemonade.

"What exactly do you mean?"

"My aunt, Barney's mother, was a serious woman, quite unlike his father. Uncle Ted was fun-loving and easy going. He made his money selling livestock pharmaceuticals to local veterinarians. Barney wanted to be a vet when he was growing up. Anyway, Barney's dad died suddenly from a heart attack when Barney was eight years old. Uncle Ted was only 34. My cousin took it hard."

"I'm sure he did. It's hard for a boy to grow up without a dad."

"Is Barney in trouble?"

"We are in the middle of a murder investigation, Marilyn. These are just general questions we are asking about people who may have had contact with any of the victims."

"Is this about those horrific serial murders?"

"I'm really not at liberty to discuss an ongoing investigation. I'm sorry."

"No, that's alright. I understand. I don't know how much I can tell you about my cousin. We really haven't kept in touch for the past 20 plus years. Barney can be a very charming man, but much of that charm is simply a method to get what he wants. I guess you can assume I was never a big fan of my cousin. He is a charming sociopath, the kind of creep who makes a good, first impression on those aesthetic-obsessed wealthy ladies enamored by high profile doctors of the rich and famous."

"Barney was always a good looking man, and the combined attributes of physical characteristics, body posture, facial expression, and his clothing choices help observers form what they think is an accurate image of his personality, but he does not present himself genuinely."

"Interesting. Tell me more about his relationship with his mother," Lillia asked.

"My auntie was a little eccentric. She always acted as if she came from money, but they were lower middle class, like my family. She would buy dresses at K-Mart and then doll them up with a scarf, or belt or a wide-brimmed hat. Anyway, she often walked around the house completely nude, and I mean, even when Barney was postpubescent. I know she made him sleep in the same bed as hers for several years after his dad died."

Lillia sensed Marilyn relished the opportunity to purge herself of memories and opinions of her doctor-cousin that she had kept buried for decades. Marilyn's floodgates were about to be opened.

"Can you tell me anything about his personality? Did he ever show signs of violence?"

"He did have a short fuse, but I wouldn't necessarily call him violent. Barney was always a strange little kid. He would rummage through the woods behind his house searching for animal skulls, of which he had a large collection. I remember he had a coyote skull with a 22-caliber bullet hole in it. I'll bet you he had over a dozen skulls. From the tiny skull of a star-nosed mole to the mammoth skull of a cow, these were his prized possessions.

"He was very intelligent; he excelled at school. I remember his bedroom was a disaster area, but Barney always knew where everything was. He called it organized chaos. He thrived in clutter."

"He was a bookworm. He devoured books, especially ones that had a dark subject. Some of his favorite books were *Notes From the Underground* by Dostoyevsky, a great book if you want to become utterly depressed, *Strange Case of Dr Jekyll and Mr Hyde* by Robert Louis Stevenson, and *The Woman in White* by Wilkie Collins. I remember these books especially because Barney would give them to me to read. I found them disturbing. It seemed as though he never read uplifting books, books that inspire or make the reader rejoice for the goodness and benevolence of humanity."

"Let's see, what else can I tell you about my cousin. He was an introvert, a night owl, a daydreamer, and often talked to himself. He was a strange kid. He could turn on and off his alluring personality, but later in life, when he would drink, his allure would curdle. As I said, he was always very charming, especially when he wanted something. I think he was a natural-born salesman, like his father."

"The first sign my cousin was a little off was when he was caught dissecting animals and removing their eyes. He would kill a chicken, a rabbit, or a squirrel. Then he would try to replace the eyes of the chicken with the eyes of one of those rodents. I'm telling you, Barney is sick. Sick, but successful and rich!"

"Why didn't he ever get married?" Lillia asked.

"He's not gay, if that is what you are asking."

"No, I wasn't thinking that. He is a very good looking man, successful, and in his mid 40s. I would think he would be married, or possibly divorced."

"Yes, he is a handsome man. Girls were all over him in high school and college. The last I heard, he hardly even dates. Do you want to know what I think? I think no woman was perfect enough for Barney, and I don't mean personality-wise. I mean, no woman was beautiful enough for him. I remember one summer when he was home from med school, the two of us went out to a fashion show. I received comp tickets from a clothing company for whom I was working. Throughout the entire show he critiqued each of the spectacular models. Her eyes are too close together. The nasofrontal angle of this one's nose is not defined enough. I specifically remember his comments about one of the model's lips. This girl was gorgeous, mind you. He said her upper lip/lower lip ratio was far from 1:1.6. I asked him what the heck 1, 1, 6 meant and he said the vertical height of the upper lip should be less than that of the lower lip, thus, the 1:1:6 ratio being ideal."

"No wonder he went into cosmetic surgery."

"Yep. No surprise there."

"You have been very helpful, Marilyn. I need to get back to the city, although I would rather not. It really is beautiful around here."

As the two women stood up, Marilyn looked Lillia directly in the eye and said, "You think Barney is the serial killer, don't you?"

"We are just trying to cover every avenue. I will be in touch if I have any additional questions. Thanks again for the lemonade. It was delicious."

# CHAPTER TWENTY

*My senses were gratified and refreshed by a thousand scents of delight
and a thousand sights of beauty.*
<u>Frankenstein</u>
— Mary Shelley

artin, Otis, Diego, and Jake arrived at Dr. Albrecht's Condo building in two separate cars. The doctor's penthouse was located on Benjamin Franklin Parkway, across the street from the Rodin Museum. The Parkway is one of the most desirable neighborhoods in the city, a cultural mecca with world-renowned museums, and outdoor sculptures which got its inspiration from an avenue 4,000 miles away in France, the Champs-Élysées. Flags from around the world decorate the wide roadway, symbolic of the city's diverse culture and immigrant communities.

The detectives, escorted by the building manager, took the elevator to the twenty-second floor. Within the elevator, and standing behind Martin, Jake caught Otis's attention and motioned with two of his fingers as if they were climbing stares. Otis was not the only one glad Martin had not insisted on taking the stairs.

"May I see that search warrant again, please?" the short, bald, and nervous-looking building manager asked. "I really think I should call Dr. Albrecht."

"Go ahead and call him, but do it after you let us into his penthouse," Diego said.

"The doctor is going to be very upset. He is a very private man."

"He'll get over it."

The penthouse made up the entire 22nd floor, spanned more than 5,250 square feet, and included a massive outdoor space with a kitchen, fireplace, and expansive city views.

"Damn! It must be nice," Diego said.

"Alright, Santos and Sinclair, start in the back rooms. Gainwell and I will begin in the living room and kitchen," Martin said.

Otis was unusually quiet. His thoughts were consumed with Kalani. He knew she was going to survive and the doctors told him she is healing well. It is her refusal to marry him that had his stomach twisted like a pretzel. If it were at all possible, he wanted to marry Kalani more now than he had before the accident.

"Detective, are you with us?" Martin asked Otis.

"Yeah. Yeah. I was just thinking."

The living room and study were littered with books. Bookmarks indicated Dr. Albrecht was reading at least 5 or 6 books at the same time. There was a biography of Leonardo DiVinci, a complete compilation of Edgar Allan Poe's short stories and poems, and a medical book on the recent advances in plastic surgery including robotic-assisted surgery, nanofat and fat grafting, and piezotome bone shaping technology.

Original paintings decorated the walls, and a couch, loveseat and a recliner surrounded a hand-painted brass inlay storage trunk coffee table. An audio system that included a turntable and Bose speakers was positioned against the wall opposite the sliding glass doors that led to the balcony, but what captivated the eyes was an iconic white, marble bust of Edgar Allan Poe that had a stuffed coal-black raven perched upon its head. Martin's immediate thoughts were that Dr. Albrecht was the anti-Martin. That, and the fact they both were huge Edgar Allan Poe fans.

"That freakin' bird is scary," Diego said. "It's creepy."

"You are going to like this. Do you know what they call a flock of ravens?" Jake asked anyone who was listening.

"Please, tell," Diego said.

"A flock of ravens is called a conspiracy, a treachery, a rave, or an unkindness."

"An unkindness of ravens? Are you kidding me?"

After searching the back bedroom, Jake and Diego walked back into the living room.

"There is nothing of interest in the master bedroom or master bath. Even the medicine cabinet was pretty boring, other than the fact that our good doctor has hemorrhoids," Jake said.

"Okay, help us sort through this clutter," Martin said. "I don't want us to miss something simply because stuff is scattered everywhere."

"Do you really think it is feasible Doctor Albrecht, one of the most respected plastic surgeons in the country, would risk everything, his practice, his reputation, his wealth, to murder women with apparently no motive?" asked Diego.

"If by feasible you mean whether a man who makes his living surgically altering the appearances of people, a guy who is a loner and quite eccentric, and whose clientele bows down and worships him as if he were the golden calf or some other graven image—whether a man like that could commit these horrific murders, then yes, I believe it is more than feasible," answered Jake.

"In light of the grotesque murders we have seen with this case, I find it interesting he is a lover of Poe," Jake said. "He has bookmarked a half dozen of his short stories in this book that was on the table next to his reading chair. And, I might add, these are not just any of Poe's works. They are the most disturbing gothic tales: *Berenice*, *Morella*, *Ligeia*, *The Fall of the House of Usher*, *Eleonora*, and *The Oval Portrait*. They all have several things in common, beauty, death, gender, and horror. Poe wrote about beautiful women who fall ill, die, and sometimes come back to life."

"Who are you?" Otis asked. "You sound like a college professor."

"I originally majored in English Lit. in college. My plan was to teach high school. Funny how things work out. I probably would have been fired and/or sued after the first time a smart-ass kid talked back to me and I slapped him upside the head. Anyway, I changed my major to Political Science after my sophomore year."

"And you ended up being a cop? How in the world did that happen?"

"Long story. The Readers Digest version is that a friend back home in Baltimore was murdered by some degenerate. He held her captive for over 2 weeks, torturing and sexually abusing her until he finally put her out of her misery. I ended up getting a master's degree in Criminal Justice.

"Anyway, back to Poe and his dead and dying women," continued Jake. "Poe once wrote that 'The death, then, of a beautiful woman is, unquestionably, the most poetical topic in the world.'"

The conversation about Poe caught Martin's attention. He grabbed a notepad from his pocket and wrote down the titles of the Edgar Allan Poe stories Dr. Albrecht was reading. Without looking up from his notepad, Martin said, "Poe also has been quoted as saying, 'I do not suffer from insanity, I enjoy every minute of it.'"

"You and Poe have something in common, Jake," Diego said with a belly laugh.

"Funny," Jake said.

"This fascination Dr. Albrecht has with Edgar Allan Poe is more than interesting," Martin said. "If we are going to connect the doctor to the killings, we need to understand what turns him on—what his hot buttons are. The doctor is obsessed with beauty, Edgar Allan Poe, and full moons."

"A little trivia about Edgar Allen Poe. The name Edgar means 'wealthy spear', and Allan means 'handsome.'"

"Boy, you are full of insignificant information," Diego said. "So, what does the name Jacob mean, Jake?"

"Jake, or Jacob, means 'trickster.'"

"That makes perfect sense," Otis interjected. "In the Bible, Jacob tricked Isaac and Laban and you are a trickster in your own right."

"I am that, Detective."

"Here is another book, apparently, the doctor is reading. Oscar Wilde's, *The Picture of Dorian Gray*." Lane said.

"Now that is a familiar book, and no, I did not see the movie." Martin said. "It's another interesting choice of literature. This is our guy; we just need to find damning evidence."

"Okay, now I feel stupid," Otis said. "Fill me in on Dorian Gray's portrait."

"You mean, *The Picture of Dorian Gray*. Okay, Reader's Digest version. The story revolves around a portrait of Dorian Gray painted by Basil, an artist who is infatuated with Dorian's beauty. Through Basil, Dorian meets Lord Henry Wotton and is soon captivated by the aristocrat's hedonistic worldview, one who believes beauty and sensual fulfillment are the only worthwhile things in life. Knowing, like all humans, he will lose his beauty with age, Dorian impulsively chooses to sell his soul and asks for the portrait, rather than himself, to age and fade. His wish is granted, and Dorian pursues a playboy-type of life full of amoral experiences while staying young and beautiful. Meanwhile, his portrait ages and visually records every one of Dorian's sins."

"Our doctor is consumed with beauty," Otis said. "There is a deeply rooted fascination with beauty which penetrates society worldwide. The indulgence to look and feel beautiful pervades all ages and genders. Our doctor is suffering from Body Dysmorphic Disorder (BDD). A disorder of self-perception. It is the obsession with perfection. Kalani told me many models suffer from BDD."

Walking out of the doctor's study, Diego said, "Captain, I'm looking through the doctor's bank statements and checkbook. He has been paying monthly payments to a Cecil Tobiason to the tune of $10,000."

"$10,000? We'll need to track down Mr. Tobiason," Martin said. "That's good detective work, Santos. "See if you can find anything else in the study."

Martin turned around to find Otis sitting on the sofa reading a book.

"Comfortable, Detective?"

"Check this out. Our killer has been obsessed with the five senses, right?"

"Right."

"Well, this book by C.S. Lewis is open to this page."

"C.S. Lewis is the author who wrote *The Chronicles of Narnia*," Jake added. "Besides being a writer, Lewis was a theologian, and literary scholar."

"Thank you, Professor, but if I may continue?" asked Otis.

"By all means."

"Listen as I read this. Jake, you especially, since you have an English literature background. It's entitled "On Being Human." If I'm not mistaken, the notion is we humans comprehend things the angels cannot, *because we have the five senses and they do not.*

Angelic minds, they say, by simple intelligence
Behold the Forms of nature. They discern
Unerringly the Archetypes, all the verities
Which mortals lack or indirectly learn.
Transparent in primordial truth, unvarying,
Pure Earthness and right Stonehood from their clear,
High eminence are seen; unveiled, the seminal
Huge Principles appear.

The Tree-ness of the tree they know-the meaning of
Arboreal life, how from earth's salty lap
The solar beam uplifts it; all the holiness
Enacted by leaves' fall and rising sap;

But never an angel knows the knife-edged severance
Of sun from shadow where the trees begin,
The blessed cool at every pore caressing us
—An angel has no skin.

They see the Form of Air; but mortals breathing it
Drink the whole summer down into the breast.
The lavish pinks, the field new-mown, the ravishing
Sea-smells, the wood-fire smoke that whispers Rest.
The tremor on the rippled pool of memory
That from each smell in widening circles goes,
The pleasure and the pang—can angels measure it?
—An angel has no nose.

The nourishing of life, and how it flourishes
On death, and why, they utterly know; but not
The hill-born, earthy spring, the dark cold bilberries.
The ripe peach from the southern wall still hot
Full-bellied tankards foamy-topped, the delicate
Half-lyric lamb, a new loaf's billowy curves,
Nor porridge, nor the tingling taste of oranges.
—An angel has no nerves.

Far richer they! I know the senses' witchery
Guards us like air, from heavens too big to see;
Imminent death to man that barb'd sublimity
And dazzling edge of beauty unsheathed would be.
Yet here, within this tiny, charmed interior,
This parlour of the brain, their Maker shares
With living men some secrets in a privacy
Forever ours, not theirs.

"This is more than just a coincidence," Martin said.

"Captain," Diego said as he entered the living room and handed Martin a folded plant layout of a production facility. "I found something else buried in a pile of papers on the doctor's desk."

"What is this?" Martin said as he began unfolding the large, detailed drawing.

"It's a blueprint floor plan for the defunct Schuylkill Packing Company."

"Some of you probably don't even remember when that old slaughterhouse was still operational," Martin said. It's located just south of the zoo on Mantua Ave. It was a thriving meat packing plant, until the workers decided to unionize. The owner, Robert Hill, gathered the entire company's workforce together. He told them he had been overpaying them and treating them fairly. He offered excellent healthcare and a pension to his employees and so he felt betrayed when they voted to unionize."

"Wow! No lie?" Diego asked rhetorically.

"A few years later, he started another meat packing plant somewhere in the Midwest. Iowa or Missouri and, from what I hear, it is thriving. But back to the question, why would Dr. Albrecht want the blueprint floor plan for that closed facility?"

"I guess we're going to find out," Diego said.

"Yes, you are, Sergeant."

"I should have known that," Diego mumbled.

I want that blueprint to go with us back to the station. Put it in this box."

Martin sensed the blueprint would be essential in their case. It was one of those discoveries that could very easily be overlooked, but

Martin's intuition told him not to dismiss it. *What does a meat packing plant have that would be of value to our murderer? Meat trimming tables. Knives, saws, slicers, meat curing ovens and smokehouses, coolers and walk-in freezers. Freezers!* Martin remembered what Dr. Wu said about the second victim, Lan Nara. She mentioned Miss Nara's body had been placed in a freezer soon after her death.

Martin hypothesized that since the Schuylkill Packing Company would surely have a walk-in freezer, that may very well be the location of where the doctor performed his vile acts. *A deserted meat packing plant near the zoo. Isolated, quiet, very little foot traffic…the perfect place for his grotesque obsession. We need to get a search warrant for the meat packing plant.*

The door to the penthouse suddenly and violently opened.

"What is the meaning of this?" Dr. Albrecht asked with a raised voice.

Otis shoved the search warrant into the doctor's chest and said, "Stay out of our way, doctor."

"Why are you searching my residence?"

Martin walked over to the doctor.

"Dr. Albrecht, as we told you, all four of our victims were your patients. Two would be a coincidence. Three, is a pattern, and four is a trend. In our line of work, when a pattern is established with three occurrences, seeing it happen a fourth time further suggests that it's not just random chance but a consistent trend developing."

"Preposterous!"

"Have a seat and let us do our work, or you can leave. Which is it?" asked Otis.

The doctor sat on the sofa and contemplated all that was going on.

Diego walked back into the living room holding a framed piece of paper. "What is this doctor? Do you admire serial killers?"

"Be careful with that! It is the original letter Jack the Ripper sent to the police to taunt them. It's rare. It's history."

"It's sick!" added Diego. "Hey, Otis, listen to this:

*Dear Boss*

*I keep on hearing the police have caught me but they won't fix me just yet. I have laughed when they look so clever and talk about being on the right track. That joke about Leather Apron gave me real fits. I am down on whores and I shan't quit ripping them till I do get buckled. Grand work, the last job was. I gave the lady no time to squeal. How can they catch me now? I love my work and want to start again. You will soon hear of me with my funny little games. I saved some of the proper red stuff in a ginger beer bottle over the last job to write with but it went thick like glue and I can't use it. Red ink is fit enough I hope ha. ha. The next job I do I shall clip the lady's ears off and send to the police officers just for jolly wouldn't you. Keep this letter back till I do a bit more work, then give it out straight. My knife's so nice and sharp I want to get to work right away if I get a chance. Good luck.*

*Yours truly*
*Jack the Ripper*

"Seems like a lot of similarities to his work and yours," Diego said.

"I am highly agitated, as you may guess. May I play some respectable music to settle my nerves?"

"As long as you don't get in our way, doctor," Martin said.

The doctor walked into the dining room and poured himself a glass of wine, then over to his stereo and scourged through a large catalog of vinyl records. Perhaps persuaded by the arrival of evening dusk, he chose Frédéric Chopin's, *Nocturne No. 2 in E-Flat major, Op. 9*, a musical composition inspired by, or evocative of the night. Its slow tempo, and subdued dynamics create an evocative mood as the doctor reminisced of the demise of his four subjects.

# CHAPTER TWENTY-ONE

*I had proof that I had five senses, that I knew how to get myself to function!
And then I lost my childhood.*
— Yves Klein

"Y**ou** brought me a chocolate malt!" Kalani said. "You really do know how to win a girl's heart."

"Not just any girl," Otis said. "How are you feeling today?"

"Otis, I think I'm turning a corner. I'm not saying I am living pain-free. I had told the doctors I feared becoming addicted to the painkillers they were giving me, so now I'm being weaned off of the opioids and I am receiving nonsteroidal anti-inflammatory agents (NSAIDs) and acetaminophen."

"You are my hero, baby."

"Heroine."

Laughing, Otis said, "Yes, I meant heroine. You have been so courageous and gracious through all of this. I have never heard you complain or use the 'why me?' moan even once. Your perspective has been positive and your glass is always half full, a few of the reasons why I want you to be my wife."

"I certainly have my moments when I feel like quitting," Kalani said.

"I'm sure you do."

"Otis, I feel good about my progress, physically and emotionally. I haven't told you, but my doctor strongly urged me to see one of the psychologists here. I was reluctant. You know my stubborn streak better than anyone. I always have had the 'can-do-this-on-my-own' attitude, but I agreed to see her and she has been wonderful."

"That's great, Kalani. I'm proud of you."

"Anyway, if all goes well, I should be able to come home soon and continue my treatments as an out-patient."

"Excellent!" Otis shouted. "We will celebrate when that happens."

"Honey, you don't know what it means to me that you still want to marry me, and I now believe it is not out of obligation or because you feel sorry for me, but you need to understand something. I was a model. I have been told I am beautiful from the time I was a little girl. Now, I am clearly not beautiful, at least on the outside,"

"You are…"

Kalani placed her index finger upon Otis's lips to quiet him.

"I need…I want you to understand how I feel. I can't get The Phantom of the Opera out of my mind. I am the phantomess, if that is even a word. I am a churel, a banshee. I am a White Lady."

"Actually, you are a black lady."

"Funny, Otis. You know, a White Lady—the common term for a female ghost typically dressed in white, often associated with tragic stories of betrayal, loss, or unrequited love."

"Then you do not qualify as a White Lady, because your love for me is returned, tenfold! Oh, and by the way, we had to pay the balance for the reception venue by the first of the month, which was yesterday. I paid it."

"Now who is the stubborn one," Kalani said, laughing. "You are absolutely crazy and I adore you."

"I am crazy. Crazy about you. I love you with all that I am."

"Otis, I would like to marry you, that is, if you will still have me," Kalani said as she looked deeply into Otis's eyes. His eyes filled with tears.

"Have you? Have you? You are all I ever wanted. Kalani, you just made me the happiest guy in the entire world!"

~~~

Martin walked out of his office to find Otis with his head in a pile of paperwork.

"Let's head over to Reading Terminal Market for lunch," Martin said to Otis. "I have a craving for oyster stew."
~~~

"I would have made you out to be more of a snapper soup kind of guy," Otis said.

"I love both."

When the detectives left the building, it was obvious spring had arrived. Spring in Pennsylvania means fresh strawberries and asparagus from the fertile soil of Lancaster County. The Amish peddle their vegetables and smoked meats at Philadelphia's Reading Terminal Market. The early harvest of fruits and vegetables help northeasterners forget about winter and long for summer. There has always been an unwritten reciprocal summer agreement between South Jersey and Philadelphia. The heat of the summer brings Jersey sweet white corn and juicy tomatoes to Philly, while Philadelphians bring their towels and flip flops to the Jersey shore.

"You look like you are in a good mood today, detective. Want to share?" Martin said.

"Is it that obvious?"

"Hey, I'm a detective, aren't I? The evidence is pretty damning."

Otis laughed. "I'm guilty as charged. The wedding is on! Kalani agreed to marry me!"

Martin stopped walking, looked at Otis with tears building in his eyes, and gave him an uncharacteristic hug.

Otis was stunned by Martin's emotional response, but it spoke volumes as to whom Martin truly is. Underneath his sometimes gruff, no-nonsense personality, is a man of integrity who respects, cares, and treats everyone how he wants to be treated.

"Otis, I sincerely could not be happier for the two of you."

"Kalani did have one condition. She wants a much smaller wedding. We cut the guest list by almost two-thirds. Martin, the guy I would have called my best friend, took a much different course in life than I have. He got a divorce a few years ago and has made several poor choices since. He tried to convince me to dump Kalani because of the scarring she received from the burns. He told me I would be crazy to marry her and I should start shopping around for another girl. Well, that friendship is past tense. Kalani never cared much for him anyway. I know this may seem like a strange request, but would you be my best man?"

Martin looked Otis in the eyes, and responded with a thoughtful, "I am honored, Otis."

The two detectives walked into the crowded market and sat at the counter of the seafood cafe. They both ordered a bowl of oyster stew.

"You know what has bothered me the most through Kalani's ordeal? The reaction of family and friends. Not all of them, mind you, but I would say most of them. They actually believe that because Kalani is permanently scarred over a third of her body, and nearly half of her face, I would never marry her. What does that say about me?"

"It says nothing about you and everything about them. It speaks volumes that they view love as something they get that makes them feel good. It is a selfish type of love. It's all about them and nothing about their partner. You, on the other hand, are the antithesis of that type of person."

"You are a man of integrity and your love for Kalani is authentic. I understand how you feel. You think they believe the marriage would be called off by you and they wouldn't blame you at all for doing that. If they thought that would be your reaction, then that would indicate you are shallow and lacking integrity, but that is not an accurate portrayal. It is indicative of what *they would do* if they were in your shoes."

"I never looked at it that way, Martin. It's a sad reflection of our society."

Otis thought about the cliche that looks can be deceiving. The saying mostly has a negative connotation attached to it, but Otis realized that sometimes, it can also be used to describe the 'ugly duckling' or 'Cinderella' syndrome where certain common things that look quite unimpressive often have a magnificently beautiful side, if only one would look more closely.

Martin finished chewing an oyster, then said, "Why do you think there are so many divorces after 20 years of marriage? No matter how beautiful or handsome someone is, looks diminish after a few decades. Wrinkles, gray hair, gravity all are inevitable. Raising children keeps both husband and wife busy, but once the little birds fly to greener pastures, the couple has to start looking at each other again. If the marriage was based only on physical attraction and nothing more substantial, the weak foundation of the relationship will show serious cracks."

"Insightful. I think you are on to something. Our society has become a department store display window which dictates the definition of beauty: aesthetic surface beauty, void of substance and blind to the beauty which is found in one's heart."

"Amen, brother! The outer beauty of a person does not always reflect a person's character, personality, and spirit. I have met some handsome men and gorgeous women who are totally ugly people. One must invest some time in getting to know the real person to see true beauty, and most people have little interest in doing that. Why do you think those who are considered attractive receive better jobs? The interview process isn't in depth enough to see the person's true character.

A few minutes passed with no conversation as the two detectives ate their soup.

"Otis, on another subject, just between you and me, I am seriously considering retiring after this case is closed," Martin said.

"Really? I mean, I kind of get it, but you are the best at what you do."

"I'm tired of it all. Sick and tired. I'm not tired of being a detective. I am tired of the peripheral BS. I keep being told I need to change with the times, but Otis, some assimilation is impossible for me. It's more than being stuck in an old way of doing things. It's the demand for me to change my morals, my beliefs. I am sick and tired of being told to accept all of these changes and when I speak out, I'm labeled as radical and hateful. I cannot even keep up with the proper pronouns of all these LGBTQ—XYZ. Heck, I still haven't gotten over Christine Jorgensen's transition."

"Who is Christine Jorgensen?"

"She's not important."

"Martin, I am a lot younger than you, and we are obviously different in many ways, but I understand completely. Our society is changing, and not for the better."

The detectives finished their soup. Martin laid some cash on the counter and the two left the market. As they were walking back to the precinct, Otis continued to offer a monologue describing the difference between aesthetic beauty and inner beauty.

"It is the epitome of you can't judge a book by its cover. If you were to meet Kalani for the first time, you would immediately see her monstrous scars. One might be afraid to even talk to her. Sure, that scarring is ugly on the outside, but on the inside resides an angel. You really can't judge a book by its cover.

"I have given this much thought ever since Kalani's accident. People are so obsessed with the external beauty of a person. Whenever I begin to feel that is wrong, I am reminded our initial attraction to a person is the physical, external, first impression. I get that. But have we become blind to that which displays true beauty? But then again, there is the matter of the natural world. Nature's glory, colorful birds, blue skies, painted butterflies, tropical fish, are all external beauty. Aesthetics. Why should it be any different for humans? What is the difference? Ahhhh, Martin. I will tell you the difference. Only humans possess a soul. It is the soul that contains one's authentic beauty that does not diminish over time. It is also the soul that shows the ugliness in a person, even those gorgeous on the outside."

~~~

Martin received a phone call that his presence was requested in the District Attorney's office. When he arrived, D.A. Malerba and Inspector Jenson were in a heated discussion about whether or not to arrest Barnabas Albrecht and charge him with both kidnapping and murder.

"It's all circumstantial evidence," District Attorney, Edward Malerba, said. "I'm not going anywhere without corroborating evidence, Captain. No grand jury will indict with what we have."

"You have tried cases with less evidence. Heck, 75% of all evidence in cases is circumstantial," Inspector Jenson said.

"Inspector, we want to make sure every 'I' is dotted and every 'T' is crossed. We are going to have one shot at this guy and I want a jury to find him guilty on all 4 murders, have him thrown into jail and the key thrown away."
~~~

"What about finding him guilty and given the death penalty?" asked Martin.

"That is on the table. If we can get him to confess and waive a trial, I am willing to give him life without the possibility of parole."

"If there were ever a case that deserved the death penalty, this is it." Martin said with more than a little annoyance.

"Mr. Malerba, what more do you want?" the Inspector asked, rhetorically.

Martin could see that Inspector Jenson was also getting heated and irritated, so he let him do the talking.

"We know all four victims were patients of Dr. Albrecht. From surveillance videos, we know the doctor is the same height as the killer. Darius Banks-Marsette identified Albrecht as the man who made the deal involving the black Cadillac Escalade. In Albrecht's penthouse we found he has a fascination with both the five senses and serial killers, especially those who target women. We're not going to find a murder weapon. He used a scalpel, succinylcholine, and fentanyl. It is as easy to find fentanyl in this city as it is to find a cheesesteak, but succinylcholine is not, but a doctor would have access to it. A scalpel is the doctor's crescent wrench, the tool of his trade."

"The fact that Darius Banks-Marsette identified the doctor only means that Albrecht gave him a car and made him his chauffeur. Can you put him at the scene of the crimes? Can you prove any of this?" asked the DA.

"If you are asking whether we have any witnesses or viable DNA then, no, we cannot put him at the murder scenes. We do have video tape, as I stated."

"I have seen that video. A tall man with a President Obama mask on. Any defense attorney will easily dismiss that video. Mark, we simply don't have enough to convict. We need an iron clad case. I need some physical evidence," ADA Bryson said. "Where were the murders committed? You did DNA swabs of the drains in Dr. Albrecht's bathrooms. Did they reveal anything? Did you find any of the victims' DNA in the doctor's penthouse? Have you found the black Cadillac Escalade, the ladder the killer used to spray paint surveillance cameras, or the Barack Obama mask?"

"We did find the car and we were able to tie the doctor to it, but forensics found nothing. It was swept completely clean. Since the car is registered to Darius Banks-Marsette, I can't see how the car can help convict Albrecht."

"Did the doctor's financials tell us anything?" ADA Bryson asked.

"I'm meeting with Corporal Wilton and our two FBI friends this morning. They stayed late going through every little detail concerning bank statements, payments, mortgages, real estate ownership. I was on my way to see them when you asked me to drop by here."

"Alright. Well, let me know if they find anything."

~~~

Martin went back to the offices of Major Crimes thinking his time at the DA's office was time wasted. Back in the offices of Major Crimes, Martin gathered his troops.

"I hear you guys spent an all-nighter," Martin said to Buchanan, Huffman and Lane Wilton.

"Not quite, but I have been pumping myself with the motor oil you detectives call coffee, in order to stay awake this morning," Special Agent Huffman said. "We did find a few interesting things."

"Please tell," Martin said.

"We know Dr. Albrecht has an offshore bank account in Switzerland. Despite our connections with the FBI white collar crime department, we were not able to obtain information regarding transactions or even the account balance. Due to Switzerland's strict banking secrecy laws and the need for international cooperation to obtain information, it is nearly impossible to get more information without strong suspicions and substantial evidence," Huffman said.

"Captain, contrary to popular belief, offshore accounts are legal and useful for international financial management. Individuals use these accounts for holding and receiving payments in multiple currencies, reducing business tax liability, protecting investments, and ensuring privacy and security," Buchanan added.

"The question that begs to be asked is why the doctor would need an offshore account unless he is trying to hide money, or unless he is afraid the government may freeze or seize his assets," Martin said.
~~~

"Not sure. I know you are aware that Sergeant Santos found monthly payments are being made to a Mr. Cecil Tobiason. We went to his apartment last night to question him, but no one was home."

"Follow the money trail. We also need to speak to Mr. Tobiason. Keep trying to find him."

"We also found the doctor owns real estate in the Poconos. He has 86 acres and a cabin just outside the town of Canadensis."

Turning to the detectives standing next to him, Martin said, "Sergeant Santos and Detective Sinclair, why don't you take a field trip to the Poconos and see if you can find out anything."

"Grab your coat, Diego. We are off to the mountains," Jake said.

"Make sure this is not an overnight trip. Don't forget that Otis and Kalani's wedding is tomorrow afternoon. I think we all need a refreshing change of scenery, so to speak. Let's celebrate with them and have some fun tomorrow."

"I just want to see you in a tux, Otis," Lillia said.

"You are in luck, Otis. They say a tux can make any man look more dashing, handsome, successful and confident," Jake said.

"He is already handsome and dashing," Lillia said.

"Alright, people," Martin said. "If I can shift gears for a minute, next Thursday night is the first full moon of the month. I know I sound paranoid, but all four of these murders occurred under a full moon. The moon's phases repeat every 29.5 days, which is known as the synodic month. Our killer is not only obsessed with the five senses, he is also inspired by the full moon."

"He's a werewolf!" interrupted Jake, which was followed by a laugh.

Martin's look made it clear he was not in a joking mood.

"If our perpetrator doesn't kill on this coming Thursday, then he will have to wait 29.5 days, which would be May 1st. I want the doctor tailed. I want eyes on him every minute of next Thursday. I want someone on him for all 1440 minutes of Thursday, from midnight on Wednesday to 11:59 pm Thursday. Check that. I want someone on him till the sun rises on Friday morning. If he is compelled to kill under the light of a full moon, we will be there to stop him. Detective Sinclair, I want you to arrange the surveillance and who will be on what shifts.

"Ewing, see if you can charm your way into getting a search warrant for the Schuylkill Packing Company. It has been closed for over nine years. I'm hoping it should not be that hard to get the warrant."

"Will do, Captain."

"Special Agent Buchanan, is there any way you can use the FBI's resources to search Cecil Tobiason's bank and financial records? No judge will grant us one on the flimsy evidence we have. The fact that he has been receiving large monthly payments from Dr. Albrecht won't be enough."

"I'm not sure that will be enough for a federal warrant either, but if Mr. Tobiason has not claimed the $120,000 a year income and paid taxes on it, we should be able to get the warrant fairly easily."

"Good. Let's hope Tobiason is greedy and has disregard for taxation laws."

# CHAPTER TWENTY-TWO

*To me it seems that those sciences are vain and full of error which are not born of experience, mother of all certainty, first-hand experience which in its origins, or means, or end has passed through one of the five senses.*
— Leonardo da Vinci

Jake and Diego got off the Northeast Extension of the Pennsylvania Turnpike and headed east on I-80. Although being only 100 miles north of Philadelphia, the temperature was 15 degrees cooler and the early spring vegetation had yet to be visible. Other than the needle leaf evergreens, the only vegetation that appeared green was the winter wheat.

As a courtesy, Jake contacted the local law enforcement in Canadensis. Lieutenant Barrett of the Pocono Mountain Regional Police Department agreed to meet Jake and Diego at the doctor's cabin.

"Take the next exit. Turn right onto Lake Panther Road," the GPS advised.

"Do you ever come up here to get away from the city?" Diego asked Jake.

"No. I'm more of a beach guy. Girls wear fewer clothes at the shore. They put more on in the mountains. What about you?"

"Yeah, my family does occasionally. I always come up the weekend after Thanksgiving with my cousins to do some deer hunting."

"The GPS says our ETA is 3 minutes."

"Do you think Albrecht used his cabin for the dissections and murders?" asked Diego.

"Probably not. I mean, he would have all the privacy he would want up here in the middle of nowhere, but he would have to transport the bodies all the way back to the city where he dumped them. I guess anything is possible, but it would seem a little cumbersome."

"Here is the driveway," Jake said as he turned onto the dirt road.

"And here is a heavy chain across the driveway,"

Hanging from the chain was a red, black and white sign:

KEEP OUT—PRIVATE PROPERTY

"Do you have bolt cutters in the trunk?" asked Diego.

"Yeah, but remember, we don't have a search warrant. Let's park here and wait for Lieutenant Barrett."

As if on cue, a police car pulled up behind the detectives' car. Jake and Diego got out of their car.

"Lieutenant Barrett? I spoke to you over the phone. I am Sergeant Santos and this is Detective Sinclair."

Lieutenant Barrett shook their hands.

"Welcome to the Poconos, detectives. You said something about working a homicide?" the Lieutenant said as the three men began walking towards the cabin.

"Correct. I didn't want to get into it over the phone, but we aren't investigating just any homicide. We have been assigned the Senseless murders."

"I figured that. It has made national news. So you think Dr. Albrecht might be involved?"

"Possibly."

"Well, he has plenty of experience performing surgeries on women's eyes, noses, and lips."

The three men walked up the dirt road to a clearing where the house stood. The log cabin had a covered porch where a lone rocking chair sat, waiting for someone to rock his cares away while looking down upon a picturesque view of a babbling creek.

"I could get used to this," Jake said.

"Go for it," Diego said. "Hey, Lieutenant, do you have any job openings for Detective Sinclair."

"I'm sure we can find a place for him," the Lieutenant said with a chuckle. "But I'm afraid he would get bored up here. We don't get much violent crime."

"Let's walk around the house from opposite sides and see if anything stands out," Diego said.

Uniformly chopped firewood was neatly stacked behind the cabin. The wooded property had a good mix of young hardwoods and scattered conifers. The three detectives met at the front of the house. Jake walked up to the porch and cupped his hands as he tried to look through a window.

"See anything?" asked Jake.

"No. I can only see a sliver between the drapes and it's too dark in there. We don't have a search warrant, Lieutenant," Diego said.

"Well, if we don't find anything, there's no need for a warrant. If we do find something, then we'll get a warrant," the Lieutenant said. "That is the way we do things around here."

Pulling a small pouch out of his pocket, the lieutenant proceeded to pick the lock to the door.

Leaning over to Jake, Diego whispered, "Well, that's putting the cart before the horse. We find something, then we get a warrant."

"Look, do you have a better idea?" Jake whispered back. "We drove 2 hours to get here and it would be nice not to go back to Philly empty handed."

The Lieutenant unlocked the door in short order and the detectives entered the cabin.

"Do me a favor and see if the electrical panel is in that closet. If so, turn on the main breaker," Lieutenant Barrett said.

Within seconds, the lights came on in the cabin. A large stone fireplace dominated the room while a whitetail buck mount whose antlers were perfectly symmetrical, watched the detectives' every move. The walls were white pine log with tongue & groove.

"I'll check out the back bedroom and bathroom. You guys have this great room," Diego said.

After a few minutes, Diego returned from the back rooms.

"Anything?" Diego asked.

"There's nothing here. It's like Al Capone's vault."

"Well, this has been a waste of time. Let's head back to Philly."

As they were walking towards the door, Diego stopped at the kitchen.

"Hey, check this out."

Diego picked up three marbles sitting in a clean ashtray. Jake took out his cellphone and took a photograph of the marbles.

"They aren't cat's eyes, but they certainly are marbles. Let's hit the road before it gets dark."

"Hey, detectives, come here," the Lieutenant said as he pulled a small flashlight from his pocket and turned it on. Kneeling down, he asked, "Does this look like blood to you?"

Diego and Jake knelt down and looked at a small blemish between the cracks in the floorboards.

"It does," Jake said.

"I'll take a swab and get it to our forensics lab, that is, after I get a search warrant from Judge Carpenter. I'm going to need some info from your investigation for probable cause."

"Not a problem," Diego said. "I'll have the office fax that over to you ASAP."

The Lieutenant put the swab into an evidence bag and stood up.

"I have a bottle of luminol in the trunk of my car," Lieutenant Barrett said. "Let's see if we have a crime scene or simply a drop of blood from a cut. I'll be right back."

"The Lieutenant seems pretty competent," Jake said.

"What did you expect? Because he's from rural America you expected Barney Fife?"

"Pun intended? You know, as in Dr. Barney Albrecht?"

"Unintentional," Diego said.

"Detectives, I was thinking something while walking back to the cabin. You said Dr. Albrecht is a suspect in those murders down in Philly where women's facial features were removed, right? Well, this may be nothing, but…

"What?" Diego asked.

"Well, about a year and a half ago a pretty young woman by the name of Julie Kane, was found in a lake nearby with one of her eyes removed."

"And you are just now bringing this up?" Jake asked.

"It was almost two years ago. Honestly, I never made the connection. Besides, it was only one eye, not the nose, ears…whatever else. And there was only one victim."

"He was practicing, honing his skills," Diego said.

Lieutenant Barrett sprayed the bottle of luminol around the area where he had collected the swab of blood.

"Kill the lights," he said.

Part of the wall and the floor lit up like the auroras.

~~~

Lillia went to the courthouse in hopes of acquiring a search warrant for the meat packing company.

"Miss Ewing, it is always a pleasure to see you," the judge said. "I would love to think you have come to ask me out for lunch, but I fear your motives are more mundane."

"I'll take a raincheck on that lunch, Judge Collins," Lillia said with a smile. "I need a search warrant for the Schuylkill Packing Company."

"That meat packing plant out by the zoo? Hasn't that been closed for a dozen years?"

"Nine to be exact. There is a suspect we like for the Senseless murders. We fear he will strike again, perhaps tomorrow night. Through a search warrant of his penthouse we found a plant blueprint for the old slaughterhouse. We think it has some connection with the case, possibly, where the murders took place. All four of the women's murders occurred someplace other than where they were found."

"Is he the owner of the deserted meat packing plant?"

"Actually, no. Someone by the name of Cecil Tobiason is."

"Miss Ewing, even if you were so inclined to invite me on a romantic weekend in Paris with you I would not give you a warrant based on this information. You should know better, detective. You *have* heard of probable cause?"

"Yes, Your Honor, but we are in a conundrum. We don't have enough to arrest our suspect because we need more corroborating evidence, but the evidence we need may be found in that meat packing plant."

"Yes, a conundrum indeed, but you are going to have to find another way to build your case, and I would hurry. The city is beginning to think this maniac will never be caught."

"Yes. Thank you, Judge Collins."
~~~

~~~

FBI Special Agents Buchanan and Huffman parked their car in front of the address they had for Cecil Tobiason.

"So, let me get this straight. Tobiason has been getting monthly checks from Albrecht to the tune of ten grand, and he is living in this dump? He's actually living in a housing project?" Buchanan asked rhetorically.

"Yeah, this doesn't add up, does it. We'll need to find out not only why he is getting his monthly alimony, but what he's doing with all that cash," Huffman said.

"Well, he is not putting it in a bank account. Money laundering is always a possibility."

"Well, he hasn't answered his phone. Let's hope he's home," Agent Huffman said as he knocked on the door to the apartment. There was no answer.

"Knock again. Maybe he's on the can."

"He's not home," a voice said.

The agents turned to see a short and wide woman with two bags of groceries in her arms get off the elevator.

"Here, let me help you within those," Buchanan said.

"Do you know when he will be home?"

Don't know, don't care," the woman said. "I don't know if that freak is a boy or a girl!"

"Do you know where we might find him?"

"He said he was off on vacation. God knows that fool don't have no money for no vacation."

"Where did he say he was going on vacation?"

"I dunno. I think Puerto Rico. No, Jamaica. Yeah, that's it, Jamaica," she said as she unlocked the door to her apartment.

"Thank you, Ma'am. Here is my card. Would you be so kind as to give me a call when Mr. Tobiason returns?"

"I hope he don't return," the woman said as she inspected Huffman's business card. "FBI? Hmmmm, that boy done get himself in some trouble."

The lady dropped the card on the floor with indifference.
~~~

Agent Buchanan handed the woman her groceries.

"Wait just a second," Buchanan said as he bent over to pick up the business card.

Reaching into his pocket, he pulled out a 50-dollar bill and tore it in half, giving the lady one half.

"When you call to let me know Mr. Tobiason is home, I'll give you the other half."

The woman took the torn bill and shut the door.

# CHAPTER TWENTY-THREE

*There is no exquisite beauty without some strangeness in the proportion.*
— Edgar Allan Poe

Ever since the search of Dr. Albrecht's penthouse, something kept surfacing in Martin's mind. *What was so special, so important about the six short stories the doctor had marked?* Martin could not wait to get home so he could delve into his copy of the *Complete Stories and Poems of Edgar Allan Poe*. His hope was to find a hidden gem or two within the stories that might shine light on the tumultuous case.

The doctor was, if nothing else, intentional. There was no such thing as coincidences when it came to the plastic surgeon. He was calculated and purposeful. If he had been reading these six short stories, there was something within the writing that aroused the doctor. Martin wanted to creep inside the grotesquely twisted mind of Dr. Albrecht, both the mystery and the macabre.

When Martin arrived home, he found a note Mary Jo had left reminding him she had promised their daughter she would babysit that evening and that Martin's dinner was in the fridge; it just needed to be microwaved. Martin opened the refrigerator and retrieved a bowl of beef stew, placed it in the microwave and pushed the two-minute button.

Martin opened the book of Poe's works and turned to the table of contents. The first of the six short stories he read was "Berenice." He began reading as he stood, leaning on the kitchen counter. The microwave beeped. Martin continued reading with great acuteness. The story describes a man named Egaeus, who is preparing to marry his cousin, Berenice. Originally beautiful, Berenice suffers from an unspecified degenerative illness.

The microwave beeped once again. Martin took his beef stew, a spoon, and a napkin and retired to the living room and sat in his favorite chair. He turned on the light and continued to read.

Something caught Martin's attention in the story. When Berenice smiles, Egaeus focuses on her teeth. He becomes obsessed with her teeth, and for days he drifts in and out of awareness, constantly thinking about her teeth. *Yes, obsession with a body part!* Monomania, thought Martin. The mental condition characterized by an obsessive preoccupation with a single idea or subject, often leading to irrational or extreme behavior best describes the mad doctor! Martin continued to read.

Egaeus imagines himself holding the teeth and turning them over to examine them from every angle. It was then that Martin came upon a sentence which made him stop, and reread it over and over again. "How is it that from beauty I have derived a type of unloveliness?" *Were the teeth symbolically used to symbolize mortality?*

Martin laid the book on his lap and took a spoonful of beef stew. It was lukewarm. He turned to the next short story on his list, "Eleonora." The second sentence of the story, "Men have called me mad; but the question is not yet settled, whether madness is or is not the loftiness intelligence…" *The egocentric doctor definitely has a high IQ and there is no doubt he is insane!* Another partial sentence jumped out at Martin as if it had been highlighted in bold print. "…made perfect in loveliness only to die."

The stories are not long. Most are fewer than five pages. Martin continued his reading, turning to the third story, "Ligeia." He felt the unnamed narrator, his obsession with Ligeia's eyes, could be named Albrecht! "For eyes we have no models in the remotely antique. It may have been, too, that in these eyes of my beloved lay the secret to which Lord Verulam alludes. They were, I must believe, far larger than the ordinary eyes of our own race. They were even fuller than the fullest of the gazelle eyes of the tribe of the valley of Nourjahahad…And at such moments was her beauty—in my heated fancy thus it appeared perhaps—the beauty of beings either above or apart from the earth…" *Obsession with, this time, the eyes, but always centered around the indescribable beauty of a lady.*

Martin took another mouthful of stew. It was cold. At that moment, he too was chilled. He considered his obsession with Poe and his preoccupation with Dr. Albrecht's admiration and limerence for Poe. The American writer and poet was Dr. Albrecht's hero and mentor. The thought of Martin being the anti-Barnabas returned to haunt him.

Martin turned the pages of the book and found the fifth short story, "The Oval Portrait." It was in the sixth paragraph that the words on the page provided a parallel to the real-life story of the Senseless killer and his motivation to kill these young ladies. Martin read outloud, "She was a maiden of rarest beauty…" *Once again, excessive devotion to the external beauty of a woman.* "He, passionate, studious, austere, and having already a bride in his Art; she a maiden of rarest beauty, and not more lovely than full of glee; all light and smiles, and frolicsome as the young fawn; loving and cherishing all things; hating only the Art which was her rival; dreading only the pallet and brushes and other untoward instruments which deprived her of the countenance of her lover."

Martin looked at the list of short stories, then turned to one entitled "Morella." No surprise that it was the name of yet another inamorata. This story was less obvious than the others. Martin could not find the relevance behind the story that may have stimulated Dr. Albrecht's twisted obsession, so he read the story a second time. Martin came across a simple sentence. "It is a happiness to wonder; it is a happiness to dream." Martin pondered its meaning and possible symbolism. The collecting of the five sensory organs relating to the five senses and creating the perfect woman was a dream come true for the doctor. It was his fantasy!

Martin placed the open book upside down on his lap and closed his eyes, thinking of the horror the women must have felt, being alive and alert during the removal of an external sensory organ. He did not realize he had dozed off until he felt Mary Jo's hand upon his shoulder.

"Honey, honey, why don't you go upstairs to bed."

"Uh. What time is it?"

"A little past eleven. You didn't eat the stew. Aren't you hungry?"

"I'm sorry, Mary Jo. I got preoccupied with some reading."

Mary Jo picked up the book on Martin's lap and inspected it.

"Edgar Allan Poe? Light reading before bed?"

"Our prime suspect is obsessed with Poe and there were several short stories he especially liked. I wanted to read them in the hope they may shed some light on this guy's motives. I want to read one more story and then I'll be right up."

Patting him on his head, Mary Jo said, "Alright. Would you like a bowl of ice cream?"

"No, honey. I'll nuke what is left of the stew when I am finished here."

Martin turned the pages to the last short story the doctor had bookmarked, "The Fall of the House of Usher." Nothing in the story seemed relevant to the murders Martin is investigating, that is, until Martin read, "He suffered much from a morbid acuteness of the senses; the most insipid food was alone endurable; he could wear only garments of certain texture; the odours of all flowers were oppressive; his eyes were tortured by even a faint light; and there were but peculiar sounds, and these from stringed instruments, which did not inspire him with horror."

~~~

The next day the Major Crimes offices were busy with activity. Otis noticed Jake grabbing his jacket and heading towards the elevator.

"Where are you going?" asked Otis.

"I have the midnight to six shift for watching Dr. Deranged. I'm heading home to get some sleep."

"Sweet dreams," Otis said with a smile.

Minutes later FBI Special Agents Huffman and Buchanan entered the office.

"Captain, since we couldn't reach Tobiason on the phone, we went over to his apartment yesterday. He's living in The Towers, that housing project on North 11th Street. You would think he would live in a nicer place if he were getting paid $10,000 a month from the plastic surgeon," Huffman said. "His neighbor told us he is vacationing in Jamaica. Our Caribbean office is trying to track him down so they can tell him he is a material witness in a murder investigation and needed back in the States ASAP."
~~~

"Thank you, Mr. Huffman. Let me know if we need to issue a subpoena. The sooner we can question him, the better."

Just then, a woman wearing a loose, bright-colored soft top and denim pants with embroidered flowers, walked into the common room. Martin could not remember where he had seen her before. Having recognized the woman, Lillia moved closer so she could hear the impending conversation.

"Detective Gainwell, may I please have a minute of your time? It's urgent," the woman said.

"Martin, this is Autumn Fields," Otis said. "She is a clairvoyant who visited us a while ago with some visions she had about the murders."

"Clairvoyant?" Martin asked.

"A person who has a supernatural ability to perceive events in the future or beyond normal sensory contact," Autumn said.

"I know what a clairvoyant is. I would add that a clairvoyant is someone who *claims* to perceive events in the future."

"A nonbeliever. That's okay, but I could never live with myself if I stood idly by while having pertinent information on this case."

"Well then, that changes everything," Martin said. "My apologies Miss Fields. Please, have a seat and by all means, enlighten us."

Turning to Otis, Autumn said, "I have not received a call from you since I walked in here to help you. That was 4 months ago. I figured you didn't need my help."

"So you *are* clairvoyant," Otis said.

Ignoring Otis's sarcasm, Autumn continued, "I am hoping it wasn't that you don't want my help, detective. Since the last time I saw you, more defenseless women have been murdered. I think you need my assistance, Detective Gainwell."

"What exactly can I do for you Miss Fields."

"I have had some very strong visions that will not go away. I saw a dog dead and a woman kidnapped. She was placed on a cold metal table and her nose was skillfully removed."

"We never revealed to the public anything about the dog, Captain," Lillia said.

"What else have you seen?" Otis asked.

"Well, that woman who owned the dog, Susan Cranford, was found with one of those gag glasses with the nose and mustache attached."

Autumn Fields now had the attention of the entire detective team.

"Where did you get this information? And don't tell me you had some kind of vision or dream!" Martin said, reflecting his patience had run out.

"Captain, I am sensing you have an angry aura."

"My angry aura is soon going to manifest itself in some ugly ways unless you stop with this game."

"Speaking of manifestation, Captain Wallace, the expressive term 'clairvoyance' literally means 'clear seeing' and refers to my ability to perceive events or people beyond the normal range of senses. In my case, it is through mental imagery that can *manifest* as visions in my mind's eye."

"I am warning you. I do not have the time, energy, or patience for this."

Autumn continued sharing her information.

"The black SUV that is part of your investigation is not owned by the killer. He only borrows the car to do his dirty work and returns it to the owner."

"Miss Fields…"

"Please, call me Autumn, Captain."

"Autumn, step into my office. Detective Gainwell, Agents Huffman and Buchanan, please join us."

Martin entered his office last and shut the door.

"Autumn, I am going to be crystal clear so there will be no need for you to read my mind. If you do not want to be charged with accessory after the fact in a first-degree murder case which carries a possible sentence of up to 30 years, you will tell me how you found this information. At the very least, you will be charged with the crime of tampering with evidence."

"As I told you, I am…."

"Stop!" Martin said forcefully.

"You may not be a believer in the power of discerning objects not present to the senses, but…"

"That's it. I gave you a chance. Detective Gainwell, please read Miss Fields her rights and book her…"

"Okay, okay! Don't flip your wig! You don't have to be such a bummer. He told me you were pursuing false leads and you were never going to catch that serial killer unless you changed your philosophy."

"Who told you that?"

"One of your detectives paid me and told me what to say to you."

"What is this detective's name?"

"Jordan Becton."

# CHAPTER TWENTY-FOUR

*Love is the poetry of the senses.*
— Honore de Balzac

Martin and Mary Jo walked up the steps to the church, the oldest Baptist church in the city, an old stone building with a red door and a fish displayed on the steeple. Called an "ichthys" in Greek, the fish is a Christian symbol representing Jesus Christ, with the letters forming an acronym for "Jesus Christ, Son of God, Savior" in Greek. Early Christians used the fish as a secret way to identify each other during times of persecution, making it a significant symbol of faith. The church's red front door symbolizes the blood of Christ.

Mary Jo sat in the pew with the other detectives; Martin, the best man, went into a room, to the left of the pulpit, to meet with Otis. It had been quite a number of years since Martin had been asked to be someone's best man.

Lillia arrived in a charming corset dress adorned with floral details that featured an off-shoulder neckline. The male detectives, having never seen Lillia in a dress, were wowed by her enchanting look.

The sanctuary seemed large with so few people in attendance. Kalani decided to cut the invitation list from 150 to only 60. Her accident and painstaking recovery gave her a fresh perspective. She realized the majority of people she and Otis were originally going to invite to their wedding were not people with whom they had meaningful relationships. The obligatory invites for business associates, cousins they haven't seen in years, and friends of their parents seemed silly.

Once the organ began playing, the chatter ceased. Otis and Martin entered the sanctuary from a door to the left side of the pulpit and stood at the front of the church with the pastor. Kalani's maid of honor was a woman with whom she had been close friends since kindergarten. Wearing a lemon-colored dress with cerulean trim, she walked slowly to the altar where the pastor, Martin, and Otis were waiting. Once she reached the front of the church, she stopped and turned to face the rear of the church. The organ ceased for a few seconds in a dramatic pause, then began playing Mendelssohn's elegant Wedding March as the congregation stood.

Kalani wore a Vivienne Westwood timeless and classic Nova Cora bridal gown expertly crafted from lustrous satin. The gorgeous floor-length drape and train, featured a romantic, off-shoulder neckline, and sculpted, fitted bodice.

Otis smiled as he tried to hold back his tears. Kalani looked stunning.

The pastor read from Genesis 2:19-20 and highlighted the context in which God revealed the glory of marriage; specifically, the richness of the text highlights the impoverished quest of Adam to find a 'suitable helper' in all of God's good creation. Though everything God created was good, the introduction of woman was far better.

The pastor then shared Proverbs 31:30. "Charm is deceptive, and beauty is fleeting; but a woman who fears the Lord is to be praised." Those words of Scripture were more than appropriate for this wedding and it pierced the hearts of all in attendance.

Martin marveled at the simplicity of the Baptist ceremony as compared to the Catholic liturgy for weddings to which he was accustomed. It was simple, yet meaningful. The pastor wore a suit instead of a robe. There was no lighting of candles, no incense and no kneeling. There were melodic hymns, plenty of scripture and a sermon describing the analogy of Christ being the groom and the church, specifically, believing people, His bride.

Martin once confessed to Otis about his fragile faith. He also asked Otis about the "born again" thing Evangelicals often referenced. "It all comes down to your willingness to surrender *your* will to *Christ's* will," Otis told Martin.

Surrender was not a word in Martin's vocabulary. Dealing with his own carapaces of skepticism, Martin explained the god in whom he believed would not allow the suffering and pain he witnessed on a daily basis.

"The god you believe in?" Otis had asked rhetorically. "So, instead of man being made in God's image, you want to create God in your image? I don't mean to get preachy with you, Martin, but please allow me to answer your question about God allowing the chaos that goes on in our world."

"God created a *perfect* world. No disease, no violence, no death. *Perfect!* It was man who screwed it up. *Adam and Eve wanted to recreate God in their image.* It didn't work. It still doesn't work. God created us with free will, to accept or reject Him. He doesn't force Himself on anyone. And even though people flip the bird at God, He still loves them. Crazy, right? The good news, my friend, is that He will one day restore everything to its intended perfection."

Martin never forgot that conversation.

The reception was held on the legendary Moshulu, the world's oldest and largest square-rigged sailing vessel still afloat. Docked on the Delaware River, she is the only restaurant in the world located on a tall ship. Built in the Port of Glasgow, Scotland in 1904, the four-masted barque Kurt was the perfect venue for the celebratory occasion.

Otis took his spoon and tapped it 4 times. The cling, cling, cling quieted the cheerful guests.

"Before I toast my incredible bride, I am going to address the elephant in the room. When you first look at Kalani, you may be taken aback by the scars covering the left side of her face. But the amazing thing is, it doesn't take long when you are in Kalani's presence before you become oblivious to those scars. Authentic beauty cannot be diminished by scarring, or age, or, well, anything."

"Picture, if you will, a gift you buy at the jewelry store. The salesperson wraps the gift in shiny golden paper with a beautiful bow and ribbons with perfect curls. But the paper gets tossed. The real prize is inside. Kalani's beauty emanates from the inside out which makes her gorgeous to those who know her."

"Please raise your glasses with me. Kalani, I adore you. Always have, always will. Love is nothing, unless it's divided by two. May our hinges of friendship never rust, and may our years of joy be as numerous as the petals of your bridal bouquet. To Kalani," Otis said as he raised his champagne glass high.

"To Kalani," cheered the crowd.

Lillia came up to the head table and gave Kalani a hug and a kiss, then Otis.

"So, where are you two love birds heading for a honeymoon?" she asked.

"We are only going away for a few days. We have scheduled a real honeymoon for September when my rehab will be complete. We plan on going to Hawaii."

"Now that sounds wonderful. Congratulations to both of you. You really do make the perfect couple."

~~~

On Monday morning Jake walked into the office with a box of donuts and two cups of coffee. He gave Martin one of the coffees.

"Want a French cruller? It's light and airy, the least offensive of the donut family."

"No, but I'll take a Boston Cream, its heavy, offensive cousin. Did anything come of your surveillance last night?"

"Dr. Albrecht left his office a little after six, went to dinner at Aubrey's Bistro, and went home. He never left his penthouse all night. Captain, I know you are going to be pissed, but our cover was blown last night."

"How?"

"Lane decided to join me on the overnight shift. We parked across the street from the doctor's condo building. We used Lane's car because it doesn't look like a government unmarked car. He has a white Volvo. A little after midnight, some kid rides up to our car on a bicycle and hands us a pizza. We told him we didn't order a pizza and to get lost. He said it was compliments of the doctor."

"Great!"
~~~

"We saw the doctor leave for the office at 7:13 this morning," Jake said.

"Well, there is a silver lining in that. At least there were no murders committed last night that would have been connected to this case," Martin said.

From across the room, Special Agent Huffman could be heard on his cell phone, and even though only half of the conversation was audible, it garnered everyone's attention.

"I can have a car pick him up at the airport," Huffman said. "Okay. That's fine. Will that be today? What time? Okay. That's great. Hey, thanks for your help on this, Neil. I owe you one."

"Do you have good news for us?" Martin asked.

"I do, or at least I think I do. One of our agents in Jamaica found Cecil Tobiason and convinced him to fly back to Philly and talk to us. He agreed, but under the condition he comes in himself. He does not want us to send anyone to pick him up. I'm not sure why, but I'm guessing he doesn't want to be seen with cops. Cooperating with law enforcement can get you a bullet in his neighborhood."

"When does his plane arrive?" asked Otis.

"It already has. My counterpart in Jamaica said Tobiason is fragile and it is best if we don't push him. Oh, and he added we may be in for a surprise when we see him."

"What does that mean, fragile?" Martin asked.

"It means easily broken or damaged," Jake interjected.

"Don't you have something worthwhile to do, Detective?"

~~~

Weeks passed and the case stalled yet again. Having known he was under surveillance, the doctor patiently postponed his final dissection. The next full moon was now only twenty-four hours away, and the anticipation was becoming unbearable for him. He was disappointed with having to let the last full moon pass, but it did give him time to select the perfect candidate. The doctor had narrowed his search to three ladies.

The doctor realized boredom was his enemy. He knew being impulsive and failing to plan every minute detail of his mission would
~~~

be his undoing. *Patience. Plan. Execute.* One evening after work, Dr. Albrecht decided to scratch his itch. The itch was to perform his final selective surgery, and even though that would have to wait, he knew something that would suffice for the time being.

Along with the change of seasons came changes in the department store display windows. The doctor decided to take an evening stroll to admire the newly positioned mannequins. Barnabas Albrecht navigated past the museum neighborhood and down toward the shopping district of Market Street. There he found the spring displays of clothing draped upon the fiberglass and plastic human beings. Barnabas was enamored by mannequins' ability to emanate an eerie and mysterious presence. And yet, he was disappointed. More and more of the pretend human beings were becoming nothing more than eggheads, lacking eyes, ears, nose, and mouth. Most did not even wear a wig! Barnabas couldn't help but wonder if this were but another decision to be politically correct. Was this an attempt by the retail establishment not to insult any ethnic or sexual identity group as to what one may deem as the "perfect" face?

Barnabas, disappointed, headed back to his penthouse. When he arrived at his building he was greeted by the doorman. "Good evening, Dr. Albrecht."

"Good evening, Clifford."

Pausing at the door for a moment, the doorman said, "Did you forget something, Doctor?"

"Actually, I was wondering if you could do me a favor."

"But, of course. What is it you need?"

"You are about my height. How tall are you, Clifford?

"I am six foot one. Why do you ask?"

"Just an inch shorter than I am. Would it be possible to borrow one of your uniforms for 24 hours? I have an ex-girlfriend stalking me. When I come back from visiting my sick aunt, I do not want her to see me. I would like to avoid a confrontation with her. I will have the uniform dry cleaned and returned to you and, of course, I will make it worth your while with a generous tip to show my appreciation."

"You certainly don't have to do that, Dr. Albrecht and, yes, you may borrow my spare uniform. Come inside the lobby with me. I always keep a clean uniform in the closet behind the front desk."

The doorman handed Barnabas the uniform as the doctor slipped five one hundred dollar bills into the man's hands.

"Thank you, Clifford. I do appreciate your helpfulness and please keep this between you and me. You know how people talk around here."

The doorman laughed. "Do I ever!"

~~~

The next morning, Dr. Albrecht left his building and walked down to a bakery a few blocks from his condo. He returned with a Danish and a latte and took the elevator to the top floor and entered his penthouse. The place was still a scattered mess from the detectives' search. He walked over to his desk and retrieved a burner phone from the bottom drawer. The detectives had not found the phone in their search because Barnabas had it on his person.

"Hello? Is this Debbie Parker? Yes, this is Dr. Albrecht. I am fine and I hope you are as well. What's that? Oh, I am so glad you are pleased with the results of the surgery. In fact, that is why I am calling. I am following up on your rhinoplasty surgery. You told my office you were extremely pleased with the results…and, of course, I was so glad to hear that. Miss Parker, I'm embarrassed to call you on short notice, but I was just notified by our advertising agency that they need to finalize the photographs for our upcoming brochure and advertising campaign."

"You had indicated on the post-op survey that you would be willing to participate in a before and after photo comparison of your nose. Are you still willing to do that? Wonderful! Here is the catch. It needs to be this afternoon. I am actually not far from your place right now. I could pick you up in say, 20 minutes, take you to the shoot, and return you to your residence, all before your husband gets home from work…Excellent! Thank you! Oh, and to thank you for being so gracious, we will offer you a 50% discount on any future work you may want me to perform. See you shortly."

Dr. Albrecht placed his burner phone in his pocket, grabbed a duffel bag containing the doorman's uniform, and headed for the building's laundry room.
~~~

~~~

Back at the precinct, Special Agent Buchanan's cell phone rang, interrupting Martin's address to his troops

"Special Agent Buchanan," he said into his phone.

The woman's voice on the other end said, "That freak, Tobiason is back from his vacation. And don't forget to bring the other half of that Grant."

"Thank you for the call. I'll drop by tomorrow with the other half of that fifty."

Turning to Martin, Buchanan said, "Tobiason arrived at his apartment. We should be seeing him soon."

"Good. We need to talk to him." Turning to his team, Martin said, "Folks, Tuesday is the first of May, and it is also a full moon. We know our suspect wants to kill under the light of a full moon. I am convinced that since he did not strike during the last full moon, he will tonight. Once again, I want 24-hour surveillance on Albrecht. Lieutenant Ewing, I would like you to schedule that, and I don't want anyone taking long shifts. You give someone an 8-hour shift and they get sloppy and miss things. If Albrecht leaves his penthouse, I want him followed."

At a quarter past three, the elevator door opened and a tall, very attractive black woman walked into the common room. Her fashionable dress fit tight around her body. The dress had thin shoulder straps, and a deep neckline revealing perfectly round and firm breasts. Her curly hair fell below her shoulders which she threw back as she entered the room with an intentional, confident, and subtly suggestive gait. All of the men in the room stopped what they were doing to admire the scenery.

"May I help you?" asked Jake as he scampered up to her.

"I hope so. I am here to see Captain Wallace."

"I am Captain Wallace," Martin said as he walked up to the woman. "What can I do for you, Miss…"

"Tobiason. Cecilia Tobiason."
~~~

# CHAPTER TWENTY-FIVE

*Dear, my hands no longer feel themselves to be hands when they touch each other — they seek to achieve their mysterious destiny of being hands only in yours — your dear hands.*
— Rainer Maria Rilke

Martin was trying to process everything he had just heard…and seen. Apparently, each member of the team was doing the same, for the silence in the room was deafening. Martin looked at Cecilia's Adam's apple, then to her girlish figure.

"You are Cecil Tobiason?"

"Cecilia Tobiason. Cecil is dead. No more. Yes, Captain, I am transgender."

Cecilia looked around the room and the eight sets of eyes assessing her.

"Why don't we go into the interview room where you may feel more comfortable. Detective Gainwell, why don't you join us."

As soon as Cecilia, Otis and Martin closed the door to Interrogation Room 1, the remainder of the task force scurried to the observation room. Jake went into the breakroom and microwaved a bag of popcorn for the show.

"How would you like to be addressed?" asked Martin with his best sympathetic tone.

"You may call me Cecilia or Miss Tobiason, whatever suits you. Please use the female pronouns she and her."

"Fine. Cecilia, you are here because we believe you are a material witness to the serial murders plaguing our city. We also believe you are either directly or indirectly linked to these crimes. Do I have your attention now?"

Cecilia's left eye began to twitch uncontrollably.

"Captain, I came all the way here from Jamaica on my own volition."

"And that is a good thing, otherwise we would have arrested you and extradited you back to the States."

"Arrested? On what charges? I have done nothing wrong."

"Accessory to murder, to begin with."

Cecilia began to hyperventilate.

"Are you alright, Miss Tobiason?" Otis asked.

"I cannot breathe."

"Take it easy. Slow down your breathing," Otis said. "I'll be right back."

Otis left the room and returned quickly with a paper bag and a bottle of water.

"Breathe slowly into the bag. That's it. It's okay. We just have some questions. If you answer truthfully, you need not worry."

After a few minutes, Martin asked, "Are you feeling better, Miss Tobiason?"

"Yes, thank you."

"We are investigating the butchering of four innocent women. In a search of Dr. Barnabas Albrecht's finances, we discovered he is paying you $10,000 a month. Why is he doing that?"

"Do I need a lawyer?" Cecilia asked.

"By all means, if you are directly involved in these murders. On the other hand, if you have nothing to hide, and you are willing to assist in our investigation, lawyers will just complicate things," Otis said.

"The money, Miss Tobiason. Why was Dr. Albrecht paying you such a large sum every month?" Martin asked.

Cecilia hesitated, not knowing what to say.

"I am afraid of that man. I cannot tell you anything".

"We can offer you protection, but we need to hear what you know."

"Protection? Really, Captain. This girl was not born yesterday! You are going to protect me like you did that material witness in that Russian mob case last year? You had him in protective custody and someone still stabbed him with a shiv, killin' him. Am I under arrest? You have nothing on me."

"That is where you are wrong, Miss Tobiason."

Turning to Otis, Martin said, "Detective, see if the IRS has a record of whether Ms. Tobiason ever paid tax on the $10,000 monthly income she has been receiving from Dr. Albrecht."

"Not a problem, Captain. The Feds have been cracking down on white collar crime," Otis said. Turning to Cecilia, Otis added, "Tax evasion in violation of Section 7201 of Title 26 of the United States Code is a serious criminal offense. The punishment can include five years in federal prison, a $100,000 fine, or both."

Otis got up and headed for the door.

"Okay! Okay! Don't let your testosterone erupt, gentlemen. My girlfriend went to see Dr. Albrecht about a nose job. Tonya's a beautiful girl, but unfortunately, she got her father's Serbian nose. Anywho, I asked her to ask the doctor if there was any way I could get a discount on a boob job. You know, since both Tonya and I would give him business, maybe he would cut me a break on a set of boobs. I work at Starbucks and I just don't have that kind of cheddar. The doctor told Tonya to give him my number."

"The doctor called me and told me to come in for a consultation. What I thought was strange was that he wanted me to come into his office at 9 o'clock in the evening, well after they were closed for the day."

"Go on," Martin said.

"Well, I met with Dr. Albrecht. He said he had a proposition for me. He would perform breast augmentation on me for free if I would agree to put my name on the property deed for a building he wanted to purchase."

"What building did he want to buy?"

"The Schuylkill Packing Company. He would send me $10,000 every month to pay for the mortgage and insurance. After making the payments, there would always be something left for me. I was hesitant, of course. I'm not one to look for trouble. I'm a lover, not a fighter. My shilly-shallowing caused the good doctor to sweeten the deal. He asked if I were contemplating gender-affirming surgery. It was like he could read my mind, my desires, my dreams. Besides being charismatic, the doctor is a very persuasive man. And handsome to boot! Anywho, he said he would perform breast augmentation on me for free and if all goes well with me paying the mortgage and property insurance, he would arrange for the gender-affirming surgery, too!"

"Darlin', I thought, this was too good to be true! So, I agreed. I took the downpayment money, the doctor forged someone's signature as the cosigner for the loan, and I got myself this fine pair of ta-tas."

"Looking at Otis, she said, "Feel them, detective. They really are magnificent!"

"Yeah, I'll pass."

"You have been very helpful, Cecilia," Martin said as he stood up. "We will be in touch."

They all left the interrogation room. As Celicia was walking down the hallway towards the elevator, Diego, who had not been in the common area when Cecilia arrived, walked up to Otis and Martin.

"Who is that? She is bodacious!"

Both Martin and Otis broke out in laughter.

"What?" Diego asked.

"That was Cecil Tobiason," Otis said as he slapped Diego on the back.

"What? No!"

"He is now a she and goes by Cecilia."

In an attempt to change the subject at the speed of light, Diego said, "ADA Bryson is looking for you. She's over there talking to Lillia."

ADA Bryson turned around when she heard Martin walking up to them.

"Captain. I was just telling Lieutenant Ewing that Robert Newell of the *Inquirer* gave us the courtesy, if you want to call it that, to inform us that tomorrow morning's paper will have an investigative piece about the case. The story is about surveillance that had, or is, being conducted on Dr. Barnabas Albrecht, the world-renowned plastic surgeon. Newell wanted to know if the DA's office wanted to comment; we declined. Do you have enough to make an arrest?"

"We have believed for quite some time he is our guy, but we still do not have enough evidence; however, that is going to change very soon. How did Newell find out about the surveillance?"

"Believe it or not, from the doctor himself."

"This guy is beyond arrogant! He thinks he is untouchable! Miss Bryson, we just interviewed someone who has been paid by Albrecht to hide his purchase of the old Schuylkill Packing Company. We think he performed organ retrieval there. I need a search warrant. I think we now have more than probable cause."

"I'll go to Judge Goldberg. What all do you have?"

"All four victims were patients of Dr. Albrecht. We know he is the silent owner of the meat packing plant. Darius Banks-Marsette identified the doctor as the man who arranged the deal with the black Cadillac Escalade. He has been unbelievably careful. We have no DNA or fingerprints to link him to the crime."

"Motive, means, opportunity?" Bryson said.

"Linda, it's a conundrum. The means and opportunity are tied to the meat plant. I need that to establish his involvement. As for motive, who in the world knows. The doctor is a sick egomaniac whose life philosophy is inundated with beauty."

"I have an idea which may not be totally kosher, but it will get us into the meat plant to investigate. We can take a team over there and simply say they heard a scream coming from within." Lillia said.

"And when they find there is no one in the plant, what will your excuse be?" asked Bryson. "Failure to obtain court permission for such a search invokes the 'fruit of poisonous tree' doctrine. In other words, any evidence discovered as a result of the search is inadmissible against the occupant or property owner."

FBI Agents Huffman and Buchanan overheard the conversation and decided to join in.

"What about using a regulatory scheme?" Buchanan asked. "We can contact the owner of the meat packing plant to tell him an inspection of the plant is necessary. We can pose as code enforcement officers or building inspectors who monitor conformity with city regulations."

"That might be walking the tight rope," Bryson said. "This type of administrative inspection may violate the constitutional rights of the owner to be free from unwarranted searches. The problem is that when a municipal officer wishes to perform an inspection, but does not have the owner or occupant's permission to do so, he must obtain an administrative search warrant."

"Judge Goldberg owes me a favor. I think I can persuade him to give us a search warrant of the meat packing plant," Linda Bryson said as she excused herself. Turning her head back to the team as she walked towards the elevator, she added, "I'll call you once the warrant is in hand. Oh, and Martin, where is Darius Banks-Marsette being held?"

"County," Martin replied.

"Bring him in. I don't want him interviewed over there. Maybe he'll be more talkative now that he's spent a few weeks in a cell. I want to see if he knows anything about the meat packing plant and about that evidence he planted to frame the Mayor."

~~~

Barnabas took the elevator to the basement of his building. It was nearly 4 o'clock which meant the laundry service the condo building used would soon be pulling into the garage. As a courtesy to the residents, the laundry company came by every Tuesday to drop off dry cleaning and pick up soiled laundry. Every resident was given a blue laundry bag with a tie string, identified by a number designated by the laundry service. The doctor did not have to wait long.

The van backed into the building's loading dock.

"I so appreciate a hard-working man who keeps a tight schedule," the doctor said to the man who was opening the barn doors at the rear of the van. "I do believe you never are more than five minutes on either side of 4 o'clock every Tuesday afternoon."

"It's my last stop of the day. I try to stay on schedule."

"May I ask for a small favor from you, my good man? I will make it worth your trouble."

"We don't do alterations," the man said as he placed clean suits, shirts and dresses covered in a light plastic wrap on a hotel trolley.

"I'm not interested in any alterations. You see, my ex-girlfriend is in her car waiting for me to come out of the building. She follows me
~~~

everywhere I go. I won't bore you with the details, but if you will allow me to remain hidden in the back of your van till you drive a few blocks from here, I will be grateful."

"Not a problem. I had an ex who punctured three of the tires on my car and smashed the windshield with a hammer. I called the cops and they didn't do squat! They said I had no proof she was the one who did it! Women! Let's go. I want to hit my local bar by 4:30."

The laundry truck pulled out of the garage, turned at the side street and passed the unmarked car where Jake and Lane were sitting. After traveling five blocks, the van pulled over and Barnabas got out. Barnabas pulled a wad of bills out of his pocket and gave the driver a handsome tip. He then walked two blocks east to where his car was parked and got into it.

Dr. Albrecht knew by watching the news broadcasts about the murders, that the police were looking for a black Cadillac Escalade, so he drove his other car. The British Racing Green Jaguar XJ220S TWR pulled up in front of Debbie Parker's home. Debbie came out of her house before the doctor approached the front door.

"Miss Parker. I certainly appreciate your willingness to help me on such short notice."

"Don't mention it, Dr. Albrecht. It will give me an excuse to tell my husband that I didn't have time to cook dinner and we will have to go out to eat this evening," she said with a smile.

Barnabas opened the car door for Debbie.

"Wow! This is some car!" she said.

"Thank you. It's a Jaguar XJ220S TWR. Only five were ever made. Very rare. I took the liberty to pick you up a cup of dandelion— pineapple, green iced tea from Tea for Thee."

"How in the world did you know this is my favorite drink?"

"You wrote that on your questionnaire the first time you came into my office."

"How thoughtful," Debbie said as she took a swallow. "There is nothing quite like this drink."

"My advertising company is wonderful, but sometimes they have these time restraints and I have to work around their schedules," Dr. Abrecht said. "Oh, and the photo will not be on your entire face, so you don't have to worry about friends or family recognizing you. It will only be a horizontal shot of your nose."

"Dr. Albrecht, I am starting to feel very woozy. I cannot move my arms and legs."

"Just relax, my dear girl. The good doctor will take care of you."

The green Jaguar pulled into the parking lot of the abandoned Schuylkill Packing Company. Barnabas got out of the car, opened the passenger door and picked up Debbie Parker placing her across his shoulders in a fireman's carry. He unlocked the door to the meat plant and walked in. While hanging over the doctor's shoulder, Debbie's face was pointed towards the floor where she first saw drains painted with dried blood. The doctor placed Debbie on a large metal table and fastened the restraining straps to her four limbs. Paralyzed, Debbie's eyes moved rapidly around the room where she saw boning tables and meat hooks dangling from the ceiling.

The sun had set and the darkness of the night was transformed into a serene sanctuary by the radiance of a blood-red moon. It was not only a full moon, it was a total lunar eclipse. The doctor had a lunar love affair created by the soft, ethereal light over the darkened city, against a starry night sky. Full moons have been known to have noticeable effects on nature, such as influencing animal behavior, particularly in nocturnal animals. Barnabas was no exception.

"I must confess I am experiencing a happy kind of sadness. My quest to find the perfect set of eyes, ears, the perfect nose and lips, and now the fifth of the five senses, touch, is coming to an end. Oh, how I will miss the challenge…the pursuit. You are to be admired, Debbie. You have a quintessential set of hands."

"I will soon have the pentad of perfect sensing organs. The perfect eyes, ears, nose, lips and hands—all of which I will transplant into a, yet to be determined, young lady. I will create the perfect woman. You should feel proud you will be part of my ingenious creation."

Debbie tried to speak, but what came out was unintelligible garble.

"Hush, my darling," the doctor whispered as he placed his index fingers on Debbie's lips. "I have saved my most favorite classical piece of music for the finale…for you. Did you know Claude Debussy actually wrote three Clair De Lunes? It is true. He got the idea from a poem written by Symbolist poet Paul Verlaine in his collection entitled Fêtes Galantes. Allow me to recite this beautiful poem for you."

*Your soul is a chosen landscape*
*On which masks and Bergamasques cast enchantment as they go,*
*Playing the lute, and dancing, and all but*
*Sad beneath their fantasy-disguises.*

*Singing all the while, in the minor mode,*
*Of all-conquering love and life so kind to them*
*They do not seem to believe in their good fortune,*
*And their song mingles with the moonlight,*

*With the calm moonlight, sad and lovely,*
*Which makes the birds dream in the trees,*
*And the plumes of the fountains weep in ecstasy,*
*The tall, slender plumes of the fountains among the marble sculptures.*

Barnabas's eyes remained closed after he had finished reciting the poem, as if resting upon the emotion the poem evoked.

"Truly beautiful, is it not? But even this beautiful poem fails as it is compared to the musical masterpiece. I want you to enjoy this exquisite composition and the beauty of the melody. The music must be perfect to compliment the matchless beauty of your hands."

"Why should I desire to steal your hands, you say? An exquisite pair of hands is the last of the five senses I need to complete my set. It has been extremely difficult to find the perfect eyes, ears, nose, mouth and hands, my dear, but finding utopian hands may have been the most difficult. Flawless hands are underappreciated. It has taken me nearly six months to find those four women and, of course, you make five. And what in the world am I to do with these five marvelous facial features, you ask? Well, the difficult part of my quest is now complete."

"I will soon be searching for a specific face shape, which actually should be much easier than the five sensory features. I will be looking for a woman with an oblong face which I consider quite beautiful because these women have a wide jawline which makes the distance between the eyes quite wide. This makes the eye quite prominent and also emphasizes the smile of the person. The women who possess this facial shape have broad and beautiful smiles, which adds to their stunning beauty."

"The climax to my ingenuity will be when I transplant each of these perfect features onto the woman I end up choosing. She will be the most beautiful woman in the world, and she will be mine alone. My bride, my pet, my love, my obsession, my possession. I will place her in the ivory tower of my penthouse and, of course, I will take good care of her."

The doctor put on a surgical mask, a gown, gloves, and a cap, all to help protect him from blood which would be plenty. Dr. Albrecht had put on surgical loupes, magnifying glasses to help a surgeon see clearly and precisely during surgery, but since this operation would not require intricate cutting, he decided to remove them and instead, replaced them with a face shield, as he anticipated significant blood splatter.

Debbie's eyes filled with tears reflecting the horror of her environment. The doctor brought a small pan with surgical instruments over to the table where Debbie was strapped. He left the room briefly, then returned with a saw.

"I know, you must be wondering what I am doing with a saw, right? It appears I am better equipped to be a carpenter rather than the world's finest plastic surgeon," he said as he threw his head back and laughed. "This, my dear, is a Gigli saw. A Gigli saw is a flexible wire saw surgeons use for bone cutting. It is used mainly for amputation, where the bones have to be smoothly cut at the level of amputation."

"Let me begin with the music," Barnabas said as he walked over to the portable CD player and pushed 'play.'

"*Clair de Lune* is a French title meaning 'moonlight.' Join me as we take a journey to introspection. It is a journey of adventure and understanding the soul in all its phases. This journey reflects life, and as we both know, life is filled with joy and sadness. No one is immune to both, but this unique melody helps us to better know ourselves. It will take us from triumphant love to sadness. It is an awkward dance. It is a radiant beauty."

Dr. Barnabas Albrecht picked up the Gigli saw and began to remove Debbie's hands.

# CHAPTER TWENTY-SIX

*Creation is a book proclaiming the Creator. It is a book of beauty that our
intellect reads, but through the passageways of our five senses.*
— Thomas Dubay

D arius Banks-Marsette could be heard before he was seen in the detective's common room. ADA Bryson had arrived a few minutes earlier when she was informed of Darius's arrival.

"Yo, I don't want nothin' to do with your murder investigation. I know somehow you all are trying to lay this on me and that old white guy you are looking for will walk. It's racial injustice."

"Relax, Darius, you know we cannot talk to you without your lawyer, but if you were willing to revoke your right to counsel, and are willing to cooperate, I am willing to offer you a plea deal for planting the evidence against the Mayor," Miss Bryson said.

"Mr. Banks-Marsette, planting evidence is a serious offense," Martin said. "You are going to do time. The question is how much time."

Darius looked to his right, clearly contemplating his options. Martin decided to coax him.

"If you can identify the man who made the car deal with you, we will actually have someone to pin these murders on instead of you."

"Okay. I'll talk to you without my lawyer. My public defender is as useless as tits on a boar hog."

Martin placed the stack of photos that included eight photos of white middle-aged men in front of Darius. "Take your time. Do any of these men look familiar?"

Darius looked through the photos one at a time. It didn't take long for him to strike gold.

Almost immediately, Darius said, "This is the guy! This is the cracker who gave me the Escalade. It's a sweet ride, but I almost regret meeting that guy."

Martin, Otis and Linda Bryson looked down at the photograph of Dr. Barnabas Albrecht.

"Tell me about planting the evidence against the mayor," asked Miss Bryson.

"Look, this same guy who gave me the Escalade called me the other day and said if I could convince that hooker to keep the Mayor's love custard he would give me five grand cash. He said that whatever it took to convince her to do it, the rest of the cash was mine. I started with one G, but she wouldn't budge. Finally, when she got me up to $3000, she said she'd do it and keep her trap shut."

"Well, I've got good news and bad news for you, Darius," Bryson said.

"What's the good news?"

"You are free to go. The last time you are going to see me is when you testify in court."

"Damn, lady, what's the bad news?"

"We are going to confiscate your sweet ride."

Turning to Martin, ADA Bryson said, "Now, you can arrest Dr. Barnabas Albrecht. Charge him with four counts of murder and three counts of kidnapping. I'll be at the arraignment. Oh, and I should have your search warrant for the Schuylkill Meat Packing Plant within the next thirty minutes."

~~~

Otis, Martin, Jake, and Lillia arrived at the Bryn Mawr Aesthetic Plastic Surgery Center in two cars.

"We want this to be quiet and easy." Martin said. "We are taking the stairs."

"What is your refusal to embrace the technology of an elevator, Captain?" Jake asked.

"You need the exercise. You appear to be a little soft in the middle, and by that I do not mean you have become sensitive or softhearted."
~~~

Otis laughed and slapped Jake on the back. "Let's go, Pillsbury Doughboy."

As the detectives entered the lobby of the plastic surgeon's office, the familiar face of the receptionist welcomed them. Seeing four detectives enter the lobby she realized this was not a social visit.

"Captain Wallace and Detective Gainwell, it's good to see you again."

"You have an excellent memory, Miss Wesoloski. Unfortunately, I wish we were here for a more friendly purpose. Is Dr. Albrecht in his office?"

"Actually, he took the afternoon off. A rare occasion for him. He is a workaholic."

Martin nodded his head, indicating he wanted his three detectives to search for the doctor, just in case the receptionist was asked to lie about Albrecht's presence. Miss Wesoloski watched with a concerned look as the detectives walked past her desk.

"Do you know where he is this afternoon?" Martin asked.

"No. The doctor is a very private man and he keeps his personal life just that, private."

Otis came back into the lobby a few minutes later.

"He's not here," Otis said.

"Alright. Let's head over to his penthouse." Turning to Miss Wesoloski, Martin said, "Do not contact Dr. Albrecht and warn him we are coming. Do you understand me? If you do, I promise you will be charged with obstructing an investigation."

"I understand. Is this about all those murders? Do you believe Dr. Albrecht is the killer?"

"Have a good day, Miss Wesoloski," Martin said, ignoring her question.

~~~

It was dark when Dr. Albrecht turned the corner onto his condominium's street. When he was two blocks south of where his building is located, he pulled over and parked his car. Barnabas had changed into the doorman's uniform at the meat packing plant. He
~~~

reached into his duffel bag and pulled out a wig and a fake mustache, put them on, and walked toward his condo building.

When Barnabas was less than a hundred feet from the front door of his building, two unmarked cars sped around the corner with their hideaway lights flashing.

*They cannot possibly know I am the Senseless Killer. I have been more than careful, and I am much more intelligent than any of those Sherlocks. Sure, they searched my penthouse, but found nothing. Then again, they would not have obtained a search warrant unless they suspected me. However, even if I am their number one suspect, all they have is that my fair ladies were all patients of mine; certainly not enough to convict me. Besides, I have completed most of my objectives. My risk of exposure has been greatly reduced.*

The detectives' cars with tires screaming their arrival, pulled up to the doctor's condominium building. They parked awkwardly in front of the building, just in front of the entrance canopy.

"I'm sorry. You cannot park here," the doorman said. "We need to keep this space open for taxis."

"Tell your residents they will get their daily exercise by walking a hundred feet to the corner to catch a cab," Jake said as he flashed his detective badge. "Have you seen Dr. Albrecht today?"

"I don't believe I have," the doorman said.

Barnabas pretended to look at his watch, his face turned away from the detectives and the doorman as he walked right past everyone and entered the front door of the building. He decided to take the stairs to his penthouse, rather than the elevator.

"Is he in some kind of trouble?" the doorman asked.

"We'll soon find out," Martin said. Turning to his detectives he said, "Let's see if the doctor is home."

The detectives entered the elevator as Martin pushed the button for the 22nd floor.

"Great! Some wise ass pushed the button for every single floor. We should have taken the stairs," Martin said.

"You want to climb twenty-two sets of stairs?" Jake asked.

Martin ignored the question.

After what seemed to be a half hour, the detectives reached the top floor where Dr. Albrecht's penthouse is located. Otis pushed the doorbell and followed that with some vigorous knocking. The door opened.

"Ah, good morning, detectives. What a glorious spring morning," the doctor said as he took another swallow of coffee. "May I offer you a cup of coffee?"

"Barnabas Albrecht, you are under arrest for the kidnapping and murders of Farah Darvish, Lan Nara, Katrina Alvarez, and Susan Cranford. You have the right to remain silent. Anything you say can and will be used against you in a court of law. You have the right to an attorney. If you cannot afford an attorney, one will be provided for you."

Dr. Albrecht's mind was in hyperspeed. He was a calculating man and now that he was arrested, his thoughts went immediately to an escape plan. He was in self-protection mode. He denied the anticipation of the inevitable.

As they were leading the doctor out of the lobby of the building, Dr. Albrecht turned to the doorman and said, "Clifford, my good man. Would you be so kind as to call my office, ask for Miss Wesoloski and tell her to call my attorney, Bruce Kiper. His card is in my top desk drawer."

With a stunned look on his face, the doorman said, "Yes, Sir, Dr. Albrecht."

~~~

Dr. Albrecht was escorted into Interrogation room 1 and was left there for over an hour while Martin and Otis met with Special Agents Huffman and Buchanan.

"Captain, I don't have to tell you we are dealing with a psychopath. I know you have outstanding interview skills and an excellent history of closing cases. I would just like to remind you of a few things when interviewing a psychopathic serial killer. Special agent Huffman and I have had some experience with these killers."

"I'm all ears," Martin said.

"Understanding psychopathy becomes particularly critical upon the arrest of a psychopathic serial killer. Psychopaths are not sensitive to altruistic interview themes, such as sympathy for their victims or
~~~

any feelings of guilt. They do possess certain personality traits that can be exploited, however. You should target his inherent narcissism, selfishness, and vanity, perhaps by focusing on praising his intelligence, cleverness, and skill in evading capture."

"Thank you. I appreciate that. We want to make sure every 'I' is dotted, every 'T' crossed. We want to hand the DA an open and shut case."

"Now that is what I love to hear," a voice said coming from the far side of the room.

"ADA Bryson!" Martin said. "You are just in time to witness our interview with our perpetrator, Dr. Albrecht."

"I have been waiting for this," she said.

"Haven't we all," Otis said.

When Martin and Otis entered the interrogation room, the doctor's attorney had joined him.

"Dr. Barnabas Albrecht," Martin said as he placed a manilla folder on the desk. "You have been charged with some serious crimes. I would like to have a little conversation with you before your arraignment."

"Why don't you show a little compassion for the victims' families and do the right thing. If you want to prevent the embarrassment of a trial and all the gruesome details that will come out of that, confess to the murders and we will work a plea with you. We will take the death penalty off the table. Otherwise, you will be tried by a jury of your peers."

"That will never happen, Captain Wallace. A trial by a jury of my peers, I mean"

"Why is that, Doctor?"

"Because I have no peers. I have no equal. The people you select for my jury are simple people, inferior individuals who do not have the capacity to comprehend my abilities, my desires, or my genius."

"Baranbas, let me do the talking, please," Mr. Kiper said. Turning to Martin he asked, "All of your evidence is circumstantial. Do you have any DNA linking my client to these crimes? What evidence do you have against my client?"

"All four victims were his clients. He was identified as the person who drove the black Cadillac Escalade seen at several of the crime scenes. He financed the purchase of an abandoned meat packing plant, the location of the murders, and he had someone else's name on the title to avoid any suspicion. We are in the process of obtaining a search warrant for The Schuylkill Meat Packing Plant, and I am sure we will have plenty of DNA that will put the final nail in Dr. Albrecht's coffin."

"He had both the means and the opportunity."

"What possible motive would I have to harm these women?" Dr. Albrecht asked.

"Psychopaths don't need a motive," Otis said.

"Insulting my client is not going to get you any answers," Mr. Kiper said.

"You have the wrong man," the doctor said with a smile. "I did not murder anyone."

"Barnabas, don't say anything. Leave the talking to me," his lawyer said.

"I know, Doctor. OJ didn't do it, Al Gore invented the internet, and Bill Clinton wasn't close personal friends with Jeffrey Epstein," Otis said.

Martin decided to take Special Agent Buchanan's advice and appeal to the doctor's ego.

"Doctor, I have to admire you. Really," Martin said. "I have worked on a variety of murder cases in my thirty years with the department. Never have I seen the ingenuity, the intricate planning, and the high intelligence needed to commit these murders. You will go down as one of the most creative and idiosyncratic serial killers in U.S. history."

A cynical smile came over the doctor's face.

"I do have one question, Dr. Albrecht. Why would you use your incredible skill as a surgeon to enhance a woman's beauty only to destroy these four women's beauty? It seems counterintuitive to me."

Dr. Albrecht slowly leaned forward, looked deeply into Martin's eyes and said, "God makes human beings. I make them perfect!"

"Barnabas, will you please keep your mouth shut?"

"What is the perfect woman?" Otis asked.

Anxious for the teaching opportunity to edify his inferior opponent, Dr. Albrecht answered, "Dark hair, olive skin, blue or green eyes—the genome perfection—the rare and perfectly beautiful woman."

"Doctor, the DA is willing to make you a deal."

"Ah, I love, let's make a deal. My twisted mother would watch that show every day."

"Barnabas, don't say anything! Please!" his lawyer said.

"Relax, Bruce. You are my employee. I am paying you, remember? I think I am intelligent enough to handle these questions."

"Dr. Albrecht, if you confess to these killings, it will save you the embarrassment of a lengthy and public trial, and the DA will be inclined to work a deal with you," Otis said.

"Detective Gainwell, is it?" Albrecht asked.

Otis nodded.

"It is a real shame what happened to your fiancée," the doctor said as he stood up and walked to the end of the table.

"Shut up and sit down!" Otis yelled.

Albrecht reluctantly sat back down and leaned forward, studying Otis's face.

"Detective, have you ever considered having rhinoplasty? You are a handsome man, but that nose. Hmmmm. That needs some reconstruction."

"Pennsylvania has the death penalty, but there have been no executions in the state since 1999, and only three since 1976. The U.S. Government, on the other hand, has the death penalty and does not hesitate to use it. In fact, the federal government has carried out 13 executions in the past 5 years. Our task force investigating these serial killings has been joined by two FBI Special Agents. They have been pressuring me to turn this case over to the Feds so they can pursue the death penalty. If you give us a confession, we will try you in a Pennsylvania court and you will end up getting life, instead of death."

"You call that a deal, Captain?" Mr. Kiper asked.

"We'll take our chances in court," Dr. Albrecht said. "No jury will believe I could have done such a heinous thing. It's my word against that street urchin, Darius Banks-Marsette."

"I think he will make a credible witness. Oh, and Doctor, any time now we should have DNA results back from blood found in your upstate cabin. We believe it will link you to a fifth murder, that of Julie Kane."

Barnabas Albrecht leaned over and whispered something into his lawyer's ear.

"We'll take our chances in court. See you at the arraignment."

~~~

ADA Bryson walked into the court room for Dr. Albrecht's arraignment to find Judge Steven Connors sitting on the bench.

"Oh great," she mumbled to herself. "The biggest case Philadelphia has seen in the past 25 years and I get Judge Connors, the most liberal judge in Philadelphia. This guy is known for handing out "Get out of jail free" cards. Thus, his nickname "Easy-Stevie.""

But ADA Bryson did her homework and was prepared.

"Docket number B-17367, 'The People versus Barnabas Albrecht,'" the court bailiff announced. "Four counts of murder in the first degree and three counts of kidnapping."

ADA Bryson stood up. Dr. Albrecht and his attorney did the same.

"Dr. Albrecht. I do not surprise easily, but I must say your appearance has me dumbfounded. How do you plea, Doctor?"

"Not guilty, Your Honor."

"Do you have a bail recommendation, Counselor," the judge said as he looked at ADA Bryson.

"Your Honor, I would ask you to recuse yourself due to a conflict of interest."

"To what in tarnation are you referring, Miss Bryson?"

"You have a personal connection to this case. Your wife received cosmetic surgery by the defendant."

"Please, Miss Bryson, I will not be hearing this case. This is simply an arraignment."

"I appreciate that, Your Honor, but I'm afraid your conflict of interest may lead to leniency in setting bail. I am sure you do not want even the appearance of impropriety."
~~~

"Thank you for your concern, Miss Bryson, but I certainly will not recuse myself in this arrangement. Now step back. Bail recommendation?"

"The prosecution requests remand. The brutal nature of these crimes leaves no other option."

"Mr. Kiper?"

"Your Honor, Dr. Albrecht is an upstanding pillar of our community, has no criminal record, not even a speeding ticket, and he's one hell of a plastic surgeon to boot. We would request a reasonable bail."

ADA Bryson immediately interjected, "Your Honor, Dr. Albrecht is charged with four heinous crimes and the dissection of his victim's body parts. Any amount of bail would be inappropriate. He has the financial resources to flee the country. The State would also request that Dr. Albrecht surrenders his medical license."

The doors to the courtroom opened and Otis entered and walked briskly up to ADA Bryson and whispered something into her ear.

"Your Honor," she said. "We will be amending the charges to include a fifth murder and four kidnappings."

"Bail is set at two million dollars," the judge said. "Cash or bond."

"Your Honor, offering bail to a serial killer makes a mockery of the justice system. Allowing Dr. Albrecht to be back on the streets causes a huge public safety issue."

"Don't you think you are being a little melodramatic, Miss Bryson? The evidence you have is largely circumstantial and presumption is weak."

The defendant will surrender his passport and will wear an ankle monitoring bracelet until his trial. You are not permitted to leave your residence, even to go to your practice. Do you understand, Dr. Albrecht? If you defy the court's orders your bail will be revoked."

"I understand, Your Honor. Thank you."

# CHAPTER TWENTY-SEVEN

*Heaven may have happiness as utterly unknown to us as the gift of perfect vision would be to a man born blind. If we consider the inlets of pleasure from five senses only, we may be sure that the same Being who created us could have given us five hundred, if He had pleased.*
— Charles Caleb Colton

Hello, Cecilia? Cecilia Tobiason? Yes, this is Dr. Albrecht. How would you like to earn a cool $5,000?"

"5Gs? I'm listening, darlin'."

"I need you to run a quick errand for me."

"Doc, I would like to help you out, but the police have been up my ass about those murders, and it's uncomfortable. I'm sure you understand."

"What murders, Cecilia?"

"The reason you're under arrest. I just watched the news. I'm not judging, mind you, but man, didn't you have a Mr. Potato Head growing up? You know, where you get to plug in the ears, nose, mouth, eyes anywhere you want on a potato? Obviously not, 'cause if you did you wouldn't be goin' round murdering and doing it on real people."

"Are you through? These murders have been going on for nearly six months. They needed to make an arrest. I am a plastic surgeon. That is why they came after me. And I am not just any plastic surgeon. I am the most famous, the most competent plastic surgeon in the country. They love high profile cases. Cecilia, I help women, I do not hurt them. You do love those perfectly round and symmetrical breasts I gave you…for free, don't you Cecilia?

"You know I do. I am truly appreciative, doctor. What do you need?"

"There is nothing illegal in what I am going to ask you to do. Go to the animal shelter on Passyunk Avenue and pick out a dog for me. Medium size. A mutt. Mix breed. One that looks energetic. I would go myself but, unfortunately, the court has me wearing an ankle monitor."

"Damn! Ankle shackles?"

"Yes, so you see my conundrum. Since I will not be leaving my penthouse for the foreseeable future, I would like the company of a four-legged friend. I had a dog growing up, but my extensive college education and the long hours I spend at my practice has prevented me from owning a pet. I think it is time for me to acquire man's best friend."

"Okay, that I can do, but this is the last favor. I hope you understand."

"Oh, I do, Cecilia. I do."

"What are you going to name the dog?"

"Poe," responded the doctor.

<div align="center">~~~</div>

Springtime. A time of new life, regeneration, beauty, and new beginnings...for all but Debbie Parker, whose life was prematurely taken from her. Her body was found at a bus stop in the Greys Ferry neighborhood, where Mill Creek debouches into the Schuylkill River. Her hands were removed and replaced with hands of a mannequin, and she was holding a newspaper dated May 1st. It was opened to an article about the Senseless Killer.

"Who found her?" Martin asked.

"Unfortunately, three young girls. They take public transportation to school. When they got to the bus stop this morning, they saw this lady sitting, and what appeared to be, reading the paper. She had sunglasses on, so they did not detect the victim's fixed gaze," Lane said.

"Fixed gaze?"

"That is what the medical examiner called it. He explained that fixed gaze can occur due to muscle relaxation immediately after death, sometimes causing the eyelids to remain fully open."

"Anyway, one of the girls threw her backpack onto the bench and the vibration caused one of the mannequin's hands to fall off the victim's arms, freaking out the girls. They all ran into that corner convenience store and the owner called 911."

"Where is Dr. Wu?"

"Don't know. The medical examiner they sent is Steve Pacyniak."

"Was there any ID on her person?" Martin asked.

~~~

"Hey Captain," Otis said walking up to Martin and Lane. "There was a full moon last night. The Schuylkill Packing Company is not that far from Greys Ferry. It almost seems as though Albrecht did not want to risk taking the body very far from where he murdered her."

"The question I would like answered is how did Albrecht leave his penthouse undetected if we have 24-hour surveillance on him? I want answers!"

"Captain, we took six four-hour shifts. There was never a point that we did not have eyes on his building. You were clear about that…it being a full moon and all," Lane said.

"I'll get the video footage from Albrecht's building to see if we can figure out how he left the building and returned without detection," Otis said.

In an attempt to change the subject, Lane said, "As you might have expected, there is a number '5' painted in orange nail polish on her stomach."

ADA Bryson pulled up in her dark blue BMW and walked toward the detectives.

"Here is your search warrant for the meat packing plant. Since Dr. Albrecht is not listed as the owner of the property, it wasn't easy convincing Judge Herman for the warrant."

"Judge Herman would do anything for you, Linda," Martin said.

"So now Dr. Albrecht has completed the circle of his obsession with the five senses. He had not received the ankle monitor when I got word they found the fifth victim, so obviously, this happened last night."
~~~

"That is what we are thinking. Counselor, have you given any more thought about the doctor's motive for the killings?"

"Other than he is a psychopath? I have given it thought, but nothing really makes sense. He has an extreme preoccupation with sensory experiences. The stimulus was the collecting of the eyes, ears, nose, lips and hands from five victims respectively."

"But, the question that begs to be answered is, what has he done with those body parts?"

"That, you will need to discover, Captain."

"Miss Bryson, would you be able to get Albrecht's bail revoked now that we have the fifth murder?"

"No. I got word they found this body when I was at the arraignment. I told the judge we wanted to amend the charges to five murders and four kidnappings, but he still offered Albrecht bail, albeit with an ankle monitoring bracelet. Considering how heinous these crimes are, it is unconscionable Judge Connors would not refuse bail to Albrecht. And to top it off, I am livid he didn't recuse himself. His wife got a facelift from Albrecht. It is a clear conflict of interest."

"Connors gave bail to that illegal immigrant who raped and killed that teenage girl, and what happened?" Jake added. "The perpetrator never showed up for his court date. What a surprise."

Lane walked briskly up to Martin and said, "I just got off the phone with headquarters. Her name is Debbie Parker. She was married and lived in Manayunk. Her husband has been at the 35th precinct all night. She was nowhere to be found when he got home from work. Mr. Parker said that she is always home by five. At midnight he drove over to the station and filed a missing person's report. He called her sister to wait at their house in case she showed up, but he refused to leave the police station."

"Alright, at least we have an identification. Listen up, everybody. Lieutenant Ewing and Corporal Wilton, I would like you to interview the husband and see if you can find out any pertinent information. Obviously, ask about any cosmetic surgery she may have had. The rest of us are going over to the Schuylkill Packing Company."

~~~

Diego took a pair of bolt cutters and cut the chain fastened on the door of The Schuylkill Packing Company. The heavy chain fell in a heap at his feet. The large metal door opened with a deep groaning sound as if it were announcing the macabre the detectives were about to experience. Immediately, the team was met with a stench of death, comparable to a combination of rotting meat, feces, mothballs, rotting cabbage, and garlic. Simultaneously, Diego and Martin reached for a pocket size container of Vicks VapoRub, placed a dab under their noses, and handed it to the closest detective.

Some say blood has no odor. That would be incorrect. There is a faint, metallic unmistakable smell. And the more one works around blood, the more one distinguishes it from everything else. When Otis turned on the lights, the first thing the detectives saw was a pool of blood that tried to maneuver its way toward the floor drains.

Leaning against a deep sink was a collapsible step ladder and resting on the third rung was a Barack Obama mask. Martin picked up the mask and said, "No surprise. Albrecht is definitely our guy!"

Otis walked over to a metal table with four restraints. A jury-rigged LED, task light dangled above the table. A smaller table sat nearby with scalpels, forceps, and several different types of scissors, and the Gigli saw. A CD player with several classical CDs next to it accompanied the surgical tools.

"Captain, back here!" yelled Lane.

In a backroom where multiple meat trimming tables were positioned, Cecilia Tobiason's body was hanging from a meat hook connected to a rail system for hanging and moving animal carcasses throughout the butchering process. A crimson puddle of blood pooled beneath her body.

"Great Caesar's ghost," Martin said. "Albrecht is eliminating any witnesses, or anyone who can connect him to these murders. Call Inspector Jenson and tell him Albrecht is going to kill Darius Banks-Marsette and that he needs protection.
~~~

"We are going to need some help processing this crime scene. Otis, call for the CSI team and have them process the scene and to collect all this evidence."

While Otis was on his cellphone, Lane and Diego followed Martin up a small set of metal stairs that led to the floor supervisor's office which overlooked the meat trimming floor. Martin turned on the light and entered the office. On the desk, neatly laid out were photographs of the five ladies Dr. Albrecht had mutilated and killed. There was also a basin with a preservation solution of gluconate, hydroxyethyl starch, and a synthetic colloid. Within the solution were two eyes, two ears, two hands, a set of lips and a nose.

Next to the desk stood the mannequin whose hands Albrecht removed so he could place them on his fifth victim, Debbie Parker. The mannequin was similar to the one the doctor had seen while taking an evening walk a month earlier. The face of the mannequin was one devoid of eyes, nose, ears, and lips. It dawned on Martin what the doctor's motive was. Albrecht is trying to create a superficially perfect woman. A woman devoid of substance, personality…soul. Barnabas Albrecht's addiction to aesthetics has driven him mad!

Otis entered the floor supervisor's office. He joined the other three detectives who were trying to process what they were observing. Diego spoke first.

"It's not unusual for serial killers to keep trinkets or mementos, but this…this is…

"Yeah, there are no words, are there? Otis asked rhetorically.

"This was Albrecht acting out on his God-complex. Do you remember what he told us? God makes humans, but Dr. Albrecht makes them perfect. He is obsessed with creating a woman of visual perfection. He is a modern day Dr. Frankenstein."

Martin reached for his cellphone and called ADA Bryson.

"Linda, it's Martin. Contact Judge Connors and get Albrecht's bail revoked. I want him behind bars. We are at The Schuylkill Packing Company and this is the scene of all five murders. Make that six. We found Cecila Tobiason's body hanging from a meat hook. We are processing the scene, but with Miss Tobiason's testimony that the doctor gave her monthly checks for the mortgage on this place, coupled with what we are finding here, you should have more than enough to lock up our serial killer…Okay, great! I'll see you back at my office."

~~~

ADA Bryson was waiting for Martin by the time he returned to his office.

"Judge Connors did not apologize for allowing Dr. Albrecht to be released on bond, but he was quick to revoke his bail once he heard the damning evidence that has since surfaced. I filed the motion to revoke his release, so your team can get the doctor and take him back into custody. He will remain in county jail until his trial. It looks like you might get a good night's rest this evening, Captain."

"I won't rest till Barnabas Albrecht is behind bars. Thank you for taking care of this, Linda. It does seem like this case is finally coming to an end. I regret we were unable to solve the case before Albrecht had murdered six people. We will go and pick him up now."

"Captain, this has been the most convoluted case I have ever worked. With all the twists and turns, and the obstacles, I might add, I think your team did an excellent job," ADA Bryson said.

Miss Bryson and Martin turned to see Lane running towards them.

"We have a problem, Captain. We just received electronic notification that Albrecht's ankle monitoring bracelet was removed and then reattached. The data showed it was off his body for 42 seconds. We weren't very alarmed at first, because it could have simply been a temporary glitch in the system, however, the GPS is tracking the doctor's location and he has left his penthouse. He's on the run!"

Martin's eyes grew large as he immediately went into combat mode. Turning to the rest of his team, Martin said, "Albrecht is on the run. I want everyone pursuing him. Corporal Wilton will be monitoring the GPS signal through his tablet and will communicate to us via radio the direction Albrecht is going. We will need to head him off at the pass.
~~~

"Wilton, tell Chief Conwell what is going on and that we need uniforms to aid in apprehending Albrecht. Let's go, people! DO NOT LET HIM GET AWAY!

"He is heading down Benjamin Franklin Parkway toward the art museum," Lane said. "It looks like he is in a car because the GPS indicates his movements are too fast for him to be on foot."

"He drives a green Jaguar, but do not assume he is in that vehicle. He no longer has access to that black Escalade. He could be driving anything."

The detectives, in pursuit of Dr. Albrecht, took off in three cars, Otis and Martin in one car, Diego and Lillia in another, while Jake and Lane were in the third. Lane had his tablet on his lap which provided Albrecht's GPS movements.

"He's heading down Kelly Drive towards Boathouse Row," Lane called out over the radio.

Kelly Drive is a popular running and biking destination which hugs both sides of the Schuylkill River in its nine-mile loop lined with weeping cherry trees with stately, pink blooms.

The scores of runners, bikers and rowers sculling down the river were all oblivious to the frantic chase going on around them.

Jake looked across the river and said, "So Elton John was thinking about Dr. Albrecht when he wrote Mad Man Across the Water."

"Turn here," Lane said, ignoring Jake's humor.

"He's not moving very fast. I think he may be on a bicycle or a moped," Lane announced over the radio. We should be approaching him soon."

"We are taking North 33rd Street, in case he heads east," Martin said over the radio. Ewing and Santos, go over the Girard Avenue bridge and head north on Martin Luther King Drive. This way we will have him surrounded."

"We have an ETA of 2 minutes," Lane said. "Oh, great! He's now on the Strawberry Mansion Bridge. He's heading for Fairmount Park! We'll never catch him if he heads into the park!"

Developed in the 19th century to protect Philadelphia's water supply and to preserve green spaces, Fairmount Park is more than 2,000 acres of rolling hills, hiking trails, and shaded woodlands. Being one of the first nice Saturdays of early spring, the park's pedestrian traffic was teeming with people off-road cycling, horseback riding, and deep-woods hiking.

Jake and Lane arrived at the park before the other two cars. Lane's tablet indicated Albrecht was near. The two detectives looked around, scanning a 360-degree perimeter. They saw a couple kissing on a park bench, three bicyclists in racing gear, a stray dog, and five young African American boys throwing a football.

Looking down at his tablet, Lane said, "He just headed into the woods!"

Otis and Martin had just pulled up next to Jake and parked their car. Seconds later, Lillia and Diego arrived.

"Alright, you two take the west perimeter of the park along Edgely Avenue," Martin said to Jake and Lane. "Santos and Ewing, enter the southern section of the park at Montgomery Drive. Otis and I will head into the park at Greenland Drive. Go!"

The three unmarked cars zig zagged through the park like lightning bolts across a summer sky. Every time the detectives thought they were close enough to see Dr. Albrecht, the signal took a drastic turn, as if the doctor knew he was seconds away from being caught.

"He now is heading into the woodlands, so obviously he isn't in a car. Probably he's on a dirt bike," Lance announced over the radio.

"You know, I hate to admit it, but this guy is smart. Very smart," Jake said. "He knew we would pursue as soon as we received the GPS signal he had left his penthouse. He also knew we would be in cars. A dirt bike enables him to go wherever he wants, dirt trails in the park, sidewalks away from roads, heck, even up or down steps. He could ride up the art museum steps, ride around the back of the museum to the grassy open area, down to the Fountain of the Sea Horses, and then across to the Fairmount Water Works Trail and Boardwalk. All places a car can't go."

"The department has cops on bicycles. Maybe we should call the local precinct and get some of them in Fairmount Park," Lane said.

"They have been notified; they are part of the pursuit."

On any given day there are at least four bike cops and another four mounted police within the sizable park. They were all notified by radio and joined in the pursuit. By changing their radio channel, they tuned into Lane's communications informing everyone of Dr. Albrecht's position and the direction he was heading.

"We're in luck! He's heading down Parkwyn Road, a dead end! Let's get over there and box him in."

"We are only 3 minutes from there," a mounted police officer replied over the radio.

"We'll arrive at about the same time," Otis added.

Two policemen on horses exited a trail onto Parkwyn Road where two unmarked cars were coming toward them, Martin and Otis in one car and Diego and Lillia right behind them. The four detectives were talking with the mounted police when Lane and Jake arrived.

"That's weird. The GPS shows he should be right here."

The words were barely out of Lane's mouth when he pointed to the edge of a wooded area.

"There! See that zone LED blinking red? That's his ankle monitor indicating he has violated the perimeter zone set up for him. It's Albrecht!"

Simultaneously, all of the law enforcement personnel pulled their guns.

"Dr. Albrecht, come out of the woods with your hands up!" Yelled Martin. "We will not shoot if you come out peacefully!"

Suddenly, a taffy and white dog with prick ears came out of the woods wagging his hair. He was wearing an ankle monitoring bracelet around his neck. A small red light was blinking.

"Come here, boy," a uniformed cop said.

The mongrel willingly ran up to the officer who scratched him behind the ears as he removed the bracelet.

# CHAPTER TWENTY-EIGHT

*The strong man is the one who is able to intercept at will the communication
between the senses and the mind.*
— Napoleon Bonaparte

"Ewing and Santos, head back to Albrecht's penthouse and see what you can find. I doubt he will go back there, but we need to check. Corporal, contact the Chief and have him put out an APB for Albrecht with his picture. Tell them he could be in a green Jag convertible, or a black Cadillac Escalade. They should focus on I-95 and the PA turnpike. Lieutenant, call FBI Special Agent Huffman and ask him to get the FBI's Criminal Aviation Investigations unit involved. Tell them to get a bird in the sky. Gainwell and I are heading to the airport. We need to know if Albrecht has purchased an airline ticket. Sinclair and Wilton, head over to Northeast Airport. A lot of private jets fly out of there."

Turning to the uniform police officers, Martin said, "Thanks for the help, guys. Sorry it was a false alarm."

"Not a problem. Good luck apprehending this freakin' animal," one of the officers said.

Otis and Martin jumped in their car, put their flashing lights and siren on, and headed down the Schuylkill Expressway towards the airport at an impressive speed. When they arrived at the airport, they parked in front of Concourse C.

"Let's divide and conquer," Martin said. "You take Concourse A, B, and C. I'll cover D, E and F. Remember, he surrendered his passport, so he will be using an alias."

Martin walked up to the Delta ticket counter and asked, "Have you seen this man?"

"No," said the agent.

Martin and Otis went from counter to counter, airline to airline, asking the same question and receiving the same answer. It was another Parkwyn Road, a dead end.

When Otis got to the last ticket counter, he asked the same question to see if anyone noticed Albrecht that day.

"No, I haven't, but if this guy is trying to avoid the police, you may want to check Northeast Airport. Being a much smaller airport, they get a lot of private jets flying in and out of there."

"Thanks. We have detectives searching there, as well," Otis said.

Located 25 miles north of Philadelphia International Airport, Northeast Airport, acts as the general aviation reliever airport for Philadelphia International. It is also the headquarters of the 1st and 8th Districts of the Philadelphia Police Department.

When Martin and Otis were back in their car, Martin called Lane on his cellphone.

"Hey Captain, I was just about to call you," Lane said. "We met with the Flight Service Station personnel. He is responsible for recording and handling flight plans. Pilots submit flight plans to the FSS before departure, outlining their intended flight route, altitude, and other relevant information. He told us no one with the name of Barnabas Albrecht flew out of here today, so we spoke with the airport's Communications Director. He had nothing for us. Just before you called us we interviewed a gate agent who identified Dr. Albrecht as having chartered a private jet this morning to Miami. We contacted Miami International a few minutes ago only to find out the plane landed a few hours ago. Oh, and he is traveling under the pseudonym Beau Ravenscraft."

"Of course. How ironic. Beau means beautiful and Albrecht is a huge Edgar Allan Poe fan, thus, the raven in the surname. Have they found him?"

"No. There is no record of a Beau Ravenscraft ticketed on any flights leaving Miami."

"Captain, there is a possibility he is traveling by boat from Miami to a Caribbean island," Otis said.

"If that is the case, I would think he is heading to Cuba. He would want to go where there is no extradition treaty with the U.S. Let's get back to the office. I want you to contact INTERPOL and request a Red Notice," Martin said.

"I'm sorry, Captain. Red Notice?"

"A Red Notice is a request to law enforcement worldwide to locate and provisionally arrest a person pending extradition, surrender, or similar legal action. They are published by INTERPOL at the request of a member country; however, they must comply with INTERPOL's Constitution and Rules."

~~~

By the time Otis and Martin arrived back at their offices, the place was a hive of activity. The Major Crimes team, FBI officers, besides Huffman and Buchanan, DA Malerba and ADA Bryson, and several uniformed police were buzzing around the office with the same objective, to help in the apprehension of Dr. Barnabas Albrecht.

Hours passed as day turned into night. No one left his post.

"Captain, I have been on the phone with the Miami Major Crimes Unit for the past half hour. They are using highly sensitive face recognition software to try and identify Dr. Albrecht. They said it may take a while."

"Alright, that's a step in the right direction. Problem is his plane landed in Miami sixteen hours ago. He could be halfway across the world by now."

Hours passed with little progress. Finally, in the wee hours of the morning, the team got a break.

"They found him!" Special Agent Huffman shouted.

Everyone in the room became like statues with their heads pointed towards Huffman, waiting anxiously for more information.

"Well, kind of," Huffman said. "Albrecht changed his false identity once again, and had a counterfeit passport to match his new name. He is going by Isaac Visage. Visage is a French surname meaning 'face.' I took French in High School."

"He boarded an Emirates flight to Dubai around two this afternoon. Miami FBI is reaching out to law enforcement in the United Arab Emirates. The flight landed 20 minutes ago. FYI, extradition between the UAE and the USA *is* provided only for murder, so that is
~~~

a good thing at least. We're waiting for word from Miami about what the officials in Dubai find."

Turning to address everyone, Martin said, "Folks, you have worked tirelessly for the past 24 hours. Go home and get some sleep. There's not much to do here but wait."

With a shared look of helplessness, the group dispersed. Martin's cellphone rang. It was Mary Jo.

"Just checking in to make sure you are okay." she said.

"I am so sorry, Honey. I should have called you. It has been an insane 24 hours. Dr. Albrecht removed his ankle bracelet and has been on the run."

"I know. I spoke with Kalani. Otis called her around midnight last night."

"Well, there's not much else we can do. We know he left the country and has landed in the United Arab Emirates. I am just waiting to hear if their police have found Albrecht or, God forbid, he has boarded another flight and is heading somewhere else. In any case, I'll be home shortly. I need some sleep. I'm living on coffee and adrenaline."

"I am more than ready for this case to be closed, Martin, and not just so this psychopath is behind bars, but for selfish reasons. I miss you terribly," Mary Jo said.

"I miss you, too, Honey. I know even when I have been home, I really wasn't home. My body was; my mind wasn't. I do have some good news for you though. I decided I will retire. I will give you a month before you beg me to go back to work," Martin said with a chuckle.

"Never! I love you. I'll see you when you get home."

"Love you, too."

Martin had no sooner put his cellphone in his pocket when Special Agent Buchanan walked up to him.

"More bad news. The UAE found Albrecht. The reason it took them so long to identify him is because even though they had a passenger list that included the name of one Isaac Visage of French citizenship, and that same person went through customs in Dubai, and face recognition software identified the individual as Dr. Albrecht, he out-foxed law enforcement again. Our counterparts in Dubai searched all passport photos scanned and recorded for every passenger boarding *outbound flights* and found a visual match. He used yet another passport, this time in the name of Felix Mooij. It is a Dutch passport."

Martin took his cellphone and began a Google search.

"What are you searching?" asked Mr. Buchanan.

"I'm looking for the meaning of those two names. Albrecht never does anything randomly. Everything has some kind of symbolic meaning behind it. Here it is. Felix is from a Roman cognomen meaning 'lucky or successful' in Latin. Mooij is Dutch meaning 'beautiful, handsome, neat, or fine.' No surprise."

"Anyway, as we speak he is on a flight to the Maldives. The flight will be landing in Malé in about an hour. He then has a connection to Dharavandhoo Island. Population under 800 people and famous among divers around the world. Martin, the beautiful island nation of the Maldives does not have an extradition treaty with the US."

"Of course it doesn't."

~~~

At noon the next day, after getting only four hours of sleep, Martin arrived at his office. The office was like a baseball park in January, as he had given his team the day off. Martin was tidying up his desk when he heard Otis's voice at his office door.

"Did you get any sleep?" Otis asked.

"A few hours. I needed to get in here to finish some paperwork. What are you doing here?"

"I had a thought last night that we may be able to freeze Albrecht's assets. I realize that Swiss bank secrecy laws offer some protection, but the U.S. has agreements with Switzerland, including mutual legal assistance treaties, that facilitate the freezing and seizure of assets if there's evidence of criminal activity or tax evasion. I figure if we can't throw him in jail for his crimes, at least we can make his life miserable by making him broke."

"You are one hell of a great detective, Otis. It won't be long before you have my desk, and it may be sooner than you think." Martin got up from his chair and walked over to Otis, taking his hand. "Otis, I
~~~

have enjoyed working with you. You are a man of integrity and I want you to know I appreciate you."

"This sounds like a farewell speech."

"Well, I guess in a way, it is. I have handed in the paperwork for my retirement. Officially, I'll be retiring one month from today. I have three weeks of vacation coming my way. I am going to take them beginning tomorrow. I'll come back to work for that last week just to tie up loose ends."

"I guess I shouldn't be surprised. I apologize if I don't appear overjoyed. Martin, you have taught me a lot about how to be a good detective. Man, am I going to miss you. As unhappy as I am for selfish reasons, I am genuinely happy for you and Mary Jo. I'll be praying for Mary Jo. You better find something to occupy all that extra time you are going to have or you will end up driving Mary Jo crazy!"

"Funny man you are. Years ago, when I was a boy and even into my twenties, I loved to head up to the Poconos to do some flyfishing for trout. I think I'll dust off my rod and start tying flies again."

"Sounds like a plan. Where are you going on vacation, Martin?"

"I thought some warm weather would be nice. The spring brings too much rain in the northeast. The Jersey shore really doesn't open up till Memorial Day. I need my toes in some warm sand."

"Have a Pina Colada on me," Otis said as he shook Martin's hand.

# EPILOGUE

Barnabas laid upon the remarkably comfortable chaise as the waves beckoned him to take a nap. Sparsely scattered upon the beach were other chaises in the colors of mango-orange, papaya-yellow, avocado-green, and watermelon-pink. Tourists, mostly from India, Russia and China, occupied the chairs, enjoyed the warm weather, and the turquoise water.

The warm wind randomly flowed and with it came a vague smell of tropical island fruit.

"Omar, please bring me another Biyadhoo Special," Barnabas said as he took one last swallow of his drink.

A group of divers boarded a boat to fulfill their quest for a sanctuary that included a variety of marine life. Behind the long pillowy-white beach sat lush green vegetation and a thick jungle. Considered the flattest country in the world, the low-lying islands always provided a breeze since there were no mountains to obstruct the wind.

A stunningly beautiful woman placed a towel on the chaise next to Barnabas and laid down. She wore large sunglasses and a wide-brimmed hat to protect her skin from the sun. It was her complexion that first caught Barnabas's attention. It was smooth, even-toned skin with a healthy glow, devoid of blemishes. Her complexion was free from excessive redness or dullness, and had a refined texture. Barnabas smiled with admiration at the color of her skin which had a wheatish tone with warm undertones and a slightly golden hue.

Barnabas caught the woman's eye and asked, "May I buy you a drink? These Biyadhoo Specials are the perfect accompaniment to a perfect beach afternoon."

The woman used her index finger to pull her sunglasses just below her eyes and smiled back at Barnabas.

"Biyadhoo Special?" she said with an English accent.

"It is a fruity and refreshing drink, made with vodka, pineapple juice, and melon liqueur. You will love it."

"Thank you, I will try one," she said with an enticing smile.

Barnabas smiled again at the young lady and asked, "Has anyone ever told you, you have the most impossibly, beautiful eyes?"

Omar interrupted the impromptu conversation as he brought Barnabas another of the tropical drinks he was enjoying so much. The drink had a vibrant yellow/orange hue and was accompanied by a little umbrella. Barnabas took a sip and let the pineapple, melon liqueur, and local fruits linger on his tongue before swallowing.

Barnabas turned his body and raised his hand to garner the waiter's attention. "Omar, please bring this beautiful lady one of these and put it on my tab."

"Very well, Sir."

Turning to the woman, Barnabas asked, "Have you been to Dharavandhoo before?"

"Once, when I was a teenager my parents brought me here on holiday. I am recovering from a bad breakup and I decided I needed to get away."

Before Barnabas could respond, a tray with the Biyadhoo Special appeared between them. The drink was handed to the lady.

"Without turning to view the server, Barnabas said, "Omar, these drinks are going down too smoothly. I cannot let this lady drink alone. Bring me another, my fine Sir."

"I think you have had enough," a voice, clearly not Omar's, responded.

Barnabas abruptly sat up and turned around.

"You can run, but you cannot hide, Barney," Martin said.

Suddenly the doctor began feeling woozy and dizzy, coupled with an overwhelming sense of dread. Barnabas knew he had been bested. He tried to stand but had great difficulty. He stumbled onto the sand.

"Yes, Barney, your drink has been spiked. I used a roofie. Mexican Valium? Ahhhh, that is street slang. A language beneath you. You may be more familiar with the medical term, Rohypnol, or flunitrazepam. One of the date rape drugs. I thought it was only appropriate."

"I have absolutely no pleasure in the stimulants in which I sometimes so madly indulge. It has not been in the pursuit of pleasure that I have pearled life and reputation and reason. It has been the desperate attempt to escape from torturing memories, from a sense of insupportable loneliness and a dread of some strange impending doom," Barnabas said, quoting Poe, his words beginning to slur.

Martin responded with his own Poe quote. "I intend to put up with nothing I can put down."

Barnabas tried to respond, but garbled nonsense only.

Martin helped Barnabas stand, put his arm around the doctor's back and under his arm to steady him.

"Come with me, Doctor. We have a plane to catch."

As Martin helped Barnabas walk towards his rental car, he whispered into the doctor's ear, "'Quoth the raven, Nevermore.'"

# AUTHOR'S BIO

G. Bradley Davis is a natural-born storyteller who can't help but pull readers into his world of unforgettable characters, unexpected twists, and richly imagined adventures. Be it truth, half-truth, or pure fantasy, his stories always captivate.

A Navy veteran, Temple University and Bethel University alum, and lifelong wordsmith, Davis brings humor, mystery, and heart to every page. Senseless is his third work of fiction, following Bellamy and Makin' Waves, continuing his mission to craft stories that spark curiosity, paint vivid pictures, and keep readers guessing until the very end.

G. Bradley lives on Marco Island with his best friend and wife, Carolyn. When not writing, you may find him traveling, golfing, on the softball field, or dreaming up his next plot twist.

Follow him at:
http://gbradleydavis.com/
Instagram at:
https://www.instagram.com/authorgbradleydavis/
Facebook at:
https://www.facebook.com/authorgbradleydavis